Y0-BEO-923

Breakers of the Dawn:

Book 1 of the Dawn Saga

ZACHARIAH WAHRER

Copyright © 2014 Zachariah Wahrer

All Rights Reserved. This book or any portion thereof may not be reproduced or used in any manner whatsoever without the express written permission of the publisher except for the use of brief quotations in a book review.

First Print Edition, 2016

Wahrer of the Worlds Publishing
www.wahreroftheworlds.com
publishing@wahreroftheworlds.com

ISBN: 0692616586
ISBN-13: 978-0692616581

DEDICATION

For my dad.
I only had 3793 standard days, but I appreciate everything you taught me.
You live on in my memory.

CONTENTS

ACKNOWLEDGEMENTS

I would like to thank all those that helped me with this book: Shanese Furlow, Megan and Lois Rahal, Frank Frey, Shreve Fellars, Ron Davis, Ryan Collins, Björn Arnór Sveinbjörnsson, and Ignacio Tripodi. These individuals made great contributions and their help is immensely appreciated. I would like to give a special thanks to Sarah Rahal: Without your help, love, motivation, and support, this wouldn't have been possible.

May the fires of the black star be quenched in your life,
Zachariah Wahrer

"Chase the sun as hard as you can, but remember it will always rise behind you."
- Dygar Proverb

"Chaos, that need deep inside.
The end is here, you can't hide.
Ascension, where I'm going.
Blood is coming, deep and flowing."
- Lyric excerpt from "Ascension" by The Black Fire

"Violence is despicable, except when your enemy is despicably violent."
- Alnos Azak-so

01 – FELAR

Felar enjoyed the feeling of fitting a rail weapon stock snugly against her shoulder. To her, it was unlike anything else in the world and she loved it. The joy and elation was just as strong now as when she had first picked up the weapon, even after all the time she had spent training.

"For as far back as I can remember, I've wanted to wield this weapon as a Founder's Commando," she told the latest group of Initiates. "I devoured the histories and legends of that elite group of warriors as I grew up on the underworld streets of Qi-3. My parents were poor and barely able to provide food for our large family. This made me tougher, and when we had to go hungry at Dog School, it felt just like old times." The Initiates watched her with awe, obviously engrossed in her story.

"When I was old enough and had learned some FC training protocols, I tried to replicate them on my own, training my body to be resilient and strong. I fought the local toughs to gain experience. My defeats helped me learn more than my victories ever would, just as yours will. Then, on the day I turned 19, I joined the Ashamine Forces. I was exemplary in my Initiate class and was sent to the FC qualification course. I passed and was given the option to continue on with full FC training, known as Dog School.

"Becoming a Commando requires an extreme amount of determination, especially for a woman. The selection process is stringent and the number of Dogs passing each successive portion of the course dwindles. The wash out rate is high. Of my starting class of 192, only 54 successfully graduated the school and earned the right to be called a Founder's Commando." Felar eyed each of the Initiates in succession, wondering if any of them had what it took.

"For now, focus on getting through your Init training, but keep the Commandos in the back of your mind. Some of you might just be good enough to make it to FC Qualification."

1

Felar pushed all thoughts out of her consciousness and looked through her scope at the target downrange. She triggered the weapon and a tungsten alloy projectile blew a ragged hole through the target exactly where she had been aiming. Deftly moving the rifle to the left, Felar focused and fired on the next target instantly. The results were the same. She repeated the procedure until all the targets were hit.

"Shooting like this requires dedication and focus. Practice is key. You will now break into squads and your instructors will demonstrate technique and safety. If you have any inclination towards wanting to join the FC's, make sure you are in the top percentage of your Init class for marksmanship. Give up hope if you are anything less."

The Initiates saluted Felar until their instructors started barking orders at them. Her demonstration was over. *Hopefully some of these bright eyed, fresh faced Inits will have what it takes to be a Commando. If not, the Ashamine Forces always needs front line troops.*

Felar left the shooting range, moving towards one of the many indoor training buildings. It was a large, hangar like structure that had been built many years ago at the beginning of the Ashamine expansion. She had a few more demonstrations to give before combat maneuvers began in the afternoon.

Entering through a small door, Felar breathed in the reassuring smell of sweat and physical toil. There were row upon row of new recruits going through part of their daily conditioning. She reflected back on her own time in training, not long in the past. The commanders had pushed them to—and in some cases past—the breaking point. Remembering the few Initiates in her class that had died in the process made her sad, but the memories of camaraderie between those that had survived lightened her mood. *All that excruciatingly hard work paid off in the end,* she thought. *I'm actually one of the Founder's Commandos.* She could hardly believe it, even though her black camo fatigues and crimson beret proclaimed it to anyone who saw her. A burst of pride welled up in her as she observed that many of the new recruits took notice of her passage.

"3rd Class Enlightened," a voice hailed, "May we have a moment of your time?" She turned towards the voice and saw, to her annoyance, Initiate Trainer Harmoth and his flock of trainees. They stood by one of the facility's many training rings, apparently in the middle of a sparring session. The rings weren't anything more than a large circle drawn on the dull gray cement, their purpose solely for teaching unarmed physical combat.

She could feel their animosity radiating towards her in waves as she walked towards the group. It wasn't unexpected. Harmoth had been in the same class as Felar in Dog School. While in the school, Harmoth had been antagonistic towards Felar and the few other females in their class.

He had been fond of saying the women in the group were good for only one thing, and it wasn't combat. When those same women scored higher than Harmoth, he had raised allegations of them giving sexual favors in turn for good marks. The fact he had been cut from Dog School, while all those women graduated, had soured him even more.

She stopped in front of Harmoth, close enough to hear him over the racket, but far enough away to be respectful. She waited for him to salute, his requirement as a junior officer, but all she received was a condescending smirk. None of the men in his group saluted either.

Their lack of respect disgusted and enraged her. It wasn't just a formality, but an honored tradition. She was an officer and a Commando and deserved respect from this subordinate and his underlings. This wasn't the first time she had faced this kind of disrespect. Macho, male soldiers often assumed since she was an attractive woman, she had paid her way through Dog School with sexual favors. Felar felt anger boil up in her, just as it had every other time she had been confronted with this type of situation. She would teach them respect and prove to them she had earned her crimson beret.

"Look at that rack!" she heard, followed by low laughter. More remarks about her appearance were exchanged, brazen and obvious. This infuriated her. *How dare they!* Stifled laughter and smirks made her realize her emotion was plain to them. A scream of rage resounded through her mind, then the declaration: *I'll beat down every single one of them if that's what it takes. I'll rip off their arms and gouge out their eyes. I'll break every bone in their body.* At this point, Harmoth broke into her thoughts.

"Enlightened Haltro, I was wondering if you could show these soldiers a thing or two, since you are a Founder's Commando," he said, a jeering tone in his voice. "Your physical *prowess* is known to many," he continued. "I thought you could demonstrate to these recruits how *you* do *it.*" He raised his eyebrows and licked his lips.

Felar quit grinding her teeth long enough to growl, "As you wish." She felt the need to prove herself propelling her into a situation it would be best to avoid. She took off her tactical combat belt—a few whistles and lewd comments greeted this action—and moved to the center of the circle. In the process, she emptied her mind, going into the trance like state the FC's were trained to adopt before combat. She began to breathe deeply and embraced the uncertainty of battle.

"You don't mind if I pick your *partner*, do you?" Harmoth's voice grated against Felar's void state, condescension infusing every word.

Her response was almost inaudible as she said, "Your choice, IT Harmoth." Harmoth shouted to his group of trainees, ordering them to form up. Moving along the line of twenty men, he selected out the largest and most imposing of the group.

"This is Initiate Alexhion. He is one of my top trainees. I've drilled him personally and he has sparred against, and beaten, every opponent in this group." As he was selected, Alexhion moved to his side of the ring. *The difference between us is ludicrous,* Felar noted calmly as she sized up her opponent. Huge, hulking, and very intimidating, Initiate Alexhion overshadowed and outweighed her.

Felar, however, was unaffected by the imposing man standing in front of her. She looked him up and down with an appraising eye, as she had been taught and had practiced many times before in drills. She came away unimpressed. Despite his large size and menacing demeanor, he was soft. Even with his training and long hours of PT, he was inexperienced. He didn't have the hard look of a veteran. He had no scars. And despite all this, his biggest weakness was underestimating his enemy. Alexhion was too busy making jokes and smart remarks to even give Felar a second look.

Harmoth brought Alexhion's antics to an end by stepping into the middle of the circle. "Lets try to keep anyone from getting too injured, OK gentlemen? Oh—sorry, I mean gentleman and lady." He stretched out the last word, turning it into a jeer. "First one to tap out, go unconscious, step out of the ring, or sustain a fight stopping injury loses the match." Felar bowed to the IT, though she hated to give him respect, and Alexhion did the same. This formality completed, Harmoth left the ring and the combatants turned to face each other. Felar started to bow to Alexhion, but as she did so, he moved forward to engage her.

OK, so he is going to continue his disrespect of the Ashamine traditions, she thought as she moved quickly away from him. He pursued her around the edge of the ring, but she easily kept out of range. This fight would be on her terms and by her rules. After a few minutes of this, he tired of pursuing her, and stopped in the middle of the ring. "Afraid of me, pole sucker? Don't want to let a drop of blood soil your pretty new fatigues? I wasn't aware they let weak little pink holes into the Commandos, even if they do have such hot bodies. How many officers did you have to pleasure to get through Dog School?" He made a suggestive gesture and looked to the audience for approval. It was at this moment, while he was looking away and playing to the crowd that Felar made her first strike.

She deftly closed the distance and drove her fist into Alexhion's lower back, punishing a kidney for his lax attention. A flicker of pain crossed his brutish face, but he quickly controlled it. Felar wasn't bothered. She knew how that pain lingered there, how it bored deep into you. *Aim here,* she remembered a trainer telling her, just before he had driven a solid fist into her kidney. It hadn't been a crippling blow, but over the course of the instruction, each subsequent hit had added up.

Felar quickly moved back to a safe distance from the hulk, her mind still void and her face composed and serene. She knew she had the edge in this fight, but she wasn't getting over confident. That would be a huge mistake and would likely end in a painful loss.

Alexhion began grunting and bellowing like some kind of incensed predatory animal. He was no longer strutting around with a proud look on his face, waving his arms in the air as if he had already won the fight. Spittle was flying from his mouth as he breathed and his eyes had a crazed, maniacal look in them. *Good,* Felar exulted, *the madder he gets, the more mistakes he will make.* Sure enough, Alexhion charged, and this was another opportunity Felar was ready to exploit.

Dodging to her left, she dropped low to avoid his grappling arms and kicked out her right leg, tripping up Alexhion as he ran past. His forward momentum kept his upper body hurtling forward, while his legs, having made contact with Felar's trip, stopped abruptly. Her body shuddered from the impact of his massive, tree-trunk legs, but she was well braced.

His arms kept him from smashing his face into the cold, hard cement, but the strain of his bulky frame was too much for the bones that supported it. With an audible snap, Alexhion's left arm broke below the elbow. As he rolled to that side, the splintered and shattered bone tore its way through his skin. The wound shone, glistening red and white, the blood already starting to flow.

Felar looked down on the prone form with regret. She had not wanted to hurt him like that. Of course she had meant to win the fight, but not with this result. Now this man would be out of service for at least a week while the nanomachines helped his body knit the bones back together. And whether she supported the war or not, every Conscript, Initiate, Enlightened, Separate, and Ascended was needed for the final, massive offensive.

Felar felt guilty for needlessly injuring Alexhion. She didn't enjoy his pain. Someday he would be a good soldier... *Hopefully... Maybe...* She approached him, intending to assess his injuries. Her conscience would not allow her to watch this man suffer, even if he had wished her so much harm. IT Harmoth and all of his Initiates were just standing around the circle, doing nothing, looking shocked. *He is losing blood. Their squad medic should be doing his job,* Felar thought, becoming irritated.

She reached the fallen man and bent down to start first aid procedures. At this range, she realized Alexhion was mumbling something. At first she thought the man was delirious and speaking incoherently, perhaps having sustained a head injury as well as the one to his arm. Once she leaned in closer however, she could make out what the words were. He was cursing her, using livid, horrendous profanities, some of which Felar had never heard before. She considered herself well versed in swear, so hearing new curses was quite a surprise. She'd have to make sure to use a couple of the more colorful ones. They were actually pretty good.

Not touching him and remaining out of his reach, Felar looked closely for any additional injuries. She saw nothing. His head seemed to be uninjured as well, as evidenced by his vocal abilities.

Her initial assessment complete, Felar decided there was nothing she could do for him. If the squad medic wouldn't help Alexhion, she would have to call in support from the medical unit. They would do a more thorough examination, set the arm, and see if it would require direct surgery or if nanomachines alone could repair the damage.

Rising back to her feet, Felar became aware of the malicious looks of the men standing around the combat ring. Earlier, they had all worn expressions of perverse delight at what they thought would be a fast, brutal fight. The fight had been fast and brutal, but the result had not been what they were anticipating. Now they were furious. None of them appreciated she had bested and injured Alexhion in combat.

The Initiates began closing in around her, eyes burning with vengeful intent. Felar tried to regain her void state, but she was finding it impossible to maintain the cool demeanor that had served her so well through the fight. Panic shone in her beautiful green eyes. Her body started tensing up. Her head swiveled around furiously, trying to anticipate who would strike at her first.

Felar regretted having taken off her tactical belt, knowing if she hadn't, she would now have access to her twin combat swords. Their vicious, tungsten alloy blades would cut through these horrible monsters and she would be able to break through their circle before they injured her. She knew they wouldn't kill her, but that knowledge didn't comfort much. Killing her would require much explanation and would most likely result in a court martial. The sentence to Bloodsport would be more brutal than the murder that brought it about.

No, they won't kill me, she thought desperately, *but who knows what they'll do to me once I'm down.* A flash burst through her mind as the whole world turned into a black, warm mass that engulfed her.

02 – WAKE

Wake stared out across the jagged, snow covered peaks of Traynos-6, his gray eyes taking in the panoramic vista below. He found the barren landscape comforting. The bleakness helped him forget the events of the past two days.

He felt responsible and knew the deaths were his fault. When he inadvertently looked in the direction of the accident site, his eyes slid past the point and his mind tried not to recognize the familiar landmarks.

"Wake!" a friendly voice said, breaking him from his reverie. He turned to face the doorway that accessed this small perch on the great icy mountain. Raimos, his superior officer, stood in the entryway.

"Oh—hey," Wake said in reply, his tone distracted and lacking enthusiasm.

"It's almost time for third meal," Raimos said. "Just wanted to make sure you didn't forget to eat, like earlier today."

"I'm not too hungry. Maybe I'll get something later." Wake responded, turning back to the desolate vista. He knew Raimos wanted to help, but right now he needed to be left alone, needed time to think.

"Well... OK," Raimos responded after a brief pause. "Look, I know you're torn up about the miners, but they were *just* miners. They signed up for duty here and were compensated well for taking that risk. They knew the dangers and they still came to Traynos-6."

"You don't think I know that?" Wake shot back, his tone harsh. After a brief pause he continued, but this time his voice was softer, more conversational. "I understand they knew what it was like here. What they didn't realize was there would be danger in using a well maintained, Ashamine built structure."

Raimos didn't say anything for a while, his gaze fixed on the mountains. "There is something I need to tell you," he finally said, his voice taking on an official tone. "I was going to wait until you healed up and recovered from the shock a bit more, but the Elder Council is moving quicker than I anticipated. I've done all I can to block it, but it will go through anyway. They are going to put you on trial for the accident. So you need to pull yourself out of this slump and start thinking about how you're going to defend yourself at the hearing."

Wake felt as if he had been punched in the stomach. A flood of new emotions merged with those he had been dealing with earlier. It produced a rancid cocktail of grief, remorse, and, interestingly enough, suspicion.

"Anyway," Raimos continued after several ticks of silence, "I'll keep doing all I can to stop the trial. It may or may not help, but I'll do my best." Wake smiled weakly at his friend, feeling gratitude. "Oh and one more thing: Orders came through not to reopen the area of the incident. I don't know why, but Command says it's not to be reestablished." He gave Wake a moment or two to respond. When Wake didn't reply, Raimos continued, leaving the deck as he spoke, "Wake, pull yourself out of this blightheart. Grief is one thing, but beating yourself up is another. It was an accident. Come down and get something to eat."

Wake sighed heavily, his breath misting even though the observation perch was climate controlled. The outside air was so frigid that it was hard to keep the fully windowed room much above freezing. He tried once again to lose himself in the barren landscape outside, but after a few minutes he realized it wasn't going to happen. Raimos' revelation had pushed him over some unknown edge and now it was impossible to *not* think. Wake decided he had to reason the whole thing out, had to find a better way to deal with his grief and guilt. Maybe it was time to quit mourning and start processing. He felt his attitude shift.

The twelve miners had died on a structure Wake was charged with maintaining. That would mean he would be held liable. He hadn't anticipated the trial though. These types of accidents weren't rare. With an empire as big as the Ashamine, things went wrong quite regularly. What was rare was a trial. It was strange. Also out of character for the Ashamine was the decision not to reopen the affected mining area. Wake didn't know much detail about the mining operation here on Traynos-6, but he had heard the effected area contained some of the richest frozen gas deposits on the planet. *Why would they leave it closed?*

His mind drifted back to the events leading up to the accident. He recalled typing a report that used the words "unsuitable for use" and "obvious manufacturing defects" in reference to the materials he had ordered for maintenance. The reply had been: "Requested material was inspected before and after shipment. No flaws were found. No new materials will be sent. Use previously shipped materials." He had up-channeled more reports and requests, but each time he did so, increasingly strong orders came down to use the original parts. In the end, he had been forced to do so.

Am I completely sure it was the bad parts that caused the failure? Wake thought about the plans, maintenance schedule, and memories of time spent on site. His workmanship had been good, he was certain of that. It had to be the materials. There was nothing else left. Then a new thought, something buried deep in his mind, rose to the surface. *Why did they force me to use faulty materials? Why didn't they just send new ones like procedure dictates?* His sense of unease rose as he thought about the implications of those questions.

Wake had been raised to be devoted to the Ashamine. All the meetings, rallies, and his time in Youth Core had showed him just how great the human interplanetary government was. His parents were diplomats and had wanted Wake to follow in their footsteps. He had been sent to several elite schools in preparation for his "great service", as his parents had put it. But Wake didn't want to be a government functionary, going to formal events and fighting for political power. He wanted to make a real difference by helping people and making their lives better. So Wake had rebelled against his parents and enlisted with the Engineering and Building Division. "We are extremely disappointed in you," his mother seethed at him the day she found out. "You were meant for bigger things. Building colonies? You're wasting all your potential and everything we invested in you. You could do so much more for the Ashamine!"

He had been with the Engineering and Building Division for six years and his parents hadn't contacted him since he had left home. He knew initially they had been shunning him with the hope he would change career paths. As time passed however, they had forgotten him in their fervor for the Founder and the war against the Entho-la-ah-mines.

When Wake had left home, his devotion to the Ashamine had equaled that of his parents. He had chosen the EBD because he knew he could help both the people and government of the Ashamine through his service there. Once out in the real world however, he had seen many things that had caused him to rethink his absolute faith in the government of humankind. Not that he was ready to forsake the Ashamine—or even wanted to—but he felt like he had a more balanced view now. He was still very impressed by the Founder, feeling a deep conviction that he was a great man and faithfully did what he could to help humankind advance in the Akked Galaxy.

Slowly, thoughts about the building materials returned. Was he being set up? This added a new crack in the weakening structure of his faith in the Ashamine. He was truly sad the miners had died and wouldn't try to duck the responsibility for his workmanship. He would not, however, take the blame for careless manufacturing, inspection, or shipping. He wouldn't allow himself to go down for a crooked bureaucrat's gain.

Raimos would do his best to stop it, but Wake *knew* there would be a trial. He also knew it would be pivotal to his continued belief in the Ashamine. If he was tried justly and fairly, based on his maintenance of the structure, he would be able to keep his faith in the colossal government. *Otherwise...* Well, if it was handled otherwise he would fight against the injustice as hard as he could.

03 – MAXAR

Maxar Trayfis drove the thin metallic spike through the faceplate of the environmental nominizing suit, shattering it. The man inside began to suffer as all his air was sucked violently into the void of space. *Inexperienced*, Maxar observed as the man attempted to hold his breath. It was a major mistake. His lungs would burst. He also failed to bring his weapon to bear on Maxar. *Rookie.* Almost immediately the man dropped his rifle in shock and opened his mouth. In another twelve seconds, he lost consciousness and fell limp. Maxar figured the man had two minutes of painless rest before the final oblivion took him. *Lucky,* he thought, his emotions a mixture of remorse, boredom, and envy.

Maxar slid stealthily back into the shadows of the ridge, a ghost of darkness. As he moved, he spotted a momentary glint of light near the edge of his faceplate's vision field. He dropped prone. *Sniper,* he thought, wondering how he had been spotted. He brought out his optical enhancer and looked for the threat, but saw nothing. He waited several moments more, dialing up the magnification, zoom, and all other enhancements the device was capable of. *Nothing.* He knew if there was anything to see, he would have spotted it. His pale blue eyes were abnormally sharp and with his optical enhancer there was little chance of missing anything as large as a human. This left only a few options, mainly that of either a communications satellite or a personnel observation drone. Both were extremely hard to spot, and as long as it wasn't an opposing player, it really didn't matter anyway. Maxar rose to his feet and cautiously continued on. His skills were leading him through the process of ending human lives in a methodical, precise way.

Back on the move, his thoughts crowded in. He wished it hadn't been necessary to kill the man. The death had been quick and painless relative to what usually went on during the games, but Maxar would have rather just let him be. That wasn't an option though. Had the man spotted Maxar, he would have called in reinforcements to this sector and it would have complicated Maxar's mission. The man, whoever he had been, had never sensed Maxar's approach. *Focus,* he thought, dragging his mind back to the processes that had kept him alive for so long in such a deadly environment. He had work to do.

The match had begun only a few hours ago, but to Maxar it felt like a lifetime. "This game is pretty standard," their team leader had said. "Each side has a secure terminal in their base. First team to hash the opponent's terminal wins. All vehicles except space craft are permitted. All weapons except for nuclear are allowed. There will be a hundred players to a side. All the new players will form infantry quads. I have assignments for all veterans, but they won't be a surprise to you."

After the group briefing was over, his squad leader had given him more detailed instructions. "You're on solo duty Maxar. I need you to go in and soften up the approach to their base. Snipers, anti-tank guns, mines, and whatever else you can take out. You're the best player we have for this. We need all the help we can get."

"What about a stealth hash," Maxar said, referring to a tactic that kept the battle from turning into a bloody frontal assault.

"Nope. The Orator won't allow it. Apparently there are some important people watching this game and they don't want it to end too quickly, too easily." Maxar's hope sank. The stealth hash had worked a few games ago and both sides had suffered few losses.

"OK, softening duty it is." And that was what he had been doing ever since.

This is true blightheart, Maxar thought as he worked his way along the ridge. There were usually several snipers in this area. They used the high vantage point to get a good line of sight on the enemy in the valley below and call in troop movements to their officers. *I wish someone would kill me like I did that guy. If I was a hardman, I'd do it myself.* He hated the repetition and pointless death of the never ending games. No matter how hard you fought, how many you killed, or how many matches you won or lost, there were always more games to come. It was eternal, and the only way out was to die or escape. And with the security on Bloodsport, the only real way was death.

Being in the game always made Maxar remember his past life and what had sent him to Bloodsport. He had been born and raised on Noor-5, a bustling stellar hub full of trade and rich merchants, along with a great deal of poverty and crime. He and his sister Emili grew up in a government care facility which was little more than a prison. Emili joined an indentured servant program when Maxar was 9 and she was 14, taking her out of the facility and sending her to Ashamine-2. She had written him through the Terminal Network for almost a year, but then had gone silent. Maxar looked for her in the Ashamine records when he got older, but there was no trace.

When he was young, Maxar had wondered where his parents were, or if they were even alive. He had been in the facility since his earliest memory and had no recollections of them or friendly adults of any kind. By the time he had the skills to hash the Ashamine records to determine his parents' fate, he no longer cared to know. They were dead to him, whether living or deceased.

As typical of many low class youth on Noor-5, Maxar began a life of crime. He remembered a time early on when he had been approached by a wealthy merchant's son. The other boy had offered him a substantial amount of Ashcreds to kill one of the rich boy's peers. The merchant's son had said the boy was mercilessly bullying him and Maxar felt inclined to exact justice. After several hours of research and surveillance, Maxar could see the target was actually the one being bullied and viciously tormented. A few hashes later and the truth became apparent: The target was amassing a case against the rich boy, for raping his sister. In the end someone had died, but it wasn't the original target and Maxar didn't get paid.

Maxar's natural talent allowed him to quickly learn the skills needed to become an expert assassin and thief. His reputation grew, and the highest circles of the criminal organization on Noor-5 took note of him. Before long he was being commissioned for high profile jobs, ones that required extreme stealth and cunning. True to his ethics however, he would only accept certain jobs. If the mark was an innocent official, devoted family man, or an honest merchant, Maxar refused. Fortunately there was plenty of corruption on Noor-5, and Maxar stayed busy.

He found his work fulfilling, both monetarily and as a lifestyle. He was free, stable, and controlled his own future. All had gone quite well for almost a standard decade until one of the major officers within the underground had been caught. Maxar never found out all the details, but from what he could gather, the officer had been one of his direct contacts within the organization. This officer had rolled over on Maxar and given the Ashamine more than enough evidence to prosecute him.

Maxar had been captured, tried, and convicted. "Let it be known that Maxar Trayfis has been censured for the malefactions stated at the beginning of this convocation. We shall now move to sentencing. For crimes of this nature there is but one option, the remainder of life spent on the Bloodsport asteroid." He'd been wishing for the death sentence ever since.

04 – TREMMILLY

The beautiful girl sat beneath a shade tree, reading. A large wolf-dog lay beside her, sprawled out comfortably in the heat. The girl's black hair shimmered in the bright light of mid-day, her green eyes intently focused on the book in her lap. The wolf-dog's gray and black fur swayed gently in the breeze as he napped. It was just the kind of peaceful scene the girl enjoyed so deeply. It was one of the best things about Eishon-2.

Her mind deep in thought, the girl absentmindedly scratched behind the wolf-dog's ears. His legs twitched in enjoyment, something the girl always laughed at, even after all the years they had been together. She quit scratching to flip a page in her book, and the wolf-dog rolled over so he could warm his other side. Minutes passed, the two enjoying the tranquility of the deep wood.

The wolf-dog heard someone drawing near their secluded spot, but let out no sign. He knew from the scent that the newcomer was friendly. The girl failed to hear the snap-crackling of someone moving through the underbrush, her attention totally focused on the large book in her hands. She did, however, hear her name when a strong male voice called out.

"Tremmilly?" the voice questioned, its tone melodic. She shut the book, careful to mark her page before doing so. After gently setting the book down, she gave the wolf-dog a hearty belly scratch. This time she focused her full attention on him and looked into his large blue eyes.

"Well Beowulf, it looks like we aren't safe, even way out here." Her eyes sparkled as she smiled at the wolf-dog. Turning to face the direction where the foot falls were coming from, she called out, "Over here!"

After a few moments and more crackling in the underbrush, an elderly looking man came into the small clearing. Tremmilly began to rise, but he motioned for her to stay seated. The old man smiled at the wolf-dog and sat down on the soft tree needles next to Tremmilly.

The trio lounged in contented silence for several minutes, the humans taking in energy from the surrounding landscape and the wolf-dog dozing lazily in the warm sunlight. Finally, the old man rose to his feet and spoke. "Walk with me, if you will." His tone was friendly, his manner loving. Both Tremmilly and Beowulf rose and started following the elderly man.

"Psidonnis," she said, as they had topped the crest of a small rise, "what brings you out so far to find me?" Psidonnis continued walking, his pace brisk. He was silent for a long time. This reticence was unlike him and Tremmilly began to grown uneasy.

"There are heavy matters afoot," Psidonnis finally replied. His wrinkled face showed care and concern, but also resolve. "I dread having to turn our friendly relationship to one of a religious nature. There are other members of my Sect that Terra could have chosen, but it was I who received the prophecy. And I think it is because of our friendship, rather than in spite of it. I believe Terra wants me to convey it to you."

A feeling of anxiety crept over Tremmilly and she stopped walking. "You raised me with the knowledge of Terra, and you know I respect your beliefs. You also know I have no wish to partake of the Dygars Sect. If there is a prophecy, how could it apply to me, a non-believer?"

The old man shrugged his shoulders, but Tremmilly thought he knew more than he let on. "I do not know how this came to be, only that it is. As I taught you, our prophecies are always for, and about, a member of the sect. This occasion has been somewhat of an anomaly."

"Psidonnis, you know I love you, but I really don't want anything to do with this prophecy. My parents came here for the Dygar Sect, but I have no faith in it. I have my own beliefs, and they aren't the same as my parents." She hoped she wasn't being too strong, but she had to tell her friend how she felt.

Looking him in the eye, she saw Psidonnis looking back, absolutely expressionless. At first she thought he was angry, but no, that wasn't right. She looked deeper and realized he was vacant, some place else entirely. Tremmilly could see it. The animation seemed to drain out of him, to seep away even as she watched. Each moment, it progressed further, his eyes becoming empty, vapid, soulless. A startled gasp escaped her as his lifeless looking lips opened and the void man began to speak. His voice had lost its normal qualities and had been imbued with a harsh, primitive tone that made Tremmilly shiver.

"When the Breakers rise, there shall be six on whose choices the worlds do lie. The choice of virtue or corruption will bring an ancient existence to many, death to more still. Persevere and strive, the Acclivity will bless those who survive.

"Six shall have great influence, many choices when the Breakers rise. Woe to six, that Breakers have experience when they have none. Six shall have need of all their will.

"The first be of a light most bright, spirit most pure. Her life touched by death before cognition, her desire only for peace. She shall start the fire that kindles the worlds to the Acclivity. Woe to the Breakers.

"The next shall have hands that shed blood, his blood in motion with machines. He does not know his heart, yet through course of life he shall learn what to see. He shall be the strong hands that guide the Acclivity, albeit he is not gentle. Woe to the Breakers.

"She of battle will fight beside the hands, her heart ferocious, yet kind. Her path has been strange, her child not of her blood. She shall be a strong pillar, the Acclivity magnified through her strength. Woe to the Breakers.

"Next is a man of character, the dead that is found, wearing that which is ancient, the icon of legends long past. His heart is good and powerful, a mighty man to lead the Acclivity. Woe to the Breakers.

"He that is green has strength of mind, his people are his weapon. He is dissimilar, but his heart is good; send him not away. He shall unite a people unspoiled, he shall be the salvation of those of his kind. He shall bring his kind to the Acclivity, and the worlds will tremble at their might. Woe to the Breakers.

"Last is he smallest of all, but a boy in the eyes of the world. He is descended from power, full of power, wielding power. His mind is a weapon, though his hands be frail. His heart is strong, though his body may fail. He has the power of life, the gift of death. The Acclivity rests on his shoulders. Woe to the Breakers.

"All six shall have friends and foes alike, some from within and some from out. Many more shall sway the Acclivity, many more essential. Some will live and many more will die. Come forth you adventurers, you seekers of battle. The Acclivity calls, though the Breakers may yet decide the fate of the worlds.

"But to you who would stay in comfort and safety, not yielding to the call: Blightheart shall establish itself on you and the worlds will be sundered by the Breakers."

After Psidonnis quit speaking, Tremmilly stood in stunned silence, afraid, not knowing what to think. The life slowly returned to his eyes and after several minutes he was fully reintegrated into his body.

"Did it happen?" he asked, his voice sounding dry and papery thin, bereft of its normal joyfulness. She didn't reply. "Ahhh, yes. I see by your face it did." He looked down at his feet and sighed heavily, but whether this was out of shame or another, more obscure emotion, Tremmilly couldn't tell. She was speechless and didn't know how to react to his strange behavior. She felt violated.

Tremmilly was about to say something, although she was still unsure what it would be, when Psidonnis raised his head and spoke. "I had hoped it would not happen this way, that I could be myself when I told you the prophecy, but it seems Terra had a different plan and wanted to communicate in a more–direct manner."

"What does it mean?" Tremmilly blurted, finally unable to contain her emotion any longer.

"I don't know child, I honestly don't, at least not exactly. We Dygars are an old order and we keep meticulous records, but there have been many times when we lost information. When you are fleeing for your life, dusty old tomes and records are often the last thing on your mind." With this statement, some of his warm personality and joking humor returned, his voice regaining a measure of its former vitality. This comforted Tremmilly and she felt her own emotions begin to settle, even if it was only fractionally.

"Do you know why I was meant to hear the prophecy?" Tremmilly asked. "I need some kind of frame work or perspective. It doesn't make sense."

"You don't see it?" He had the look on his face she had seen when he tutored her, the one that said, "You know the answer Tremmilly. Look harder!" She thought for several moments. Psidonnis remained quiet and allowed her to think, just like he always had.

"I honestly don't," she replied, her mind failing to connect anything in her life to the vague and poetic prophecy. "None of it sounds familiar or connected to anything or anyone I know."

"Well then," he said with a sigh, "I suppose it's time to bring you in front of the elder council and let them explain some things to you. Perhaps you'll see the connection then." As he said this he turned away from her and began to head in the direction of the Dygar enclave. Tremmilly looked down at Beowulf, seeking and finding comfort in his familiar pale blue eyes. She gave the wolf-dog a confused but determined expression and turned to follow her oldest human friend and benefactor towards the unknown.

"Before we go to the council Tremmilly, there are a few things I should tell you. I think they will make more sense coming from me than from the elders." Tremmilly tensed up, sensing she wasn't going to like what he was about to say. "You are the one the prophecy refers to as being 'of a light most bright, spirit most pure.' I think it is time for you to leave Eishon-2. I think you need to go search for the other five people referred to in the prophecy."

05 – LOTHIS

"Arise," the atonal voice announced, interrupting Lothis' trance-like sleep. It was the end of his three hours of rest. His vibrant orange eyes flicked open and he was instantly aware of his surroundings. This was simple because the room was his world.

Lothis looked at the space, its features drab and metallic. Every surface was made of brushed stainless steel. He was used to the surroundings, comfortable in them. He couldn't remember any other place. His eyes ran over the dull walls, seeing, yet not seeing the lavatory area in one corner. More wall brought his eyes to another corner and what he thought of as his training area: a terminal, running device, and several other training apparatus. Another brief section of wall and then he saw the final corner of the room. It contained the device that dispensed his meal of the day, along with a terminal and a table where he could work on projects. In the center of the room sat an angular metal chair and a terminal, this one far larger than those in the training or project area. Everything in the space was as it had been when he had closed his eyes, unchanged, immutable.

Rising from the flat metal platform that was his bed, Lothis walked over to the lavatory area. It was here he started the daily routine that was the entirety of his short life. He knew he was young. His calculations showed he had repeated this daily, twenty-four hour cycle 3785 times.

Finishing up in the lavatory, he returned to the central area of his small room and sat down in the chair before the display terminal. The synthesized, atonal voice returned as the terminal's large screen came to life. "Lothis, lesson, begin," it sounded, lacking any emotion. The screen began to display complex math equations which Lothis solved instantly. His orange eyes flicked back and forth across the display, comprehending the information as quickly as it was shown.

After a span of time, the terminal's display changed, the math replaced by intricate diagrams and specifications. Lothis' eyes continued to play across the screen, absorbing everything. Later, the diagrams changed to what appeared to be random symbols, scrolling by so fast they began to blur.

Several hours passed and then the screen went black. Lothis rose from the angular steel chair. Moving across the small room, he stood on top of a wide belt that was recessed into the floor. The belt turned and Lothis ran. The pace became furious, but he never stumbled, never missed a single step.

Hours went by, the belt slowed, and Lothis moved on to his other exercises. He did each with superior physical prowess and dexterity. His small ten year old frame was deceptively weak looking, hiding the incredible abilities it contained. His exercises complete, Lothis stretched methodically, from head to toe.

With the day's physical training finished, he moved on to other tasks. Guided by the voice, he built several small electronic devices, all of which he easily and accurately assembled.

Lothis sat and ate his one meal of the day in silence. He swallowed the protein compound bars and liquid vitamins with no enjoyment, no pleasure whatsoever. They were bland and tasteless.

After his short meal, he sat in front of the main terminal, which once again began to rapidly flash numbers, symbols, and colors in a seemingly random pattern. This continued a while longer, but then the screen went black. The monotone voice spoke saying, "Lothis, sleep, begin."

Lothis rose from the chair and returned to his metal shelf. His mind was empty as he lay back. He never considered his life, never questioned his existence. Every day was exactly the same. Thoughts and speculation about the past were pointless. Thinking about tomorrow was also futile. It was all so predictable, like knowing the future.

He closed his eyes, slowed his breathing, and fell asleep instantly. The voice would return in three hours to wake him.

06 - THE FOUNDER

Seated in his massive chair at the head of the conference table, the Founder seethed with rage. *What more can be done to crush this uprising?* He had to find a new tactic. This situation was causing him more frustration than anything else he had experienced in his 130 years of life.

One of the Classad, the Ashamine government's highest council, made the unwise decision to break the heavy silence, "Perhaps, if we met some of their demands and change some of—"

"We have already discussed that!" the Founder roared, his vibrant orange eyes burning into the man. He felt the fires of the dark star roaring within him. He wanted to release all his rage on these old men, to burn them for their failure to destroy the dissidents.

I must calm myself, he thought, pulling back to diplomacy. *These men are of no use to me if I alienate them all.* Why had he been so prone to anger lately? He had never been this way as a younger man.

"What I mean to say," he continued, almost recapturing his usual charisma and poise, "is that we have already thought that idea out to its logical conclusion. The Divisonist's propaganda is particularity virulent. Their strongest weapons are peaceful protest and the ability to spread false information as if it were a disease. If we give into their demands, we'll look guilty and they will use that to infect and recruit more of the Ashamine population. We cannot negotiate. We are the ones with the power and we must use it to fight their insidious agenda."

He paused, his mind once again running through all the history, tactics, and information that had been discussed in prior sessions. This took little time, and his mind leaped to a conclusion it had previously missed. *What if...* he thought, a sadistic grin touching the corners of his mouth. He would have to approach this carefully though. Most of the

Classad would be opposed to it, unable to bring themselves to do what had to be done. That was fine. The Founder was used to issuing such orders. He had the perfect person in mind to perform the task. If not knowing the plan would keep the conscience of the Classad clean, then so be it. They didn't need to know anyway. Their purpose was to offer advice and carry out his edicts.

The Classad hadn't always been this weak. The Founder remembered when he'd learned the secret history, how the first Founder had answered to the Classad.

The Ashamine Charter stated: "The Founder is to lead, but he is directed and held accountable by the Classad." The creators of the Charter had chosen a man much too smart and determined to be ruled by committee though. Twenty years into his term, the Ashamine was under the total control of the first Founder. Of course, no one but the Founder himself knew this secret history, and that was all for the best.

The first Founder would have approved of this course of action, he observed, the thought bringing him out of his reverie. "For the time being," the Founder resumed, fully back in his relaxed persona, "let's continue to try to think of alternative solutions. Now we should move on to other, more gratifying business." He could see the Classad relaxing as he spoke.

"From the intelligence briefings we've received, it seems fairly evident the Entho-la-ah-mines are nearly annihilated and the war is almost at an end. They only remain on a handful of planets, and their forces grow weaker by the day. " This statement brought about a buzz of excitement and anticipation the Founder enjoyed. "Furthermore," he continued, "I'm told by the Ashamine Forces that we are close to discovering the hidden Entho worlds. The Engineering and Building Division has also informed me they will be ready to start developing these new Entho worlds as soon as they are cleared of the insects." *Everyone in the Ashamine will cheer my name when we annihilate those bugs and open up new colonies. Everyone except for the Divisionists.* This thought drove the thorn of the rebellion back into the Founder's mind and his mood soured again. Humanity needed the resources that were on the Entho worlds, and if the way to get them was to destroy a bunch of interstellar insects, then so be it. *The Divisionists can go bugger themselves in the fires of the dark star,* the Founder thought. *They can protest the war all they want. The Ashamine will take those worlds.*

The discussion about the war continued a while longer, a few members of the Classad talking about this or that until all felt the matter had been fully reviewed. The Founder brought the meeting to an end by dismissing each of them personally.

After they left, the Founder returned to his chair at the head of the table and brought out his personal communicator. "Crasor," he said into the device, and after a few moments a clear, soft spoken voice replied.

"Yes, Founder?"

"Are you back on Ashamine-2 yet? I have need of my Facilitator."

"Yes, I just arrived and can be at the Ashamine Complex shortly."

While he waited for the Facilitator, the Founder thought about the man. Crasor Tah Ahn was amazing. He wouldn't be the Facilitator if he was anything less.

The Founder remembered the time he had spent meticulously researching personnel who would best fit his newly created title of Facilitator. At the end of the search, he had summoned Crasor and asked, "1st Class Enlightened Tah Ahn, how would you like to be my aide?"

"I will do anything you ask of me", Crasor had replied, his devotion evident.

"Anything? Anything at all?"

"Of course. You are the supreme leader of the Ashamine. Your word is law."

The Founder's Commandos had been sad to lose Crasor, and with good reason. The man's skills were far superior to any other operator the Founder had researched. Over the eleven years Crasor had been his Facilitator, the Founder had grown quite fond of the man. He wouldn't call him a friend, but he was certainly closer to him than he was to anyone else.

"Founder," a voice said, and he looked up to see Crasor entering the room.

"Facilitator," the Founder replied, using the title because he knew Crasor enjoyed it. "Thank you for coming." He gestured at the chair to his right and Crasor sat down. "How did everything go on Traynos-6?"

"The bridge fell," Crasor replied, his excited eyes betraying his calm voice.

"Everyone was taken care of?"

"Yes. The scene was compelling and contrary evidence non-existent."

"Perfect," the Founder said, smiling at Crasor. He was glad that, unlike the Classad, his Facilitator could get things done. "I have a new project for you."

"What do you have need of?" Crasor asked, leaning towards the Founder.

"There is some business I need you to conduct on Noor-5," the Founder answered. "I have a surprise for the Divisionists, a bit of a message in fact." As he explained the details, Crasor's mouth curled up into a sadistic grin the Founder delighted in. He felt the same smile grow on his lips, knowing Crasor would execute his plan perfectly.

07 - CAZZ-AK-TAK

Cazz-ak-tak lumbered out of the entrance to the Entho-la-ah-mine tunnel system that lay below the surface of Lith-elo-hi-rosh. The emerald green of his exoskeleton shone brightly in the blue light of the primary star.

The beauty and vastness of the landscape on this planet never ceased to inspire wonder within him. Tall, emerald green grass waved gently in the bright light, looking like a deep green sea. The leaves on the mighty palos trees rustled lightly in the breeze, small groves of the huge hardwoods breaking up the endless fields of grass. In the distance, grand mountains reached for the sky, their heights unknown, unexplored.

Cazz-ak moved out into the long grass, his six legs quickly taking him through the waving plants. He followed a well defined path, one that he could see both with his eyes and his mind.

As he moved out into the prairie, he startled a tak-ai, a small rodent-like animal indigenous to Lith-elo-hi-rosh. Its green body blended into the grass perfectly when it stood still, but the animal was very skittish. As it fled from Cazz-ak, it inadvertently ran full speed into a calath plant. The sharp leaves sliced the poor tak-ai, and after a few moments it fell over, dead. The neurotoxins produced by the plant were fatal to most wildlife on the planet. Cazz-ak walked by both the plant and the tak-ai, not taking any special precautions. His exoskeleton was armor against the sharp leaves and the chemical was a psychedelic for the Entho-la-ah-mines, rather than a neurotoxin.

After a few minutes of walking, a huge canyon appeared before Cazz-ak, the emerald grass growing all the way to the edge. He continued on the path, and soon it wound down into the canyon and entered a tunnel. After a short distance in the narrow tunnel, Cazz-ak reached an enormous, vaulted chamber that housed numerous gleaming ships. Each vessel was made from a substance the Entho-la-ah-mines secreted, a substance that was close in composition to their exoskeleton. It was a very useful material, easily molded into whatever shape was needed, whether it was a food basin for a family or hull plating for a ship.

Cazz-ak thought about how much life had changed for the Entho-la-ah-mines within the past few years. The initial contact with the humans had been amazing. Both species had come together, had exchanged knowledge and information about themselves. Unfortunately, something about the way the humans had evolved caused them to see the Entho-la-ah-mines as resources rather than friends. It hadn't been long after the Unification and Harmony Tour that the humans invaded their first Entho-la-ah-mine world.

Cazz-ak could hear and feel his fellow Entho-la-ah-mines throughout the galaxy, and they in turn could feel and hear him as well. Everyone was connected through the central mind known as the Great Thought. He felt the joy and harmony of those on peaceful planets still undiscovered by humans. He also felt the pain and agony of those suffering from the human expansion onto the Entho-la-ah-mine worlds. The suffering of his kin was like the edges of many calath leaves being drawn slowly across his mind. The pain was excruciating, yet somehow he and all his people managed to bear it.

It was this call, this alarm, that Cazz-ak-tak was answering. Even though his race was peace loving and had never fought in the past, Cazz-ak-tak was going to war. He felt ill-equipped to perform his mission, knowing the humans' warfare technology was far advanced compared to that of the Entho-la-ah-mines. It had been just a few decades since the Entho-la-ah-mines had even learned about the concept of war. Now they were being forced to fight for their survival.

Cazz-ak approached one of the many ships arrayed in a triangular pattern inside the cave. They were massive objects, crewed by up to five hundred Entho-la-ah-mines at a time. The ships looked like two pyramids stacked bottom to bottom, a bi-pyramid. They hovered in the space above him, silent, hulking, their organic hull plates shining bright green in the artificial light. The bi-pyramid shape had been chosen because of its efficiency in focusing the mental powers of the Entho-la-ah-mines.

Cazz-ak used his mind to reach out to the hatch on the exterior of the ship above, identifying himself to the security protocols. It was an easy task that he did subconsciously. Stopping below the vessel, he focused hard on drawing power from the Great Thought. Cazz-ak then channeled this force towards the ground below him and he rose into the air.

He floated upwards towards the mind hatch and the aperture lensed open at his approach. It was just big enough to fit his awkwardly shaped six legged body. Once inside the entrance, he began to walk again. The corridors were oval, one body wide by two tall. As he continued through the ship, a few of the crew passed over Cazz-ak's head, mentally greeting him as they went by. After passing several branching corridors, he finally came to another mind hatch that blocked his passage.

This hatch led to the uppermost area of ship, to the apex of the top pyramid. Cazz-ak went through the mind hatch and the orientation of gravity changed. He now stood on what he previously thought of as a wall. The shift in perspective was easy for him as it often occurred on Entho-la-ah-mine ships. Each of the five points of the bi-pyramid was its own "up", which allowed them all to be observation points and command bridges in case of damage. Now that he was on the main command deck, he was able to look out through the hull plating on all three sides, seeing the upper points of the other bi-pyramidal vessels. He was amazed they had been able to build so many ships in such a short period.

Images flashed through Cazz-ak's mind. He saw his people systematically exterminated on Kii-la-ta, the first planet to be taken by the humans. They had been unable to defend themselves and the massacre was still excruciating to remember. He saw the great councils meet, saw the philosophical debates about violence and warfare, about what they must do as a species. None of them understood at the time that they were being killed so the humans could exploit the resources of their worlds. Then more planets fell and the councils had resolved to fight against the extinction of the Entho-la-ah-mine species. They had to do it in their own way though, had to use the tools evolution had given them.

This was where the bi-pyramid ships came in. The Entho-la-ah-mines knew they could not resist the humans in battle. Cazz-ak himself had seen the power of the human ships and it would be many years, even at Entho-la-ah-mine speed, to develop the abilities to fight them. In the end, considering all the circumstances, the Great Thought had decided it would be best to abandon the home worlds and leave them to the humans. The bi-pyramid ships would evacuate as many as possible, but there would still be countless left behind.

Cazz-ak found himself wishing he was evacuating his fellow Entho-la-ah-mines, but he knew his mission was far more important. Instead of saving several hundred Entho-la-ah-mines, he would be attempting to save his species as a whole.

He forced his mind back to the present and hailed his Hax-ax-ons, a group of three Entho-la-ah-mines that controlled the ship's systems. They returned his salute and he instructed them to begin departure procedures. Each was standing in their control focus point, a Hax-ax-on at each of the three angles of the pyramid. Cazz-ak took up his position in the center of his officers, the focus point known as the Hax-at-tory, his title as commander of the vessel. It was his channel to the Great Thought that would ultimately power and move the vessel.

In his mind, he could feel the readiness of his crew, as well as their nervous apprehension. Transporting the cargo that was on board was dangerous, but it was far more dangerous to keep it on Lith-elo-hi-rosh. It was also an immense honor to be part of this mission, to help bring about the continued existence of their species. These facts created a swirl of emotion that had everyone on edge.

Cazz-ak observed as Ak-lah-hum, the officer in charge of the ship's mind, soothed and comforted all those aboard, instilling confidence and unity within the group. Cazz-ak was proud of his Hax-ax-ons and his crew. This was not their first deployment, *And with the Great Thought's aid, we will continue to help our people.* His orders and what he and his crew had to do would not be easy, but Cazz-ak knew he would do his best to serve the Entho-la-ah-mine race.

He sent out the signal to depart. All around the ship, the Entho-la-ah-mines gathered their thoughts and focused on the apex of the ship. Cazz-ak felt the power enter him and drew it in deeply. Once had pulled in all the power available from the crew, he invoked the might of the Great Thought, bringing it into himself as well. Cazz-ak reflected and magnified the might of both power sources into Raa-alk-mi. As the ship's propulsion officer, Raa-alk-mi turned the mighty force towards the fabric of space-time around the vessel. He warped it such a way that caused the massive vessel to rise out of the hangar chamber.

Cazz-ak gave the order and the ship accelerated through the atmosphere. As it left the planet, he gave a course towards the edge of the system. Cazz-ak continued to listen to the thoughts of all those who suffered because of the actions of the humans. The more he listened, the more his sorrow and resolve deepened.

Once they were outside the Lith-elo-hi-rosh system, Raa-alk-mi slowed the ship, bringing it to a stop in empty space. The propulsion officer refocused his attention on a point in space just in front of the huge bi-pyramidal ship. The stars visible behind the focal point disappeared, but were quickly replaced by a new, different set.

As the ship began moving towards the distortion, Cazz-ak fervently hoped their return to the Entho-la-ah-mine origin world of Haak-ah-tar would not end in the extinction of their species.

08 – WAKE

Wake stood on the bridge, getting ready to begin his maintenance routine. This far north on Traynos-6, everything was hidden under a thick layer of snow, ice, and various types of frozen gas. It was bitterly cold, but his environmental nominizing suit kept him warm and safe from the brutal conditions surrounding him.

He gazed at the jagged mountains that encompassed the bridge, then down into the crevasse it spanned. *Wonder how deep it is,* he thought. He felt the bridge vibrate and looked up to find the cause. As he watched, the last of several large vehicles began crossing to the far side of the bridge. That would be miners on their way to a work shift. He wished the bridge could be closed while he did maintenance, but that would halt production, and was unacceptable to the mining base commander. On the far side, a few huge gas tankers and a couple of transports waited for the bridge to be clear. The roadway spanning the crevasse was only wide enough to allow one way traffic. Usually that was sufficient, but for some reason there was a queue at the moment.

Wake started to make his way across the bridge, his feelings about the work ahead mixed. He was doing routine inspection maintenance, ensuring the bridge remained safe for use. The harsh weather conditions of this polar region and heavy use by the miners put a large strain on the structure. The bridge had needed frequent repairs since it was first put into service nearly a standard year ago.

Wake was particularly anxious to check the new parts he had installed a few weeks ago. He needed to see if they were still in good condition. They wouldn't be, but he was hoping all the same.

Wake stopped as he reached an inspection point, checking a cable and noting it was starting to show signs of significant and dangerous wear. This was not surprising in the least because it had been one of the new, faulty parts he had been sent. The cable's yoke end was fraying just as he expected it would. He decided to radio the nearby mining base to inform them the bridge would need to be closed until he could repair it.

He turned to look as one of the huge gas tankers from the far side rumbled by. As Wake began opening the base frequency, he felt the bridge lurch slightly. A lance of panic pierced him, knowing instinctively the bridge should not move in that way. Whirling back around, he checked the cable again. Several of the finely braided strands had snapped. Running through mental calculations, he realized the remaining strands would not be enough to support any of the vehicles that were beginning to cross the span. *The cable is compromised,* he thought frantically, *the bridge is going to collapse!*

Involuntarily, he looked over the side of the structure into the chasm below. *Even if the drop doesn't kill them, unlikely as that is, it would be impossible for us to rescue them before they froze.* Wake knew he had to act, and speed was crucial. Just as he began to open an emergency frequency, a violent gust of wind caught him and threw him off balance. He tottered near the edge of the bridge, swaying back and forth, trying desperately to maintain his precarious balance. This bridge had no pedestrian traffic, and therefore had no railing.

Just as he thought he had regained his balance, another gust pushed him over the edge. He screamed in terror and felt the reverberation instantly as the sound was directed back by the confines of his helmet. He fell for only a second before his safety harness and tether caught him with a jolt. He swung violently back towards the bridge, staring down into vast drop below. There was only a moment to collect himself before he swung back into one of the thick bridge supports, dealing a savage blow across the back of his head and shoulders. All went dark and he felt himself swimming in a fuzzy haze.

Coming to, Wake stared around, dazed and bleary eyed. *How did I get here?* he stammered mentally. As his eyes cleared, he realized there was nothing but air in every direction but up. His body continued to swing back and forth in a lazy arc, the wind and his collision with the support creating an erratic path. He blinked hard a few times and then it all came flooding back to him. Horror swept through his concussion addled brain as he looked up and saw the last of the gas tankers begin to cross. *If I don't get them to stop*—he thought, cutting off the speculation and forcing himself to act.

He attempted to switch on his comm unit, but it was unresponsive. Thoughts whirled through his mind frantically. *Must have been damaged when I fell. Don't have time to mess with it. Have to climb up and give a visual signal.* He fought desperately to get established onto some part of the support structure, but the underside of the bridge was painted with a deicing compound that was as slick as the ice it prevented. Wake couldn't hold on to anything long enough to climb back up.

Trying a new strategy, he began hauling himself up his tether. He made it up the ten feet by brute strength alone, managing to get an arm up on to the deck of the bridge. Just as he pulled himself up the rest of the way, the gas tanker lumbered by and Wake felt the bridge lurch as more of the flawed cable broke. The moan was audible over the wailing of the wind. *It won't take another stress like that. It's going to give out. Any moment now, any moment!* His mind was spinning. He tried his com unit again, but the result was the same as before.

Wake quickly detached his tether and sprinted towards the mining base. His feet slammed hard against the frozen ground as he left the bridge. An alarm sounded in his helmet and a warning popped up in his head's up display telling him he was consuming oxygen faster than the suit could refine it from the atmosphere. His lungs began to burn, both from the lack of breathable air and his exertion. Wake lowered his head and pushed harder, fighting the black splotches that threatened to shut out his vision. When he looked up, the distance didn't seem to be any smaller. *I'll never make it in time. I have to go back and try to wave the drivers down. Why didn't I do that in the first place?*

Spinning on his heels, he looked back towards the bridge. With a shock, he realized there were now two transports on the bridge at one time. Didn't these foolish miners remember the rule that forbade two vehicles from crossing at once? It had been established to prevent so many different problems that it was practically common sense. The driver of the second vehicle was more interested in getting to his warm shelter three minutes faster than in being safe while doing it. He just wanted to relax after a cold and grueling day's work running a gas mining machine, but his action was foolish. His haste would kill everyone in both vehicles.

Wake ran back towards the bridge, pushing even harder than he had before. He was almost close enough to signal the driver, but the vehicle was dangerously close to the point of no return. Wake started waving his arms franticly in an attempt to signal the operator of the vehicle. They weren't stopping. It wasn't working. He knew he was close enough now for the driver and his backup to see him, but obviously they weren't paying attention. Most of the drivers set their craft's auto-nav system and paid only minimal attention while on the return trip.

The lead vehicle crossed over the section of bridge with the weakened cable and the structure gave a massive shudder, girders and supports moaning under the strain. In less than a second, a huge section of roadway tipped to a steep downward angle, the lead vehicle barely holding traction on its surface.

Wake fell as the deck steepened and started sliding towards the drop off. As he shot past an upright that rose out of the road, he tried to catch it. His body was jerked to a violent, bone snapping stop, yet Wake felt no pain. He looked down at his arm, caught between two parts of the upright. The arm was obviously broken and the sight of it made Wake want to puke.

A soft moan escaped his grimacing mouth as he disentangled himself from the upright. He didn't know why he had moaned. His arm didn't hurt, so it wasn't from pain. It was like he was watching everything happen through some amazingly realistic POV cam, feeling no physical sensation.

Somehow, even with the tilting bridge and the broken arm, Wake managed to get his feet under his body, pulling himself up using his good right arm. He took a few precarious steps, using the bridge framework for support. He looked towards the vehicles and found he was close enough to make eye contact with the people inside. That was when he knew something was very wrong. Not wrong in the sense the vehicle was going to plunge into the depths, that was different. He couldn't put words to his sense of foreboding, but it was strong in the depths of his mind.

Somehow the people just weren't right. That had to be it, but definition still eluded him. Then he noted the second vehicle was gone. It hadn't fallen off the bridge, he knew that much, but it was gone all the same. He turned his attention back to the people inside the cab: one man, two women, one child, an Entho, and a huge dog. That was incorrect for a standard mining crew, not to mention totally absurd. The crews consisted primarily of men, maybe a woman or two, but never children, dogs, or non-humans.

Breaking out of his troubled thoughts, Wake realized the situation was continuing to worsen as the seconds passed. The angle of the deck was growing steeper, and soon the transport's tires would be unable to hold on to it. He had no idea what he could do to save the people in the transport. As his mind was grasping at options, the bridge segment gave another moan and shudder, then began falling. Wake, along with the transport and the people inside it, plummeted down into the gaping maw of the crevasse.

Screaming, Wake's eyes flew open and he frantically looked around the dark room. It took him a moment to realize he was no longer falling towards the black, cold ice, that he was stationary and warm. He took long shuddering breaths, wiping the sweat from his face on to the lower part of his shirt.

This wasn't the first time he'd had this dream, but this time it was different. Every time prior, the dream had followed the events of that disastrous day quite faithfully. This time however, the dream had changed. This time, he'd fallen into the crevasse. This time, it had been a strange mix in the vehicle, not the crew who had actually been there. Wake didn't know what to make of it. He didn't recognize the people who had replaced the mining crew, yet he could see their faces in his mind as clear as if they were his close friends. Their visages were permanently etched in his memory.

He climbed out of his narrow bed and walked over to a small basin on the far wall. Using a tap, he dispensed some water into a small cup, drained the cup into his mouth and swallowed. He filled it again, and drank it again. His throat shuffled up and down in time to the gulps. His hands shook from the remnants of the dream.

He let out a long sigh. The feelings during the day were bad enough, but the dreams were worse. Setting the cup down, he walked over to the nearby window. It was small, but still allowed him to see the stars and some high clouds moving by at a steady rate. *Who were those people?* He wished the dreams would stop. He had enough to deal with at the moment without them. His trial date was fast approaching.

09 – FELAR

Felar's throat felt like it was full of dusty gravel. Her head was throbbing in sync with her heart, big painful pulses that made her want to cry. She opened her eyes slowly and blinked several times, trying to remove the gritty feeling from them. She experienced a stab of panic when everything remained black, but after a moment she realized the room was in darkness.

Just as she became fully conscious, the illumination came on. The sudden light nearly blinded her, but Felar's eyes quickly adjusted. A tall, dark skinned male combat physician walked in a moment later. He began checking the various machines she was hooked to, making notes on a hand held terminal. The man looked to be in his middle years, which was old for the position his dress denoted. He had a fit, elegant grace that suggested he could handle himself if the need arose.

"Don't try to speak yet," he said, noticing her eyes were open. His voice was deep, melodious, and rich. "You sustained a severe head and neck injury. Some medications we had to gave you have noticeable side effects. Nothing too serious mind you, but one of them causes an inflammation of the vocal cords. We are no longer administering that particular drug to you, so the inflammation should diminish in a day or so. In the meanwhile, you can use this," he pulled another hand held terminal out of his pocket and handed it to her. " Use it to communicate as you feel necessary. I'm Doc Hase, by the way."

Felar began to type on the terminal screen in quick, precise strokes. As she completed each line, a voice emitted from the computer. "How long have I been unconscious? Where am I?"

"In answer to your first question, you have been in a drug induced coma for two weeks." A slight frown crossed his mouth as he spoke the words. She began to type on the pad once again, but he caught her wrist gently and continued, "I know what you are going to ask. Let me save you some time." Letting her go, Hase walked over to a small window set in the wall opposite the door.

"No one knows what happened to you. Some witnesses saw you inside the Init training facility on Ashamine-4, but no one is willing to admit who assaulted you. Someone found you in a side corridor, unconscious and in need of medical attention. Medics were called and you were brought to the training hospital."

Anger filled Felar as she heard his words. *No one knows what happened to me? How is that possible?* She typed furiously on the pad, the auto-correct having to work hard to fix all her mistakes. "How could no one have seen what happened? That building is always full of Inits and officers. Someone had to have seen something. And why can't I remember what happened?" Her synthetic voice lacked the emotion Felar felt, and this only increased her anger.

"You'll have to speak to the officer in charge of the investigation. He can explain the details. I only know a brief overview. You sustained a blow to the back of the head, as well as many other injuries. Your short term memory of that time was erased. Thankfully, all the scans show your brain function is normal and it is unlikely you will experience any long term effects." Hase gave her a consoling smile, his eyes soft.

"Thank you for telling me," she typed, and he nodded in response. Hase continued looking at her, and she could tell there was something else he wanted to say. He looked uncomfortable, and Felar guessed whatever it was, it was unpleasant. A sinking feeling began to gather in her stomach.

Hase's smile faded. "We have reason to believe you were raped," he said, his voice flat. "The evidence, little as it was, was transmitted to the investigating officer."

Felar was stunned, felt numb. She didn't know how to respond. After several moments of silence between the two, Hase resumed speaking. "Since no witnesses stepped forward, Command decided it would be best to get you off of Ashamine-4 and away from whoever did this to you. The theory is that the perpetrator would be caught by the time you returned and wouldn't be able to try to silence anything you happened to remember. You were issued transfer papers for a new tour of duty, effective as soon as you are cleared for combat."

The thought of her attacker roaming free made Felar angry and afraid. She was glad Command was reassigning her, thankful she would have separation from the person or persons who had done this to her. Given this new assignment, Felar now had more questions than ever, so she began to type. As she finished the inquiry, the synthetic voice intoned, "Where to?"

"Haak-ah-tar, one of the old Entho worlds." Hase seemed relived to be off the subject of what had happened to her and his warm demeanor returned. "Things are supposed to be pretty messy in that area. Apparently the Enthos have been gathering forces on the edges of Haak-ah-tar space and seem to be preparing for something. We in turn have been sending ships there in an effort to maintain the blockade. I've also heard the Enthos landed some of their forces and are engaging our troops. It would be the first place those alien buggers actually put up any resistance. It's strange, we take the planet from them and they wait over fifty years to attempt to take it back. Now they face a massive buildup of forces there."

Feeling some relief, Felar began to write again, "I'm so glad to hear they aren't going to put me on some blighthearted administrative duty. When do I ship out?"

Hase chuckled, his big smile also shining in his eyes. "Strange you should ask. I'd think an experienced soldier like yourself would feel the ship's worm drive powering down, but you're probably still groggy. We are in Haak-ah-tar space and the Separate Commander said we should arrive there in a few standard hours."

10 – LOTHIS

"Arise," the atonal voice announced, interrupting Lothis' trance-like sleep. It was the end of his three hours of rest. His vibrant orange eyes flicked open and he was instantly aware of his surroundings. The room was his world, and the world never changed.

But today something was—different. Lothis could feel it, sense it somehow. He couldn't see it, but the weight of it was all around him. Something was wrong.

There was a new sound. He had never heard that sound before. His routine was filled with only a few noises other than those emanating from himself. The commanding voice and occasionally the sounds of faint footsteps were all that broke into his world. This sound was different though. It was too loud to be his imagination, but not loud enough for him to be able to discern its origin or source. He could feel the sound's rumbling bass frequencies, and it came from all directions. It set him on edge and filled him with a sense of foreboding.

And the air—something was different about the air. He had never noticed the air before. That was strange.

Another disturbing development was that the room was moving. That was impossible. The room had never moved.

Curiosity flooded his mind. *What is causing all this? Why is it happening?* And then a new thought materialized: *Where am I?* That question felt dangerous and he shied away from it.

Lothis began to be troubled. In his whole existence, he could not remember a time when his life had been different, where any day had even the slightest change to it. So many new things were happening, so many new thoughts and concepts were assaulting him. He realized he was breathing faster and shallower than normal and his heart rate was elevated. Clinging to routine, he walked to the lavatory and cleaned himself as he had done every other day. It didn't bring the calm focus to him as it normally did.

Once this task was completed and his attention no longer buried in routine, his mind quickly returned to his plight. The air was still different, the rumbling noises and oscillations still came and went, and he still felt a foreign emotion his brain tried to classify as fear. He sat down in the angular metal chair in front of the terminal and waited for the voice to instruct him to begin his lessons. He waited. And then waited some more. It was most certainly past the time the voice should tell him to start, but silence still prevailed. Just as his panic began to spill over and take control, the voice spoke. But this too was different, increasing the fear instead of allaying it.

"Lowwwwwthhhhissssssss leeeeeesooooooon beeeeegiinnnnnnnn," it said, its tone slurred and deepened, words drawn out almost to the point of being undecipherable. Lothis stared at the terminal, horror etched on his face. Never had he heard such a thing. It terrified and fascinated him.

The screen began to display images, but they too were all wrong. They scrolled slowly, the symbols and colors distorted and meaningless. Strange sounds begin to issue from the console, sounds Lothis didn't recognize. Then, as if some strange mechanical heart was pumping its last, fading beats, it all slowed even further and then stopped.

The panic quickly rose to a level Lothis could no longer control. He leapt out of the seat, a cry of terror escaping his lips. Hearing that sound come from his own mouth scared the small boy even more.

Lothis had to get away from the terminal, but he didn't know where to go. He ran a few steps then fell, his head striking the edge of his raised metal sleeping surface. Immediately blood flowed from the point of impact and a new sensation filled his head. *Pain,* he thought dully, then wondered what the word meant. Pain was abstract, something he had learned about, but had not personally experienced. Was this what it felt like? Was this what pain actually was? It was horrible.

The sensation in his head was growing, placing more of a demand on his attention. Blood continued to stream down his face and he finally found the courage to touch its source. "Ahhhhhh," he yelled, the sound surprising him as much as the surge of pain.

Lothis had no idea what to do. Change was everywhere and he couldn't cope with it. Before he even realized or understood what he was doing, he blocked the change out. He shut the blood, the pain, the sounds, the air, and the memories of the voice that was not the voice out of his mind. He couldn't take the change, couldn't adapt.

He sat down on the metal bed and decided, for no particular reason he could understand, to go back to sleep. True, it was not normal, but at least the action was familiar.

In the short seconds between wakefulness and sleep, he thought maybe the prior events had just been a dream. Then he wondered faintly, in the instant just before sleep, what a dream was. It was his 3,793rd standard day.

11 – MAXAR

Finally, the game was over. Maxar was deeply relieved. He wasn't happy, but he was about as close as he ever came these days. *That was a close one,* he thought, remembering the final seconds before victory. *Good thing Benson took out that sniper or I'd have been buggered.* His whole body hurt and he limped as he walked. The games were always exhausting and this one had been no exception. He was just glad it was over. That was all that mattered.

Finding a seat in the personnel transport vehicle was easier than he would have liked it to be. *We lost far too many guys out there. Both sides took a hard hit,* he thought, slumping into the most comfortable position the hard composite seat would allow. *It's blightheart! We accomplish nothing but empty entertainment with all this bloodshed. At least if we are to die, send us out against a real enemy like the Enthos.* He began to curse under his breath, but none of the vehicle's few other occupants noticed or cared.

The match had lasted a grueling 48 hours. He had not slept in that whole time and hadn't been given much to eat or drink. Midway through, when they normally would have gotten a break and a real meal, it was announced that High-Elder Hatcholethis was watching the match and desired a test of endurance. No rest or food had been given and the fighting had continued. *What a bastard,* Maxar thought in disgust. *How could someone promote the suffering of his fellow humans this way, even if we are convicted criminals?* As a result of the High-Elder's presence, the game had been far more brutal and lethal than usual. It had been a spectacular show, but it had come at an extreme cost. Almost all the combatants in this match had been killed in the intense fighting that had been waged underground, on the surface, and in near-asteroid space.

"Hatcholethis should burn in the fires of the black star," the man next to Maxar mumbled, mirroring his thoughts. Everyone within earshot nodded, curses and expletives flowing freely. It was widely known that High-Elder Hatcholethis enjoyed watching the games, and whenever he watched in person, there was an unusually high death count amongst the participants. It was rumored he had donated large amounts of Ashcreds to Bloodsport. Most likely this was why they allowed him to modify the match rules whenever he liked.

As Maxar drifted in his thoughts, the personnel transport came to an abrupt stop. "Buggering blighthearted Founder's cursed reception," he swore under his breath, unable to muster the energy to say it louder. He despised the meeting more than the match itself. All the most powerful fans would be there, asking lots of stupid questions. Just the thought of what he had to do next made him want to puke. Having outsiders glory in his pathetic existence was humiliating. And the thought of the body shackles made him even more nauseous.

He exited the carrier, his stomach tied in knots, on fire, and pierced with daggers. All the surviving combatants made their way from the debarking area into the prep room for the reception. They had done this many times before, but few actually enjoyed it.

Restraints were placed on Maxar along with the rest of the group and then they all moved into the meeting hall, Maxar ending up at the back of the line. *Maybe since I'm last they'll be tired of asking questions and will leave me alone.* The thought was a bitter hope, one that was unlikely to be fulfilled. His stomach continued to ache and churn as the line slowly crept forward. He wanted to hold his belly and hunch over in agony, but the restraints limited his movement.

The group of combatants crossed the length of the room to where a line of well dressed people were eagerly waiting for them. Maxar immediately picked out the pudgy High-Elder Hatcholethis along with his stunningly beautiful wife. They were at the front of the line of VIPs, and Maxar desperately hoped Hatcholethis wasn't interested in him. The two lines met and slowly passed each other, each member of the VIP group getting as much time as he wanted with each combatant.

Time dragged by as the fans got to question their doomed heroes. Maxar failed to recognize any of the other VIPs, but he wasn't surprised. Most of the really high profile Ashamine officials didn't have time to visit Bloodsport. He waited in agony, his stomach pains rolling in like waves of fire. Finally, Maxar stood before the High-Elder and his wife. By this time his frame of mind was as foul as his stomach.

"That was an amazing performance you put out there. Simply amazing! The way you were able to sneak up and kill that man with your bare hands without anyone else noticing was amazing! You were featured on all the displays at that moment. A few of us were following you before then, but it was going to be such a good moment that we told everyone to switch to you. Simply amazing! How does it feel to kill a man like that? Good? I should think that..."

The man is insufferable. I don't want to relive these kills. They don't make me proud. Maxar only did these things because he had to, because in this world it was a given that you had to kill. *I'm very good at killing, but that doesn't mean I enjoy it. I'm not like this man.* It was as if Hatcholethis' words were a poison, a sickness that was being deeply injected into Maxar. It was more than he could bear and there was no way for him to escape this verbal onslaught.

"Blood everywhere!! It was fantastic!" Maxar heard the man say, his gruesome accolade never ending. Maxar physically couldn't endure it any longer. His head was throbbing, his guts burning, and this fool wouldn't leave him alone. And then he felt the rising bile. The contents of his stomach were going to make an explosive exit. He began to strain against the body shackles, but they wouldn't permit him to turn away from the High-Elder or his wife. If he spewed his partially digested rations all over this high official, his life would certainly be forfeit, good performance or not.

His throat began to convulse and spasm. He fought desperately to hold his body in check. He clamped his mouth shut and tried to calm his stomach, fighting the urge with all his might. Still, the convulsions and spasms continued. He could feel the burning acid working its way up through his esophagus.

"By the Founder!" High-Elder Hatcholethis blurted in the middle of his never ending description of blood, gore, and killing. "I think this man is ill! Someone send for aid! He is a champion specimen and I don't want my winnings forfeited because of some technicality."

A foul, greenish-brown liquid erupted from Maxar's mouth and Hatcholethis jumped quickly to the side, the stream narrowly missing him. It made a wet splattering noise as it hit the composite floor and began to slowly puddle in the low spots.

"By all that is right and righteous!" Hatcholethis blurted out, his wife emitting a short, high pitched scream. His pudgy, overweight face flapped, his jowls reminding Maxar of an ugly neighborhood dog he had known as a child. "Someone has poisoned my player to invalidate my bet! Where is the medical aid? If I lose so much as one Ashcred, I'll order an investigation. I have a lot of currency riding on this man. Where are the medical personnel?" He was practically foaming at the mouth, his eyes crazed. Spittle flecked the comically thin lips that contrasted so horribly with the rest of his overweight face.

If there had been anything left in his stomach, Maxar would still be vomiting. *Even now he won't stop blathering, even when I almost blasted him with vomit.* He tried to ignore Hatcholethis, but the man's voice pierced deep into his mind. *Passing out would be really nice right now.*

Just as Maxar was deciding he had enough will power to make himself spontaneously combust—anything to silence that piercing voice—the medical personnel came rushing into the room. *Finally!* he thought ecstatically as the techs took him towards the med facilities.

Just as they reached the exit doors, Hatcholethis' frantic babbling crescendoed as he called after Maxar, "You must stay healthy! You really must stay healthy. I have a lot riding on you. It's really important you see! Don't let them kill—" but whatever he continued to say was lost as the large doors closed, finally cutting off the annoying man's stream of words.

12 – TREMMILLY

Tremmilly sat in a cramped seat as the engines of the ancient passenger ship powered up. "What are we doing Beo?" she asked, scratching behind the wolf-dog's ears. The familiarity of the action calmed them both and helped mitigate the stress of the situation. "We are going on an adventure because of a prophecy made by a religion we don't even believe in." She smiled at the wolf-dog, and he pulled back his lips into a friendly snarl. Tremmilly loved how happy it made him look. "But we'll get to see new places, and I'm excited for that." She paused for a moment, feeling apprehensive. "I suppose we'll be meeting a lot of new people too." She'd lived in the same small village for all of her 21 years. New people were intimidating.

"It's a good thing we know how to take care of ourselves," she continued. "Psidonnis did a good job of teaching that. I'm so grateful he was there for us after my parents died." She could only remember small wisps of her parents, but the recollection of their deaths was vivid. Fifteen years had passed, but she could still recall the way the plague had twisted their bodies and made them almost unrecognizable. Death, for them at least, had been a blessing. Psidonnis had cared for her ever since, had raised her like she was his own daughter. She loved and missed him, but not nearly as much as her parents.

Tremmilly's mind was a jumble of thoughts, feelings, and emotions. She had been studying the prophecy ever since she had heard it and had memorized each word. Unfortunately, even though Tremmilly knew the words so well, the meanings still escaped her. The talk with the Dygar council had been—unsatisfying. They hadn't answered enough of her questions. She didn't know if that was because they were ignorant or if they were concealing something from her.

A few parts of the prophecy were very prominent at the moment. The bit about: "*The first be of a light most bright, spirit most pure. Her life touched by death before cognition, her desire only for peace,*" actually made sense. She definitely desired peace and her life was touched by death, but she wasn't completely pure or bright. Both Psidonnis and the council said the prophecy was referring to her, but she wasn't totally convinced. She would need to be on the lookout for someone who better fit that description.

"*But to you who would stay in comfort and safety, not yielding to the instruction of this prophecy: Blightheart shall establish itself on your head and the worlds will be sundered by the Breakers.*" Now that part was clear and scary. And while it hadn't been the reason she had left Eishon-2, she couldn't deny it had played a part in the decision.

The rickety vessel began to shudder, groaning as it lifted off the ground. Tremmilly hardly noticed, despite it being her first time in a space craft. The contemplation of the prophecy consumed all of her attention.

"I don't even believe in the Dygar faith, or any god for that matter," she told Beowulf. Somehow she knew the prophecy was true though, its connection to the religious order irrelevant in her mind. Maybe it was her trust in Psidonnis. Perhaps there was a higher power in the universe that had chosen to use her. Maybe it was just the first real reason to leave Eishon-2 and she was using the prophecy as motivation. It could be that it was all of these things. She didn't know. What she did understand, despite her initial skepticism, was that the prophecy had the feeling of truth. Something bad was coming and she had an obligation to fight it.

Beowulf growled softly and let out a few muffled whimpers, sounding his commentary on the situation. His head was firmly in her lap, his eyes closed, but still awake. The rest of his body lay crunched into the seats beside her. She had never thought Beowulf was large, but when removed from the lush forest and placed in this confined environment, he looked massive.

"I won't take him," the commander of the ship had told her when she was trying to book passage. "He's a threat to the other passengers. Besides, he's too big. There is no way you'll get him to fit into a single seat."

"I can't leave him behind," she protested. "I don't have many Ashcreds, but I can pay for the extra seat." She was angry the skinny, seedy man was extorting her for more money.

"That won't make him any less vicious. He looks like he could tear my arm off. If he hurts one of the other passengers, I'll be liable and they'll take my ship along with every Ashcred I have."

"You obviously don't have many passengers, and I'm offering to purchase three seats. If you don't take me, you'll be losing a lot of credits." Tremmilly was beginning to feel desperate, stuck between leaving Beowulf and not following the mandate of the prophecy.

"Fine," he said, turning his back on her. "But if that dog barks, bites, or blighthearts on the buggered floor, you're the one to deal with it. I take no responsibility."

Hail Terra, she thought, the ship now moving through the upper atmosphere. *If he hadn't changed his mind, I would still be on Eishon and who knows what the consequences would have been.* Tremmilly felt the turbulence fade as the ship passed into space.

"Look at all those stars, Beo," she said in amazement, gazing out the small window beside her. The points of light were far more numerous than anything she'd ever seen back on Eishon-2.

"Hopefully we'll know what to do once we get to Noor-5," Tremmilly said, turning her attention back to Beowulf. "Psidonnis said it is located on one of the major shipping lanes. Guess that means there will be a lot of people there." That made her nervous, but she would push on. There was no turning back now. "It would be nice if we could find all the answers on Noor-5, but if not, we'll have to keep going. And that means another transport. And that means negotiating for passage with another commander." Her resolve to pursue the prophecy was strong, but she knew her love for Beowulf would over ride any other conflicting desire. She could never leave her best friend, even if it meant sacrificing the entire Akked Galaxy.

13 – CRASOR

The Facilitator, Crasor Tah Ahn, deftly slid his way through the crowded capital plaza located on Noor-5. He moved in and out, sliding with the grace of an elegant serpent in the grass, barely brushing each blade. No one thought about him or even seemed to see him. He felt like a shadow.

Crasor was on Noor-5 to exact the vengeance of the Founder. He would make the Divisionists pay for their heretical idealism. And he would do it in such a way that no one would realize it had been the Ashamine.

What a blighthearted dump, Crasor thought disgustedly. *These are the people that will burn in the fires of the black star.* Compared to the glory of Founder's City on Ashamine-2, it was dirty and run down, a dump ready to be demolished. *Once the Ashamine has finished with the buggered Enthos,* he thought with a sadistic pleasure, *it can turn its might on these small, backwater planets. Founder damn them all.*

He continued to make his way towards the front of the large group listening to a preaching Divisionist. The speaker's rhetoric sounded like the same clichéd garbage every one of them spewed out. Crasor wasn't paying much attention to what the man was saying, however. His attention was focused on the crowd, and remaining an invisible entity inside it.

The situation between the Divisionists and the Ashamine continued to degrade. The Founder's Proclamation was clear: "Those who chose to follow the teachings of the Divisionists shall serve five standard years hard labor on the newly established colony worlds. This is education so they might see the justification of the war against the Enthos. For those who lead the Divisionists and cause a rift in the Ashamine, a harsher punishment must be enacted. They know the truth about the Enthos and they know they speak falsehoods. Therefore, all of them will be sent to prison worlds to live out the remainder of their lives." Crasor didn't think these punishments were nearly strong enough, but the movement was gaining more popularity by the day. The situation had to be handled carefully.

The real problem, however, lay in the fact that governing officials on certain planets, like Noor-5, were turning a blind eye to the Divisionists, allowing more of their strongholds to spring up. Crasor was happy to tear down the enclave here. He would bring the situation back under control.

"Up until now," the Founder had told him back on Ashamine-2, "we have tried peaceful tactics in dealing with the Divisionists. But it isn't working, and they continue to cause disruptive protests and dissension as well as a loss of morale amongst the Ashamine Forces. With the final offensive against the Enthos occurring soon, we cannot afford these types of setbacks.

"I've come up with a plan I feel you are perfectly suited to execute. We will fabricate a patriotic organization that will strike against the Divisionists. The Ashamine itself cannot be associated with terrorism, but a group of concerned citizens certainly could. Travel to the worlds with the highest concentration of dissension and strike at them. Make it look like a patriotic group is doing it. You must be extremely careful and let no ties be made to the Ashamine. If all goes as I think it will, the sentiment amongst the masses will swing towards patriotism and the Divisionists will wither." Crasor, after doing some research, had decided Noor-5 would be the best place to start his retribution against the traitorous group.

As he made his way through the clueless multitude, Crasor broke into an empty pocket quite unexpectedly. A young woman was standing in the center of the void, a massive, wolfish dog at her side. The dog turned to look at Crasor and their eyes met. Crasor could see malevolence in the dog's pale blue eyes, malevolence directed at him. The dog bared his teeth in a snarl, but emitted no sound. The girl didn't look at Crasor, didn't even notice her animal's behavior. She was completely focused on the adherent and his heretical doctrine of peace towards the disgusting Entho-la-ah-mines.

Crasor quickly merged back into the crowd, hoping the dog didn't follow. He would find a different path, one that didn't involve the strange pair. The girl was definitely an oddity. Her clothes, hair style, and most of all, her pet, set her apart from those around her. Maybe she was another of those strange, para-political religious types. So many new groups had been springing up lately, but none were having the success the Divisionists were experiencing. Crasor put thoughts of the girl out of his mind. At this moment, he had more important things to focus on.

It took Crasor a considerable amount of time to get to the front of the assemblage, but that was to be expected. Stealth required caution in this situation. He reached into one of his pockets and pulled out a compact respirator, thinking about his appearance as he did so. His disguise was impeccable and would keep him from being identified by anyone who survived. The security devices recording his image would come up empty if they tried to find matches in civil or criminal databases. He was a non-person.

Crasor would rather have been in the center of the huge crowd, right where the strange girl had been standing. His weapon would have the most effect there, but the Founder had been very specific in his objective to primarily target the Divisionist preacher and his immediate contingent. He also wanted the listeners dead, but that was a secondary concern. It was also important there be some survivors to recount the horror.

In just moments, Crasor thought, *the Divisionists will begin to feel the wrath of the Ashamine. This is only the beginning.* Those who practiced the heresy would be punished, and perhaps citizens who heard of this event would think twice before listening to seditious speech. The local government of every planet who allowed the verbal insurrection to continue would feel the pain as Crasor assassinated officials who didn't punish Divisionist adherents. "I have already begun writing a speech to be given after your first strike," the Founder had said. "It begins: 'The citizens of the Ashamine are unhappy with the unlawful, traitorous acts of the Divisionists. They seek justice and an end to the divide that grows amongst our population.' I should add a line about how these patriotic citizens are heroes. That will help shift the public opinion. And also something about how the innocents that perished were martyrs on the altar of justice." The Founder truly was a genius, and Crasor was glad he could serve him.

Crasor placed the respirator over his mouth and nose and began to breath through it. Immediately, the air had a sterile, stale smell. He reached into his pocket and grasped the triggering mechanism, but didn't engage it.

This is it, he thought, his mind running through a last minute check of all his preparations and plans. He knew his equipment and tactics would work flawlessly. The small pump and tank concealed under his jacket, the respirator, the decontamination pod on his waiting starship, the packed crowd, the Divisionist scum—all were where they should be, just waiting for him to trip the switch. He was calm, at peace, and ready to serve his Founder.

As he began to pull the trigger, a high pitched scream assaulted his ears and the ground shook beneath him. *What is this?* Crasor wondered as the noise and the earthquake both intensified. The sound made his head feel like it was going to implode. His hands left the trigger as he attempted to cover his ears, but they did little to keep the sound from penetrating his skull. He stumbled a few steps from the disorienting effect of the noise, trying his best to remain standing.

Fighting through the pain, Crasor could see the surrounding mass reacting to the acoustic assault. First there was disorientation, then the panic grew and people started to scream and wildly flee the area. Those who didn't keep up with the herd were knocked to the ground and quickly trampled.

The rumbling in the earth worsened as the seconds passed. The square started shaking violently and many of those fleeing fell to the ground. Crasor watched as thousands tried to crawl to a safety that didn't exist. *They're disgusting,* he thought, his well trained body keeping its balance. His composure had returned, and he was able to assess the situation. Knowing the longer he waited, the less effective his weapon would be, he removed his hands from his ears and went for the trigger in his pocket. Once it was firmly in his grasp, he tripped the switch.

14 – CAZZ-AK-TAK

Cazz-ak-tak felt a shudder run through the ship as it touched down onto the hard desert of Haak-ah-tar. He could feel the power of combined thought trickle away as each of his crew uncoupled their minds from him. In turn, he lessened the connection between himself and the Great Thought. He could still sense the thoughts of all living Entho-la-ah-mines, the suffering of those under human aggression a dreadful ache in the back of his mind.

This mission was presenting many new challenges to Cazz-ak, and he wondered if he was up to the task. Thankfully, with his leadership and some new technology, they had been able to sneak through the human blockade around Haak-ah-tar. Cazz-ak sent a mental signal to the scientists that had developed the stealth ability. "The humans failed to see the ship, at least so far. The crew was able to handle the demands of the cloaking and all is healthy with them."

The moment they had passed onto the other side of the worm hole, Cazz-ak had been on edge. The scientists had said the technique would work, but it had never before been tried in a hostile situation. "Ti-el-loth, make us unseen," he had ordered, and the weapons Hax-ax-on had done just that. None of the human battle starships they passed had attacked. Their invisibility was based solely on the fact they had tricked the human mind into incorrectly interpreting their instruments. It was now a race against time as their ship's logs would give away the Entho-la-ah-mine presence if anyone decided to review them. They wouldn't be on Haak-ah-tar for long, but every second they were there, Cazz-ak worried the fleet above would discover the Entho-la-ah-mine presence.

Cazz-ak's ship had landed near the edge of a slot canyon in the middle of a vast desert. At the bottom of the canyon was the entrance to a complex system of caves and caverns the Entho-la-ah-mines had inhabited for as long as the Great Thought could remember.

The day Cazz-ak had been forced to evacuate Haak-ah-tar had been one of the worst moments of his life. Each planet that had fallen to the Ashamine aggressors was a supernova of pain in the Great Thought, and Haak-ah-tar had been worst of all. It was the home-world, the origin planet, the place where all Entho-la-ah-mine life had begun. It was also the place Cazz-ak had been born.

Growing up on Haak-ah-tar had presented many opportunities to see the history of the species, to be educated at the hub of Entho-la-ah-mine existence. Being hatched in the First Hive was an amazing experience, especially when he was old enough to see it from the historical view of the Great Thought. And to have developed in the same hive as the queen was a prestigious honor. Now, the whole planet was controlled by the humans. The First Hive was destroyed, the city of Entho-hal-is empty, and most important to the survival of the species, the Crystal Chamber was lost. Without the Crystal Chamber, the species couldn't produce a queen connected to the Great Thought, and lacking that, the species lost its leadership.

Cazz-ak's mission, even if completely successful, would be a temporary solution. It was also only half of the plan the Entho-la-ah-mines hoped would save their species. All over the galaxy, Cazz-ak could see Entho-la-ah-mine ships evacuating the colonized planets as quickly as possible. They would have to find new worlds to live on, places hidden from the humans. *Is that even possible?* Cazz-ak wondered. What he did know was his current mission was vital to the continued survival of the Entho-la-ah-mines. If he failed, the species would likely go extinct whether the humans found their new colonies or not. *We need a queen to bind us together, to give us hope.*

Cazz-ak and his detachment left the craft through the lower mind hatch and headed towards the lip of the canyon. Directly behind him was a female carrying a large Entho-la-ah-mine egg on her back. The egg was a shiny, iridescent green that shone brightly in the mid-day star. Cazz-ak had a hard time taking his eyes off it. He hadn't seen a queen egg since he had left the hive after his birth. Behind the female were eight other males, all of highly advanced age.

When they reached the lip of the slot canyon, Cazz-ak turned to survey the group. They had everything they needed to perform the ceremony, but did they have time? He felt the weight of the orbiting battle starships far above, their unseen presence menacing. He turned back to the canyon, knowing he had no choice but to proceed.

The black stone of the slot canyon did little to reflect the bright day light, cloaking the canyon's interior in darkness. Cazz-ak walked over the edge of the precipice and began to plummet. He quickly passed into the blackness that inhabited the lower regions, gaining velocity.

As he fell, Cazz-ak could sense the floor of the canyon rapidly approaching. When the time was right, he began using the power of the Great Thought to slow himself down. He landed lightly on the rocky floor, immediately knowing where he was, both from his memories and those contained in the Great Thought. All of his party gently landed around him, including the female.

Although the darkness was absolute, Cazz-ak could sense a path the Entho-la-ah-mines had traveled over their millennia of existence on this planet. Part of themselves had been left on top of the black, unforgiving stones, like the path had been paved with their mental images and emotions.

Following this winding path, Cazz-ak and his detachment made their way through the blackness. He was grateful for his six legs, and wondered how the humans were able to do so much on just two. This pathway would be extremely hard for humans to navigate, the rocky terrain treacherous to their fragile bodies. *Their technology has imparted abilities evolution never would have given them,* Cazz-ak thought. He had often compared the evolution of the Entho-la-ah-mines to that of the humans. *Why do they hate us so much? What does it gain them?*

Abruptly, the pathway ceased. Before them lay The Way, a shaft cut deep into the mantle of the planet. The Great Thought had no memory of how or why the shaft had been created. The bore was perfectly symmetrical and smooth sided, just big enough for an Entho-la-ah-mine body to fit into it. It was one of the Entho-la-ah-mine mysteries, one that, with the human invasion, would never be solved.

Just as Cazz-ak was getting ready to lead the group down The Way, he felt a wave of energy resound through the Great Thought. His mind was bombarded by images of gore and destruction and he fell to the floor under the onslaught. Mutilated Entho-la-ah-mines wished for death and couldn't find it. His people were tortured by ghastly figures who never left the shadows and delighted in their pain. The Great Thought was perverted, destroyed, and shattered into a thousand agonizing pieces that cut their way through him. Cazz-ak could feel the core of his being slipping away, but he held fast, knowing that to do anything else would mean death.

When it was finally over, Cazz-ak realized none of it was real. The Great Thought was still there, still pure. He could sense his connection to it, and that gave him comfort. When he felt he could stand once again, Cazz-ak rose back to his feet. "Is everyone OK?" he asked of his group, particularly concerned about the egg. All the males responded positively.

"I am alright," the female replied. "I believe the egg is intact as well, but we will have no way of knowing for sure until we begin the Awakening." This response worried Cazz-ak deeply, but he knew there was nothing he could do about it at the moment.

He sent a question out to the Great Thought, its intent merging with every other Entho-la-ah-mine who was asking the same question. The response wasn't good. "We do not know. Nothing like this has ever occurred before."

Was it some weapon the humans had developed? That seemed unlikely. Their mental capabilities were far from being able to produce such an attack. Maybe the scientists would be able to figure it out, but right now, he had to continue the mission.

"We can't let this distract us from what we must do," he sent, mentally gesturing towards The Way. "We must proceed to the Crystal Chamber."

Cazz-ak dropped into The Way, using the Great Thought to keep himself stable as gravity pulled him down. The shaft was deep, and if possible, even blacker than the canyon above it. It had a feeling of disuse and partial decay that made Cazz-ak despair. This never would have happened if the humans had left them alone. Cazz-ak was still leading the group, and after a long fall, they reached the bottom. He continued following the path paved in mental images, the particularly strong ones distracting him.

Cazz-ak saw the corridor as it once had been, lit in beautiful colors with thousands of Entho-la-ah-mines visiting the Crystal Chamber to see its marvels. He smelled the enticing aromas of foods being prepared by the finest Entho-la-ah-mine chefs. He breathed in the intoxicating aroma of the Enlithas, the young females looking for mates. Everything was so joyous, carefree, and festive. The memories, both his own and those that paved the pathway, made Cazz-ak homesick for a place no longer in existence, a time of innocence forever shattered.

Cazz-ak pushed on towards the Crystal Chamber, trying as best he could to shut out the images he so desperately wanted to enjoy. "We will have peace and harmony once again," Cazz-ak sent to the group, trying to infuse it with as much positivity as he could. "Someday we will find a place far from the humans. Peace and happiness will once again be our way." He felt the morale of the group rise, and he tried not to let doubts enter his thoughts. *What caused that polluted wave of energy in the Great Thought?* he wondered, his shield slipping. *No. There is no time for that now. We have to complete the Awakening and get away from Haak-ah-tar before the humans realize we are here.*

Whether he was successful or not, Cazz-ak knew the Entho-la-ah-mines would continue fighting for their survival, no matter how scant the odds. He would do anything he could to preserve his species, no matter the personal cost. Cazz-ak shut out both the residual happy memories and the polluted ones, hardening himself. He had to focus. The most dangerous parts of the mission were yet to come.

15 – WAKE

Wake bit down into the krakori fish morsel, savoring the bold flavor. "Very good, no?" the vendor said. "Just one Ashcred for an entire skewer."

"I have business to attend to, but when I'm finished, perhaps I'll return." The vendor immediately lost interest in Wake, and began looking for a new potential customer.

Pushing his way through the dense crowd, Wake left the fish stall and made his way towards the Lower-Elder Council Building. The food market was quite popular with the government officials in this area and being lunch time, it was packed.

Wake's trial was due to start in thirty minutes, but since it had already been rescheduled three times, he wasn't sure it would happen today. From what he had heard on the news, the Elders were busy trying Divisionists, sentencing most of the offenders to hard labor on the newly colonized Entho worlds. *I wonder if that's where they will send me?*

He had been on Ashamine-2 for seven standard days, waiting for his trial to actually go through. He was on the third repeat of the cycle: Get up, kill time until the trial, have the trial be postponed, spend the rest of that day and then the next exploring the city.

The impending trial was mentally taxing, but Wake tried to make the best of it. On the days between postponement, he wandered around, marveling at the amazing buildings and their impossible architecture. It staggered Wake to think the entire planet was covered in some type of structure or well manicured park. *Ashamine-2, the city-planet.* He'd never seen anything like it, not during any of his extensive travels with the EBD. Wake knew he didn't want to live here, but he was glad he had been able to see it, even if it was under stressful circumstances.

"I'm Wake Darmekus and I submit myself for trial," Wake told the guards stationed at the entrance to the Lower-Elder Council Building. They said nothing as they led him inside. His boots, and those of the escorting guards, made rhythmic tapping sounds as they struck the highly polished marble floor. White pillars lined the entry hall, the bright lights causing them to shine. He had never been allowed into the building in times past. *That probably means the trial is going through.* He straightened up, forcing himself to look calm and composed.

Wake tried to walk naturally in his new boots, a fancy pair he had to buy in order to meet the dress requirements of the summons. They made his feet hurt, probably because they were not yet fully broken in. Thankfully, his Engineering and Building Division dress uniform fit the rest of the dress requirements.

The weight of the synth-diamond sword at his hip felt strange. The weapon had been a gift from his parents when he was a boy. Ashamine diplomats carried some type of ceremonial armament, although few actually knew how to use them. "A diplomat must always look strong and ready for battle, be it with words or with action," his mother had always said. In keeping with their desires for Wake, his parents had gifted him the blade. Possessing a sword he could not use had seemed stupid to Wake, so he pestered them for fighting lessons until they gave in. He had learned from every swordsman on his home world of Psinar-3, eventually besting them all. As an adult, he wondered at his boyhood obsession. Occasionally, during his travels, he would find someone who practiced the archaic art and they would spar, but he now lacked the fiery passion of his boyhood. *So why am I wearing it now?* Wake was no diplomat, but the dress code contained in his summons said a formal armament was allowed. It didn't quite represent his role within the Engineering and Building Division, but it did represent something of who he was and where he had come from.

Wake grew increasingly nervous as they approached the massive doors at the far end of the hall. The Lower-Elders rarely conducted trials face to face. Usually, the Elders reviewed the cases and transmitted their verdicts back to their point of origin. *Why is my case different?* He couldn't think of a way to interpret their actions in a positive light.

Finally reaching the door, Wake and the members of his escort stopped. The commander of the guard fixed Wake with his hard eyes. The man's uniform was crisp, clean, and well maintained. It told Wake a lot about this man's regard for his duty and position.

"Sir, please go in immediately. The convocation is awaiting your presence." The commander had a clipped voice, harsh, but not disrespectful. "Please only speak when directed to, show the deference due your station, and please keep yourself under control at all times. Your sword will stay in its scabbard for the duration of the trial. It is a decoration for this ceremony, and will only be used as such. It is impossible to harm the Elders as they are shielded against attack. If you start to act in a threatening manner however, preventative action will be taken. That will result in your death. Do you understand these instructions?"

Wake nodded his head and looked down at his sword apprehensively. He still wondered whether it had been the right decision to wear it, mainly because he didn't want to appear militaristic. The Engineering and Building Division was not deployed to combat zones, but Wake wanted to show these men he was strong and confident.

Two of the guards pushed the doors open and stood at attention. Their crisp, military manner made Wake even more nervous than he already was, but he pushed the feeling down as best he could. The commander motioned Wake to walk through the door and he did so, entering a room unlike any he had ever seen.

It was enormous, the ceiling so high Wake couldn't make out any of its details. The walls curved, making the room a perfect circle. A wide ledge came out from the walls at a height of twenty feet. Large, ivory colored banners bearing the Ashamine insignia hung along the walls above the ledge. It was extremely bright in the room, and since most of the surfaces were white, there was little to diminish the harsh light.

The Lower-Elders were seated on platforms along the ledge at perfectly spaced intervals. They were old men, not as old as the High-Elders, and certainly not as old as the Classad were rumored to be, but old all the same. When he neared the center of the room, he realized they were in a circle around him. This fact made Wake even more uncomfortable, but he made conscious effort not to let it show.

"Stop!" a curt voice commanded as Wake reached the center of the room. He did as commanded and also lowered his head in deference to the power that surrounded him. A long silence followed and Wake could feel every eye on him, evaluating, testing, probing.

Time dragged for Wake until a new, flat voice broke the silence. "Hear all present: This is an official convocation of the Lower-Elder Council, appointed and sanctioned by the Founder, Classad, and High-Elder Council."

"Can we dispense with all the worthless formality?" an older, tired sounding voice interrupted. "We have many Divisionists to try and they are of far more importance."

The man directly in front and above Wake on the ledge rose to his feet. He was tall, and his platform was slightly higher than all the others. *That must be the Presider.*

"My dear Odameesi," the Presider said, "we have plenty of time to settle both this man's case and those of the Divisionists. Besides, this trial was mandated by the High-Elders. We must give it our full attention." He then turned and addressed the group. "We are here to decide the fate of this man, known by all as Wake Darmekus, of the Engineering and Building Division of the Ashamine. Let it be known to the ends of the Akked Galaxy that he is charged with the malefactions of delinquency of duties, disregard for safety, and the murder of twelve colonists."

Wake felt the Presider's words hit him as if they were a physical blow. *The High-Elders mandated this trial? And they are going to charge me as if the accident was totally my fault? What about my protests of faulty materials? I was forced to use them!* Anger roared in Wake as he realized he was being set up to take a fall for some greedy bureaucrat that had ties to the High-Elders.

"How do you respond to these charges?" the Presider asked, his face expressionless. Composing himself and straightening to his full height, Wake looked the Presider directly in the eyes.

"In the evidence log, you can see I submitted several reports prior to the bridge accident. In these reports, I state clearly that the materials I was sent were faulty." Wake had to calm himself, realizing his anger at their accusation was bleeding into his words. "I submitted several requests for replacements, but was continuously ordered to use the original parts. The choices I had were to either use the parts or disobey a direct command. Under these circumstances, I don't see how I can be at fault for the accident or the deaths of the colonists. The officer who continuously ordered me to use the parts should be held responsible. Have you even looked at the evidence?!"

As the last word left his mouth, the room erupted in shouts. He shouldn't have asked the last question, shouldn't have let his temper get away with him. These men demanded respect and were used to receiving it. Wake stood tall, knowing that backing down now would make him look weak and guilty. All around him a verbal inferno raged.

"I see no reports filed!"

"He is a liar!"

"This man was negligent! He must be punished!"

"There is no evidence of faulty parts!"

"How can he disrespect us with such blatant lies!"

After several moments passed, the tumult quieted. One of the Elders, a tall man with pure white hair, spoke out in a clear voice, "Surely this man seeks to place his blame on others. This defense has been perpetrated since time immemorial. We have no record of his reports, and the Ashamine inspector who went to the site said it was faulty workmanship. What do you think of that, sir Darmekus?"

"This Wake Darmekus is a fool and an idiot if he thinks we will be taken in by such blightheart," a short, dark Elder proclaimed. The Elder then uttered a curse and glared at Wake, his expression as hot as the fires of the dark star. Immediately, an uproar of insults, curses, and rejoinders flew around the large room. Wake now had no doubts he was being set up. His workmanship had been flawless and his reports had disappeared. *Lies,* he thought, sliding even deeper into despair.

"Order! Order!" the Presider said, fighting to regain control of the situation. Eventually, the clamor calmed to a soft buzz and the Presider addressed the assemblage. "We have all heard this man's testimony and have viewed the statements of his senior commanders as well as that of the inspector. With these things in mind, we must come to a decision." He paused momentarily to look around at his fellows. "All those who feel this man, Wake Darmekus of the Engineering and Building Division of the Ashamine, is innocent of the malefactions he has been charged with, please stand."

Around the room, five of the thirty Lower-Elders stood, including the Presider. Wake began to feel a horrible emptiness in his guts. It was as if something was draining everything he was, siphoning out all he felt until only an empty void remained.

"All those who feel Wake Darmekus is censurable for these malefactions, please stand." Now, the remaining twenty five Lower-Elders stood, their faces grim. A few even had malicious expectation blazing in their eyes.

The Presider, a look of surprised terror on his face, stared at Wake. But that wasn't quite right. The Presider was looking past Wake, at something behind him.

Wake whirled around and saw a form crouched along the wall near the doors. This puzzled him, because the figure hadn't been there when he had entered the convocation hall.

The world took a violent spin and Wake went crashing down to the floor, his left leg awkwardly twisting beneath him. Just as the pain was building to an agonizing crescendo, the limb slid out from under him. He looked up from his prone position as a figure strode past him, the person's features obscured in a billowing black robe. *How did he move so fast?* Wake dazedly thought.

He tried to push himself back up to his feet, but his abused left leg and ankle screamed with pain and he fell back to the floor. Remaining prone, he swiveled around to watch the progress of the figure. *The guards should be arriving any second now.*

The figure stood below the ledge where the Presider sat, hooded head tilted up. Then, an instant later, it stood on the ledge directly in front of the Presider.

"I am of the Brotherhood of Azak-so," the figure said, its deep voice booming in the large chamber. "I bear a message from myself and my fellow Brothers." Then, before the words had finished echoing in the large chamber, the figure disappeared.

"We have tried to convey this message through more subtle means, but you refuse to unstop your ears." The voice was now coming from behind Wake. He scooted his body around on the hard floor, and sure enough, the figure still stood on the ledge, only now it was directly across the room from where it had been. "We are forced to unstop them for you, through any means necessary. For many years, this government—this *Ashamine*—has become more and more repulsive." He said the word Ashamine like it was something profane. And then he was gone again, moving to another portion of the platform. *Why aren't the guards here yet?* The whole situation seemed surreal, like he had fallen into a vivid dream.

"You have denied the poor and enhanced the rich. You have made a mockery of justice and have made profit your highest goal. You have slain the innocent and have sought to annihilate the peaceful Entho-la-ah-mines. You have failed humanity."

Suddenly, the man was next to Wake again, back in the center of the room. Wake could smell him, a mixture of fury and musty cloth. The man's clothing was made of ancient material, its construction simple and crude.

The hooded man raised his hands high into the air and slowly rotated, taking in the whole room. "And though you oppress many, there are those who will bring you low. Misery to you who are mighty! You who will soon be brought to your knees!"

Wake tried to stand once again. He almost fell, but managed to leverage himself to his feet. His ankle and leg still protested bitterly, but at least he was able to move.

Having no clue of what to do now, Wake just stared at the intruder. Quick glances at the Lower-Elders confirmed they were doing the same. From what the commander of the guard had said, the intruder should be dead by now. He was clearly threating the Lower-Elders and blaspheming the Ashamine.

"Destroy corruption and cut out the cancer eating at the heart of humanity. For if humanity does not forsake our wicked endeavors, we shall be consumed. The Breakers are coming!" At this final declaration, the man turned to face Wake, drawing a long alloy rapier from his robes. Glaring directly at Wake, he muttering under his breath, "Boy, cut me down, for if you do not, these men will surely hand a sentence of death."

Wake drew his translucent synth-diamond katana, but went no further. He didn't understand the situation. Everything was moving too quickly. He needed time to think.

When the man lifted his own sword and attacked, Wake automatically defended himself. He deftly deflected the other man's strikes, easily falling into the forms that had been drilled into him in his youth. The man was an expert swordsman, his movements fluid and effortless. Wake knew he didn't have a chance against him. *Don't give up,* he thought, trying some of his best forms and finding no success. Then, there was an obvious opening. His opponent's sword strayed too far past a normal arc, exposing his entire left side. It was as if he really did want Wake to cut him down.

Wake instinctively made a quick slash across the exposed area, feeling sick about the blood that would be spilled. *Not too deep. Only want to incapacitate him.* But no—just as the sword was about to cut into him, the man disappeared.

Assuming a fully defensive posture, Wake glanced quickly around the room, expecting to see the man on the ledge somewhere. He was gone. Only the horrified looking Lower-Elders and Wake himself remained in the dazzling light of the large chamber.

Realizing the threat was gone, the Elders broke into chaos. Everyone began to talk at once, their voices shrill and much louder than normal. These men were not used to being threatened and verbally abused.

"How, in the name of the Founder, did that man get in here?"

"Blightheart, where are the guards and why were we not defended?"

"I could have been killed, we all could have been. I could be lying here in a pool of my own blood!"

The clamor continued on for quite some time. Voices overlapped each other. The room got louder and louder, no one listening to anyone else.

Wake was still standing in his defensive form, his sword high in the air, when a throng of guards rushed in. They were all wielding high powered rail guns and they were aiming them at him. "Drop the sword! Get on the ground! Drop the sword immediately! Get on the ground now! Get on the ground!"

Wake, let his sword fall and dropped to the floor. He had no idea why they were coming after him and not hunting for the figure. "Leave him be," the Presider intoned, the appearance of the security forces restoring the Lower-Elders to their composed state.

Instantly, the guards were scanning the room, looking for new threats. *These guys are well trained and disciplined. Where were they when we needed them?* The Presider, seeming telepathic, voiced Wake's thought, "Where were you when we needed you?" Wake then noticed he didn't recognize any of the guard squad. It was made up of entirely different men than those he had been escorted in by.

"Distinguished Elders," the commander said, straightening up to attention. "My squad was dispatched to your chambers by Ashamine Command, priority urgent. When we reached the outer vestibule, we found the on-duty squad, unconscious. We rushed in to secure your personages, fearing the worst. That is all the information we have been given."

"Truly strange," the Presider replied, narrowing his eyes in thought. "Thank you for your service commander." Murmurs and hushed conversations sprung up around the room, the Elders speculating about the recent events. A silence came over the room and time passed uneasily for Wake.

"This Brotherhood of Azak-so, has anyone heard of it? Or the Breakers he warned us of?" Wake recognized the speaker as being one of the men who had derided him at the beginning of the trial.

A new speaker, his voice dripping with disdain, shouted "Let us finish the matter at hand. We should not be discussing this in front of outside ears."

"I believe some sort of additional consideration should be afforded to this man," the Presider stated. "He was our only defense in this crisis."

"He didn't do much, didn't even kill the intruder," a voice said, barely audible.

An Elder to Wake's left cut in, "We shall put it to a new vote. Will that satisfy you, Presider?"

"Indeed it shall, and keep in mind what this man did for us when you vote."

The voting process was repeated. The same five Elders stood to vote in Wake's favor, with the remaining twenty five standing against. *Just like the first time,* Wake thought. *How could the vote have stayed the same?* Despair washed over him. *Not even one Elder appreciated my defense of them? Maybe they didn't buy into the show. Or maybe someone bought their votes before the trial even started. What happened to all the reports I filed? I'm being set up!*

The look on the Presider's face was stern as he stood once again and looked down on Wake. "Let it be known Wake Darmekus has been censured for the malefactions stated at the beginning of this convocation. We shall now move to judgment. For crimes of this nature there is but one sentence, execution by asphyxiation in the void."

16 – FELAR

Felar had been on Haak-ah-tar for several days and was fully recovered. She felt great. It had taken some minor rehab to restore regular strength and fitness levels, but that was all in the past now. She knew it was time to move on, to put everything that had happened on Ashamine-4 behind her. *How can I put the assault behind me if I can't even remember it?* Maybe not remembering was for the best.

While she was happy to be back on combat deployment, she wasn't ecstatic to find she would be leading a squad of newly graduated Initiates. She had nothing against any of them personally, but it would have been much better to be on duty with other FC's.

"Sir, I'm used to being deployed with other Foundies," she had told her commanding officer. "I fear their inexperience might lead to problems in the field. I need troops I can count on."

"They are a good group, graduated top of their class," her commander had replied. "You have a day to run drills with them and make sure they are up to speed. If you have a problem with any of them, let me know and we'll find a solution."

And so far, she hadn't had any issues. They were smart, capable, and looked up to her with an awe that bordered on reverential. During training exercises it was fairly obvious they were trying to impress her by out doing their fellows. She even noticed a few of them had picked up on her speech and mannerisms. None of it bothered her, and she was flattered in a way. It was a far cry from the flagrant disrespect she had so recently experienced.

I'm even beginning to grow attached to these Inits, she thought. *Have to stay professional though, I'm their CO. And if the mission gets dangerous, I can't hesitate to send them into harm's way. Completing the mission is the highest priority.*

"OK, squad," Felar said, snapping out of her thoughts, "we've received some new sit-reps." The armored personnel carrier jolted hard, throwing her against her seat restraints. "Ackerson," she barked, "try to keep us off the worst of the rocks. My brain's feeling rattled enough as it is."

"Yes ma'am," he responded, swerving the large vehicle around some new obstacle.

"Anyway," Felar continued, trying to hold herself steady so she could read the terminal screen, "it appears the Enthos have come back to Haak-ah-tar. Seven of their bi-pyramid ships just appeared inside the AF blockade. Nobody understands how they got there." Felar paused, wondering how such a technologically backwards species could pull off that kind of trick. "That's some creepy blightheart," she resumed, finding where she had left off in the report. "We've managed to hunt down two of the ships and destroy them, but the rest have evaded us. It looks like the remaining vessels have been bombarding the surface with some kind of force or gravity weapon. The sci guys apparently have no idea how it works, but it causes earthquake like effects and seems to emanate from their bi-pyramids. They've been sending their ships over areas with little to no tactical significance though, so their intel must be bad. Some of their vectors have taken them over Ashamine targets, but it seems almost accidental.

"AF analysts are saying the Enthos are trying to take Haak-ah-tar back from us. That doesn't sound right to me. Their tactics are all wrong for something like that and unless they have a lot more firepower and ships coming, they can't hope to push us off world. I wonder what they are really up to." Felar thought about the question for a moment, then looked back at the terminal screen, knowing she needed to focus on her mission and not the overall campaign. Leave that job to the Separates.

"It looks like we've also received a briefing on our current mission, thank the Founder. I was wondering if they were going to keep us in the dark forever." Felar quickly scanned the report, assimilating everything she needed to know.

"We're headed to some kind of classified research facility, Inits." She looked around inside the cramped quarters of the APC, making eye contact with each of them. "This is a big deal guys. We've all received clearance to enter the installation, but none of us is to look at any research information. This is strictly a search and rescue op. An Entho vessel passed over the facility a few hours ago and AF Command hasn't been able to establish contact since. We are to find out what happened, render any aid we can provide, and report back to AF Command."

Felar had a bad feeling about this mission. There was so much secrecy surrounding it. The information in their mission briefing had been scant and she hated that. Lack of information got people killed. And the fact it was a classified installation made it even more ominous. *What are they researching there? What are we going to run into?*

A notice popped up on her terminal that they were straying from the navigation track. "Initiate Ackerson, why are you are deviating from the nav coordinates?"

"The point's all screwy, Enlight Haltro. Nav was having me go over some big buggered hills. Decided to go around, ma'am," Ackerson responded, his tone cheery. She could see he needed praise for his actions, so she gave it to him.

"Well done Ack. Glad to see you aren't just blindly following a machine." She had known why they were slightly off course, but keeping these Inits on their toes was vital. While she didn't expect an ambush—or even any Entho ground forces for that matter—it was good to build a habit of vigilance for when such things could occur.

"Are there any other details about the facility, ma'am?" This was from Initiate Shanbek, a tall gangly looking youth, barely old enough to join the Ashamine Forces.

"Nope," she replied, "and since it's a classified location, I doubt they'll send anything else. We're gonna be in the dark and on our own, so best stay sharp." Turning to her tactical readout, she addressed Ackerson, Shanbek, and the three other Initiates that were in APC. "Now that we aren't just driving off into the desert to find a nav coordinate, we can formulate a mission protocol. When the blightheart comes, there is rarely time to stop and think. It has to be instinctual, so pay attention!" She paused for a moment and looked at everyone, using her eyes to reinforce the seriousness of her tone.

"First off, let's go over squad assignments. Ackerson, you are running tech on this mission. We shouldn't come across anything you haven't been trained on yet. Intel says this is a standard Ashamine facility, so doors, computers, AI, and just about everything else should—and I stress *should*—be Ashamine standard. If you run into something over your head, let me know. I have some advanced training in tech, so I might be able to help. Just don't panic and we'll be OK.

"Shanbek, you will be on scout and recon. Remember to calibrate to the highest sensitivity you can without receiving too much interference. Since this is primarily an SAR mission, any contacts you get on your readout should be friendlies. *Should* and *are* can be very different things in the real world though, so keep your weapons ready, but don't get too trigger happy. We can't be blasting scientists or any other non-hostile that may be down there. That makes us look bad.

"Edwards and Unthar, you'll both be on primary weapons duty. From what we know of on-site conditions at this point, you shouldn't be doing much. That isn't an excuse for laxness or inattentiveness! I've seen *easy* missions go to the fires of the black star so fast it would knock you out of your boots. So stay on your toes and make sure you watch your buddies' backs.

"Malen, you are on support weapon duty. You'll be manning the big rail gatling weapon. I know you are certified on it, but make sure you respect it. Wield it wrong and you will kill us all. Use it correctly, and you can knock down anyone or anything. That gun has some awesome power, as I hope you fully realize." Felar stopped, looking at each at her troops to make sure they understood her. "Is everyone clear?" They all nodded their affirmation.

Felar's terminal popped up a notice they were five minutes out from the facility. "Check your weapons and gear load out," she commanded. Felar inspected her primary rail gun to make sure it was properly loaded and ready to go. She did the same to her side arm. Felar also checked to make sure her short swords were in their scabbards on her back. She had sharpened them this morning and knew they were ready for action. Her own preparations complete, she made sure the Inits were doing likewise. They were somewhat slower than she had been, but by the time Initiate Ackerson stopped the APC, they were all ready. "Line up for deployment," Felar barked, and they quickly did so.

When the deployment ramp dropped, the Inits all hustled out of the vehicle, running in a slight crouch with their weapons all pointed at specific fields of fire. Felar brought up the rear, the position she had always taken when the squad had drilled. Ackerson led them over to a small entrance door and began working the access panel. *Good thing we didn't try to use the vehicle door,* Felar thought as she eyed the larger entrance. *They definitely didn't design that to fit an APC.*

Felar looked back to the squad and experienced a moment of pride as she watched the green Inits functioning as a team. *True, it's not a combat drop, but at least they are staying in formation. Good to see all that blighthearted drilling we did got through their thick skulls.*

"Damn it!" Ackerson swore as he focused intently on the access controls. "Apparently everything is locked down. It's not letting me open the door. Giving me some kind of nonsense about not having an authorized access code. Didn't we get this code from AF Command?"

"Affirm Ackerson." Felar's voice was commanding, but her tone was troubled. She clicked on her long range comm. "Overwatch, this is Tango-5."

"Tango-5, Overwatch has you with synced signal," a strong male voice replied.

"Overwatch, the supplied code for entry to the facility is non-functional. Request new code." The officer was silent for several moments before responding.

"Tango-5, the supplied code is correct."

"You sure you entered the code correctly Ackerson?" Felar asked.

"Yes ma'am," Ackerson promptly responded. Felar trusted him, so there must be some other issue.

"Overwatch," she said, reopening the long range comm, "the code remains non-functional. Request updated orders." The officer was once again silent for several moments and Felar wondered if they would be heading back to base.

"Tango-5, the mission is still a go. Use any means at your disposal to gain entrance. This is a high priority mission."

"Affirm," Felar responded, "Tango-5 out." She looked at the door, wondering if they would be able to penetrate it. They'd have to try. *A remote research facility is high priority? I wonder what's behind this door. Blightheart. Maybe I don't want to know.*

"Squad," Felar barked, "either Intel has got this buggered all the way to the fires of the black star or this base is on some type of extreme security lockdown. Either way, we are on this side of the door and our objective is on the other. I, your ever resourceful Enlightened, have a plan." She said all this with a big smile on her face, even though she was beginning to feel some serious apprehensions about the mission.

"Malen, use your rail gat to create an entrance for us." After giving Malen and the rest of her squad more precise directions, Felar moved everyone back to a safe distance. Watching the rail gatling weapon spool up and launch was a sight to behold. Its large barrels circled slowly, pounding out a shot every quarter second. The tungsten alloy slugs packed an enormous punch, but they only put dents in the door at first. Felar thought it sounded like some demon in the dark star was beating on a horrible, tremendous metal drum. She increased the active sound dampening of her combat helmet, hoping to block out some of the shrieking cacophony. Sparks flew as the rounds began to penetrate the heavily reinforced door. Fragments of the door pelted her and Felar was thankful for her combat armor. A gat round ricochet would be deadly otherwise.

After thirty seconds of punishment, Felar called a halt. The door was bowed inward and many holes penetrated its surface, but the door still barred their entry. "Another thirty second burst would probably finish the job, but I don't want to deplete all your ammo. We'll try a new tactic." She pulled a small package of explosives from her combat vest. This compound was distributed exclusively to the Founder's Commandos, and with good reason. She molded some into a shaped charge, placing it on the door. As she set the timer, Felar directed the squad to take cover. Running back to safety herself, she counted down: *Four, three, two, one...* The concussion wave boomed around them, and Felar was glad she hadn't been any closer. The helmet's dampening had maxed out, but still her ears were ringing.

The door had finally yielded, a small tunnel piercing it. Felar's apprehension ratcheted up a notch as she noticed the full construction of the entrance. It was three feet thick, with several inches of steel covering a core of concrete.

Once inside, Felar looked for the mechanism securing the door, hoping she could open it so the survivors wouldn't have to climb out through the hole. She found nothing. The interior was completely smooth. *The door must be controlled remotely*, she thought. *That must mean they needed to keep people from leaving as well as entering. What exactly are they studying here?*

Ackerson led the way down the long, steeply pitched corridor. It was almost completely dark on the ramp and Felar was reluctant to leave the brightness of the star streaming through the doorway. She switched on the light at the end of her primary weapon and watched the rest of the squad do the same.

It took some time, but they finally reached the bottom of the ramp and entered the complex proper. The air felt heavier here and Felar could somehow feel the weight of the ground surrounding them. It was oppressive. Most of the lights were off here as well, leaving the long corridors in an eerie pallor. "Must be running on some kind of backup power," Ackerson noted. "At least it isn't completely dark." He stopped at a wall monitor and tried to check the compound's systems. As Ackerson worked, Felar wondered just how deep underground they were now. The ramp had seemed to go down for at least a mile and was fairly steep. She ran some quick mental math and figured they had to be at least five hundred feet below the surface of Haak-ah-tar, maybe more.

"Bugger it all," Ackerson swore, breaking into her thoughts. "It's unresponsive. Enlightened, all the monitoring and system control access is disabled on this terminal. We could try another one?" The squad looked at Felar expectantly, waiting for her to tell them what to do next.

"If the complex is on lockdown, they'll all be the same." She tried to signal Overlord to give a sit-rep, but nothing happened. Her eyes flicked to the HUD on her face plate. It showed her comm status as up for local and down on long range. "Blightheart," she cursed, her expression calm, but her voice beginning to betray her unease. "The command link is down, so we are on our own for now. I'm guessing it's because we are too far underground. The APC should be relaying the signal to AF Command, but apparently our signal isn't reaching the APC."

She paused for a moment to think. It would not be wise for her to share her sense of foreboding about this facility with her squad. Fear had a way of infecting minds, and she, more than any of them, was better equipped to handle it.

"We all stay together and work as a fire team. No one leaves the squad for any reason. We search this facility from top to bottom and find anyone still shaking and bring them out. Search and rescue is our mission. Stay alert. Keep your weapons hot. Most likely we will only find scientists, but be prepared for anything."

Felar took point, alert, but on edge. The situation felt too serious to let an Init lead the team, even an Init she had trained. They searched room by room, corridor by corridor. The first few rooms contained desks and terminal screens flashing "Lockdown. Report to secure quarters," but no people. They also discovered a rec room which had giant terminal screens flickering the remnants of gaming software. The same lockdown message flashed across the huge screens, making the room look like one of the dance clubs on Ashamine-2.

Continuing the search, they found more of the same offices. Their plainness allayed Felar's fears at first, but then she realized something. *There is nothing personal here, no decorations, no individuality.* It looked sterile, unused. There were no people here either, which was strange. *Where is everyone? Where are the 'Secure quarters'? And if this is a research facility, where are the labs? Down,* she thought, her foreboding deepening.

"We need to find the lift," she commanded the squad. "Everyone must be on the lab levels." After more searching, they found an elevator. Ackerson quickly touched the screen and selected the option to call for the lift.

"It's asking for a security code ma'am," Ackerson said, his voice sounding resigned. Felar watched as he typed in the code supplied by Intel. She wasn't surprised when the screen displayed "Code Denied".

"Damn it," Felar cursed. "I don't want to have to blast through this door. We risk damaging the lift and that would make evac into a nightmare." She tried to think of other options, but nothing came to mind. Her squad stood around her, looking nervous but keeping a strong perimeter. "We don't have much of a choice," Felar finally decided. She began to take out more of her special explosives, but as she did, the control panel switched from a flashing red hand to a green thumbs up symbol. Seconds later, a rumbling sound emanated from below.

The entire squad tensed up and sighted down their weapons at the lift doors. "I didn't do anything to cause that," Ackerson said, stress evident in his voice. "Maybe someone could have initiated it at AFC through remote access?"

Felar made her voice sound confident and commanding, "Alright, when the lift gets here, we clear the interior and then we all get on. This should take us straight down to the lab areas. We'll find any survivors and escort them back to the APC. Keep your weapons hot and your fields of fire sharp. No mistakes."

They finished getting in combat formation just as the elevator door opened. Its interior alternated between bright and dark, the lights flickering in a disturbing syncopation. Dread and unease were apparent on the faces of the Initiates. She hoped they could handle whatever faced them down in the deep unknown of this eerie place.

17 – LOTHIS

Lothis awoke, his head pulsing a rhythmic thud of pain. His hands were coated in a crust of red. *Dried blood?* He was scared. Everything was foreign and unfamiliar. *There is no voice, no instructions. What do I do?* He stared at the wall that was half open. *No, no, that's not a wall. That's a–door?* There had never been a door there before. *Why is this happening?*

His routine had been broken, his strict rituals lost forever. The voice was silent, the screen dark, the exercise apparatus still. No meals had come. New sensations were now growing in his abdomen. It felt as if it was gnawing at itself, as if there was a hungry creature in there. *Is this hunger?* His mouth was dry, his throat raspy. It was difficult to swallow. *Thirst?*

Now the hunger and thirst were starting to drive him, almost as much as his routine once had. He must find something to eat and something to quench his dry throat. At the rate the feelings were growing, he knew they would force him to leave this room before long.

Leaving was impossible though. *Or is it? What is on the other side of the door?* And then Lothis' cognition shifted, jumping forward to a new model of his environment. *This room, my world, is but a tiny part of a larger world, all interconnected by doors. How could I not have thought of this before?*

Lothis crept towards the door, hesitant to go through it. *What if there are other beings, like myself, but different?* He couldn't make himself go through, couldn't force himself to go into the unknown. He returned to his bed and sat, his mind racing. He felt unstable, both physically and mentally, his small body shaking with the stress.

Time passed, Lothis' hunger and thirst increasing. He tried staring at the terminal, but its blank screen couldn't distract him for long. Always, the door drew his attention back, tempting him. *What's out there?* The hunger became a dull ache in his stomach. His throat grew more parched and his tongue began to stick to the roof of his mouth. Curiosity and a need for water soon overcame his fear of the unknown. Lothis had to know what was on the other side of the door, had to know what the rest of the world looked like. *And maybe there will be water out there.*

Rising from his seated position, he crept closer to the door. His bare feet fell silently on the cold metal surface as he moved. Cautiously peering out of the slight gap, he noted the lights on the other side were dim. A negative feeling welled up in him. A feeling of—*dread?*

Lothis wanted to stop, wanted to go back and sleep, but he had to know what was *outside*. He understood now that the protein compound bars, liquid vitamins, and water had been the fuel for his body. *I'm still learning, even without the terminal,* he thought, his mood improving slightly. Something like a smile crossed his small face.

Once out into the corridor, he was forced to make yet another decision. Left or right? Having no information to base a choice on, he stared one way and then the other. Blank hallway ran in both directions, fading into obscurity in the dim light. Both directions looked identical. Lothis was disappointed. *What was I expecting?* He made a random choice, and went left.

As he crept down the hallway, Lothis began to feel more confident. His shaking steadied and his breathing slowed. He became used to the bigger, less confined space. When he reached the next intersection, he could see the right corridor opened up to a larger room a short way down. Lothis moved towards the room, excited, and nervous, to see something other than the hallway.

Upon entering the room, he noted there were large, jagged fragments of some type of clear material lying all over the floor. There were also large gaps in the walls. Lothis quickly determined the pieces would fit perfectly into the gaps, forming compartments within the larger room.

Observing the space more clearly, he realized there was a tremendous amount of blood all around the room. There were pools of it on the floor, sprays on the ceiling, and crimson smears along one of the walls. It puzzled Lothis how so much blood could have been spread onto the various surfaces of the room. *How was it produced? And why?*

Something moved and Lothis' heart hammered in his chest. A hunched form crouched in the darkest corner of the large room. Lothis' small ears picked up a wet, crunching noise coming from the shape. Moving to one side, he could see the form was crouched over a dead, half eaten body.

His dread increased exponentially, and a cry of terror escaped his pursed lips. The form turned towards the sound and rose to its full height of three meters. *What is it?* he thought, eyes widening in horror.

The grotesque figure had a layer of matte black skin, spattered with fresh red blood. It was unlike anything Lothis had ever been educated about. It was humanoid, with long, stoutly muscled arms that looked like a gorilla. Broad, blunt claws tipped the ends of its stumpy three fingered hands. Short, spindly legs were attached to it's thin, graceful torso. The creature's five toed feet had long, scythe-like claws extending from them. The narrow head had black eyes and a single slit for a nose. A gaping maw of dagger like teeth was left exposed by non-existent lips.

The monstrosity let out a bellow and locked eyes with Lothis, its slit of a nose taking in rapid breaths. Lothis stood still, his mind having no knowledge of how to deal with this situation. The monstrosity glared at him a moment longer. It seemed to decide Lothis was not a threat and turned back to its meal, the wet slurping sound resuming after a moment.

As the creature's gaze left him, Lothis was able to move again. He backed out of the space as quickly and quietly as he could. The world was surprisingly dangerous compared to his room. He was afraid, but yearned to learn more. Cautiously, he returned to his exploration.

Stopping outside a partially opened door, it occurred to him blundering around without any knowledge of the world was illogical and hazardous. He needed to find out where he was and formulate a plan of action. Adapting to these challenges was exhilarating compared to his previous life.

Lothis felt himself changing, his mind expanding in ways he never knew possible. His routine, which had once been his lifeblood, seemed stifling and claustrophobic now. The boundary of what was imaginable was growing exponentially.

Peeking his head cautiously inside the room, he saw nothing of interest. *No threat. No dangers.* He ducked inside, deciding it was a good place to hide and form a plan. He momentarily considered barricading the door, but discarded the idea. The thought of trapping himself inside a small room reminded him so much of his old quarters that his stomach began feeling nauseous. Staying undetected would be a better defense, so Lothis kept his movements silent.

Once inside the room, he found there were several pieces of furniture and equipment he was unfamiliar with. In the middle of the room was a large table with several chairs around it, all made of a white composite material. The walls were display screens, but at the moment they were dark. On another, smaller table were several box shaped items made of the same material of the tables and chairs. Lothis guessed they were used for scientific analysis, but their specific purpose was unknown.

Continuing to scan the room, something caught his eye. It was a terminal screen that resembled the one in his room. He had a hunch the terminal might help him gain knowledge of this new world. A feeling rose up within him, a powerful emotion that made him excited and positive for what was about to happen.

He nervously touched the screen, thinking of how much he had learned in front of a terminal just like this. The memory caused several mixed emotions, conflicting and powerful. Lothis loved learning and the screen had provided it. Now he could see how he had been kept confined, each day spent in a cage. This angered him, another emotion that was new. Surprisingly, melancholy was also mixed in this strange, toxic brew of feelings. He knew he'd been abused, yet habit and nostalgia made him want to go back to that time. *And who or what was keeping me there? The monstrosity? Something unknown?*

Lothis jumped in surprise as the screen turned on, its brightness glaring in the dim light of the room. He squinted his small, orange eyes and tried to read the words, but it took a moment for his pupils to adjust.

Once focused, Lothis realized the interface on this terminal was unlike the one in his room. Lessons were the only available feature on his old display, but this one had cascading menus and options. On the main menu he saw "Personnel Status", "Experiment Status", "Security Systems", "Defense Systems", "Lock Down", as well as several others that were less interesting.

Lothis selected "Personnel Status" and saw a long list of names and a system to track their vital signs. Something had to be wrong with the interface though, because everyone was non-responsive. There were over two-hundred people listed, and not one had a heart rate. *Odd*, Lothis thought. *Perhaps a receiver malfunction?* And then he thought about the creature and began to wonder if perhaps the data wasn't in error after all.

He returned to the main menu and started to select "Experiment Status", but was interrupted when a notification box popped up. The box read: "Complex in lockdown. Lab access requested from main lift." Also in the box was a video of six humans in front of a metal door. Below the video were three options, "Allow", "Deny", and "Defend".

Lothis was captivated, all his attention focused on the video. One of the figures was working on the terminal next to the door, while the rest were nervously watching him and their surroundings. One figure stood out from the rest. It was a female. She was gesturing to the others and they were responding immediately. Lothis wished the feed had audio, but he saw no way to enable it.

He sat and pondered which of the three choices to select. Either they had come to save him or destroy him. As he watched the woman, he felt a connectivity, some kind of channel between them. It defied logic, but it was there all the same.

If all the personnel inside this place really were dead, these people must be from outside. *They might be my only way out.* Between his connection with the woman and his lack of other options, Lothis decided he had to make contact with them.

Quickly, and without any further hesitation, he selected the "Allow" option and watched as the door opened. The figures went through the doorway, looking wary. Once they were all gone from view, the display disappeared.

Wondering what to do next, Lothis stared at the menu options that had returned to the screen. He needed a view that would show him the layout of the corridors, something that would help him find the people from the video. He selected "Security Systems", deciding it was the one most related to what he was trying to find. Lothis was rewarded with a map of the complex, complete with indicators showing the status of the various doors throughout the facility. Scanning the map, Lothis saw three different icons, one type labeled with names, one with "U", and the other prefixed with "E" and ending with several numbers. All of name icons featured a single letter followed by a name. None of these were moving. *Those must be the facility personnel.* The fact they were stationary further confirmed his suspicion they were all dead. A pattern of movement in the map caught his attention and he quickly forgot about the named icons. All the "E" prefixed icons were converging towards a door near the bottom of the screen. Behind that door lay all the "U" icons. Looking closer, Lothis saw the door was labeled "Main Lift".

An awful, sinking feeling began developing in Lothis' gut as he realized what was about to happen. With even more agony, he realized it was his fault. He had let his rescuers in and led them into a grotesque ambush.

Hurriedly, Lothis tried to memorize the map and orient himself. *Where am I? Where am I?* he thought, panic stabbing at him. And then he noticed another icon, one that was alone and unmoving. It was labeled "F" and was in a room tagged "Conference 4". When Lothis thought back about his path here, it matched up with the map. *Am I the "F"? What does that mean?*

Without time to confirm his hypothesis, Lothis memorized a series of turns that would take him to his rescuers and then jumped up from the terminal. He looked around the room, hoping to find something he could defend himself with. Nothing was readily apparent, so Lothis raced out into the corridor, thinking he might find something along the way. He immediately accelerated into the fast pace he was used to performing every day, confident all the danger of the "E" icons was concentrated closer to his destination. As he headed towards the elevator, Lothis was uncertain of what he would find when he got there.

18 – MAXAR

It felt good to be out of the games for a few days, not having to fight for your life every moment. But Maxar was well and he was being thrust back into the same old blightheart. He wished his stomach ulcer had been worse. *Well, maybe not worse, but at least it could have kept me out a few more days.*

"So what happened to you?" asked a small, wiry man named Benson. His voice was filled with a strange, lilting accent characteristic of some colony worlds. It had been difficult for Maxar to understand him at first. Both men were sitting in the staging area, waiting for the briefing that would begin Maxar's first game back.

"The blightheart we live with day in and day out has been wearing on my one frayed little nerve, and apparently, it gave me a stomach ulcer. Who'd of thought this place would be bad for your health, right?" Maxar gave Benson a sour grin. "Anyway, the med heads gave me some kind of experimental nano-tech that's supposed to heal me up. I guess it worked, because after they injected me, I was feeling alright in no time. In fact, I think I feel better now than I ever have in my life."

"You do look a lot better," Benson replied. "No denying. Man, when we unloaded from the death wagon after that last game, you looked terrible. I thought maybe the sniper had nicked you or something before I terminated him. Can't deny we were all bummed your spew missed that bugger Hatcholethis though. Woulda been a good ending to a blighthearted day, and at least you would have gotten some kicks out of your pain."

"Yeah? Well, I don't think it would have gone well for me had I hit him. I suppose the fact I scored him a ton of money would have helped. And thanks for taking that sniper out before he got the shot off. You really saved my ass." As Maxar finished the sentence, a tall blond man entered the staging area and stood on a platform at the front of the room.

"If I could have your attention," he said, his voice harshly ringing off the metal walls of the room. Maxar and his teammates quieted down and listened intently. The briefing was important in developing a strategy for the upcoming game. No one wanted to risk their life by ignoring it. "Today's game will be a bit of an irregularity," the blond man stated flatly.

Upon hearing these words, Maxar became extremely interested. Irregularity meant a possibility the security of Bloodsport might be compromised somehow. Somebody, somewhere might make a procedural mistake. He focused even harder on the briefing, trying to spot any kind of weakness.

No one had ever escaped off the Bloodsport asteroid, and many had tried. Maxar could remember several that had been killed in the attempt. He had been forced to watch the lethal hand-to-hand cage matches of those who had been captured. All the would-be escapees had been experienced operators with good plans. *But then again, none of the runners were me.* A small, wry smile crossed his face.

"As some of you know," the briefer was saying, "Entho ships have been bombarding Haak-ah-tar with a new kind of weapon. The bastards don't seem to know how to use it though, because they haven't inflicted much damage. Since the Enthos are in system, attendance for this next game will most likely be low. In accordance, we will be scaling down the match." He then went on to read the list of those who would be participating and those who would be sitting out. Maxar heard his own name in the latter list and was excited. If he was in the game, any chance of escape was seriously decreased. The security was too tight. *In the barracks though...*

The briefer continued, "Those of you who are still on for the game—" A screeching alarm drown out the briefer's words and he looked around wildly.

A frightened voice flooded the area at an ear splitting volume, "Bloodsport is under attack, I repeat, Bloodsport is under attack! All participants will return to their dormitories immediately! All security and gaming personnel please perform your emergency duties. This is not a drill. Bloodsport is under attack!" Maxar's hope soared. *This is more opportunity than I've ever dreamed of!*

For a moment after the message ended, everything was calm. Maxar could see the ramifications of the situation became apparent in the eyes of everyone around him. A roar of mingled hate, rage, and elation rose as everything began to happen at once. Chaos exploded like a malfunctioning worm drive. People were dashing everywhere, their intentions a mystery to everyone but themselves. Maxar remained in his seat, his mind finishing his escape strategy.

Maxar caught sight of Benson, who was staring intently at him with a gleam of excitement in his eyes. He too was still seated, as calm and composed as Maxar. *Benson was never very intelligent,* Maxar speculated, *but he has a soldier's mindset and follows my lead well.*

Maxar turned to Benson, feeling more hope than he had in years. "If we can get to the shuttle dock, we might be able to use this riot to get off the asteroid. The spectators will be trying to get away and security might just be buggered enough not to notice extra people on a shuttle."

Benson's eyes narrowed and he looked thoughtful. Maxar could tell he was unsure of the plan. Just then, several chairs came hurtling through the air. Maxar dove away from the danger and came up unharmed. He saw Benson had also avoided the projectiles. "Damn," Benson sputtered, making a profane gesture towards the group who had thrown the chairs. "This is getting out of control!"

Maxar understood their pent up rage at the Bloodsport, but he would use this opportunity for more productive endeavors. Most of the rioters had a natural, unrestrained penchant for violence that had landed them here in the first place. They were now focused on fulfilling their blood lust. Maxar watched the briefer and his aide get bludgeoned to death by a crowd wielding chairs, fists, and boots. It was a grisly sight. Other rioters were bent on destroying as much of the facility as possible, using their chairs to break down doors and the meager decorations that were part of the participant area.

"It's a full on riot," Maxar agreed with Benson, his voice calm and steady. "And you are more than welcome to stay here. I'm sure if you go join the action you'll do fine, for now anyway. What's going to happen when the Blood gets back on its feet and starts to exert control though? I doubt any of you live to fight another match, even if you want to. Of course—" he then paused dramatically, a crooked smile ruining the seriousness of his tone, "you could come along with me, just for the fun of it. At least then you would have the chance of escape offsetting the certain death awaiting here."

Benson's eyes once again narrowed in thought, only this time, no chairs came flying their way. After another moment or two, Benson said, "Sure Maxar, why the buggers not? When you put it that way, how can I say no?"

"You can't, and that's why I like you. No matter the situation, you always see sense and act on it." Maxar rose up, grabbed a piece of chair that would serve well for a club, and turned back to Benson. "Grab something and let's get going. We don't know how long this damned opportunity will last." Benson did as instructed, finding a piece smaller and more suited to his size. Both men started to make their way out of the briefing room, dodging rioters and security personnel who were locked in heated combat.

Maxar didn't count on having much time to complete his plan. As expected, the security forces were already cracking down hard. Hopefully the Enthos would continue their odd attack, further confusing and hampering the Bloodsport overlords.

To his amazement, he realized he had a huge toothy smile on his face. Its presence felt unfamiliar, yet welcome and good. To his further amazement, he felt a strong emotion welling up deep inside his soul. It was so foreign to him it took a moment to identify it. *Happiness*, he thought, *happiness...* It was so strange, so out of place. It felt so good.

He didn't understand his elation though. Maybe it was because he was doing something productive. Maybe it was the hope of a real future, even if it was always on the run. Whatever the cause, it was good. It was exhilarating and amazing. It was like liquid sunlight coursing through his veins.

Maxar ran towards the exit of the participant sector, dodging other Bloodsporters and security personnel alike. He dodged down several smaller corridors, bypassing huge groups of combatants that would take too long to fight through. It had taken Maxar a long time to memorize all the more obscure areas of the participant sector, but that work was paying off now.

When they reached the exit that would lead them to the shuttle dock, Maxar was both elated and crushed. The door itself was unguarded, but was in full lockdown. Two security guards lay on the floor, blood pooling around them. "Guard my back," Maxar said as he ran over to the door control panel. He quickly ran through several menus, using all of his hashing skills to break deeper and deeper into the interface. In his time on Bloodsport, he had talked to all the hashers he came in contact with, trying to learn every trick he could for just such a day as this. *The matrix tile overload exploit,* he thought, remembering one of the more obscure hashes he had been told about. A few more taps on the screen and the door opened.

"Woah," Benson said in awe. "You'll have to explain how you did that later."

"Sure thing," Maxar replied. Raising his voice, Maxar called to the nearest group of rioters, "Hey! This door just opened." As if it were controlled by one mind, the group turned and ran towards the exit. Maxar and Benson stood off to the side letting the group run through. "That should help soften the way ahead."

After several moments, Maxar set off through the door. The exit was the first of many major obstacles to overcome. The way ahead was still fraught with danger. *This might actually work!* he thought.

19 – TREMMILLY

Beowulf began to whine, startling Tremmilly out of her thoughts. The room seemed to shift and Tremmilly felt herself rise. She saw her body below her, Beowulf nudging her anxiously. Noor-5 fell away and she began to accelerate. Stars blurred, leaving bright streaks across her vision. Tremmilly knew logically she should be frightened, but something about the experience made her calm, at peace.

After an indefinable amount of time, Tremmilly slowed down. She passed by a barren, desert planet, it's surface sparsely habited. Soon, an asteroid came into view and she slowed even further. She stopped above the asteroid, noting extensive structures. Directly below her was a complex that had a military look about it. People were fighting outside the complex on the pale gray surface of what she thought of as an asteroid or moon. They were killing and being killed, which filled her with sorrow.

Then, she was moving again and the whole scene shifted dramatically. Tremmilly wasn't herself anymore, yet she knew *she* still existed. Looking out of *his* eyes gave her a different perspective on the world she had seen earlier. Now she was inside the complex. And it was chaos—pure, absolute chaos. She had never seen anything like it in her life, yet *he* stayed calm, keeping Tremmilly the same. Her new perspective was exhilarating. She could feel his muscles moving, could sense his emotions. Tremmilly couldn't control his actions or hear his thoughts, but felt totally integrated otherwise.

He was running through the chaotic melee, dodging small knots of people that were brutally slaughtering each other. His strength was evident to her and she felt he was capable of handling anyone they ran by, but could feel fighting wasn't necessary at this point. Moreover, she knew it would harm their escape, but she didn't understand what they were escaping from. Yes, she wanted to get away from the fighting, but it was a deeper, more complex desire that drove their body forward.

There was a man following behind, but she sensed he was an ally. Tremmilly felt their movement slow momentarily to get through a group of rioters blocking the corridor. *He* became nervous. Time was precious.

The mental pressure eased somewhat as they halted in front of a wide door. Above it was a sign labeled "Shuttle Service". She sensed this was the destination. Tremmilly felt his tension rise as they crept cautiously through the wide doorway. Once inside the large room, she could see many small shuttle craft lined up in neat rows along the deck. Their swept back wings and elongated fuselages gleamed brightly in the artificial lighting.

With a jolt of awareness, *he* spotted a group of security guards. The small man ran into the hangar and stopped next to them. Simultaneously, the guards noticed there were people in the room with them. They drew large flechette pistols from their shoulder holsters and fired at them and the small man.

The first round whistled by *their* head, and she felt the wind of its passage on his cheek. Before the guards could tighten up their aim, *he* dove behind the nearest shuttle. The small man was not as quick.

As he and Tremmilly watched in horror, their ally took a round directly in the stomach. The tungsten alloy needles were merciless. His midsection exploded. A spray of blood and tissue flew out behind him in a gruesome fountain. A silent scream escaped Tremmilly's lips and he bellowed in rage.

She became sick, dizzy, and disoriented, but she sensed he had been through much worse and had controlled these light emotions. Staggering to their feet, Tremmilly felt his sadness as they ran through the rows of ships in a haphazard pattern. From the small glimpses she caught, the guards were starting to spread out and lose sight of each other. She felt he was satisfied and knew this was what he hoped they would do.

Carefully making their way through the ships, they doubled back behind the guard that was the furthest away from his comrades. He had no idea anyone was there until it was too late. Tremmilly felt his flesh as their hands twisted his neck until she felt a grinding noise, then a quick pop. The guard fell to the deck, dead. Picking up his flechette pistol, she felt his happiness to be armed and have more equalized odds. Tremmilly found it strange they had killed the guard without remorse for the action. Instead, the revenge felt right. Their ally had been murdered. They would have found the same brutal end if the guard had been more skilled.

Over the course of the next few minutes, Tremmilly experienced additional killings as each guard was eliminated. Having a weapon made things so much easier. Each body was then thoroughly searched. Tremmilly could feel his desire for something. Much of what they found was of little use, but then he spotted it. The laser key was such a small,

ZACHARIAH WAHRER

mundane object, but it brought him so much joy.

Key in hand, they ran over to a terminal screen and began entering commands. The first command opened the hangar's exterior doors. A plasma barrier kept the area pressurized and separated from the vacuum of space. The bright blue barrier shimmered, the magnetic lines of force evident in the swirling of the plasma. The next command entered powered up the closest shuttle. It was sleek, streamlined, and looked expensive. It lacked a wormhole generator, so leaving the system would be impossible.

They quickly hopped through the shuttle's opening hatch, hitting the close button before the door could fully open. Sitting in one of the six spacious chairs, they watched the terminal as the ship began a short self-diagnostic procedure. It listed their destination as "Bloodsport Dock" and that the craft was on auto-nav. Tremmilly noticed that the seats were plush and comfortable, but *he* seemed intent on other things. Once the self-diagnostic was complete, the ship rose off the deck and exited the shuttle bay. It passed effortlessly through the plasma barrier and began accelerating. They watched out the large view window as the asteroid fell away below them.

"Thank you for visiting Bloodsport," a voice said, startling Tremmilly. "Remember to register to watch upcoming matches. If a return journey is not convenient, all matches are streamed live over the Terminal Network. Check the Bloodsport Information Channel for more details." The farther they got from the asteroid, the more relieved he felt. He was calm, at peace, and most of all, happy.

As the shuttle moved towards the large orbital ship dock, Tremmilly felt a tug. She was then outside *him,* moving quickly away. After another indeterminable amount of time with stars streaking by, she felt herself falling and then a snap. It took Tremmilly several moments to get oriented and then she recognized the dull gray walls that had been boxing her in for the better part of a standard week.

As her cognition formed back into the reality that was her and only *her,* Tremmilly felt her lungs screaming for air. It took her a few seconds to realize she was holding her breath. Stale air exploded from her mouth. She gasped in fresh breath, taking in huge lung fulls that made her head swim. She had no idea how long she had been holding her breath and even less understanding of why she had been doing it.

What was that? Tremmilly wondered, her mind still reeling with shock. Beowulf was still nudging her, whining anxiously. Looking at the clock on the room's display, she realized a significant amount of time had passed. *Was that real? Was it a vision?* She embraced Beowulf, pressing her face into his long fur.

In addition to this experience, Tremmilly had been having strange

80

premonitions and feelings lately. She felt like she was on the cusp of a new reality, like she was touching something massive and unknown. It was scary, but also exhilarating. Sometimes if felt like she might even be able to see *through* reality, to see the underlying fabric of space-time. *This all began when Psidonnis told me the prophecy,* she observed, her breathing and heart rate gradually slowing as she calmed.

Tremmilly tried to analyze the experience logically. "I left my body and traveled," she said and Beowulf's whimpers subsided, "so that seems to lean towards it not being a vision. Why go through the trouble of moving if it wasn't my actual consciousness that was there. That seems to rule out a vision. And since time passed, it makes sense I was there in real time. But how, or why, did it happen?" The last question had no answer and was part of what was troubling Tremmilly ever since she had left Eishon-2.

Now she was on the orbital dock above Noor-5, but the reason why eluded her. Tremmilly smiled sardonically, finding it amusing her life was now being guided by a mysterious force, just like the Dygars. The sect was peaceful, loving, and to be totally honest, somewhat laughable. It had seemed obvious their consumption of farcanthis leaves had caused their strange experiences, but now Tremmilly wasn't so sure. She hadn't been anywhere near the plant's powerfully hallucinogenic leaves, yet had just experienced something she couldn't explain. There was a difference though. Psidonnis had told her about the Dygar visions, and they were not nearly as vivid as what she had just experienced. *Maybe their visions are because of farcanthis,* she thought, *but what caused me to leave my body?*

And even if she had the answer to that question, did that explain what she was supposed to do with the experience? Why was she connected to the man she had been a part of? Was he the important part, or the location? So far, she felt influenced by some kind of entity or power greater than herself, driven to do things she would normally never do. Leaving Eishon-2, her birth world, had never been a part of her plans. Thinking back now, Tremmilly realized leaving Eishon-2 was allowing her to explore more of the galaxy. Perhaps the "influence" was just a strange way of convincing herself to go. *Maybe I'm going crazy... Maybe I should have stayed on Eishon. It's where my parents wanted me to live.*

"Your parents came here a few years before you were born," Psidonnis had told her when she was old enough to understand. "On other worlds, the lower class citizens can only afford to live in the densely populated city states. These places are not pleasant and your parents sought to escape the urban wasteland. They wanted space to live and clean air to breath. They sold every possession they had and used all the Ashcreds to buy passage to Eishon-2. Arriving here with nothing, your parents homesteaded a small plot of land several miles away from any other settlers and made life work for them.

"You were born a few years later and your parents were delighted. Six years passed in happiness, some of which you probably remember."

Tremmilly stopped there and wiped tears from her eyes. Her parents had died at their homestead from the terrible plague. She hadn't meant to remember that much. Remembering was painful, even after fifteen years. *What caused the plague?* she wondered. *Was it carried here on a cargo ship or was it spread by the Ashamine?* It had been a vicious, nasty illness, causing intense pain. The victim would run a high fever, fall into a coma, and then bleed out shortly thereafter. There was no cure, no answers, no proof about where the plague came from or why it had died off almost as quickly as it began. *Why did it kill my parents and not me?* Tremmilly hoped that perhaps she might be able to get some real answers while she was traveling. It seemed like such a small chance, but anything was possible.

After what had happened on Noor-5, she was definitely willing to believe in small odds. She and Beowulf had been listening to a Divisionist orator as he rebuked the Ashamine and its war on the Entho-la-ah-mines. In all honesty, she had found the man quite boring, but his words had some truth to them. It was unclear to her what had happened, but an earthquake had struck the area and released some type of poisonous gas that had killed many of the onlookers. A few minutes before the ground began to shake, she had felt a strong *push* to leave the area, so she did.

When the earthquake hit, Tremmilly was knocked to the ground. Thankfully, there were no tall buildings around her, and she escaped the quake without serious injury. The poison gas had been localized to the vicinity of the crowd and Tremmilly had been far enough away it posed no threat.

The many deaths and her narrow escape upset Tremmilly. She felt it was time to get off the planet. The people she was looking for were elsewhere. Noor-5 was in chaos after the disaster. It took time for her to find a transport, but eventually she'd been taken to the orbital dock above the planet. Now she was stuck at the dock, sleeping in the cheapest lodging—which she still couldn't afford—not knowing where to go next. *Maybe this experience is the key to the next step.*

As she replayed the memory in her head, more details began to pop out. The voice had said, "Thank you for your visit to Bloodsport." She'd heard that name before. Wasn't it the place that had been on the news?

Tremmilly hurriedly accessed the small terminal in her room, pulling up the archived footage. "We don't have much information at this time, but it appears the Enthos are trying to take back Haak-ah-tar, a world they fled over twenty five years ago. They've broken through the

Ashamine blockade and attacked several installations on-world. The nearby Bloodsport asteroid's security was compromised by the attacks and is now in security lockdown. Players are rioting, causing a disruption in the games. All scheduled matches are postponed until further notice. Bloodsport officials say they will be releasing "Best Of" footage of the riots on the Terminal Network. We will keep you updated on the Entho attacks and Bloodsport riots."

The reporter went on to interview several celebrities and highly placed Ashamine officials. They all complained about the interruption of the games and the fact Bloodsport wouldn't be streaming live footage of the riots. Tremmilly switched off the terminal in disgust. It made her feel sick to her stomach thinking about what occurred at the "games", even if they were convicted criminals.

The backdrop of violence and rioting in her experience made sense now. *I was seeing a Bloodsport participant escaping in real time.* The fact that he was a convict gave her pause. *He was helping the other man escape though, and he only killed those guards because he had to.* Tremmilly felt the man's heart was good, that his motives were pure.

Am I supposed to go to Bloodsport to help him escape? That seemed like the obvious conclusion. It would be risky, but Tremmilly was starting to develop trust in whatever had been guiding her. She didn't know if it was coming from within or without, but if it had taken her this far, why wouldn't it guide her the rest of the way? She questioned her next move, but felt finding the man from the experience was the key.

"Come on Beo," she said, gathering up her few belongings. "We've got a place to go now!" Leaving the decrepit room, Tremmilly and Beowulf made their way down to the docking sector of the orbital facility. Tremmilly knew it would be a challenge to find a captain that would be willing to take her into a war zone.

"I'm seeking passage to Haak-ah-tar and the Bloodsport asteroid," she told one captain, trying to sound casual.

"Are you a buggering blighthearted idiot?" he said, laughing disgustedly. "Haven't you heard the Enthos are back? Founder curse you to fires of the dark star as a fool." Beowulf's ears pinned back and his lips rose in a snarl at the man's tone. He moved between Tremmilly and the aggressive captain. The man fell back, angry at having to do so. "Get your buggered dog away from me!" Several other seedy looking captains and crew members began to take notice and Tremmilly decided it was time to move on.

After asking several friendlier looking captains and receiving negative responses, Tremmilly sat on bench, realizing this next move might take more craftiness and deception. "Who would be going to that asteroid?" she wondered aloud. "Military personnel maybe, but there is no way they'd let me tag along. And I don't think we'd be able to slip through security and become stow-aways." She continued to think, scratching Beowulf behind the ears in his favorite spot. "Let's walk around some more," she said finally, hoping it would give her a chance to think like she once had while wandering the great open spaces of Eishon-2 with Beowulf.

After an extended period of walking through the facility, she came to a ship she had missed on her first pass through the area. When she looked closer, she realized why. It was small, stuffed into a corner, and looked like a derelict.

As she drew closer, she was amazed at the terrible condition the ship was in. Maybe the mechanics were fine—she didn't know about that kind of thing—but the hull was mottled with corrosion and a needed a new coat of paint. Presumably the interior of the ship was even worse. The captain of this vessel was probably too lazy to work for what little money Tremmilly could offer him. She had to try though. "He certainly won't be worried about his ship getting damaged," she said to her friend.

"Hello?" she asked into the darkness of the open hatch. No answer. "I would like to speak to the captain of this vessel." Still no answer except for a faint echo bouncing off the inside of the ship. Stepping further up the ramp, she peered into the ship's interior, but there was nothing discernible in the blackness.

She waited a few moments longer, then backed off the ramp, a troubled look crossing her face. *Thwarted again,* she thought. Then, inspiration dawned on her and she grew excited. Hope blossomed, and she *knew* how she was going to get to Bloodsport.

No captain will go near the Haak-ah-tar system, so I need a ship without a captain. And since I can't afford to buy a ship, I'll have to borrow one. Here it was, unguarded and empty of personnel. She had little experience in piloting and knew next to nothing about ships, but she would figure it out. Maybe there would be a vision or someone would come along at the right time to help her. *I have to try. I feel like this is meant to be.*

She walked back up the ramp with Beowulf, entered the ship, and groped around in the darkness looking for the interior light switch. This was made difficult by the large amount of what felt like refuse strewn about the floor. The stench was terrible. *Those who break a wheel shouldn't complain if the spare one squeaks,* she thought, a saying her father had told her many times.

Finally managing to hit the illumination switch—more by accident than design—the pale lights revealed what her nose had already suggested. Piles of junk and refuse littered the floor, coming up to knee height at the highest places. Dust sat heavy on the support structures of the bulk heads. Grime caked the dingy walls. Beowulf began to sniff several of the piles and Tremmilly had to command him to return. "You don't know what kind of nasties are in there, Beo. Leave off." The wolf-dog looked disappointed as he returned to her side.

Carefully picking her way around the worst of the garbage, she stalked towards the command deck. *That might be an overly grand name on a ship like this,* she thought, trying not to breath too deeply. Upon entering the deck, she was glad to see garbage and refuse was absent from this area. It wasn't clean by anyone's standards, but at least it wasn't full of junk and rotting whatever-they-weres.

Tremmilly sat in the captain's chair and tinkered with the ship's terminal, wondering if she could pilot the vessel on her own. The menus seemed easy, but she wondered if there was more to it. She tried to remember her trip to Noor-5, but she had been in the passenger compartment, unable to see what the captain had done. "No help there," she said. She began navigating through menus, hoping something would stand out. A file labeled "Checklist" caught her eye and she opened it. Scrolling down past headings for "In-System Travel", "Worm Travel" and "Arrival", she finally found "Departure". Tremmilly began reading.

20 - THE FOUNDER

The Founder sat behind his expansive hardwood desk, his fingers steepled. He had a look of calm on his polished exterior. Inside, he was seething with a bitter rage.

How had everything gone so wrong lately? Now, in addition to the Divisionist problem, the Enthos were striking back on Haak-ah-tar. *They've been on the run for twenty five years. What changed?*

And where was Crasor? He'd heard nothing from his Facilitator. This was the longest he'd ever been out of contact with Crasor, and he was desperately in need of the man's skills.

Worst of all was the loss of communication between himself and the Legacy Genetics Project facility on Haak-ah-tar. He could find a new Facilitator, but if the Enthos had attacked the LGP, it was quite possible all the vital progress that had been made there would be lost.

Priority first, the facility on Haak-ah-tar, he thought. *That needs to be resolved. I need to know what is happening. The potential loss of development there could destroy the Ashamine.* He checked his terminal yet again for a report from Ascended Rathis on Haak-ah-tar. *Nothing.* He gritted his teeth, wanting more than anything to have a report from his officer. *I need Crasor for this!*

The LGP was a tricky situation. The fewer people who were exposed to the information contained in the LGP facility, the fewer people who would have to be silenced. The Founder didn't mind needing to dispose of personnel, but he wasn't stupid either. The consequences of a security leak on this project would be catastrophic. And the loss of highly skilled officers and soldiers would be a detriment as well.

When he had failed to contact Crasor, he had ordered Ascended Rathis to dispatch a team to investigate. "Send a Founder's Commando with a squad of Initiates for support. They will report directly to you when they return, and to no one else. This mission is classified Ascended or higher. The team is to be fully quarantined after the mission. I will issue further instructions upon their return." Those orders should compartmentalize the squad and minimize the loss of personnel. *Just one FC and a squad of Inits. The FC is regrettable, but I need someone leading that team that has experience.* And the LGP would have to be relocated immediately, regardless of its functional status. *Not even an Ascended can be trusted with the knowledge of the facility's location.* The Founder's orange eyes lost focus as he thought about the history of the LGP.

Started almost as early as the Ashamine government itself, the secretive Legacy Genetics Project was started by the original Founder as a way to insure an individual of his caliber would always control the government he had created.

The product of the LGP, while not clones of the original Founder, were close to it. The Ashamine populous was told each successor was the son of the former Founder, but this deception was meant to engender support for the successor. The Founder didn't want to think about what would happen if the Ashamine people discovered his true origins. Clones, or anything even remotely resembling them, were deeply feared and hated by the citizens. The memory of the Archetype War kept the prejudice strong, and the Ashamine priests reinforced that sentiment. Humanity could never again experiment with genetic modification or enhancement. The consequences were too great. *Except for where the Founder is concerned...*

The location of the LGP facility had been moved several times due to security concerns. After a near-discovery by a zealous Terminal Network reporter, the program had been moved to the isolated planet of Haak-ah-tar. Buried deep under the desert, the LGP had been able to advance its goals in privacy with a minimal chance of discovery.

What if the Entho bombardment killed my successor? That thought was horrific. The chain of succession would be broken and the government would be thrown into chaos. The total collapse of the Ashamine was a real possibility if there was no successor, especially with the rising popularity of the Divisionists. *Hopefully the attack just damaged the facility's communication capabilities.* That would explain why he had stopped receiving his weekly sit reps from the Director.

I don't trust Gerald Kasol, the Founder thought scornfully, a grimace marring his beatific face. The new Director had been appointed after the former head had committed suicide under questionable circumstances. Gerald Kasol was brilliant, that was the reason he had been appointed. Recently though, the Founder had come across some dark bits of history about the man's past. It wasn't much of a stretch to think Director Kasol had some experiments on the side he had conveniently forgotten to tell the Founder about.

Frustrated, the Founder tried the communication link to the LGP facility and received the same blighthearted message stating the link couldn't be established. He then immediately tried the link to Crasor, wanting his Facilitator to go figure out what in the fires of the dark star was going on at the LGP. The device said Crasor too was unavailable for an unknown reason.

The Founder experienced a feeling of helplessness, something that was completely foreign to him. Never in his long reign over the Ashamine had he felt this powerless. It triggered recollections of his childhood, something he had worked hard to forget. He raised both his fists and slammed them down.

The outburst brought the Founder back to his senses. He sat in bemused introspection and thought about how he was losing the tight grip he kept on himself. He had to get control, had to form a plan. Knowing it was crucial, he began once again to prioritize the situation, *First I must secure my successor. Concurrently, but with a lower priority, I must get in contact with Crasor. Tertiary, I must meet with the Classad and discuss how to handle the attack on Haak-ah-tar. At least the potential security leak from the discovery on Traynos-6 has been resolved and research is up to full production.*

Feeling more at ease and empowered now that he had started developing a plan, he rocked back in the beautifully styled antique chair and steepled his fingers once again. "Tohnn," he said to his assistant through the voice comm, "prepare to dispatch orders." It was time to bring his power down on all those opposing his will.

21 – CRASOR

Crasor was baffled by the events that had unfolded on Noor-5. An earthquake had struck a geologically stable planet. And why had it occurred just as he was about to strike at the Divisionists? It could have been an unfortunate coincidence, but it felt planned. The timing was too perfect. *If the Divisionists had access to Ashamine technology, I might believe they had orchestrated it. But they had no way of knowing I was there, and using an earthquake to disrupt my attack would be like using a rail pistol to repair a worm drive.*

It was getting harder to think about the events of the past few days though. The burning—the burning in his Founder's cursed head was driving him insane. It felt like a hot rod was being forced through his mind. And whenever he moved, the sensation turned around in his skull, continuously pointing towards *something.* It made no sense. He could find no explanation for its presence or why it had started simultaneously with the earthquake. The chemical agent he had released into the crowd didn't cause this type of reaction. Besides, he had used all the necessary protection and decontamination procedures.

Crasor wasn't the only one experiencing this strange sensation. From the window of his rented room, he watched as people walked out of town, seeming like dazed automations. The thing that really bothered him was that the people were all heading in the direction the burning line pointed to. *Where are they going? Am I going to end up like them?*

As days passed the burning continued to build, crowding out anything else. Then it began to pulsate, its rhythm creating an atonal beat in his mind. *Why is it in my head? Where is it pointing?* Crasor successfully resisted the pull, but he often forgot why he did so. He supposed he should probably report back to the Founder, but that seemed so trivial. The line was all he focused on now. He was being moved towards a place, and he was having a harder time fighting it. Crasor dully realized he no longer had his highly sophisticated, miniaturized comm device. *Why am I so apathetic about my duty?* he fleetingly thought. Deep down he felt a slight twinge of anger at how his strict discipline and regimented lifestyle had been swept away, but the feeling quickly passed. *The line. The line. The line.* The burning line was all that mattered.

***

Crasor stood at the edge of a giant fissure that scarred the crust of Noor-5. Its depths black, unfathomable, and mysterious. *How did I get here?* He had no recollection of the journey, but from the way his feet hurt he could tell he had walked a great distance. The burning line pointed straight down into the fissure. The pain had lessened, from the burning of a fiery inferno to that of a torch. *Why am I here?* That question was the most terrifying, and Crasor shied away from it.

Time passed as Crasor peered intently down into the depths. Slowly, a soft, hazy glow began to emanate from deep within the blackness. It grew brighter, but the fog like quality remained. As the intensity of the glow increased, so did the intensity and pain of the burning line in his head. Every molecule in his body strained to reach the light.

Before he could stop himself, he started to climb down the vertical walls of the crevasse. *This is insane,* a small, logical voice protested. *Why am I doing this? What am I going to find down there?* Crasor didn't care though, and the voice of protest shrank and shriveled into insignificance as he drew closer and closer to the light. The pain in his head also lessened as he climbed.

The loss of logic made him realize, remotely, that something had a strong hold on him. He vaguely wondered why, in the name of the Founder, he was climbing down the side of a crevasse that could close back up at any moment if there were aftershocks or another quake.

Crasor's will attempted to reassert itself as his hands began to bleed from the sharp edges of stone he was down climbing. Pain gouged its way through his logic starved head, a torrent that made him feel better because it loosened the hold of whatever was drawing him here. Sharp edges continued cutting his palms and fingers like rough daggers, causing him to bleed more profusely. This too helped him surface a little more, but it was not enough to stop the compulsion that drew him down towards the glowing light.

After several long minutes of climbing, Crasor neared the glow. Just as he reached the light's edge, his hands, now slimy with blood, betrayed him. His foot slipped off a small hold and his hands were too slick to support the additional weight. He grasped desperately at the rock, but he was already moving too fast to arrest his fall.

Crasor fell towards the unknowable depths of the crevasse, terror enveloping his mind. As he passed into the light, his consciousness changed. His memories were pulled from him, extracted in one violent motion that he couldn't comprehend. All his secrets were known, all his vile acts exposed. He was helpless, violated, naked.

***

Crasor woke up. Not back in the small sleep room he had rented in the city, but on an uneven surface in near darkness. There was light, but it was weak and far above him. He rose, a throbbing ache pounding at the back of his head. He reached up and touched the area and immediately drew his hand away as a bolt of pain shot through his head and out his eye. And then he realized the burning line was gone. *I've arrived,* he thought, not understanding exactly what he meant.

Vaguely, Crasor remembered how he had gotten here. Not understanding why he had entered the crevasse, he hoped he would find out soon. In addition to the line being gone, his mind had cleared. Self-control had returned to him.

His hands were raw and bleeding, his head throbbed, and his whole body ached. *It's going to take some time to recover completely,* he thought, checking over each part of himself.

As more of his training, memory, and logic returned to him, he remembered the Founder and his failure to report. He needed to get in touch with the leader of the Ashamine, but after a brief examination of his pockets, he realized his comm device was missing.

"You were brought here for a purpose," a light, harmonic voice said. Crasor wheeled around looking for the source, causing his head to throb in protest. He couldn't see much in the darkness, but he thought he knew the direction from which the voice had originated. Strangely, the vast stone walls produced no echo.

He crouched down close to the floor to lower his profile, hoping whoever had spoken could not see well in the dark. The action was futile. "Ah, you bow down already Facilitator. So smart of you." The woman's tone carried sarcasm and this time he could not intuit its direction.

Figuring he was at her mercy anyway, Crasor spoke as he rose from the rough stone floor, "Who are you?" The words felt like a lame response, but he wanted to know the answer.

"We, oh Crasor of the Ashamine, are everything you have ever wanted, everything you have ever dreamed of," the feminine voice said. "You were drawn here for a purpose and now we offer everything to you. Yet we know you have questions, so ask."

Indeed, Crasor did have questions, and he supposed the statement had been a logical guess, but something in the woman's tone suggested she knew more. Crasor had studied voice inflection, amongst many other things, and all his senses were telling him something was wrong with hers. A vague memory of feeling violated passed through his mind, but was gone as soon as he tried to grasp it.

"Forgive me for my impertinence, but could you explain your answer to my first question in more detail?" As he said this, he began to edge his way towards the wall, a plan forming that involved climbing his way back out of the deep crevasse.

"Simply put, *we are*," the voice said, placing special emphasis on the last two words, making them sound like a title. "We are life. We are power. We are control. We are... *the ultimate*." Again, the emphasis on the last few words.

By this time, Crasor had made his way to the wall and discovered, to his dismay, that there was no possible way for him to climb. His hands were too raw, too damaged to function. The second he touched the rock, hot pain crackled through his hands and he jerked them away as if he had touched a shuttle's hot exhaust cowling.

The feminine voice laughed delicately, and Crasor guessed she had known he would make the attempt. Dread began to well up inside him. The force that had drawn him had completely vanished and now all he wanted was to get away from this Founder's forsaken place. Since that was impossible, at least temporarily, he decided to play along.

"OK," he said, his voice impassive. "You said I was led here for a purpose. Please tell me, what is it?"

"Your destiny depends on a choice, one of greatest importance. It is simple. You can either watch as the universe comes under the control of a superior power, or you can become the wielder of that power. We can give you the universe, Crasor of the Ashamine." Crasor cocked his head, intrigued. His desire to escape diminished slightly.

"It is my experience that gifts often require a reciprocal favor. What is it you would ask of me, were I to agree?"

"Only for you to become the driving force behind a new array of this universe, to be at its center, its quintessence. No more will be required of you, Crasor." From what he could tell, the voice was speaking truth. He could hear when a lie was birthed and he sensed no such falsehood.

"Let me ask you then, will this new order be humanitarian in nature?" As he continued, a greedy note entered his normally flat tone. "Or will it be subjugation?"

The woman's voice laughed delicately. "Subjugation—most definitely." All the mirth, fake or real, was gone from the voice now. It was cold, final, a fist to the face. "Crasor, we *know*." He certainly didn't like the emphasis she put on the last word. "We know what you are qualified for, and what you are willing to do. We know your actions prior to coming here, how many have died, and how many more have suffered from your actions. We know the joy you took in everything you did. You were selected for this destiny because of who and what you are. If we had wanted a humanitarian, we would have selected the girl." Crasor wondered what girl the voice spoke of, but had no time to think it over. "Any more questions?" The voice now had the note of mirth—*And sarcasm?*—back.

Crasor knew he could say no to her proposition if he wanted to. All the mental direction that had been used to get him here was gone. He was being allowed to make this decision completely on his own, and he appreciated that.

"What do I do next?" Immediately after asking this question, he felt a *directive* in his mind. The voice said nothing, and Crasor decided that was his answer. He began to follow the crevasse down its length and even though it was nearly pitch black, he had no problem navigating it. He never faltered or stumbled. It was as if the *directive* was a map in his mind, leading him around jagged rocks and steep drop offs he couldn't see. He felt empowered, like a new ability had been unlocked in his mind. After a short walk he felt a weighty presence over his head and knew the crevasse had turned into a cavern. His footfalls echoed and the floor begin to slope slightly downward.

After a few more minutes he could see a soft glow which grew brighter as he neared its source. Rounding the next bend, his eyes were forced into a squint. After a moment, a small chamber came into focus, illuminated by harsh, cold light.

There was power in the air—thrumming, awe inspiring, terrifying power. It felt like the electricity was arcing invisibly through the air. The place was malicious and dangerous. He momentarily thought about turning back. He could escape the blightheart his deepest self knew was coming. Crasor forcibly squashed the desire and entered the chamber, his lust for power dominating his every action.

The enticing light emanated from a multi-faceted crystalline prism jutting from one of the chamber's rough walls. Surrounding the crystal was seared and melted rock.

Immediately, the crystal's beauty entranced Crasor with its complexity. The light was not shining through it, rather from it, producing a yearning within him. The power he felt from this object was overwhelming. *I'll do anything,* he thought.

"Kneel," the woman said, her voice as hard as diamond. He bent his knees and settled down to the floor. He kept his head held high, pride burning fierce in his brown eyes. He had no idea what to expect, so he readied himself for anything.

A small, dark core appeared inside the crystal. As he watched, the core enlarged and began to swirl, its edges granular. It became fractal in shape, growing larger than his fist. An appendage grew off the darkness, stretching in Crasor's direction. When it reached the wall of the crystal, a tiny stream of what appeared to be dust fell on the floor. The dust flowed in a line towards Crasor. When it was ten feet away, the line stopped advancing and started to mound up. More dust continued to flow from the crystal as the pile grew higher. In less than a minute, a humanoid shape was standing before him. The indistinct shape grew more defined, making up a familiar one—that of a woman.

As the details were worked into the woman's face and figure, Crasor realized he knew this person. It was Emili Trayfis, his first and only love from back on Ashamine-2. Her eyes were closed, her breathing soft.

Conflicting emotions raged in the depths of Crasor's heart. Should he run? Should he embrace her? Should he kiss her familiar lips? But Emili was dead. Had been for eighteen years. And there was no doubt she was dead, because Crasor himself had been the killer.

When the doppelganger opened its eyes, Crasor had to choke back a scream of horror. Hard, shiny crystalline orbs were in place of the cool, refreshing blue ones he had stared into.

"Does my appearance please you?" the doppelganger said, flashing a sultry smile. He didn't know how to answer, but the question was apparently rhetorical because she continued without pausing to let him reply. "True, this body is not actually Emili, but it matches hers in every way that matters. Every detail is as you remember it, even the dark, warm spots you loved so much. And this Emili will never die, no matter how you please yourself with her. The same can't be said of the original, now can it? Are you ready for your transformation?"

The second question was so abrupt and off topic it took a moment to sink into Crasor's excited mind. "Transformation?" was all he could say in response.

"Surely you've had experience with nano-machines? My appearance, my voice, my substance, is all created from the aggregate of these machines. The technology you are familiar with is in its infancy by comparison. Imagine the difference between a starship and a pebble, such is the difference in magnitude. Your transformation will be accomplished by these machines. You will be empowered and networked. You will become an entity of domination. You will *become.*" The woman's last word contained an emphasis Crasor was drawn to. His desire was fully aroused and all the misgivings he had earlier had been discarded.

"I am ready," he said, voice rich with anticipation. The doppelganger's visage wavered momentarily and then shattered, individual nano-machines falling to the floor like dust. The black carpet of machines flowed towards Crasor. It reached his kneeling form and swarmed over his skin. He threw his head back and bellowed a cry of triumph that echoed harshly off the chamber's walls.

Once the nano-machines had totally enveloped him, there was a moment of calm. In the stillness, Crasor could feel the legs of the tiny machines, although he knew that was impossible because of their microscopic size.

Then there was pain. It felt as if every cell in his body was being rent in two. He was being invaded, penetrated, consumed. More than just physical anguish, this pain was also in his life force. It was excruciating, engulfing, all consuming. The nano-machines, being microscopic, should have been able to pass into his body without this punishing sensation. "What-is-happening?" he screamed in agony. Crasor thrashed around on the floor, his body battering and tearing itself on the jagged rock.

In the midst of the pain, an image and a voice developed, not just a voice, but *the* voice. It was huge, booming, and epic beyond any size or proportion."We *are*, Crasor Tah Ahn, and now you *are* as well. You were chosen and now you will *become*." Crasor felt it. The rending was replaced with a mending, a knitting of the fabric of his being back together. And something had been added, something mysterious and powerful.

In the next instant, Crasor felt another shift, although this one was solely in his mind. He could feel his body still on the floor, but his vantage point was high on a building far above a vast city. The star of this particular planet was a cold red and the air was dry and arid. A battle raged on the streets below. "We are ancient, Crasor Tah Ahn, and now you are *One*. We are immortal, Crasor Tah Ahn, and now you are *One*."

One side of the combatants, which was obviously human, fought on foot as well as with armored vehicles Crasor was unfamiliar with. They rolled on a track system and had a large tube protruding over the front of the main body. Every so often the tube would let out a great boom, launching an explosive projectile that caused great geysers of dirt to spray from the ground.

The force attacking them was composed of strange looking creatures Crasor had never seen before. While they looked humanoid, many of their features told him they were definitely not human. At this distance Crasor couldn't pick out details, but their major features were plainly visible. Their skin was a pale gray, absorbing more light than it reflected. The creatures' heads were narrow and tall with jaws full of sharp, symmetrical teeth. The vertical leading edge of their heads glinted brilliantly, suggesting it was made of some type of metal. An elongated, powerful neck joined the head to a lean, strongly built body. The creatures' lengthy legs propelled them swiftly over the broken terrain of the battlefield, effortlessly leaping over ten meters at a jump. Their arms were much longer than those of humans and each forearm had a jutting appendage that stuck out past the elbow and reflected light. It reminded Crasor of a sword. Long, slender fingers tapered down to sharp points which also shone in the waning light of the red star.

"Gaze, Crasor Tah Ahn, and see the subjugation of your forebears in a former age." Crasor watched in awe as one of the creatures jumped towards a human target twenty meters away. As it landed, the man was easily cleaved in two by the attackers slender head. Others used their forearm weapons to brutally dismember their human adversaries. Not all the humans attacked fell to their deaths. The fingers of the creatures would penetrate the human's thin flesh, causing their bodies to spasm and convulse. After several minutes of writhing agony, the human would rise and begin attacking their comrades.

Crasor watched with a twisted grin on his cruel face. A booming voice confirmed his assessment, "Those who are not chosen are killed. Only those with a certain penchant can become *One*. It will take time for them to mature, but they serve and are loyal immediately." As if to illustrate this fact, one of the converted staggered his way towards a human. The convert managed to knock the woman down, and after a brief struggle, tore through her throat with his teeth. He raised his blood spattered face, looking for his next target. Crasor delightfully exulted in the dominance of the creatures. Excitement pulsed through him as he thought about his own transformation.

"This is but a small foretaste of what is to come. In times past when we ascended, the universe was disinclined to us. Now, there is richness for harvest and we can sustain. We will fully consume and the universe will ascend to the high plane with us. But first many things must be broken, and you, Crasor Tah Ahn, will break. The humans and the Entho-la-ah-mines will be crushed under you. Both young and old will fall to you. You will break the weak and you will obliterate the strong. Terra and space are no match for what you will become. The stars are setting on the dominion of flesh as they settle in decay. Their ascension will not come— cannot come—because you, Crasor Tah Ahn will break their Dawn."

22 – CAZZ-AK-TAK

Cazz-ak marveled at the crystal cave's fractal structure and wondered, for the thousandth time, how it had formed. Thousands of Entho-la-ah-mine queens had been brought to this Great Chamber in order to usher them into adulthood. Its walls glowed with a pale blue luminescence that made his exoskeleton glow with iridescent fire. Cazz-ak could feel the group's excitement grow as they walked further into the depths. It was a special place, a structure revered and treasured by their race. There was no Entho-la-ah-mine species without it.

Cazz-ak led them into the center of the chamber, forming a rough circle directly beneath the enormous main crystal. Elth-eo-lan and her ward stood in the center of the circle, looking nervous, but excited. As long as everything went well, there would be a new queen at the conclusion of the Awakening. Once the group settled down and aligned in the proper formation, they began focusing their thoughts.

The ritual was precise, the formula ancient. Remembering the Entho-la-ah-mine history in unison was the first step. The circle would relive the path of the species through the mind of the Great Thought, using the power of the crystal to bind it to the ward's mind. It was important the group be big enough, so the history wouldn't be interpreted through the eyes of the individuals. There needed to be balance. The ritual would show it all, no matter how brutal or gory, so the new queen could understand their history.

***

The group's sense of fear heightened as they stared down into the shaft. The proto-Entho-la-ah-mine whose memory they were reliving thought there might be food down there. He was scared though. There might also be predators. There was no scent trail leading that way. None of his kin had ever been there before. The hive was hungry. He needed to check.

The creature made his way down the shaft, tenuously clinging to the unnaturally smooth walls. He carefully placed each of his six legs. One slip and he would be dashed to pieces at the bottom of the shaft. He felt very exposed to predators. There was no place to hide. It took him quite some time to get to the bottom, but when he finally did, he quickly hid behind one of the large crystal structures and listened. Nothing. He tried to smell out any possible food sources, but again, nothing.

Coming out from behind the pillar, the creature began exploring the large cave. Inadvertently, he wandered under the large central crystal. A surge of energy flowed through his brain, opening unused pathways and springing complex cognizance to life. New emotions welled up within the creature as he saw the world around him in a totally new light. He was processing an incredible amount of information at once with such ease. *Who am I?* he questioned. This new level of focus brought about by the crystal had sparked a consciousness that evolution never would have reached.

As the ancestor left the cave, he noticed details that had escaped him before. Questions about his surroundings flooded through him. It was overwhelming and it took him time to organize his thoughts and emotions. *There is so much I have been missing about the world around me,* he thought, excitement welling up within him.

When he ran into another of his species, he tried to explain what had happened to him. *I have found something great and wonderful. It is a place that brings your mind to life.* The other of his species rubbed his front legs together, signaling he did not understand. *Come with me,* the proto-Entho-la-ah-mine mentally sent, desperately trying to make him understand. Without further communication, the other left.

The proto-Entho-la-ah-mine's new found intelligence made him realize he was the only one of his kind anywhere. *I wish I had someone to talk to,* he thought, wishing for a friend. This desire inspired a plan: *I can signal another that there is food in the cave and they will follow me. Then they too will be changed and able to communicate with me.* So he did just that.

The group watched through the eyes of the proto-Entho-la-ah-mine as he and the newly evolved members of his population slowly converted their whole hive. Eventually, the only one left without cognizance was the Queen. *She is too frail to climb down The Way,* the first ancestor, now called Del-ele-ex, told the hive through the newly discovered group mind. Sadness ran through them, but they all knew it was true. They had barely been able to help the other old members of their species down the steep tunnel, and the Queen was far less agile than worst of that group.

As the years went on, Del-ele-ex and his mate had children, as did all the other mating pairs. Each egg hatched and produced offspring connected to the group mind without going to the crystal. The species had fully evolved, or so they thought.

When the revered Queen passed, her daughter succeeded her, which was the custom of the species. The queen, while not required for procreation of the species, was a vital component in the structure and leadership of the Entho-la-ah-mines. They could survive without her, at least for a little while, but morale dropped and the species' growth faltered. She was a vital binding agent for the society, a benevolent leader who was able to analyze their path and psyche.

Del-ele-ex was there when the new Queen's daughter was born. The egg hatched and the Queen-to-be was healthy, but she had no connection to the group mind. This was easily solved by taking her to the crystal chamber, but no one understood at the time why she was born without the connection. In later years, Entho-la-ah-mine scientists found the male genetic component was needed for the reproduced connection to the group mind. Since the queens procreated asexually, they still had the increased brain capabilities, but lacked the ability to pass on the connection.

Now the group watched the history of his species through the perspective of the group mind, which over time had evolved into the Great Thought. The hive, now much more intelligent and able to communicate more efficiently, quickly built many new colonies on Haak-ah-tar. As generations passed, the mental power of the species grew stronger and science became a beloved field of study. They were able to build starships and venture first to other planets and then to other solar systems. They built underground colonies on planets that suited them and studied the universe.

Their harmonious hive mind allowed them to be peaceful, and lacking wars, they developed quite quickly. Soon after the Entho-la-ah-mines developed interstellar travel, they ran across the humans. Initially, the Entho-la-ah-mines were overjoyed. It was great to know there was other life in the galaxy and they were excited to share their culture and scientific discoveries.

The humans were on the brink of extinction, their planets polluted and overpopulated. The Ashamine seemed a good government, but its citizens weren't united behind it. The Entho-la-ah-mines had offered to share some of their resource rich planets and the Ashamine gladly accepted. At first everything had worked quite well, but then the humans started breaking their agreements. They encroached on Entho-la-ah-mine settlements and mining areas. Then the Slaughter of Kii-la-ta had occurred.

The group watched through the eyes of the Entho-la-ah-mines on Kii-la-ta as the humans came for them, raiding their city with rail guns and long swords. None had been spared, not even the young. The entire hive had been wiped out.

After the Slaughter of Kii-la-ta, many meetings had been held. The group watched some of them through Cazz-ak's eyes. The Ashamine tried to explain away the actions of the humans, saying it was self defense. That was a lie and Cazz-ak knew it. Looking back, it was obvious the Ashamine had been trying to stall the Entho-la-ah-mines and keep them from developing a military. The humans had needed time to convert their newly gained resources into war ships. The group felt Cazz-ak's sadness and anger—an emotion new to their race—that the humans would deceive them. The human mentality was totally foreign to the Entho-la-ah-mines. It was so foreign, in fact, that it was hard to place the humans into a framework of the universe the Entho-la-ah-mines could understand. The Great Thought wondered if they had ever wanted to coexist or if they had been planning xenocide all along. Based on the human history, they suspected the latter.

Even with all the extensive research into the humans and their culture, they were still a mystery. If it was resources they wanted, the Entho-la-ah-mines had offered them freely. They had done everything possible to try to help the humans. The group thought the best hypothesis was simply that the humans didn't understand how to share or co-exist with another intelligent life form. They seemed to even have a hard time co-existing with each other.

Millions of Entho-la-ah-mines had been slaughtered over the past few years, the aftershocks of which would reach many generations into the future. Until recently, this slaughter had gone unchecked, and a feeling of hopelessness pervaded the Great Thought. Now though, things were changing.

Although a peaceful species, the Entho-la-ah-mines had a self-preservation instinct that rivaled humankind. The group knew it was just as strong, but that it wasn't perverted and misused in the human way. Once their existence had been threatened, the Entho-la-ah-mines began developing defensive military hardware and a small amount of tactical offensive weaponry. The group relived the joy that had been felt the first time one of their ships had withstood an attack by an Ashamine ship. The enemy vessel had been small, but that was tremendous progress. It had taken years to get to the point they were at now, but the harmonious Great Thought had allowed them to make a lot of progress during that time.

The Entho-la-ah-mines took no joy or pride in their newfound combat prowess. The entire species mourned the loss of any type of life—including that of their enemies—no matter how many of their kind were slaughtered. The action went against the nature of their species, but the humans had forced them to this point. Otherwise, there would be no Entho-la-ah-mines left in the galaxy.

Coming to the present, the group saw several Entho-la-ah-mine ships causing destruction and possibly even death amongst the humans on Haak-ah-tar. They were attempting to create a credible distraction, one that would keep the humans from coming after the group. Hopefully, when it was time for the Entho-la-ah-mines to once again withdraw from Haak-ah-tar, they wouldn't leave too much destruction behind. It was such a beautiful planet. It was home.

"Cazz-ak," Elth-eo-lan thought, bringing Cazz-ak-tak out of the group mind. "We are ready for the next part of the ceremony." He realized the Remembrance had been completed, the memories of the hive mind copied into Elth-eo-lan's ward. It was time to move on to the next part of the Awakening ceremony.

Elth-eo-lan, taking the place of the deceased Queen-to-be's mother, took the egg off her back and carefully cradled it. She stroked it with her forelegs, signaling the egg's occupant it was safe to hatch, that the time had come. A small crack formed in the surface as the infant pushed. Soon it grew, fracturing the iridescent green surface. A small head poked out, and in another moment, the egg broke in two and a small Entho-la-ah-mine stood before them. All those assembled bowed, joy soaring in their hearts. The Queen-to-be wasn't able to communicate psionically yet, but she did wave her limbs in acknowledgement of their deference. She was small at the moment, but would rapidly grow to full size now that she was outside the egg.

With the Remembrance complete, all that remained was to allow the power of the Focus to bind the memories and responsibilities within the young Queen. Cazz-ak melded his thoughts with the group, the psionic force of the members becoming one. They strengthened their connection to the Great Thought, allowing all the Entho-la-ah-mines in the galaxy to see the event. Tapping into the Focus, they pushed the Remembrance into it. Next, they brought the resulting energy out and directed it down towards the Queen-to-be. But something was wrong.

A dark presence pushed in at the edges of their psionic gathering, probing for a weakness. They could feel it trying to snake its way in, a putrid energy that wanted to corrupt and infect them all. Acting as one, the group pulled in strength from the Great Thought and built a shield around Elth-eo-lan and her ward. They flexed their mental abilities, pushing them to their limits in an attempt to protect the Queen-to-be. The corruption struck back, lashing at the mental barrier with a force that staggered the group. They held strong however, and after several more fierce attempts, the intruding energy vanished.

The group kept the shield up for several minutes, nervous the attack might resume. *We must continue. The queen must be brought forth if there is any hope of survival,* the group thought. They cautiously lowered the shield, ready to put it back up at the first sign of danger. But the corruption was gone.

Once again they grasped the energy of the Focus and brought it down towards the Queen-to-be. They fused it inside her, binding psionic ability, memories, and the connection to the Great Thought into her mind. The group split its psyche back into the individual states and Cazz-ak felt himself return to a mix of emotion.

The Great Thought was excited, nervous, worried, and overjoyed. Cazz-ak felt the same and for the same reasons. There was great rejoicing and thanksgiving at the bringing forth of a new queen. The old Queen had been killed by a human attack on the colony world she had been forced to flee to. She was still young, and her loss had been devastating. This young—almost too young—protégé had been the only candidate available to take her place, and the odds of getting her into this cave safely had been bad. But Cazz-ak and his crew had over come all the obstacles and had completed the ceremony. He was truly happy.

Even with the new queen a reality, Cazz-ak-tak was not totally at ease however. There was still so much that could go wrong. What if the humans dispatched more ships to Haak-ah-tar and destroyed the Entho-la-ah-mine diversion? They might be able to sneak out using the psionic trick that had worked on the way in, but that worried Cazz-ak. There was too much at stake. He would try his best, and he knew every Entho-la-ah-mine would lay down their lives for the new Queen, just as he would if it were needed. The Queen, now consecrated and psionically enabled, was still no safer than her mother had been. Cazz-ak just hoped more human ships didn't arrive before they could get through a worm hole.

And what about the dark energy that had assaulted them earlier? *It wanted to corrupt the Queen,* Cazz-ak worried. *We barely stopped it. What if it had gotten through?* It had to be connected to whatever had assaulted them on The Way. *We can't fight another enemy, especially not one that is so psionically powerful. We are doing all we can just to survive the humans...*

23 – WAKE

Wake shook with fear as he thought about his future. Raimos had been right to worry about his safety. He had been set up and now he was going to be executed. *And what is this Brotherhood of Azak-so?* he wondered. Had they tried to help him or hurt him during the trial? More importantly, regardless of what had been meant to happen, the end result was catastrophic for him.

He had been taken to the ASN Antadroga, a Rubicon class ship, after his trial. Although he knew this was the end, he could not help but be amazed by the vastness of the vessel. Wake's previous experiences flying had only been on small transport ships. And the latest ship completed, the ASN Founder's Hammer, was supposed to dwarf the Antadroga, a feat he hardly believed possible.

Wake looked up as the door to his cabin opened and a large marine came in. "Come with me," the stone faced man commanded, motioning Wake towards the door. Wake followed the guard, taking measured, calm steps. Keeping himself under rigid control was his only hope of staying calm. They entered a lift that easily raised them up several levels to the main deck.

Exiting out into a large, open area, Wake immediately noticed the crimson colored environmental nominizing suit displayed in the middle of the command deck. It was the universal symbol of the damned. Everyone who knew anything about the Ashamine had heard of this suit. Wake couldn't take his eyes off of it. It held a beauty that captivated him, making his eyes want to follow its graceful curves. He had never seen a suit constructed or a colored like it.

"I see you've noticed your ENS," a deep, gruff voice said. Wake pulled his eyes from the execution apparatus and turned to face the commander of the Antadroga, Commander Yaladon. He was a short man, stout and gruff with close cropped gray hair. He faced Wake squarely and looked up at him with a stern expression on his hard face. "I won't make this any harder on you than is necessary. I'm here to do the will of the Ashamine, not torture you. Within the constraints of the orders, I will try to make this as quick and painless as possible." He turned to face the subordinate officers standing at attention across the command deck. "The ceremony shall now begin. Wake Darmekus, formerly of the Engineering and Building Division, censured by the Lower-Elders of the Ashamine for the malefactions of delinquency of duties, disregard for safety, and the murder of twelve colonists on the planet Traynos-6, please don the Clothing of the Iconoclast."

Wake, saying nothing, nodded his thanks to the Commander for his consideration. It was the closest thing to kindness he had received during this whole ordeal. He walked over to the suit, his heart pounding so hard, it made his chest hurt.

As he approached, he continued to marvel at the suit's beauty. Silver scroll work, intricately detailed, drew the eye and contrasted beautifully with the deep crimson color. The ENS appeared ancient, yet its uniqueness gave it a futuristic look. It was unlike any suit Wake had ever seen.

After a brief period of study, Wake began to don the Clothing of the Iconoclast, and in a short time, all that remained to be fitted was the helmet. The suit felt elegant and Wake wished he could see himself in it. He turned to face Commander Yaladon, feeling a small amount of gratitude towards the man for his fairness. Once he had made eye contact, he pulled the helmet down over his head and sealed it.

"Wake Darmekus," the Commander's voice said over his suit's comm, "this very suit has been used to execute all those who have turned traitor to the Ashamine or committed crimes of great magnitude against its people. You will be sent through the airlock of this ship and set adrift in the void. Contemplate your crimes while you drift, but do so quickly because your oxygen will only last so long. Once your life expires, we will send your body out to roam the galaxy as a witness of your crimes." After a brief pause the Commander pointed towards a large, circular door and said, "Please enter the airlock."

Wake looked down at his ENS clad feet, motionless, immobile. He couldn't force himself towards the airlock. Panic began to enter his mind, knowing that in a moment he would lose control and try to escape. A sudden jab in the back propelled him forward and he barely managed to keep himself from falling. He looked back in time to see one of the guards resuming his rigid stance.

"Enlightened Alexhion, stand down!" Yaladon's voice was hard as tungsten. Alexhion made no further movement, but also showed no remorse. Yaladon was obviously on the verge of taking further action, but instead, escorted Wake to the threshold of the airlock. Wake continued alone into the chamber. The airlock's bright light caused the ENS's crimson finish to glow and the silver scroll work to shine brightly. Wake wondered absent-mindedly how many people had worn this suit and taken the one way trip through an airlock.

"Turn," Yaladon's gruff voice intoned and Wake did so, stopping midway inside the airlock's deep expanse. "Watch Captain, seal the inner doors." Even as he was speaking, the doors began moving silently, sliding in from each corner with a circular motion.

A clanging sound resounded through Wake as the corners met. The finality of the sound made him shudder. Wake took a deep breath and tried to calm his nerves. Some people claimed images of your life flashed before your eyes as you began to die, but all Wake saw was the gray finish of the dull walls around him. *Maybe I'm not dead enough yet,* he thought, the morbid humor bringing a smile to his lips.

The little amount of levity he had built up vanished as the outer doors opened swiftly. They had not equalized the airlock so the blast of escaping atmosphere would force him out into space. *No chance they were gonna let me hide in there while I die. They want to see it. They are probably recording everything.* He found the thought sickening, not because it was his own death, but because it would probably be televised. Recording it for evidence was one thing, but recording it for the sick pleasure of the masses was quite another. Wake had always found the televising of executions to be distasteful and demeaning to the citizens of the Ashamine. Now, ironically enough, he was seeing what it was like to be on the other side of the camera.

The hemorrhaging air violently propelled his body into the void, but his quick reflexes kept him stable and graceful in flight. He was weightless, with a slight rotation causing him to spin lazily. This wasn't his first time in zero-g, but every time caused him to marvel at how he could think of any direction as "up". Wake looked around, seeing the desolation of this remote sector of Ashamine space. The stars were vivid, bright points of light in a vast blackness.

Soon he was growing increasingly distant from the ship, watching the huge vessel become smaller and smaller. He knew they wouldn't let him continue on indefinitely, so it was no surprise when he felt his speed slow, then reverse. The ship was focusing its gravity-mass beam on him in order to draw him back. It was a strange sensation, having the tug of gravity pull only on his chest. That area became "down", but his head had a hard time shifting perspective since it was only his core that was effected.

When he was within the proper distance, he stopped completely. Now the waiting began. He knew it was important to breathe slowly in order to maximize the time he had remaining in this world.

Earlier, he had been frighted into paralysis, but now he was beginning to grow progressively calmer. This was contrary to logic, but it felt right. Perhaps he was learning to control his emotions better.

Thoughts of his parents flashed through his mind. It still pained Wake greatly that they couldn't accept his decision to join the EBD, that they no longer talked to him or even acted like he existed. He would never be able to change any of that now.

The more he thought of his parents, the more he despaired and regretted how things were going to end with them. Upon hearing the news, they would think of him as a traitor. His parents would trust what the Ashamine said about him. No doubt would linger in their minds.

Wake began to grow angry at his parents for their absolute belief in everything the Ashamine said. If Wake's experience had been any indicator, things were very wrong within the government. He wished he could have seen the depth of the corruption sooner and been able to fight it. *Who am I kidding,* he thought, *I couldn't even win my own trial.*

Wake had been so devoted to the Ashamine. Seeing his efforts wasted on such an unworthy cause made him feel sick. Adding this emotion to his anger and sadness created a caustic cocktail. In an instant he decided he would be better off leaving this world and its greedy, deceitful inhabitants. Death would bring nothingness, a true void the deep shadow he floated in now could only poorly imitate. He welcomed the darkness, the eternal nonexistence appealing to him. The longer he floated, both in his agony and in the void, the more he realized that maybe the Ashamine were doing him a favor. He welcomed death.

Wake had no illusions of an afterlife of bliss where he would float in eternal joy. Those peaceful, happy images were a luxury only those such as the Dygars and other cults had the benefit of. Even the Ashamine used the promise of bliss in an afterlife to promote their state religion.

And then his air ran out. It was there one moment and gone the next. There was nothing to breath in, nothing at all. His chest struggled to draw in oxygen, but the result was a jerking spasm that made his body flood with panic. He fought to remain calm and to keep his mind focused, but he knew it really made no difference.

As Wake's body tried to bring in the oxygen it so desperately needed, his logical mind calculated how much longer he had to live. Two minutes was probably the maximum, he decided. *What to do, what to do, what to do?* he queried, but there was no viable answer. Death was now unacceptable to his lucid mind, his body fighting desperately to cling to its spark. In the abstract, death had been fine. The reality of the end of life was turning out to be something else entirely.

Black spots began to form in his vision like little splotches of oil floating in water. As time passed the splotches converged and the mass grew larger. "Hold on Wake," sounded somewhere in his head, but it made no sense. "We're trying to get to you, but this Ashamine ship is making it difficult." The noise was buzzing in his ear, nonsense to be ignored.

An urge to take his helmet off grew inside Wake's mind. He knew it was crazy because the void was worse than the inside of the helmet. As his precious seconds ticked away, the idea grew more and more appealing however. His hands rose towards the release controls around the neck of the suit, but he forced them away.

By this time, his sensory input was dampened by the lack of oxygen. The impulses that did make it to his starving brain were relegated to a low priority. Wake vaguely noticed the Ashamine ship was accelerating rapidly away from him. The buzzing continued in his ears, but it was growing faint.

Wake could barely control his panic and his hands once again rose to his helmet controls. There had to be air outside the helmet, it was that simple. He had been stupid to wait so long, had almost killed himself being so stubborn. In just a moment the refreshing air would be in his lungs, purging the burn that was consuming them.

He couldn't seem to work the fittings that held the helmet in place. Wake cursed, dimly wondering why his fingers were so sluggish and far away. Finally, after several long moments of struggle, he found the fittings and began to operate them.

As the helmet came off, Wake was blinded by a bright light, his body feeling a tremendous acceleration. The punishing g-force lasted for a few seconds and was gone. *Whaaa,* Wake thought dazedly, unable to understand what had just happened. Once his eyes adjusted, he realized he was laying on the floor of a cargo hold. *Magnetic deceleration,* he thought, explaining the earlier g-force. His whole body felt bruised. His first breath in caused a stab of pain to surge from his rib cage.

The joy of the air filling his lungs eased his pain and he welcomed the stale air of the cargo hold, drawing it deep into his lungs. It tasted so sweet. After a minute passed he managed to rise to his hands and knees, lungs still drawing in the refreshing air. He knew he wouldn't take oxygen for granted ever again. The pain of its absence was excruciating. Never had he experienced such a painful, horrid sensation.

A man strode into the cargo bay as Wake rose unsteadily to his feet. Both men stared at each other for a moment before either spoke. The newcomer broke the silence, his voice echoing hollowly off the metal walls of the bay. "Sir Darmekus, we are so happy we were able to save you. Thankfully surprise was on our side." The man was speaking rapidly, but

Wake understood. "We are still not safe and I'm quite sure the Ashamine ship will bring its big guns down upon us as soon as we are within range. Captain Malesis is an amazing commander, but I fear this situation will push him past his limits. We were able to get in easily because they had all their attention focused on you. Now though, they only have eyes for us." The man smiled and motioned Wake to follow him. "We'll do our best though, as that is all we can ever do. Come with me. We must move fast to get strapped in before the shooting starts."

Wake rose and made his way towards the man who, once he was sure Wake was following, strode quickly back out the way he had come. Their journey was short and ended in a small flight deck containing four other humans. The man escorting Wake sat in one of the seats at the back and motioned Wake to sit in the single remaining seat. "Strap in tight, things could get bumpy." A look of frustration crossed the man's face as he rolled his eyes and smacked himself in the forehead. "I always forget to introduce myself to new folks. My momma says it's a character flaw. The name is Ralen Call, member of the Brotherhood of Azak-so."

"Wake Darmekus, although you already know that," Wake said, a tentative smile crossing his face at the man's openness and gentle demeanor. "Is there anything I can do to help? I have some skill with computers and machinery."

"Captain Malesis here, Brotherhood of Azak-so," a man in one of the front seats said. "I don't know if there is much you can do. We are trying some tactical maneuvers to stay in close to the Ashamine ship and out of their weapons range. That ship is too small to carry fighters, thank Azak-so, so we don't have that to worry about. We are in a precarious situation here. Too close to the ship and it can ram us, too far away and it sends tungsten ripping through our hull. The only thing that has kept us alive so far is smooth flying—not meaning to brag mind you, just stating the situation. Do you have any ideas?" Wake looked thoughtful as he removed the crimson gauntlets covering his hands.

"I may have something," Wake said after a brief moment passed. "Let me check your systems and then I'll be able to tell you more." No one else in the room spoke. None of the three remaining men introduced themselves. They were engrossed in their displays, totally focused on their tasks. Captain Malesis and Ralen were also busy with their stations, but both were listening. "OK, here is what I'm thinking: Your ship is obviously more maneuverable than the larger vessel, but far out gunned. We need to use our maneuverability to get into a position where we can strike at a vital system. I know what you are thinking, 'All the vital systems are well armored' and in that you are correct. But I was just on that ship, and I had a pretty good look around. I was paying special attention since it was my first time on a vessel of that size. One thing lacking in their impeccable design is the view port on the main deck. One of the crew told me that during battle they lower an armor plate over it to keep it from being compromised. In order to watch my death, they had it wide open. I'm guessing since we are such a small ship they won't have bothered to lower it since then. If you can–"

"If I can get a couple of rounds through that window," Captain Malesis interjected, "they will experience a very unpleasant explosive decompression."

"Exactly," Wake said, a beaming smile on his face. His emotions had risen to a level they had not been to since his arrival on Ashamine-2 for his trial. His face turned somber as he thought through the situation more. "I feel terrible we will be killing everyone on the command deck, but I guess it's us or them at this point."

Ralen gave Wake a strange look as he said, "Considering what they were about to do to you, I'm surprised you aren't excited for it. We can fill you in on some of the terrible things the Ashamine has done to the human and Entho-la-ah-mine races if you feel guilty afterwards. Trust me, if your plan works out, you are doing a service to the Gods and the Universe." Ralen did have a point about the death they had planned for him. It had been a close call, and a painful one at that. The fact his sentence was unjust and unfair mitigated some of his anticipated guilt.

"Ralen," said Captain Malesis, "I'm going to bring the ship in on a vector that will allow us to get a clear shot on the main deck window. If you miss, we won't get a second try. They'll bring the armor down, game over. I'm not trying to stress you out, but you need to know the stakes."

"Sure, sure," Ralen said speaking in his characteristically quick manner and not bothered in the least. He continued speaking in a low mumble Wake couldn't understand. After making some adjustments on his screen, he looked back towards Captain Malesis and nodded to indicate he was ready.

Captain Malesis brought the ship in low over the top of the Ashamine vessel, moving fast and skimming low. After a few seconds they were to the front of the ship and Captain Malesis pulled up sharply into a tight loop.

Ralen began mumbling, and all Wake could make out was, "Great, great, great," said in a tone that sounded less than enthusiastic. Ralen's mumbling ceased as the Brotherhood ship reached its apogee from the Ashamine vessel. Wake monitored his console, still trying to think of anything that would help them succeed. In a moment, they would find out if his plan was enough to keep them alive.

As they dove towards their target, the interior of the deck flared brightly as a rail projectile passed within meters of the Brotherhood ship. "Damn them to the fires of the dark star!" Captain Malesis cursed.

Just as Wake was feeling it was time to fire, Ralen did so. The ship bucked as four tungsten projectiles left their barrels. Four bright ion tracer trails streaked towards the Ashamine ship. It briefly appeared the volley was a complete miss, that the rounds would pass in front of the enemy ship. Ralen's calculation and Wake's gut feeling had been correct, however. Wake watched as the Ashamine ship flew into the line of fire just as the projectiles were about to pass it by. All four tungsten alloy rounds hammered directly into the deck window. The plasti-glass fractured and exploded outwards in a shower of debris. Wake saw the bodies of the deck crew fly into space and knew they would be experiencing the fate he had just escaped. *Us or them,* he thought.

Captain Malesis pulled out of the dive as hard as he could, trying to avoid a collision with the Ashamine ship. "This is gonna be close," Captain Malesis yelled. Wake checked his harness straps, knowing they wouldn't save him if they struck the other ship at such a high speed.

We're gonna hit, Wake thought, the enemy ship growing huge in the main window. Collision alarms began to sound, too late to change anything. Closing his eyes Wake braced for impact. His body felt the extra g-force of Captain Malesis pushing the ship to its limit, barely missing the larger vessel. A few bodies who had been ejected from the enemy ship bounced off of their front window and hull as they passed. The muffled thumps made Wake feel queasy.

He thought they were away from the debris cloud until a familiar figure came streaking towards the window, the large body spinning wildly in the air. It was Enlightened Alexhion, unmistakable due to his hulking frame. Striking squarely against the main window, his head exploded, leaving a smear of blood and brain that froze instantly. And then he was gone, his body consigned to the void for eternity unless the Ashamine decided to retrieve it. "Damn," Captain Malesis muttered.

Wake felt no sympathy for Alexhion, knowing the man had felt no sympathy for him. He had the impression Alexhion had been a cruel, nasty individual, brutalizing those who were unfortunate enough to cross his path. His death would probably benefit the Universe.

"We cheated the fires of the dark star once again!" Captain Malesis proclaimed, breaking the silence. "I won't say I'm happy those people died, but..." After a beat or two passed, he spoke again. "We have the needed separation from the Ashamine ship and are far enough inside the worm zone to engage the drive. Carson," he said as he glanced towards a dark skinned man Wake had yet to be introduced to, "it would be quite unfortunate if the Ashamine were able to track us from the worm impression, so forty for seven." The man called Carson raised his hand and nodded to acknowledge the order. He didn't look up from his console, his attention completely focused on entering the formulas the

Captain had requested.

Wake didn't know enough about worm travel to understand what the Captain had said, so he turned to Ralen and quietly asked, "Forty for seven?"

"Yeah, forty false signatures for each of seven worms," Ralen replied quickly, looking up from his terminal. "No way to get rid of our actual worm impression, so we try to keep the odds in our favor by using false trails." He let out a short bark of a laugh. "Carson will make sure that some of the false impressions come out near black holes or in star forming regions. Attempting to follow us would be really hazardous."

"Sounds like it," Wake replied, impressed by their resourcefulness. Silence once again returned to the deck, each of the crew members focused on their tasks. "Captain," Wake said after a minute had passed, "is there anything I can do to help? I appreciate what you did for me and would like to do all I can in return."

Before Captain Malesis could answer, the ship shuddered as a blackness sprung up at its nose, enveloping it. The void soon swallowed the entire ship, the darkness outside complete. And then the stars were back, but in a different configuration than they had been just moments before. Wake let himself breath again, glad their passage through the worm had been successful.

"Don't worry about it," Captain Malesis said, picking the conversation back up. His voice was straightforward, his tone frank. "We simply did what was right. We know the failure of the bridge on Traynos wasn't your fault. The Ashamine is to blame, and mind you, they are completely to blame. We intercepted some intel that the Ashamine was planning the accident, but we weren't able to get there in time to stop them. When we arrived, the bridge had already collapsed. After that, we kept an eye on you. The Brotherhood figured the Ashamine would try to take you out in order to eliminate any conflicting stories. We hoped our demonstration at your trial would scare the Elders, that you defeating Karthis would show them your loyalty and patriotism. We thought it would change their decision to have you take the fall."

"Wait, wait," Wake interjected, a confused look on his face. "Why would the Ashamine kill those colonists? They were miners. Those people wouldn't show up on anyone's sensors."

"All you say is true, or at least it was until a few weeks before the accident. What brought those twelve miners onto the Ashamine High Command's sensor array was what they discovered while mining. We don't know all the facts, mind you. The Brotherhood can only hash so deeply and all the details are *way* deep, like High-Elders deep. We did manage to find out it's something ancient, and obviously important to the Ashamine. They seem to think it could revolutionize humanity.

Ashamine HC didn't want the discovery to become public knowledge. The logical thing was to get rid of those miners and blame it all on the engineer responsible for the bridge. Simple, clean, and easy. They took some gambles though, especially when they sent you the faulty materials, but all that fell into the crevasse. And the data evidence disappeared too. We looked for it. They were very thorough."

Wake had not believed the claims of those who were critical of the Ashamine, at least until his trial had become such a joke. Now, with what Captain Malesis had told him, he was completely convinced. "I knew the components they gave me were sub-standard, but they would have been serviceable for at least a few standard months. I was even on the bridge doing maintenance. I saw it all happen..." Wake trailed off and fell silent, eyes falling to the floor.

"It wasn't your fault," Captain Malesis tried to comfort Wake.

After a moment, Wake looked up, a supernova's worth of fury burning in his eyes. "They set me up. They tried to execute me. I felt guilty, felt responsible for the death of the miners. Now I find out the bridge was sabotaged somehow?" His voice boiled with rage. "They killed innocent people to keep an archaeological find secret? That's despicable and horrendous. I hope they get blighthearted while they burn in the fires of the dark star. It would be the smallest part of what they deserve!"

Captain Malesis' face lit up with a broad smile. "Welcome to enlightenment, Wake. You are experiencing what every one of us in the Brotherhood of Azak-so has gone through: the realization the Ashamine government you love and trust isn't the pure, altruistic entity you thought it was.

"Any one of us here could tell you our own stories about how we discovered the truth, but it wouldn't sound a lot different from your own journey. Different circumstances, same blightheart. We are here to try to hinder and remove as much of the Ashamine corruption as we possibly can, using any and all means necessary. That's partially why we came to your aid. Innocent men being executed in the selfish interest of government is not acceptable. The Brotherhood won't allow it. You were a special case, as I mentioned, because we could not stop the murders before they happened. We didn't want you take the fall. Once we discovered their plans to execute you, we were honor bound to intervene."

Wake felt drained after his outburst, overwhelmed at the implications growing exponentially in his mind. The system he had served was rotten and putrefying. "What do I do now?" he asked, unsure if he was questioning Captain Malesis or himself. Captain Malesis answered first.

"I'm sure you realize you can never go back to any planet controlled by the Ashamine, at least not looking like or being identified as Wake Darmckus. So here are your options as I see them: you can either live out your days hiding on some outer planet or you can take a stand against the Ashamine and fight for the good left in humanity.

"Obviously you know what decision we would like for you to make, but we will help you regardless. We read your personnel file and we know you have skills that would be valuable to us. We also took note of your high integrity. If you decide against joining us, we will drop you off in a safe place and give you enough Ashcreds to start a new life. If you decide to join the Brotherhood, you have a home amongst us. It's dangerous, but what worthwhile thing in human history was not worth fighting or dying for? The choice is yours, no pressure either way. Take all the time you need. "

Wake knew he couldn't live in hiding, couldn't stand by knowing the corruption that festered in the heart of the Ashamine. He had to do something about it and the Brotherhood seemed like the best way. There was still many good things about the Ashamine, and maybe he could be part of restoring it to the just and honorable system he once thought it was. "I want to join the Brotherhood. I'm ready." Wake looked into Captain Malesis' eyes, confident. "I need to make a difference. I want to help restore the Ashamine back to what it once was.

"Well now, that was a quick decision. I don't think you'll regret it though. We're a good group of people and we take care of our own. Let me be the first to formally welcome you, Wake Darmekus, into the Brotherhood of Azak-so."

24 – FELAR

Darkness. She couldn't hear anything over the sound of her own frantic heart beat and ragged breathing. Felar was terrified. Blackness enveloped her. *Have to slow down, have to get control,* she thought. *Remember your training and your experience.* None of her past combat situations had been anything like this though. She focused on controlling her breath, which in turn calmed her heart rate. She had to regain full control of herself if she wanted to stay alive.

Felar took stock of her current situation, both assets and liabilities. She couldn't see anything in the darkness, but she felt like she was in a small room, perhaps an office or utility closet. *That door is definitely a problem.* She knew it was flimsy from when she had entered. *Those things won't have any problems breaking through it.* Felar hoped that perhaps, in all the chaos that had just occurred, she had slipped away from whatever had attacked them.

In the way of assets, she had little. Her whole squad was dead. She had lost her primary weapon—boy, would her instructors have lit into her for that back in Dog—leaving her with a semi-automatic rail pistol that had a wicked recoil. She also had a few illum sticks, her combat short swords, and a small amount of the special explosives. When listed, it sounded like a lot, but Felar knew all of these items were a weak set of tools to combat those *things* out in the corridors.

Everything about the current situation was a liability. She was pitted against a foe she knew next to nothing about, and those things had easily decimated her squad. She now had no back up whatsoever. How in the fires of the dark star was she supposed to extract herself from this place? It seemed impossible, yet she had been taught to do just that.

The carnage, gore, and death of her squad members was burned indelibly into her memory. They had been attacked by a small group of the things just as they had left the lift. "Keep your fields of fire tight,"

Felar had ordered after the initial attackers retreated. Everything within her told her she needed to go back, had to retreat. But an FC didn't retreat, an FC completed the mission. So they ventured further into the facility, and all the fires of the dark star broke loose.

"We're being flanked," Shanbek shouted. "What are these things?!"

"More attackers inbound from my sector," Malen reported.

"Full defensive posture," Felar ordered. "Fire when ready."

And they did just that, Malen's rail gatling mowing down the creatures with Unthar guarding his back. But the things were too fast, too agile, and far too smart. A minute into the battle they switched tactics and instead of full frontal assault, they started focusing on short hit and run attacks. They darted in and out of corridors and rooms until Malen's gun ran out of ammo. And then they reverted back to full assault. Felar and her squad were overrun.

Felar shook her head, trying to forget what had happened next. It was too much to process right now. She had to focus on saving herself. Regret, guilt, and remorse could come later.

Control yourself, Felar thought, pushing the memories out of her mind. She had to embrace the mental state she had been taught at Dog School. *Isolate yourself from fear, pain, and hopelessness. Embrace the now.* She pushed out the pain from losing her team, tried to forget the guilt of being the only survivor. She could do nothing about that in this moment. She pushed out the terror and loneliness of being isolated in a situation this alien and frightening. Emptiness and stillness enveloped her, shielding her from external pressures.

Pulling out her side arm, Felar checked the weapon to make sure it was ready to fire. The creatures could be taken down with a tungsten alloy rail round. She wouldn't have to discharge her weapon if her plan was successful. Stealth was her best tactic. *Will they continue to hunt as a pack or will they split up to search for me?* Felar didn't know which option was worse.

She carefully peaked her head out of the small room she had holed up in. A few small emergency lights allowed her to reconnoiter. Felar couldn't make out any targets or threats awaiting her. Low light optics would greatly increase her effectiveness at this point, but neither she nor her squad had deployed with it, not anticipating any need for it at the time. *If they had told us where we were going sooner,* she thought, inwardly cursing Ashamine Forces Command.

She slipped out into the hall, careful not to make any noise. The floor was hard and her boots soft, making her task easier. The main obstacle was to avoid kicking or stepping on any fallen debris. Fortunately there was very little in this area. The darkness made every task harder, so Felar stayed focused.

Nearing a hallway junction, she slowed. Rushing the plan would get her killed, but being overly cautious would expose her to danger longer. Consistency and caution were key.

Easing her head around the corner, Felar dry heaved at what she saw. A large hulking form stood over what was once a human body. It's matte black skin was barely visible in the darkness. Felar had to look hard to make out the creature's stout arms and narrow legs. The low light obscured the monstrosity's actions, but from the sounds—wet slapping accompanied by tearing and grunting noises—she knew what was happening.

Felar felt repulsed and disgusted by both the creature and what it was doing. Why were these *things* here? They had to be some sort of genetically modified organism, something manufactured to kill. Or maybe they were an unknown type of alien species. Whatever the case, she didn't want to get closer to try to find out.

Why was the mission briefing so flawed? It had said nothing of these fiendish creatures and their powerful killing ability. *They effortlessly took out an entire squad of soldiers,* Felar thought, fear trying to creep into her focus. She would tell the blighthearted buggers about their shoddy intel when she got back to AF Command.

Felar quickly transitioned across the intersection and continued on, hoping she could find a map of the facility. The creature didn't pursue. She needed to orient herself. Getting lost in the earlier chaos had left her with no idea where she was in relation to the exit. *Another stupid mistake,* she chided herself.

Finding a terminal in one of the hallways, Felar began to hash it, trying to break through the security lockout. "Access denied," kept popping up no matter what she tried. Finally, the terminal was locked off the network and she was forced to move on. *Time for a new tactic.*

It was a crude method, but Felar figured if she kept moving in a straight line, eventually she'd reach an outside wall. From there, she'd trace the perimeter of the facility until she reached the lift, which had been on one of the outer walls. Felar continued following her current hallway until it ended and she was forced to turn. When that happened, she went right and then took the first left, thereby continuing in roughly the same direction. She did this same maneuver several more times until she reached an intersection and heard the sounds of a feeding monstrosity. She quietly detoured to the left, and then took the first right. *How many of those blighthearted things are there?*

As time passed and she continued avoiding the creatures, Felar began feeling confident in her escape. *Don't let your guard down,* she thought, focusing her attention. *There is still a long way to go and a lot of things that can kill you.*

A dark flicker of movement in the corner of Felar's eye told her she was about to die. She had the rail pistol aimed and her finger tightening on the trigger before she consciously realized what she was doing. Thunder boomed in the confined hall as the projectile broke the speed of sound. The light from the tungsten's ionization was brief but intense to Felar's dark adjusted eyes. She was momentarily blinded, unable to see her attacker. A deep bellowing roar sounded as the hulking creature crashed into her. Felar grunted as she was slammed to the floor by the creature's weight.

She struggled fiercely to free her self, thrashing and lashing out with every ground fighting technique knew learned. This thing might kill her, but Felar would leave it a few bruises to remember her by. It took her a moment to realize the form on top of her wasn't moving. It was crushing the air out of her lungs. She could hardly breathe.

Felar labored with all her strength to shift the massive creature. The more she struggled, the heavier it seemed. Then, in a moment of brief rest, she heard something that gave her chills: a distant snarling and fall of heavy feet, growing nearer and nearer. Obviously, some of this creature's friends or family heard the battle and were now coming to investigate. Investigate was probably too intelligent of a word, however— *feed* was more appropriate.

Felar, feeling terror rising in her mind again, strove for the emptiness and calm she knew would allow her to perform at her best. She summoned all her strength and pushed at the corpse as hard as she could. It moved, but not far enough for her to fully extract herself. She could breathe normally, but her legs were still pinned.

Just as Felar was figuring out the best way to extract her legs, a flash of motion in her peripheral vision caught her attention. *Damn it all to the fires of the dark star,* she thought as she snatched up her pistol and triggered a round. The same deafening sound accompanied the same brilliant flash of light. The creature's blood misted the dark air, a gaping hole punched through its bullet shaped head. The monstrosity hit the floor hard and slid for a meter before coming to a stop, its dagger like teeth exposed in a death snarl.

Her ears were still ringing when she heard a faint sound behind her. Knowing all too well what she would find, she lay back as quickly as she could. Felar extended her arms over her head in a firm shooters grip. The creature running towards her was upside down in her weapon sight, but neither this nor the awkward position of her body was a problem for Felar. The round took the creature low on its head, severing a portion of it and sending it flying through the air. The rest of the creature fell next to Felar, one of its taloned feet almost landing on her head. The sharp claws carved small furrows in the smooth stone floor. She shuddered at the thought of what those talons could do to flesh.

Looking at the body lying on her legs, fury began to rise from deep within Felar. She was sick of this damn creature just sitting there. It was going to get her killed, all because its stupid self had decided to park its fat, buggered corpse on top of her. Anger gave Felar the strength she needed to pull one leg out, and with that free she was able to push harder and extract the other.

Just as she managed to gain her feet and get oriented, two monstrosities came at her from the intersecting corridor. She dropped to one knee, quickly shot both of them, and then rose back to her feet. Previously, her situation had been severe, but now it had changed to dire. Her rail pistol held five shots, the last two of which she had just used. Felar had no reloads since the pistol was strictly a backup weapon. Now she was down to just her short swords for armament. Felar had the distinct feeling these would be less than effective against her current adversaries. She had exceptional skill with the blades, but the creatures were large and deadly at close quarters. Not having a weapon in hand made her nervous, so Felar drew the swords. They were nearly invisible in the low light, their matte black surfaces whistling through the air as she flourished them. Hoping she wouldn't have to get near enough to use them, she started forward.

Before Felar could resume her attempt to find the elevator, a pack of the beasts rounded the corner at the far end of the hallway. "Oh blightheart," she cursed as she sprinted away in retreat. She skidded to a stop a moment later as a second pack of monstrosities blocked her escape. Now she was trapped.

Looking around franticly, she noticed a door she could flee through. It was large, made of heavy gauge metal, and looked quite sturdy. She tried the handle. *Locked!* She didn't waste time jerking on the handle or slamming her shoulder into the door. The solid feeling was all it took for her to realize it was securely bolted and there was no way she was going to get it open without the proper pass-code.

Knowing this would be her last stand, she returned to the middle of the hall and assumed the sword fighting stance known by the FCs as the High Low, left sword held horizontally at head height, right sword by the hip in a reversed dagger grip. It was an excellent stance for all around defense, but she knew those who had created it had never fought one of these creatures.

When the monstrosities were less than ten meters away on either side, a strange thing happened. The lights directly above the monstrosities kicked on, dazzling the creatures. The lights above her stayed off. The creatures bellowed in surprise and pain as the bright light flooded what must be sensitive, dark adjusted eyes.

A split second after the lights kicked on, Felar heard a snicking sound beside her. When she turned to look, she saw the previously locked door had swung in slightly. Taking no time to ponder how or why any of these fortunate events had happened, she rushed through the door and slammed it behind her. She heard the bolts slide into place just as a large mass slammed into the other side of the door. A split second later, another heavy weight crashed into it. Thankfully the door was built for security as opposed to privacy alone and it easily stopped the monstrosities from bludgeoning their way in.

Feeling safe, at least temporarily, Felar was able to survey her surroundings. The room was lit by small shafts of soft light that emanated from recessed ceiling fixtures. It was almost as dark in here as the hallways, but the effect was not of chaos as in the rest of the complex, but of style. A large desk made of smooth stainless steel with burnished hardwood woven throughout sat near the far wall. There was also a door on the other side of the desk, but it was hard to make it out in the dim light.

Deciding she needed to reassess her situation and develop a new plan, she walked towards the desk, intending to find a place to sit. As she neared it, faint noises became evident and a new feeling of apprehension settled over her. She heard murmurs of what sounded like speech, but couldn't make out any words.

Felar stalked towards the desk, swords poised and at the ready. It wasn't until she was a couple of meters away that she realized the sounds were coming from behind the door instead of under the desk.

Felar crept up to the door, keeping her foot falls silent. Her short swords reflected no light and were nearly invisible in the pale gloom. Placing her ear next to the metal door, she strained to understand what was being said. Just as she settled in, the door burst open. Felar stumbled back, catching herself before she fell to the floor. The man in the doorway was just as startled as Felar, his fat face taking a moment to register her presence. He was obscured in blackness, but enough of his short form was visible for her to recognize him from the mission briefing.

"Director Kasol?" she asked tentatively. The man continued to stand where he was, swaying in place as if he was drunk. The briefing had listed him as the commanding officer of this installation. Felar hoped he might know what was going on and could provide some intel that would be useful in their regress from the facility.

"Yas? Blah blah blah mam ma ma ba bab lack shap have you any wal? Ra ra rah come to mah." He continued to stand in the doorway, still swaying as if drunk.

"I'm 3rd Class Enlightened Felar Haltro, Founder's Commando with the 9th Batt of the Ashamine Forces. My squad and myself were sent here to ascertain what had happened to this facility and to determine damage taken. If it is at all possible, you need to come with me, sir. We can return to the surface and report to Ashamine High Command."

"Wha? Sush good timin. I wus ghettin ungry and nah you here ah food." His voice continued to be slurred, but at least now she could make some sense of the words. "I been stuhk here. Poor deshishin on the secur syshtem. I cannu controly here. Ima still ungry, so littuh met left on hem. Huh yah gat in her?"

"The door unlocked for me at a very opportune time," she said, trying to think of how to deal with this drunk man in the middle of a dangerous situation. "Sir, we need to move out and get to the surface as quickly as possible. I can escort you and I'm sure if we work together we will get out of here just fine." She had no such confidence, but they needed to get moving.

"I donneed an escurt, this is muh facilty and I runit. Whu I ned is met. Luts and luts of red met. Yuh have met and yuh were led har by gohds, gohds that wannut me to hab met." Felar did not like where this was heading. Now he wasn't sounding drunk, he was sounding deranged. She took a step back from him, not wanting to be forced to hurt him. Obviously something had gone terribly wrong in this installation and this man was responsible for it.

As she reflexively moved back, the Director stumbled forward out of the doorway. Now she could see details that had been hidden in the dark. His hands, arms, and face were coated with dried, crusty, reddish brown blood. His wispy hair was in disarray, as were his formal clothes. Felar glimpsed the remains of a body in the room behind Director Kasol. All that was left were scraps of clothes and clean white bones. The floor around the body was covered in dried blood.

"Met! Met! I ned teh met!" Director Kasol chanted as he stumbled towards Felar. He wasn't moving fast, but he was determined, despite the fact that Felar had weapons and he did not. The closer he came, the farther she withdrew, until she backed up against the exit door.

"Sir," she said in a tone of command, "stop where you are. I don't want to hurt you." She flourished her swords, the blades whistling through the air.

"Met! Met! Met!" he chanted, a burning insanity in his eyes. He kept coming, inexorable, steadfast. She knew she had no choice. It was him or her at this point. If she ever made it out of this blightheart, she would have to explain her actions to her commanding officers. She hoped they would understand why she had injured such an important official. He was obviously deranged, but would her superiors believe her report?

All these thoughts played through Felar's mind in the short time it took for Director Kasol to cover the remaining meters between them. Once he was within the range of her swords, she performed the Spinning Blossom. Feinting to Kasol's left and then spinning to his right, she slashed the back of his knees, severing his hamstrings. At the end of the maneuver she was behind Kasol, with the full length of the room to maneuver. His knees crumpled and he fell to the floor, slamming down with a sickening thud that sent chills through her body.

"Grahhhhh," Kasol growled in agony. "Muh met, I ned muh met!"

"I don't want to kill you Director Kasol, but if you continue to attack me I will be forced to do so." While Felar spoke she searched for a way to escape the room, but there was no way out. She couldn't stay here, not with Kasol attempting to eat her. Even now he was crawling towards her, moaning and sighing in what sounded like a combination of agony and ecstasy. As Felar watched from across the room, he stopped, fingering the bloody wounds at the back of each knee. He moaned, sounding euphoric. Sticking his fingers into his grinning maw, he licked the warm blood from each finger. Felar shuddered in deep revulsion at the man's actions. It was inhuman and intensely sickening. She felt it would be doing Director Kasol a favor to kill him, but that was not her decision to make.

Leaving the Director to his perversion, Felar scouted the small room at the back of the office. It was only a closet and contained only bones. She turned back to the main room and saw Kasol had resumed his crawl after her. Obviously he wasn't a true threat, but all the same, it made her feel defiled just looking at him. "Met! Met! Met!" he continued to chant and she wondered if his madness was caused by a contagious pathogen. The thought scared her.

When he was close enough to touch her, she leapt agilely over his crawling form and stood by the exit door she had no way of opening. During the time it took Kasol to crawl back across the room, she wondered how the man had operated the door before the chaos had begun in the facility. There was nothing obvious in the room and she was sure any inquiry to Kasol himself would only result in him chanting "Met! Met! Met!" Just as Kasol was nearing her again, she heard a familiar snicking sound. When she turned to look, the door had swung slightly open. *Who or what is controlling all these doors?*

Before she could ponder her question, she felt something grasp her ankle. The pressure was tight and immediate. She turned and looked down, dread forming in her stomach. Kasol had her ankle grasped tightly in both of his bloody, disgusting hands. As she watched, he began using her leg to pull himself closer, arching his back to bring his head to a level where he could bite into the meaty part of her calf. He bared his teeth, manic light burning fiercely in his eyes. Felar's light combat armor didn't go down that far on her leg, so the only thing protecting her from his filthy, possibly diseased mouth was the cloth of her combat fatigues. She knew what she had to do before he touched her skin with any part of his loathsome body.

Felar brought her blades down, rotating them in her hands so the edges pointed inwards and towards each other. She then hooked the sharp edges under Kasol's stretching neck and brought them up and out in opposite directions, using the deadly edge of each blade to its full effect. Blood spurted from severed arteries and both body and head collapsed to the floor. The head rolled over, and before Felar could look away, maniacal eyes looked into hers. Their insanity and desire were still intact, even in death. She shivered and stepped away, repulsed by the entire situation.

Felar had to get out of the room, had to get away from the severed head and decapitated body. If she didn't, she knew she would blow that morning's rations all over the already defiled floor. She fled through the door and instantly began to feel better.

The corridor was dark again and there was no sign of the monstrosities. *Maybe they went to look for prey elsewhere.* Even the five she had killed were gone. Did these creatures eat their own dead? *Hopefully they aren't going to ambush me.* The thought gave her chills.

Felar got her bearings and decided to resume her prior search pattern. Logically, it made the most sense and hopefully most of the creatures would be grouped towards the middle of the complex, allowing her to make her way around the outside without being disturbed. It sounded good in theory, but she held no illusions she had much chance of surviving this. If she had a projectile weapon it would have boosted her odds, but going nose to nose with these creatures would obviously be fatal.

Lights blazed on as Felar began to move. They led away in a straight line going in the opposite direction of where she intended to go. Again she wondered why these strange things kept happening around her. Perhaps someone was trying to help her escape? Certainly everything that had happened so far had been helpful. She would be dead if whatever was operating the facility's systems hadn't flashed the monstrosities and opened the door for her just in time. The lights seemed to deter the ugly, deformed creatures, leading her to believe the intelligence operating the system wanted her to follow this newly created path. In reality, it was just as good an option, if not better, than what she had planned to do.

The lights flashed on and off a few times in measured intervals, as if the intelligence had heard her thoughts and was sending a confirmation. Of course that was impossible, but it made her feel a little better, knowing that there was a chance she wasn't alone in this hostile environment after all. Maybe she was going to make it out of this alive. Just maybe. She allowed a faint glimmer of hope to shine in her heart as she began running down the center of the hallway, following the bright beacon of the ceiling lights.

25 – LOTHIS

Lothis drove the monstrosities off from around the woman's room as fast as he could. They hated the light and he used that to his advantage. *Now, to open the door.* He checked on the video feed and was horrified to see the bad man had caught hold of the woman and was about to bite her. *Nooooooo!* he screamed in his mind. But then the woman quickly placed her blades beneath the man's neck and took off his head. The terminal showed everything in gruesome detail. Death was a relatively new idea to him, never having experienced such a thing before he had encountered the creatures. It disturbed him, but he realized it had been necessary for the woman to defend herself. She was not evil like the bad man or those *things* he had encountered in the hallways. *What exactly does evil mean?* he wondered as he watched for what she would do next.

He had not meant to trap her in the room with the man, had not even known the man had been in the room. Lothis had seen her state of distress and had opened the door and locked it again once she was safely inside. He knew he had saved her from being eaten by the monstrosities. That made him happy.

Lothis had watched as the woman discovered the man in the room with her. It surprised him there was another living human being in the complex besides himself and the woman.

At first he had been happy because he could help save another human. He had recently discovered he was one himself, relishing the concept of belonging to a group larger than one. When he realized the man had eaten another human being, he became sick, regurgitating the meager contents of his stomach. This too was a large part of the reason why he was not sad for the bad man's death.

The woman quickly exited the room, looking like she too might be sick as well. Once she got into the hall, she seemed to compose herself. The woman looked both ways down the hall and turned towards the way that would lead her straight into the largest group of creatures. *Don't go that way, don't go that way,* Lothis chanted in his mind. *Go this way,* he thought, switching on the lights behind her. She stopped and turned, seeming puzzled. Lothis? was so focused on her image, on her presence in his mind, on her energy, that he glimpsed she was worried what was operating the lights. That couldn't be right though, because there was no way he could sense that. He had been taught just such a thing by the console screen back in his *cell*—that was how he was beginning to think of it now. *Intellectual guess,* he decided, pulling up a new menu on the terminal. *I will guide you,* he thought as he flashed the lights in such a way that she would know there was intelligence behind it.

Responding to the flashes, the woman began to follow the path he laid out. It was extremely complicated to route her through the complex. Several packs of the creatures were roaming around searching for prey that didn't exist—except for the woman. A couple times he was forced to change her path at nearly the last second. Had he been any slower, the woman and one of the packs would have run into each other.

Her journey was long and circuitous, but he finally managed to lead her to a secure room adjoining the one he was currently in. It wasn't that he didn't trust her so much as his logical mind demanding he proceed cautiously. The cocoon he had occupied—the room that had been his whole world—now gave him perspective on the immense scope of things. There was a lot going on and he felt most comfortable when given sufficient time to analyze and absorb it. Hence why he brought the woman to a place he could interact with her, but not be exposed to risk.

The woman was reluctant to enter the room though, pausing outside the door warily. *Get inside,* he thought, worried a pack of creatures was about to come around the corner next to the woman. Lothis looked at her image intently, trying hard to think of a way to get her to go inside. In his mind, he urged her to enter the room. After a second or two, she did. Lothis thought it an interesting but insignificant coincidence that his desire had turned into her action. *She just needed time to make sure it was safe.*

Now Lothis couldn't decide what to do next. He had spoken little in his cell and he wondered if the woman would be able to understand him. Before Lothis could begin though, the woman spoke, "Who are you? Why have you brought me here?" He started to form a response, but she beat him again, "Are you A.I.? What happened in this facility?" She was pacing around the room, looking for clues as to why she had been brought there.

This time she was quiet long enough for Lothis to reply. He selected the menu item that activated his audio sensor and tried to speak. "I... I... am... Lo...Lothis," he said, his voice faltering and sounding feeble. He cleared his throat and concentrated hard on the words and continued, although his voice was monotone. " I'm not A.I. I do not know what happened here, but I need your help. That is why I have been trying to assist you. I do not know how I came to be here, but it seems I was being held captive. Will you help me?"

The woman thought for a moment and then replied, "I would be glad to help you, but I need to know where you are. It would also be helpful to know how to get out of here, which after the trip you took me on, I would imagine you have figured out."

Lothis thought over the situation once again, afraid to place his safety in the hands of another after he had just won his freedom and independence. On the other hand, he didn't have much of a choice when it came to trusting her. She was the only way out of this wretched place and Lothis needed to escape. He didn't know for sure that there was more to the world than this place, but there had been more to the world than the room, so it was logical.

The woman must have sensed his internal struggle, because she kept silent and waited patiently. Internal debate consumed him for a few moments longer, but the choice was inevitable. He activated the audio sensor and began speaking again, "I am in the adjoining room. I will unlock the door."

She entered his small room, her height slightly taller in person than the console screen suggested. Her light brown hair was tied back in a pony tail and her emerald green eyes burned with fire. Lothis shrank back, her visage and myriad combat gear frightening him so much he fell off his chair. He scurried away from her approach, barely noticing the look of concern and pity that had come over the woman when she first caught sight of him.

"No, honey," she cooed, "No, don't be afraid. I'm here to help. I won't hurt you, wouldn't dream of it. We're gonna get you out of here straight away. I'm going to need your help though. This place is full of those monsters and I don't know the way out."

"I...I...I am Lothis," was all he could give by way of a response. He backed himself into a corner of the room and huddled into a small ball, scrawny arms clutching his bony legs. The woman crouched over him and began smoothing his hair, her touch gentle. It reassured Lothis. He didn't understand the gesture or what it meant, but it did make him feel better somehow.

"I'm Felar," the woman said after Lothis calmed somewhat. "It's nice to meet you Lothis. We are both going to get out of here, I promise you that. It will take both of us working together to do it, but I know it can be done."

"Thank you," he responded, voice still monotone, but lacking the stutter. "I will do everything I can." Lothis didn't understand how he was able to converse with the woman so well, but so far she was understanding him and not thinking him exceedingly odd.

"Good, good," Felar responded, voice still calm and gentle. "I assume you have gained access to the computer systems in this installation? Can you show me a map? Do you have a way to track those monsters?" Lothis showed her the console he had been using earlier and she soaked up the data at a glance. After a minute of watching the creatures move on the small screen, she was ready to go. "Can you run?" she asked, eying his scrawny frame.

"Yes—very well," Lothis answered, becoming self-conscious due to her scrutiny. He felt an additional new sensation as well, a burning that was located in his cheeks. He hadn't taken much notice of his personal appearance before this moment, but now it was important. How had he missed something so vital? What else was he missing even now?

"OK, well I think our best bet in this gamble is speed. We need to avoid those creatures and get out as fast as we can. I need you to run as hard as possible and keep up with me, OK? I know you can do it." By this time they were almost to the door that led to the outside hallway. As she reached for the door handle, a thought seemed to strike Felar, and Lothis watched as she returned to the computer.

"Founder blight their hearts. It's not right. What were these people doing?" she questioned under her breath. Lothis barely heard her and didn't understand what she meant.

"What?" he prompted, voice lowering to match her soft volume.

"Nothing," Felar answered in a normal volume, "I was just talking to myself." Lothis didn't understand why someone would want to talk to themselves when thinking was infinitely faster, but he held his tongue, knowing this was not the time to ask. "Damn it," she said after a moment had passed. Lothis looked at the terminal screen and saw "Access Restricted" was flashing in big red letters across it.

Lothis, eager to help this woman who was so kind to him, stepped over and motioned her to let him have access to the terminal. She did so and Lothis began to hash the machine. Before long, he was into the restricted system. He moved aside, allowing her to directly view the screen. She scrolled through the information, reading it at a pace Lothis thought was quite slow.

"Founder blight their hearts," she said again, only this time it was said slowly and in awe. Lothis found this phrase no easier to understand than her previous self-speech, but he kept silent, assuming it would be explained if explanation was needed. Apparently it wasn't, because Felar pulled a small shiny square out of one of the pockets of her combat vest and pushed it into a slot on the terminal. She selected some items on the screen and then sat back. The square blinked a couple of times and the terminal chirped a notification. Felar retrieved the square, returning it to her pocket.

"It's time to go," she said, her voice carrying an edge of emotion Lothis couldn't identify. They walked towards the door again, but now Felar had more resolve in her step, her eyes burning even more ferociously than before. Lothis wasn't scared now though, he knew the fire wasn't directed towards him and it would soon be burning those who tried to hurt him.

As Felar opened the door, she grabbed Lothis' hand, and the boy felt another surge of reassurance and wellbeing overtake him. They were good feelings and Lothis savored them, as if they were a flavor he could taste on his tongue. But before he could fully appreciate the subtleties of these new emotions, he and the woman were sprinting.

26 – MAXAR

Maxar felt the loss of Benson more acutely than anyone else he had known on Bloodsport. The way the man had been killed right in front of him was pretty ordinary by Bloodsport standards, but he had been a true friend in a place that was barren of that commodity. Most of Maxar's teammates had been comrades-in-arms, but none had brought a smile to his face or turned a brutal day into one that could be borne in the way Benson could.

He wished he could have given his friend a proper burial, but there had been no time to retrieve what little had been left of him. The game was merciless and cared not at all for its participants. That was the Bloodsport way of life. In the end he knew Benson would care little one way or the other regarding his burial. He would have wanted Maxar to escape rather than retrieve his body if it meant capture. *Nothing I can do about it now,* was Maxar's mantra on the short trip from the Bloodsport asteroid to its orbital dock.

As he looked out of the shuttle's large view window, the dock drew nearer and nearer. He hoped the disappearance of this small craft had gone unnoticed in the chaos exploding all over the asteroid. Soon enough he would be dealing with the dock's security crew. That job would be hard even if the dock wasn't on alert.

All of a sudden the lights in the cabin seemed to wink out, but then Maxar realized something had eclipsed the light of the primary star. He turned in his seat to look out the shuttle's large side window—no expense had been spared in the creation of this lavish transport—only to see several enormous bi-pyramidal shapes silhouetted by the primary star.

The sight filled Maxar with awe and fear. Up until recently, at least if the news on the terminal was true, the Enthos had been quite ineffectual at war fighting, but things changed a short while ago. Now they were able to fight back using alien weaponry human scientists had no way of counteracting. They hardly even understood the weapons, theorizing the species had some sort of group mind they brought to bear with devastating results. How did you fight against telekinesis and mind weapons? That was the deep question apparently. Until a defense could be developed, the Enthos had attained offensive equality with their tetragonal bi-pyramid ships.

Maxar stared at the Entho Tetra ships for a moment longer until he was sure they weren't tracking a course for his shuttle, Bloodsport, or the orbital dock. Their arrival caused the chaos that had allowed him to escape, but he didn't want those ships coming any closer. That would be too much chaos, even for him.

"Shuttle 2489, please state your passenger manifest and pass-code," came over the cabin speakers. *Dammit to the black star,* he thought, *I should have been prepared for this.* Maxar cast off the self incriminations and thought as quickly as he could, knowing time was of the essence. He had to be as convincing as possible. He certainly couldn't transmit his real name. They would have a record of that. And as for a pass-code, he had none. "Shuttle 2489, please state your passenger manifest and pass-code. This is your second prompt," came again over the cabin speakers. Apparently, their operating procedures mandated a quicker response than he had hoped.

More time dragged by, and then Maxar thought of a reply that had a chance of getting him inside the dock. "This is...this...," he said changing his voice to sound quavery and old, stuttering to suggest a terror he didn't feel. "This is Joseph Gunderson, I...I...just escaped from that terrible asteroid. Several of the competitors were holding me captive. I barely escaped with my life. You have to help me!" As he spoke, he sped up his words. By the last sentence it was coming out quickly, hopefully mimicking intense panic.

A brief pause followed his transmission, silence filling the cabin. Maxar held his breath, hoping beyond hope they would swallow his deception. "Shuttle 2489," filled the cabin, "Joseph Gunderson, our record shows you leaving Bloodsport yesterday. How is it you are still on the asteroid?"

Had he been lucky enough to stumble on the name of an actual spectator? Apparently so, but it was strange because he had just said the first name that came to mind. His initial intent was to buy enough time to get him onto the orbital dock, most likely having to fight his way to a worm capable ship. That would be bloody and dangerous, but up until this point he had no choice. Now though, there might be an alternative.

"My original plan was to leave yesterday, but I hadn't checked out yet. I don't understand why it is showing me as gone. I paid the fee for another day." He hoped the lie would be convincing enough to fool the security personnel. If not, he could always go back to his original strategy.

"Under normal conditions, there wouldn't be a problem, but under the current circumstances we will be forced to detain you until your correct identity can be confirmed. Please be advised two guards will be waiting at the shuttle dock to escort you to a secure holding facility."

Diving further into the role of the rich aristocrat, Maxar became angry. "You are going to lock me up after what I just went through? How dare you!" He considered pushing it further, but he could easily handle two guards. If he protested more, they might send additional security to restrain him.

"Sir, it's simply for the safety of all. We don't want any Bloodsport participants running loose on the orbital dock. I assure you, your accommodations will be adequate and comfortable. Please do not be alarmed."

Acting sufficiently cowed, Maxar responded, "Well, when you put it in that manner, I do suppose it's for the best."

"We'll see you in a moment sir. Please relax and enjoy the journey."

Sitting back in his chair, Maxar looked out the large shuttle windows and sized up the orbital dock's defenses. It certainly wouldn't be able to hold off military ships, but it had enough weaponry to destroy a fleeing passenger ship.

He quickly revised his plan, factoring in the guns that would take out his ship before he had a chance to open up a worm. Disabling the dock's weapons systems would be a top priority, followed closely by the acquisition of a suitable escape ship. At this point, anything that flew and was easily obtainable would be perfect.

By the time he had everything sorted out in a way that was tactically sound, he was almost to the dock. It loomed large, his shuttle as a speck of dust when compared to its size. Although Maxar had never been to the dock, he had heard much about it from the spectators and advertisements that were constantly being played on Bloodsport. The orbital dock featured huge hotels and casinos, large viewing terminal areas for the games below, shops with merchandise catering to the wealthy, and many other luxurious features. In short, it was a paradise for those who loved to view the deaths of others and live lavishly while doing it.

Maxar's craft entered the shuttle bay without his hands on the controls, the dock's operators taking over the piloting. This bay looked almost identical to the one back on Bloodsport and the similarity brought back painful images of Benson's death. Maxar shook his head to clear it. He quickly spotted the two escort guards standing next to an empty space that was the shuttle's destination. Both were tall and well built, wearing neatly pressed uniforms of Bloodsport security. Their armbands were red instead of orange, denoting a different branch than the comrades down on the asteroid. *Guest services,* Maxar thought, laughing derisively. Their armament wasn't anything amazing either. One flechette pistol a piece, still in holsters. This would be easy.

After the shuttle landed and powered down, there was stillness. The guards were standing too far away, so Maxar decided to wait them out. They finally grew impatient and came to open the hatch. When they did, Maxar struck fast and hard. He had no weapons to speak of, but his body was plenty of weapon in and of itself.

The first of the two guards took a hard boot to the face as Maxar swung out of the hatchway. The man's jaw shattered, and he fell to the floor, unconscious. Maxar pivoted and shoved a heavy fist into the second man's face, knocking him out. Both men were incapacitated in seconds and there were no loud noises to alert anyone. *Perfect.*

Looking down at their flechette pistols, Maxar considered taking the weapons. If it came down to an armed battle, he would never get off the dock. He had to rely on stealth and confusion. There were too many opponents to try a frontal assault. *Move fast and never be where they expect you,* he thought, dismissing the pistols. *Besides, they will make me more obvious and I have no way to conceal them.*

Maxar dragged the two men into the shuttle, knowing they would be missed soon, but wanting to give himself as much of a head start as possible. Maybe they wouldn't be found for some time and their superiors would think they had gone off for a drink or something. *Like the fires of the dark star they will,* Maxar thought, *but you never know.*

Moving at a fast walk, Maxar began scouting for a place to hole up. He needed to perform some surveillance and plan the next few steps of his escape. He made his way out of the shuttle area, hoping he was not being tracked on the base's security system.

While not a scientist, Maxar knew the dock's defensive rail guns required massive amounts of power to function. It stood to reason that all the cannons ran off of a central power source. Disabling or destroying this source sounded like an excellent way to take out all the cannons in a relatively quick manner. He was basing everything off of assumptions, but lacking any other place to start, it seemed like a good idea.

Maxar hit a lucky break as he exited the shuttle landing area. Huge conduits ran along the ceiling of the large corridor outside the main bay, likely leading to central power. All he needed to do was follow the conduits and eventually they would lead him to his objective.

He had yet to run across any dock personnel, but Maxar had a feeling that could change at any moment. It was against his instincts to move so openly, but there was a chance if he looked confident, no one would question him.

He got to test this theory after rounding the first bend in the corridor that followed the conduits. Three security guards were running towards him, shock batons in hand and grim expressions on their faces. His disposal of the guards had not gone unnoticed. As they neared, he ran through several scenarios to dispose of them. Most were violent, risky, and used up precious time. He opted instead for trying to blend in and hope they didn't notice him. When they were only a few meters away he sprang to the side, flattening himself against the wall like any normal person would if they were about to get run down. The guards didn't give him a second look, perhaps thinking if he was their quarry he would have run at their appearance. Maxar found it surprising the guards hadn't been briefed on the Bloodsport participant uniforms. That would have made him easy to recognize, but the security on the orbital dock probably wasn't up to the standards he was used to on Bloodsport. The lack of security cameras here was another indicator of their laxness.

Not wanting to give the guards a chance to discover their error and return to rectify it, Maxar hurried on, following the conduits until they turned away from the corridor and went through a wall above a door. Maxar doubted the central power supply was behind this door, but perhaps it was a utility room that had an access way. The door was passcode protected and that led Maxar to think his hunch was likely correct.

Just as he was trying to formulate a way to gain access to the room, something flew by his neck, the heat of it causing a searing pain to blossom. A loud concussion wave passed over him, making his ears to ring in protest. Without even thinking, Maxar clapped his hand to his burned neck and dropped to one knee to lessen his targetable profile. Looking down the corridor he had come from, he saw the three guards he had dodged so easily. They had abandoned their shock batons in favor of rail pistols. *Well, they know I'm a participant now.*

Another projectile flew by him, but this time he saw its ion tracer trail after it passed. This slug wasn't as close, but he knew if he didn't bring the fight to his attackers, they would soon be scraping bits of him off the walls. He cursed himself for choosing stealth over aggression. *I should have grabbed those flechette pistols when I had the blighthearted chance.* Three against one and no weapon other than his own body wasn't the best of odds, but Maxar had faced worse and this time he was fighting for his freedom as opposed to sport.

He charged towards the guards, running low and veering randomly back and forth across the large corridor to make himself harder to hit. It seemed to be working because ion trails stitched the air all around him, the rounds making strange musical tones as they ricocheted off the corridor's armored walls. The air boomed as round after round broke the speed of sound, concussion waves breaking over Maxar as he ran.

In a dim, detached way, Maxar noted the looks of horror on all three of his attackers' faces. They were beginning to wonder if their marksmanship would bring down the terrible beast charging towards them. Round after round missed as Maxar closed the distance.

Finally, a shot hit Maxar directly in the chest. Rather than being cut in half, Maxar was knocked clean off of his feet and propelled back for ten meters, where he sprawled on the floor, dazed. He felt no pain where the projectile had hit, but the rest of his body ached from the massive acceleration and subsequent fall to the floor. It took him a moment to clear his mind and begin to make sense of what had happened. After rolling over onto his hands and knees, he looked up to see the guards were running away as fast as their legs could carry them.

Maxar rose to his feet, unsteady from mental shock rather than pain. How had he managed to survive being hit by that slug? There was no way to explain it. They had been live rounds and not dummies, that was for sure. All the rounds ricocheting off the walls were proof. Another astonishing question was how it had knocked him back so far, yet hadn't injured him. All puzzling questions that needed to be answered, but right now he should be moving and not contemplating. Those guards would be reporting what had happened and their commander would be sending more men, no doubt about that. His chances of escape had shrunk immensely.

Maxar returned to the door that was blocking his progress towards the central power center. Accessing the terminal beside the door, he tried the same hash he had used on the door back on Bloodsport. The exploit failed and he was sent back to the main screen. Maxar tried more hashes as precious time wasted away. After a particularly risky exploit, the screen flashed "Invalid" several times and then posted the message "Terminal Lockout, Contact Admin for reconnection to network." *Dark star fire take them all,* he thought viciously, frustration pulsing in his veins. *Think! What can I do?* The only option he came up with was to try to find another way to the power center, and it didn't require much imagination to guess they would be secured as strongly this one.

All this way just to be captured. So close, he thought bitterly, scorning himself. Chewing on his bottom lip in concentration, he stared at the door. Such a small thing to send him back to Bloodsport, back to all that agony and misery, back to his death.

Disgust for the life he had almost left behind flooded him. Maxar slammed his balled fist into the door in white hot rage. The door shuddered. Maxar cocked an eyebrow and examined the door closely. It was quite sturdy, a security door made to keep out the unauthorized. He slammed his fist into it harder and it shuddered more, trembling as if it were made of flimsy plastic instead of reinforced alloy.

Sensing a possible solution to his current situation, Maxar dealt the door a third blow. This time he had the intent of causing damage and he struck the door like he meant it. His blow fell slightly to the right of the center seam, the door being the type that had two panels that slid from the walls to meet in the middle.

Maxar's blow was so hard he should have broken several bones in his fist—he intellectually knew this—but instead of pain, his hand felt normal. He looked down at his fist with no small amount of wonder for its resiliency, and when he looked up at the door he was shocked even more. The right panel bowed in, not extremely far, but it was something no human hand should have been able to do. Once again he had to pull himself back from analyzing the situation and focus on the lack of time.

The problem of getting through the door was now solved and Maxar battered at it, bending the right panel farther inward until he could slither through. When he finally managed to pull himself through the door, he was in a small room connected to a long corridor. Looking up, he saw the conduits running along the ceiling like a bright arrow pointing towards freedom.

Maxar ran down the hall, following the arrow.

27 – TREMMILLY

After reviewing the checklists and the ship's systems, Tremmilly felt ready to leave the Noor-5 orbital dock. Clicking the toggle, Tremmilly transmitted, "Noor-5 control, we request departure."

"Departing vessel, what is your origin and destination?" a smooth voice asked over the ship's good sounding speakers.

"We are leaving from the orbital dock and will be traveling to the worm area in order to tunnel to–" She faltered, unable to think of a lie. Tremmilly certainly couldn't say she intended to go to Bloodsport. She'd never get clearance and they'd likely send a ship to escort her back. "What do I tell them Beo?" The wolf-dog looked back at her inquisitively.

"Didn't catch your destination, departing vessel," the smooth voice said.

"Eishon-2," Tremmilly transmitted, saying the first place the came to mind. Even just saying the words brought a twinge of homesickness to her.

"Not much out that way, but have a safe journey and hopefully we'll see you back in the Noor system soon."

"Thanks for the help, Beo," she said scoldingly, trying to find the menu for the automated takeoff procedure. Beowulf cocked his head, seeming puzzled. After several long moments of being lost in the hierarchical structure, Tremmilly became anxious. "Where did it go? It was just here!" The whole auto-nav system had vanished. The only options available were for those of manual control, and Tremmilly knew she wouldn't get far trying to pilot the ship herself.

"Departing vessel, you are cleared for exit. You are holding up the pattern on the orbital dock. Please take off immediately." The voice now sounded agitated, adding to her anxiety.

Hurriedly swiping through menu entries, Tremmilly's palms began to sweat. After several tense moments, she found the problem. "I accidentally switched over to manual controls somehow," she exclaimed, finding the option to go back to auto-nav. "Departure, orbital dock, launch authorized, execute," Tremmilly voiced as she selected the command sequence she had memorized from the checklist.

Composing her voice and trying to sound professional, she transmitted: "Sorry for the delay. We are headed out now."

"No worries, departing vessel. Safe travels."

Clearing the orbital dock, the ship accelerated for a few minutes. When the engines cut out, the ship became eerily quiet. "I guess now we create the worm tunnel and travel through it to Haak-ah-tar," Tremmilly said, trying to fill the silence. "Worm travel, destination," she said, scrolling through a long list of planet names. "Haak-ah-tar," she continued, finding it. "Execute."

"Insufficient clearance from gravity well," the screen flashed.

"What does that mean?" She tried to initiate the worm again, but the same message flashed. Tremmilly consulted the checklist, realized she was still too close to the planet, and executed the commands to take them away from Noor-5.

After an hour of travel, the terminal screen announced they had reached sufficient clearance. Tremmilly tried the commands for the worm tunnel again and this time it materialized. "Even on auto-nav, this thing takes some getting used to," Tremmilly told Beowulf as they flew through the worm. She entered more commands and they began accelerating towards the planet of Haak-ah-tar.

"You know Beo," Tremmilly said, turning once again to look at him in the seat next her, his weight completely compressing the tired foam. "I think once we've found all these people, we should return to Eishon-2 for a little break. Maybe just a year or so. Then we need to explore some habitable planets near Eishon, see what they have to offer. I think it would be good for us to get out there and explore." Beowulf looked back at her, seeming happy to do whatever she wanted. He had taken to space travel quite quickly, something Tremmilly herself was having a hard time stomaching. The drab walls and canned air smell grated harshly against her love of sunny, wide open spaces and fresh air. Despite the cramped quarters, she felt energized by this adventure. The newness of it all astounded her. Taking it in was a great joy.

Tremmilly thrust her hands out just in time to catch herself as she flew towards the console in front of her. "Did we hit something?" Tremmilly worried. "Why are we decelerating?" Beowulf, sensing her anxiety, whined in sympathy.

Something was wrong with the ship and Tremmilly had no idea what it was or even where to start looking. To add spite to affliction, she was in an area of space where help was not likely to come flying by. "Well

Beowulf, guess we'll have to see what we can do. Maybe there is a checklist for troubleshooting." Tremmilly's voice was bright, but tinged with worry. The wolf-dog raised his ears, his eyes locked on the door at the back of the small command deck.

Just as Tremmilly sensed his alertness, the door opened, and to her shock, a man shambled through the doorway. He was rumpled and disheveled, his long brown hair tangled and greasy. Swaying as he walked, the man held an antique looking glass bottle in one hand. It was partially filled with a clear liquid that sloshed gently as he rocked back and forth.

"Hure you? An why arh ya on muh ship?" he asked, voice slurred in apparent drunkenness. Tremmilly stared at him in shock for a moment before realized he must be the captain of this junk heap.

"I'm Tremmilly Octus," she replied, fixing her emerald green eyes on the man's muddy brown ones. She figured it was far past the point of using deception to attain her goal, so she decided to tell the truth. "I needed passage to Haak-ah-tar and your ship seemed available, so I took it."

"Shtole it ya mean," the drunk man said, his tall frame still wavering as he stood in the middle of the deck.

"Yes, I did steal it. I would have gladly paid the fare, but no one was willing to go to Haak-ah-tar."

"And why whould they want ta? Itsa whar zone there right nhow. No one whants their ship pulled apart by dhem Enphos." A note of disgust had entered his voice. The man looked around the small flight deck, not really seeing anything. His eyes slid right across Beowulf, who had taken up a position next to Tremmilly. The man did a double take a moment later when the huge wolf-dog registered in his alcohol muddled brain. "I don't whant nothin tado with ya," he stammered. "Gotta go back ta sleep. Need more ta drink." The last statements were said in a low voice, speaking to himself.

He turned and left the deck, his figure disappearing back into the bowels of the ship. Tremmilly hesitated to follow, but she had to figure out what was wrong with the ship. Her intuition was screaming time was of the essence and she was swiftly wasting the little extra she had. Tremmilly hoped she wasn't too late to rescue the man from her vision.

"Wait," she said after the captain, stepping quickly to catch up with him. "Please, I need to talk with you. It's vital we get back underway towards Haak-ah-tar." As she walked through the doorway after him, she saw the piles of garbage and refuse once again. How this man had let his ship fall to this condition was beyond her understanding. When she saw what he was doing, she realized why she had missed him on her initial entrance into the ship.

The drunken captain was burrowing down into a particularly large pile of garbage and filth, apparently using it as bedding. He would periodically take a large gulp from his bottle, being extremely careful not to spill any of its contents. Tremmilly felt disgusted. Beowulf, picking up on her emotions, growled softly in the back of his throat.

"Sir," she said imploringly, "I need your help. Something is wrong with the ship and I desperately need to get to Haak-ah-tar."

"Nuthin' wrong with muh ship, I jus diabled the main power. I don't let shcamps steal muh ship. Now leat me shleep." He collapsed down into his makeshift garbage bed and took no more notice of her.

Well, perhaps since he only disabled it I might be able to figure out what's wrong, she thought, optimistic. Walking through the cargo hold, she opened the door to the engine room. One look inside told her it would be impossible. It was all so complicated and foreign to her. There were too many wires, circuits, and components. Her pleasant outlook faded as she shut the door. Whatever the captain had done, Tremmilly knew she wouldn't be able to find it.

Developing a plan as she went, Tremmilly walked back into the cargo area where Captain Garbage was sleeping. She reached through the piled litter and shook the man briskly, hoping to awaken him before he fell into a drunken coma. He moaned and slapped at her hand. Beowulf saw the man's movement and was in the captain's face in a split second, growling menacingly. This had the effect Tremmilly wanted. Captain Garbage sat up, a scowl on his deeply lined face.

"What do you want?" he asked, more sober than he had been during their last conversation.

"First, if you could tell me your name, I could address you properly." Tremmilly spoke in a bright tone she hoped would not be construed as sarcastic or high-handed.

"Jaydon Erath," was the man's curt reply.

"It's a pleasure to meet you, Captain Erath."

"The name is Jaydon, Capitan Erath was my father and he's dead. What else do you want from me?"

"Can you please reverse whatever you did to cause the engines not to function?" This she said while giving him her most winning smile, although she did it unconsciously.

"Please don't take this the wrong way Trem, but you are touched by the dark star if you think you can steal my ship, flounce your way to a battle zone, and then try to sweet talk me into helping you. It's not gonna work."

"I don't have time to explain everything, but it's vital we get to the Bloodsport asteroid as quickly as possible. There is no time to waste. There is so much riding on this. It's critical." A pleading tone had entered her voice, and she was becoming hysterical.

"I'm sure it is, but you don't seem to hear me. I'm not going to help you and neither is the A'Tal's Revenge—my fine ship's name in case you were confused. Now please, leave me so I can drink and sleep in peace."

Tremmilly grew more and more desperate as the time slipped away. A new idea occurred to her, but she was loath to carry it out. As another minute dragged by and Jaydon continued to lie in his rubbish bed, she realized it was her only option and decided to put her conscience on hold. "I'm very sorry to do this, but we have to get to Bloodsport. I asked nicely, but you wouldn't listen." Tremmilly gave a quick signal to Beowulf with one hand and the dog began advancing towards Jaydon, his thick fur standing erect on his back and a deep chested growl intensifying as he got closer to the man.

"Really?" Jaydon asked, sounding exasperated. "You're gonna force me like this? Can't you just let me be till I sleep this off? We can work on it when I'm in a better state of mind." Tremmilly merely looked at him and said nothing as Beowulf continued to advance. "Alright, alright, since you are gonna let that dog take a chunk out of me if I don't, I'll fix this junky crate. I'll just warn you this is a bad idea. Personally, I couldn't care less about my hide or this wreck, but I'd hate to see that pretty face get blown into the vacuum." At first, Tremmilly thought his comment was backhanded, but then she realized it was genuine and she began to blush. She recalled Beowulf and watched as Jaydon rose and walked to the back of the cargo hold. He removed a small panel next to the engine room door, reached his hand in, and did something she couldn't see. The ship lurched slightly, ceasing its deceleration. In a moment or two, Tremmilly felt them speeding up.

"It's a bad idea to go to Haak-ah-tar right now. I admire your daring in stealing my ship and going headlong for whatever goal you're punching towards, but all it's gonna do right now is get you stuck in the crossfire between the Ashamine and the Enthos. I'm going back to sleep now. If you need anything, wake me up. But please, don't need anything. I have to sleep this off. If you're gonna get us killed, please do me a favor and make sure it's quick. The void is fine, but I don't wanna get burned to death or anything like that." Without waiting for a reply he turned and walked back to his garbage nest, taking a tug of the clear alcohol as he did so.

Feeling there was nothing she could say to the man, Tremmilly returned to the flight deck, leaving him to his drink and sleep. Once back in the pilot's seat, she scanned the ship's grungy terminal screens. According to the computer, it would be another hour before they reached the vicinity of Haak-ah-tar. She was beginning to feel a bit drowsy herself. Knowing things would probably get crazy when they reached their destination, she decided to take a quick nap. Beowulf was back in his seat, watching the stars through the dirty view window. Tremmilly nodded off after a moment, her eyelids growing heavy and sleep overtaking her mind quickly.

She awoke from her dreamless sleep with a start, nearly falling off the seat. She managed to catch herself by grabbing the control panel that ran in front of her, and it took her several seconds to fix all the buttons she had accidentally hit in the process. For a moment she wondered what had awakened her in such a violent way.

"Unidentified craft, turn away from this facility. We are not taking inbounds at this time. Please be aware this whole sector is in a state of conflict and has been declared off limits for civilian traffic by the Ashamine. Please acknowledge receipt of this transmission and turn away at once." The voice was coming from the ship's speakers, sounding tinny and garbled.

It took several moments for Tremmilly to realize what was going on. She quickly looked at the terminal displays which showed the ship had arrived at its destination. The auto-nav had automatically slowed and vectored them to the Bloodsport orbital landing dock. Apparently they weren't going to allow her to land, an obvious development she felt quite stupid for not having anticipated.

The voice came from the speakers and repeated the same message. Tremmilly began chewing her nails, a nervous habit she'd acquired recently. Beowulf began to whine softly. Just as she was about to transmit something stupid and ill prepared, Jaydon arrived on the flight deck.

"Hold on Trem," he said, using the nickname Tremmilly found simultaneously irritating and endearing. "I'll handle this one. Been in plenty of tight spaces and I know how to work the system." He was quite sober, although she noticed he was still lugging the clear bottle around. It looked like it held just as much liquor as it had earlier in the day.

He eyed Beowulf who was in the only chair other than the one Tremmilly sat in. "Can you please have him move? I need access to the controls to pull this off." Tremmilly signaled the big wolf-dog, using only her eyes, and Beowulf obliged. Jaydon took his seat and began checking over the terminal screen and the console in front of him. "Follow my lead in this and I think I can get you to the dock at least." He looked like he had cleaned up a bit, his hair a little less grungy and marginally cleaner clothes on his lanky frame.

Without waiting for a reply, he turned to the console and hit the toggle to begin transmitting back to the voice from the speakers. "This is the civ ship A'Tal's Revenge. We are declaring a state of distress." Jaydon let off the transmit toggle, turning to look at Tremmilly as he waited for the orbital dock to respond.

A moment or two passed, and just as Tremmilly began to wonder if the transmission had gone through, a harsh burst of static came over the speakers and then a voice, "Civilian ship A'Tal's Revenge, you must leave this sector. It is in a state of conflict and has been declared off limits for civilian traffic by the Ashamine. Please acknowledge receipt of this transmission and turn away at once."

Instead of following the instructions, Jaydon took over manual control of the ship, increased thrust, and began flying towards the orbital dock. Once under way, he sent: "Transmission garbled. Unable to understand. Must land as soon as possible."

"Civilian ship A'Tal's Revenge, I repeat, you must leave this sector. You may not land here. Reverse your course. I repeat, you may not land here." The voice was beginning to gain a note of panic, evident even through the poor quality of the transmission.

"Kind of odd they don't want us to land there when we declare an emergency, even with the Enthos nearby and a riot on the asteroid. I wonder what's going on there." Jaydon drummed his fingers on the console in front of him, a thoughtful scowl on his face.

Tremmilly was having a hard time knowing what to think of this man. One minute he was drunk and now he had taken control of the situation and was handling it quite well. *Hopefully he isn't going to turn me in for ship theft once we dock...*

"What do we do now?" she inquired.

"Well, it's pretty simple. I keep disregarding their orders not to land, and then we land. Hopefully they don't get it into their minds we have any mischief planned, because if they do, they'll send several slugs through this heap. In the meanwhile, tell me why we are going to Bloodsport and why it's important enough you stole my ship."

She did as he requested, trying not to omit anything. She was interrupted several times by the same voice coming over the speakers, making the same warnings and demands as before. Tremmilly told him almost everything, including her vision of the man on Bloodsport. One thing she didn't tell him was Psidonnis' prophecy. That felt personal, and she wasn't quite ready to share it with this man, even if he was beginning to show more character and strength.

"That's quite a story," he said when she had finished. A speculative light was in his eyes, but he didn't seem to be doubting anything she had told him, merely mulling it over. Tremmilly knew parts of her story, principally those she attributed to a force or power guiding her, were a bit far fetched when viewed from outside. She was thankful Jaydon didn't draw attention to this. "So you think there is a guy down on Bloodsport who needs our help, someone who will be crucial in some way to humanity?" Now he raised one eyebrow in doubt.

"Yes, that's exactly what I think," Tremmilly yelled. She had not meant to be so forceful, but her insecurity had been jabbed and that made her irritable.

"Calm down," Jaydon said soothingly. "I wasn't trying to insult you. It's just a lot to take in. You have to admit that. I'm still going along, aren't I? If I thought you were crazy I would be tying you up, turning us around, and getting the dark fires out of here."

Tremmilly shuddered involuntarily at the thought of being bound, but she quickly regained her composure. "I'm sorry for snapping at you Jaydon. I know how crazy my story sounds. It's true to me, so when it's questioned I guess it sets me off."

"I understand," he replied, still in the same soothing voice.

Time passed in silence, Tremmilly still worried he was going to turn her in once they reached the orbital dock. She tried to think of a way to be subtle, but nothing came to mind.

"Why did you decide to help me?" she blurted, surprising herself.

"Well, I don't have time to explain it all, but let's just say you remind me of someone I used to know. I missed the opportunity to help her, and things turned out pretty bad." Jaydon had a far away look in his eyes, and Tremmilly could see pain written on his face.

"I'd like to hear about her someday," Tremmilly responding, matching the soothing tone he had used earlier.

"If we get out alive, I promise to tell you. At any rate," he said, snapping out of his reverie, "we need some sort of plan for when we get inside the landing dock. I assume you—or *we* I should say—need to get down to the asteroid itself. The only way to do this is by shuttle, so we'll have to—uhhhh—procure one, as you procured my ship." This last he said with a grin on his weathered face, and Tremmilly couldn't help but smile back. "Not that I've forgiven you just yet," Jaydon said, laughing. "That one you'll have to earn."

As they continued to talk, the ship grew closer and closer to their destination. After several minutes, Jaydon was guiding the A'Tal's Revenge into the incoming area of the orbital dock. The space was expansive, but there were barely any ships present. Those here were exclusively Ashamine vessels. It was odd so many official ships were in a place used solely for entertainment. It was also strange that so many were still here even when this locale was a declared conflict zone.

"They're probably all here watching the riots," Jaydon said, sensing her question. "I'm sure they are paying a lot to do so. Most of those ships are diplomatic vessels. Probably a bunch of High-Elders somewhere on the orbital dock." Tremmilly felt disgusted. The more she learned about the Ashamine, the less she liked it.

Jaydon set the ship down lightly and pointed out the flight deck window. "Look over there," he instructed, his demeanor one of resigned determination. "I hope you understand what you've gotten us into. I need to go back and disable something so it doesn't look like we were faking when we declared an emergency." With that he rose and went out through the door, leaving Tremmilly to watch as a platoon of heavily armed soldiers double timed their way towards the A'Tal's Revenge.

I hope I know what I'm doing, she thought, unsure of what to do next. She still felt she was doing the right thing, but the situation was getting serious. *This path is right, at least I know that... I hope...*

Watching the soldiers was accomplishing nothing, so she stood up and followed after Jaydon, signaling Beowulf to do the same. When she reached the cargo hold, Jaydon was just reattaching a panel on the wall, wiping his dirty hands on his clothes. "That should hold up to cursory searches at least," he stated.

Just as he finished speaking, a loud pounding came on the exterior door and a muffled voice could be heard ordering them to open up. "Hold on, we're dealing with an emergency here," Jaydon hollered by way of response. He then lowered his voice to a whisper and looked Tremmilly straight in the eye. "We don't have long, but we need to get our stories straight. You're my daughter, your mother died when you were young. We were doing some trading when our worm generator malfunctioned and we were forced to land here. Keep it simple and straight and we might have a chance." He then spun on his heels and headed towards the door, hitting the button to open it before Tremmilly could point out the fact that unless they were selling garbage, there was nothing in the hold that was tradable. She would just have to hope no one else noticed.

As soon as the door opened wide enough, a soldier jammed himself through the opening, his comrades just behind him. They quickly secured Tremmilly and Jaydon, but were unsure of what to do with Beowulf. "He's big," she told them, "but he is completely harmless." Tremmilly quickly signaled the wolf-dog with her eyes and he became relaxed, although she could see he was still alert.

A detachment of soldiers surrounded Beowulf, guns trained and ready to fire if he showed any sign of aggression. They attempted to muzzle him using cordage, but nothing they tried worked. Finally, they gave up, settling on having three soldiers watch him at all times. "If he so much as growls, we will shoot him," one of the soldiers told her.

"As I said, he's harmless," Tremmilly replied, hoping Beowulf would continue to follow her command. As the trio watched, the rest of platoon quickly swarmed over the small ship, prodding piles of garbage and searching every trash heap and service panel. Evidently they didn't find anything of interest, because after several minutes they returned empty handed.

A large, muscular man made his way towards them, the soldiers in front of him clearing out of his way. Tremmilly was unsure of military rank and procedure, but all the men assembled were taking orders from this single individual, making him someone of import. "You have landed at this dock when expressly ordered not to," he growled, voice low and harsh. "This facility is under security lockdown, elevating the offense from minor to severe." This evidently made the man excited, his eyes burning with anticipation.

"We had an emergency. We couldn't under—" Jaydon was cut off by an open handed slap delivered by the man standing next to the commanding officer. His appearance was that of an aide and not a soldier.

"You will speak when Separate Domis asks you to," the aide said, his voice conversational. Jaydon nodded and lowered his head, playing the good, cowed civilian. The fire in his eyes gave away his defiance to Tremmilly, but none of the soldiers noticed.

"Since the security lockdown is in force, we are required to make a thorough check of this ship and its occupants. I hope this will not be a problem?" He was excited once again, eager to have it be just that.

"No, no problem, sir," Jaydon answered. Separate Domis nodded his head slowly, eying each of them in turn. After several long moments, he turned to his men.

"First and second squad, you are on search and detainee detail. You know the search procedures. After you are finished, bring the detainees to the security sector. I will give you further orders there. Remaining squads, back to ready state at your assigned duty stations. All squads, execute!" As the last word left his mouth, a flurry of action ensued. In less than a minute the Separate's orders were being carried out to perfection.

Tremmilly was briefly puzzled at why they had been left on the ship, but after a minute it was clear they were being used as a kind of measuring instrument. Their captors watched them closely, probably hoping to spot a tell if their searching comrades came close to anything hidden. Fortunately, Tremmilly had nothing to hide and if Jaydon did, he had hidden it well.

After what felt like several hours, but was probably less than two, their guards led them from the ship. They were marched across the dock's massive floor, its expansive spread made to hold ships several times larger than the A'Tal's Revenge. *This place must get a lot of business,* Tremmilly realized. The memory of her dream came back to her and the thought of what was done in the name of entertainment, sports, and justice made her nauseous.

They walked for several minutes and then came to the edge of the dock area. The group entered a small corridor through a pass-code protected door. The head of the squad leading them entered the code quickly and Tremmilly was unable to see what it was. Once they were in the corridor, she looked back and saw there was no corresponding keypad on the interior. *That's a small blessing,* she thought, even though she figured it probably wouldn't matter.

They walked a short way down the hall and stopped in front of a door with a thick pane of security plasti-glass embedded in it. The interior looked like a cell, and in combination with the view port, it was quite obvious they were being locked up. Tremmilly still couldn't see what the squad leader was entering on the pad, so she looked around instead.

She analyzed her surroundings in much the same way she had done back on Eishon-2, only here she saw nothing she liked. The small, dim lights left ugly shadows that pooled on the floor. Several huge conduits ran along the ceiling from further down the hall, a ninety degree turn allowing them to snake through the wall above the doorway directly opposite the cell. Why this area of the dock was so dark and dreary while the rest was glamorous and clean was anyone's guess, but Tremmilly figured it all part of their attempt at intimidation.

With a soft triple beep and a whir, the cell door began to slide open. The squad leader was turning on his heel and opening his mouth—probably intending to order them inside—when the door opposite the cell began to open as well. Everyone in the corridor turned to look, not because an opening door was terribly interesting, but because it was an unexpected motion that drew their eyes. None of the ten soldiers did anything but gawk.

When the door was halfway open, a figure sprang through, hitting the ground and tucking into a roll. It came up slashing with what was either a very long knife or a short sword. The blade sliced through the abdomen of one of the soldiers, sharpened edge expertly finding a joint in the battle armor the man wore.

The figure then turned towards Tremmilly and for a moment that lasted a mere fraction of a second, their eyes locked. The man—for she could clearly see his features now—had a stubbly, shaved head and pale, icy blue eyes. He was tall and lean, with a look that reminded Tremmilly of Beowulf when he was on the hunt. It was a look that always chilled her. And then, all at once, *connection.* She had looked out of those eyes once, she had shared space in that body. The man standing in front of her, blood coving the makeshift sword in his hand, was the reason why she was here. He was the reason, and now that she saw him, she was terrified of him. *Follow your intuition,* she admonished herself, the words seeming empty and useless with this killer in front of her. *What have I gotten myself into?*

And then their link broke and everything began to happen at once. The new man had caught them off guard, but these soldiers were professionals and recovered quickly. Each of the soldiers unsheathed wicked looking knives that were nearly as long as the newcomer's blade. Tremmilly realized they couldn't use their rail pistols in the small space because of the risk of friendly fire.

Surprisingly, Jaydon reacted quite quickly, but lacking a weapon, had to content himself with trying keep from getting skewered by any of the combatants. Tremmilly found herself in the same position, wanting to fight for her freedom, but unable to do much good against armed and armored foes. Beowulf had no such inhibition.

The wolf-dog sprang into the fray, teeth bared and hair raised. He and the new man sensed each other and understood the other's intent. For Tremmilly, they appeared to be a manifestation of the same being—a snarling, blood thirsty, killing entity. She was glad they were on her side.

The man danced lightly and deftly through the soldiers packed in the tight corridor, makeshift blade slashing this way and that, occasionally parrying a knife thrust, but more often delivering a fatal or maiming cut to his enemies. Tremmilly found it hypnotic in a way, but it also made her sick to see the soldiers fall in crimson sprays, their body armor as effective as wet paper.

Beowulf distinguished himself as well. He had a tougher time than the man, his large muzzle too big to slip between armor plates, but the soldier's unarmored throats fell pray to a side of her friend Tremmilly had never seen before. She didn't know who she was more frightened of at the moment: the wolf-dog or the man. Beowulf was covered in gore. His lustrous gray and black fur was stained crimson in the blood of his adversaries. From what Tremmilly could see, none of the men who faced Beowulf had any idea how to fight him. Apparently, dispatching dogs with knives had not been part of their training.

A hand grabbed Tremmilly's arm, causing her to utter a short, high pitched scream of surprise. When she looked, she saw Jaydon standing beside her, grizzled face a mixture of strong emotions. "We gotta get out of here, get back to the ship," he jabbered at a frantic rate. "That guy and your dog are buying us the time we need. We gotta get moving." He tugged on her arm and continued to do so until she slowly formulated an answer. Her mind was not running at its normal, intuitive pace.

"He's the man," was all she could come up with, her voice choked. Jaydon stared at her, his hand falling away from her arm. They both turned, as if on cue, to look at the man who was obviously on the winning side of the quickly ending battle. Beowulf had helped of course, but this man had been the originator and catalyst of this turn of events.

"What do you mean, 'He's the man'?" Jaydon asked, brows furrowed in puzzlement. He'd lost some of his frantic intensity when it was apparent the man and Beowulf had the upper hand.

"He's the one from the vision. He's the one we came here for. We have to get him out of here before he gets killed." Her voice sounded wooden, even to her own ears. The amount of blood being shed was larger than anything she had ever seen before. True, the chaos on Noor-5 had been bad—the way the ground had split open and swallowed so many people into its seemingly infinite depths still made her feel sick—but it was much more abstract than what was going on right in front of her. And the way Beowulf was acting scared her most of all. He had been a gift from her parents and she had raised him ever since he was a tiny pup. This was a side of him she had never seen, let alone suspected. He had always been protective, but this was extreme. The way he fought alongside the man, working as a pair to flank the soldiers, was a type of behavior she had never seen before.

"Well, in case you haven't noticed, I think your man can take care of himself," Jaydon said in a small voice, his words interrupting her revere. "Are you sure it's safe to take him along? Those are the outfits the Bloodsport fighters wear, meaning he's a convict. He seems pretty skilled with that blade too and it's quite likely he will kill us once we are on the ship and away from here."

Tremmilly winced as the man dealt a particularly fierce blow, killing one of the few remaining soldiers. "No, I'm not sure it's safe to take him along, but I know it's what I'm supposed to do, what we're supposed to do." Her voice had gained a steely tone of resolve and Jaydon, oddly enough, was drawing strength from it. The man and Beowulf made short work of the last soldier, fighting so well as a pair that the movements seemed rehearsed.

Tremmilly had realized early on in this strange journey that the universe held many intriguing secrets. She also knew she had only seen an infinitesimally small portion of them. How this man and dog fought so well together when they had never met was just another faint glimpse of that world of secrets. She supposed they might share some kind of linked life force or essence and this buoyed her. Anyone who was linked to Beowulf couldn't be bad, could they?

"Fine animal you have here," the man said. He sounded tired, but a spark of admiration and joy lurked deep in his voice. He reached a hand down to pet the wolf-dog and Tremmilly thought Beowulf would do his standard baring of teeth and low growl, but instead, the dog enjoyed the attention. It shocked Tremmilly to see her old friend once again acting out of character. It supported her linked life force theory though, so perhaps it wasn't bad.

"We should all be getting back to the ship and jumping the worm," Jaydon said, head swiveling so he could watch both lengths of the corridor as he spoke.

"You're right," the man said. "Thank you for your help." He paused for a moment, his eyes scanning the corridor as Jaydon's had. He then turned and noticed Tremmilly for the first time since their initial eye lock. She could feel his scrutiny. "Have we met before? I have the feeling I know you, but your face is not familiar to me in the least. My name is Maxar Trayfis by the way. I would be grateful if you would tell me yours."

His politeness and its stark contrast to the violence just moments before stunned Tremmilly and she stuttered her reply. "I...I...my...my name is Tremmilly. And this is Beowulf." She motioned towards the wolf-dog, feeling embarrassed by her discomposure.

"And I'm Jaydon," the captain said. "Now can we get going? I'd really like to get out of here."

"How do we get back to your ship?" Maxar asked. "Do you know whether or not it's guarded?" Jaydon answered Maxar's questions, giving him directions and his opinion that it was probably still being searched. Maxar took it all in stride, never faltering at the overwhelming odds. Tremmilly had just seen him take on two whole squads of well trained soldiers with an improvised knife and a dog at his side. She knew she shouldn't be surprised, but she was.

They all took a compact rail pistol from their former captors, wiping the blood from them on the clothes of the fallen men. Jaydon raised the idea of taking some battle armor, but Maxar explained that without training, the armor was more of a hindrance than a help. Maxar, calm beyond any natural ability, gave her a quick course in the use of the pistol. Jaydon seemed a little too interested in Maxar's instruction and Tremmilly guessed he did not quite understand how to use it either, but was too proud to ask. Tremmilly was unsure if she would be able to use the rail pistol, feeling it would probably be as useless to her as the armor would have been. Whether she could fire on a living, breathing being was yet to be seen, but she doubted it. Hopefully Maxar, and at extreme necessity, Beowulf, could handle any threats they encountered.

Their preparations complete, the group set off back in the direction they had come from. Maxar took point, Jaydon followed, and Tremmilly and Beowulf brought up the rear. They soon reached the doorway into the incoming dock without incident. Tremmilly thought their guards would have been missed by now, but for whatever reason, nothing had happened yet. The group, after more walking, grew close to the A'tal's Revenge. When Maxar saw the ship, he looked a bit surprised and confused, but he veiled his emotions so quickly Tremmilly was unsure if she had even seen them in the first place. It wasn't much of a stretch to think someone would be surprised to be rescued by a ship that looked like the Revenge. She remembered how, when she had first seen the ship, she had wondered if it would even get off the ground.

The same two squads were still clambering over the vessel, looking for who knew what. They had been searching for quite a while and Tremmilly supposed they would have stopped long ago had it not been for their harsh commander. A shudder coursed through her at the thought of that horrible man.

Maxar led them toward a small group of metal containers stacked near the A'tal's Revenge. Tremmilly feared they would be spotted as they approached the containers, painfully aware of how exposed they were while crossing the expansive floor. She felt a bit better after they were behind cover though. "I don't think we have time to wait for them to finish up," Maxar said in a whisper. "If we wait too long, the dead guards will be discovered and this group will form a defensive perimeter around the Revenge." He looked back and forth between Tremmilly and Jaydon, and Tremmilly could tell he was evaluating them, seeing if they could handle what he was about to say. "Instead, we need to rush in with guns firing and ambush them. If we are in close, we'll be safer from rail fire and Beowulf and myself will be able to work at close quarters."

Now that the time had come, Tremmilly was sure she wouldn't be able to point the rail pistol at a living creature and pull the trigger. Killing was not in her nature and she knew she would feel tremendous guilt if she did manage to kill one of the soldiers. Yes, they had been treated unfairly, and yes, saving this man was what she had come here to do, but did that justify killing? The thought ricocheted through her mind and she was unsure of what to do. Her companions were counting on her and if she didn't help—well, the odds weren't great to begin with and she would be making them worse. She steeled her resolve, knowing if she did manage to hit and kill one of the soldiers her conscience would beat her up. She also knew that letting—*No, causing*—her companions to die would be much, much worse.

Maxar counted down silently using his fingers. Five...four...three...two..., and just as he was about to flash the single digit, something made him pause. Then, Tremmilly sensed it. Jaydon too had noticed, his head cocked to the side to take in the sound.

There was a rhythmic stomping of boots, growing louder by the second. *We were seen*, Tremmilly thought, a cold dread falling over her already tumultuous emotional landscape. She looked at Maxar and was surprised to see he was happy. Tremmilly didn't understand. *He's a veteran. There must be something about the situation I missed.*

Maxar then motioned for Tremmilly, Beowulf, and Jaydon to follow him as he slunk down the line of containers. They reached the end of the row and slipped around the edge just in time as the soldiers who had been at the ship began to double-time their way past the other end. It had been a close thing. If they had moved a few moments later, they would have been spotted. Tremmilly breathed a small sigh of relief and Jaydon looked as if a load had been taken off his shoulders. Maxar still looked much the same, a small bit of happiness on his face.

"They made our job a bit easier," Maxar whispered. "Once they are far enough away, we can board the ship. Hopefully you can get us out of here before they get back to their operations base and realize there are a couple squads and several prisoners missing. We won't have much time, so we all need to work as quickly as possible." Tremmilly and Jaydon nodded in silent assent. Tremmilly, being last in line, peeked out to observe the progress of the soldiers. They were moving fast and had covered a large distance.

"I think they are far enough now," she said, hoping she was right. Tremmilly had the distinct impression if they were caught now, they would find their situation to be much worse than before. She was beginning to have more confidence in the tall man with the pale blue eyes. This too felt like the right thing to do, but she could not decide whether this was intuition or desperation.

Maxar slipped around the far edge of the containers, his foot falls silent. Jaydon followed, his movements producing considerably more noise. Tremmilly, with Beowulf at her side, brought up the rear. Maxar led them to the A'Tal's Revenge, which, amazingly enough, had been left unguarded. Once inside, Jaydon quickly reversed his earlier sabotage of the ship, and then hustled to the flight deck.

Tremmilly started to follow Jaydon, but Maxar stopped her with a hand on her arm. "Can we trust this captain and his ship?" he asked, eyes probing hers as if he could delve the answer from them. "Well," she responded, "he brought me this far on my word and a small threat." Maxar looked as if he wanted to know more, but they both felt a shudder run through the ship and Jaydon's voice came back to them from the flight deck.

"The engines are powered up, but there are some guards running towards us. They have rail pistols drawn." He sounded panicked, but was holding it together. Maxar left Tremmilly and ran off towards the flight deck. When she managed to catch up, she saw the situation had grown worse.

Two guards had rail pistols leveled at the view window, while another two stood behind them, apparently lacking ranged weapons. The two with the pistols were making hand motions to the effect that Jaydon was to power down and open the ship's hatch. "We all know what happens if we stop now," Maxar said. "The outcome of pressing on, while seeming dire at the moment, at least has the distinction of giving us a chance. The commander of this facility will certainly *not* give us a chance, not after we killed several of his men." Jaydon was terrified, but took heart from Maxar's words. Tremmilly was ready to put her life into the hands of this convict, crazy as it seemed. Both she and Jaydon nodded in agreement.

Jaydon put the ship into a vertical take off and then flew towards the huge doors of the dock, the stress causing the ship to groan ominously. They also heard several popping noises and then they were out the bay doors and into the void. *Space and the confines of a small ship have never felt so good,* Tremmilly reflected as they flew further and further away from the orbital dock. Jaydon let out a small whoop of triumph as he slid his chair back from the console. Maxar was a bit more stoic.

"We can save the celebration until we are safely outside their grasp," he said, settling down into one of the deck chairs.

A terrifying thought occurred to Tremmilly, "What about their defense systems? Won't they shoot us now?"

"No," Maxar said, "they can't. I disabled the power to the defensive systems. That was what I had just done before I found you."

As Maxar finished speaking, several warnings came up on Jaydon's grungy control console. "The hull has been breached and we're losing pressure." Jaydon said anxiously. "It's venting faster than the converters can keep up with. We've got about two hours until we reach critical level," he stated, voice quavering, but eyes resolved.

"You keep putting as much distance as you can between us and that dock and I'll go see what's wrong, although I'm pretty sure I can guess what it is." Maxar left the flight deck and Tremmilly was alone with Jaydon, save for Beowulf. Neither spoke, both contemplating the perilous situation they found themselves in.

After a minute passed, Maxar returned, his face still stoic. "It's as I thought. Those popping noises we heard were rail projectiles punching through the hull. We've got at least three or four decent sized holes. They are all venting atmosphere quite rapidly. Where is your emergency patch kit located?" Jaydon shook his head, obviously fearing Maxar's response.

"I sold it," he said, eyes cast down in shame. After a moment's pause he added: "For drinking credits." Maxar didn't seem to mind, and even smiled a little at Jaydon's admission.

"It'll be rough as the fires of the dark star, but we can still pull through. Once we are at worm distance, we'll just have to jump to some place we can land without attracting too much attention. Any ideas?"

"We will be safe at Eishon-2," Tremmilly interjected. "It's where I'm from. It's quiet, and I know a lot of people there. They also aren't exactly loyal to the Ashamine, so I'm sure no one there will report us. We will have plenty of time to repair the ship and figure out what to do next." Her voice was eager and she realized she was more homesick than she was willing to admit.

"Sounds fine to me," Maxar said, the small smile returning to his face when he heard her enthusiasm. Jaydon also agreed.

Minutes passed in silence as the ship accelerated towards the worm zone. "I ran the calculations," Jaydon said, "and if I push the engines to their max, we should be able to get to Eishon-2 before the air runs out, but just barely. We won't have a lot of time to spare."

"Then we will have to make sure there are no delays," Maxar said, still optimistic. Tremmilly was too nervous to join in the conversation. She had begun thinking about the air flowing out of the rents in the hull. *What if Jaydon's calculations are wrong?* The thought of being locked in this box with no air... Well, she didn't want to think about that.

Silence returned to the deck. Jaydon was busy programming in the coordinates for the worm drive and Maxar sat in contented silence. Tremmilly managed to get her fear under control somewhat, but the anxiety of the situation kept her from being her talkative self.

After an hour of uneventful acceleration through Haak-ah-tar space, the ship reached the worm zone. *Not a moment too soon,* Tremmilly thought, excited to be heading back to Eishon-2.

"Here we go," Jaydon said, initiating the worm generator. Nothing happened. He tried again. Still nothing. "The worm drive is down," Jaydon pronounced, voice sounding miserable. "I can try to take a look at it, but I'm not qualified to repair something that complex." He leapt out of his chair and left the command deck, heading for the engine room. It was right for him to hurry. They all knew their lives now depended on getting to a suitable atmosphere in less than an hour. Maxar and Tremmilly, both more ignorant than Jaydon on the subject of worm generator repair, sat in the chairs by the ship's console and waited.

An enormous burst of light filled the ship and Tremmilly thought she would be blinded. It was the brightest thing she had ever seen and she wondered for a moment if Jaydon's attempt at repairing the ship had caused some disastrous backfire. Only when the light's intensity had lowered somewhat did she open her eyes. The view window on the ship had tinted as dark as it was capable and the light was still painfully intense. "What in the fires of the dar—" Maxar began to say, but an emergency tone from the ship's speakers cut him off.

After several seconds of the tone, a voice replaced it. "All ships, this is Bloodsport orbital dock. Haak-ah-tar Primary has just gone supernova. We repeat, Haak-ah-tar Primary has just gone supernova. Suggest moving to worm area and retreating to a safe system. This is not a training exercise. Flee with all possible speed."

"That's bad luck," Maxar said with a sigh, covering his face with his hands for a moment. "The participants back on Bloodsport used to talk about how long it would be before the primary went nova. There was even a betting pool for it."

"How did it just go supernova?" Tremmilly asked, her fear of suffocation momentarily eclipsed by curiosity. "And how did anyone guess it was going to happen? It's not like there is a timer or anything."

"The primary star has been dragging material off of its smaller binary companion, gaining mass. It's been known it would go supernova, but when was the big question. Some thought years, some thought millennia. Guess we know now, and I would have lost the pool." A far away look came over Maxar's face, and Tremmilly guessed he was thinking about his friends back on Bloodsport, how the whole asteroid would be destroyed by the oncoming shock wave.

Jaydon had evidently heard the news about the supernova as well, because he could be heard cursing loudly from deeper in the ship. "This certainly makes our situation more complicated," Maxar said, pulling himself out of his reverie. His characteristic fleeting smile appeared, and it made Tremmilly feel better. "It wasn't enough for the Bloodsport to be after me. Even the star itself is pursuing us."

"Hopefully Jaydon can get that drive fixed," Tremmilly said, her fear returning. "Otherwise, we'll all suffocate in this box and then be blasted into the particles of our existence."

"On the bright side," Maxar interjected, still sounding hopeful, "at least the Ashamine won't be able to find us then." His cheerful demeanor was doing less and less to comfort Tremmilly. She was finally starting to feel a deep and paralyzing fear. Had the leading brought her all this way just to kill her? She was beginning to question what had been smoothing her path and giving her all the guidance.

Maxar stood from his chair and left the deck, perhaps heading back to try to help Jaydon. Tremmilly couldn't think of anything she could do to help. Tears welled up into her eyes and she hugged Beowulf, the two illuminated by the light of a dying star.

28 - THE FOUNDER

The Founder rose from his knees and made the sign of the Ashamine, left hand covering the top of his right fist, upraised at chest level. He then bowed his head towards the chalice displayed at the front of the enormous cathedral. *I wonder if it really is the same chalice the first Founder drank from to seal the covenant with the First Council.* It was certainly a sight to behold, original or not. The gilded pedestal it rested on was worth the price of a small colony world by itself. The cathedral around him cost many times that amount to build. It was no wonder so many citizens made pilgrimages to come see it.

All those seated behind the Founder rose to their feet and followed his example, making the sign of the Ashamine and bowing towards the Chalice of Unity. They also made a bow towards the statue of the first Founder, something that would be inappropriate for the Founder himself to do.

Seeing the statue and its likeness to himself, he thanked the spirit of Ashamine for the deliverance of the boy who would one day take his place as the leader of humanity. He had been briefed by Ascended Rathis and the news had elevated his mood considerably.

The Ascended had told him about how the Founder's Commando had gone into the LGP facility and retrieved the boy. He had been rescued, but the commando, one 3rd Class Enlightened Felar Haltro, had been the only other person to survive the mission. No word or sign had been heard of Director Kasol and the Founder was relieved by this fact. The man had been out of control, conducting experiments far outside the pale of his authorization. An investigation would need to be made into exactly what he had been doing and where he had disappeared to. Crasor would be prefect for that task, but he too was still missing. *Perhaps it is time to begin the search for a new Facilitator,* the Founder thought, eyes narrowing. It was also time to set up a new facility for the LGP, but since the successor was safe, time was no longer as critical.

The boy, known as Lothis until he assumed the title of Founder, was orbiting Haak-ah-tar, his guardians awaiting the orders of where to take him. The Founder had yet to decide on where to set up the new LGP. His top scientific advisors were still trying to find a suitable location. Many factors had to be taken into consideration, with secrecy and proper facilities heading the list. *Hopefully this Enlightened Haltro will keep her mouth shut about the LGP until she can be taken care of,* he thought. She was a hero, but she'd probably learned too much while she was down in the facility. *It's unfortunate, losing an FC.* She had served well, and while he regretted the decision to terminate a member of his namesake unit, it had to be done. The Founder had ordered Ascended Rathis to remove Haltro from quarantine and send her to recon what the Enthos were doing on the surface of Haak-ah-tar. A well hidden explosive device in her APC would detonate when she reached the mission area.

Just as the Founder was turning to leave the cathedral, an aide ran up to him, disheveled and manic. He was so erratic that the Founder's Fist, the body guards who surrounded him at all times, tensed and reached for their flechette pistols. Before the situation could escalate any further, the Founder motioned the Fist to be still. The aide, whose name was Delson, stopped abruptly in front of the Founder, almost touching him. *Well he is certainly putting on quite a show for these people,* the Founder thought, anger beginning to rise. Touching the Founder was a punishable crime and this man was causing a scene that would sow gossip and scandal.

"Haak, Haak-ah-tar, just, just, just went supernova," Delson stammered, loud enough for many of those nearby to hear. Immediately, several of those who had over heard went running out of the cathedral, looks of horror on their faces. The news quickly spread around the cathedral and mayhem erupted. The Founder stood in the middle of it all, a look of stunned apprehension on his elegant face. He turned and watched as people fell to their knees, praying to the first Founder. *That certainly should have been kept confidential until we had time to assess the situation,* he thought, a strange sense of detachment engulfing him. Oddly enough, he didn't feel any anger towards the aide—of course the man would be punished severely, but right now that didn't seem to matter. He felt hollow, empty, husked.

And then he remembered the boy. Lothis was on a ship in the Haak-ah-tar system, and now he was almost certainly dead. His heir had been saved from the crazed scientist only to be wiped out by a star. All the feelings of depression and uncertainty slammed back into place in what felt like a physical blow. The realization that years of work had been wasted and would need to be repeated stoked a blaze of fury within the

Founder.

Before he fully realized what he was doing, he struck out at Delson, his well muscled arm driving his fist into the man's face. Blood flew from Delson's nose, mouth, and lips, the ornate rings on the Founder's hand gashing and lacerating the pale aide's narrow features. Delson's eyes rolled up into his head and he went down hard, flat on his back. The Founder, rage still fueling him, began kicking the fallen man, aiming his blows for the most vulnerable points on the aide's body.

The Founder continued to attack Delson's unconscious form until one of the Fist worked up the courage to drag the Founder away. By this time however, his rage and lust for blood had been sated. He looked down at the dying man, a feeling of serenity beginning to emerge in his turbulent mind. He wasn't remorseful for what he had done, only regretful the man had caused so much chaos with his lack of discretion. Cleaning up this negative publicity would take quite an effort, but now that he had vented some of his emotions, he would be better able to handle all the work ahead.

He strode down the aisle, the Fist clearing the way through the crowd. He exited the building and climbed into his personal transport. The ship rose into the night sky and the Founder gazed down onto the city-world of Ashamine-2.

His predecessors had worked far too hard to build this empire for him to let it fail. His heir was important to the continuance of the Ashamine, but the Founder would hold the government together until a new heir could be created. There was no other option. He was old, but with careful planning and optimization, everything could be set right once again. *And perhaps the Traynos discovery could prolong my... No, it's too early to speculate and I cannot allow myself false hope.*

Once he arrived back at his residence, the Founder began reading the full reports about Haak-ah-tar. *Such bad timing,* he thought, wishing he had moved Lothis sooner. Based on what he read, the Founder guessed there was a chance the boy was still alive, that perhaps the ASN Founder's Hammer would be able to outrun the shock wave. It would take some time to know for sure. Communication with anything in the Haak-ah-tar system was down, so he had no way to signal the ship. Until it turned up somewhere, he would have to assume the worst and begin the work on a new successor.

He didn't want to give up on Crasor, but the Founder knew he needed a new Facilitator. He had waited long enough and the lack of a highly qualified operative was decreasing his effectiveness. *I need someone to be my hands, to do the things I cannot.* Pulling up a file on his terminal screen, he began viewing candidates. Time passed and the Founder only grew more frustrated. "None of these FCs is even half as good as Crasor!"

he yelled.

The memory of all the help Crasor Tah Ahn provided him caused another spike of anger to drive through the Founder. Where had the man gone and why had he not contacted him? This lack of communication was extremely atypical of Crasor. *He has either gone rogue or died.* The Founder preferred to think it was the latter, not believing a man so loyal to be capable of treason. *Anything is possible though,* he allowed, *but I won't believe he deserted until I am proven wrong.* He closed the candidate file, sighed heavily, and looked out over the city-world that spanned below him.

Where are you Crasor? the Founder part lamented, part raged. *Your help would be quite useful, now more than ever...*

29 – CRASOR

Crasor climbed out of the crevasse, relishing how strong his muscles felt. It was as if he were a spider, still using the hand and foot holds of the wall, but possessing boundless strength and endurance that allowed him to climb easily. A sadistic grin curled his lip as he saw what awaited him on the surface.

A vast sea of humanity covered this remote area of Noor-5. They lined both sides of the crevasse that led down to the temple of the Breakers. They had been drawn by the Breaker's spore, the same spore that had drawn Crasor, burning his mind with a desire to come to *this* very spot.

As the crowd caught sight of Crasor, they let out a roar. The sound was nearly identical to what crowds did when one of the Bloodsport combatants scored a brutal kill. Crasor could see into the minds of everyone gathered here. They wanted him, *needed* him, but none of them understood why.

Anticipation bubbled up in Crasor and he strode into the crowd. Feeling triumphant, he stabbed his newly elongated and sharped fingers into the abdomen of a tall, darkly skinned man. The Seed of the Breakers flowed through Crasor's fingers, injecting the man with the nano-machines that would begin modifying his DNA. The man writhed in an ecstasy of agony, and Crasor realized this was probably what he had looked like when he had received the Seed. *But my transformation will be greater, more powerful. I will transcend flesh!*

The nearby crowd shrank back from the writhing man, looks of horror on their faces. Crasor sent out a mental command and the mass of humans lined up, nervous, yet eager for the chance to receive their own Seed. Several hours passed as Crasor continued his work. He enjoyed every second of it.

After the last person received the Seed, Crasor looked out across the sea of what had once been humanity, but was now something else. They were clumsy and ungainly at the moment, unintelligent and only desiring to kill and feed. Soon, however, they would evolve into the Breakers he saw in the millions of memories swirling around his mind.

"I am the Breaker of the Dawn," he proclaimed, his mouth speaking no words. "You were chosen to serve and conquer. Go now and do so. Bring before me those who can become like you. All others, do as you will." With the mental direction complete, the horde had set off in a thousand different directions, each heading to convert or kill. *Many of them will die*, Crasor reflected, *but we are now established in the universe.* The thought gave him a savage pleasure he had experienced occasionally when in the employ of the Founder. This time, the feeling was exponentially stronger.

Days passed and more and more of Noor-5 fell to Crasor. Early on he hashed the planet's main terminal, taking it over and shutting down all communications. *We can't let anyone off world know of us just yet,* he thought, a crooked smile on his face. *They will hear about us soon enough.*

***

Crasor stood on the main street of the once bustling capital city, its boulevards empty except for the hand full of Breakers he had picked to help him. The five of them stood before the Ashamine Planetary Governor's house, a lavish residence that embodied the wealth and opulence typical of the Ashamine. Seeing it made Crasor rage with envy and lust. Why had he never been acknowledged? Why had the Founder never rewarded him for all his sacrifice and devotion? Hate burned within him like the fires of the dark star, and he wished for something to kill or maim to sate his craving.

He calmed down and focused. He needed to give this situation all of his attention. Death was still a distinct possibility. Compared to a fully ascended Breaker, he was still weak and frail, his followers even more so. Going into this dangerous place and getting back out alive would require the full use of his burgeoning powers: mental, physical, and spiritual. He desperately wanted to use them, wanted to bring them to bear on the nearest manifestation of the power of the Founder. Since he couldn't destroy the Founder yet, the man's authority on this planet would have to satisfy Crasor for the moment. He would fight through the soldiers and bodyguards to reach the Governor and kill or convert him. Crasor would be willing to put a wager on convert, but he was too new to the process to be totally sure.

Crasor's growing intelligence force had discovered the Governor and his family had sequestered themselves in their estate when the fighting had broken out. Apparently they had thought it a safe place to wait out the storm. Now, the storm had come for them. There was no one left to defend the family except for those on the grounds. No more military, no more government. Still, the force they retained was strong and well trained. Crasor knew what he would be up against from his Ashamine days, and he wouldn't allow his new found strength and power to make him less vigilant. He just hoped there were no Founder's Commandos inside or his work would be more difficult, maybe even impossible.

Crasor stepped forward, approaching the massive gate that led into the estate grounds. His acolyte Breakers followed, their gait lurching and ugly. When they all reached the barrier, Crasor drew back his arm and struck, flat palm hitting the gate at its middle seam. The heavy panels flew inward as if blasted by a charge, sturdy metal screaming in agony. The two halves of the gate burst off their hinges and tumbled across the estate grounds. His acolytes said nothing, but their eyes widened in amazement. Crasor could also see into their thoughts and knew they were amazed at the force exhibited. *I even surprise myself a little,* Crasor thought, the side of his mouth twisting up in a vicious parody of a grin.

With the gate removed, Crasor strode onto the Governor's estate, four acolytes following. The grounds were quite large and contained several buildings that might be harboring the Governor. Crasor would search every one of them if he had to, but his best guess was that the man would be in his house. They headed across the well manicured lawns, eschewing the immaculate pathways running in every direction. Abusing the pristine grass lent a little touch of disdain that Crasor liked. The details were always the most important things.

Soon they were closing to the range at which the soldiers in the buildings would be able to fire on them. Crasor reached out with his mind, touching the air around the group. Without fully understanding what he did or how he did it, Crasor bent the fabric of space-time. Nothing visible happened, but he could feel a strangeness in the atoms surrounding them.

In the next instant, projectiles came flying towards them, ion trails blazing brilliantly even in the bright daylight. They seemed to pass right through Crasor's bubble, emerging on the other side without harming any of those inside it. Crasor let out a whoop of exultation and started to jog. His followers had a hard time keeping up, their shambling gait not well suited to the faster pace. Crasor slowed, but still maintained a brisk walk. If one of them were to slip out of the area he had generated, they would be cut down by the rail weapon fire.

Crasor was amazed by the lack of defenses for the highest official on Noor-5, but he supposed there had been no real threat to this man before now. Soon, the Ashamine would learn how ill prepared they had been. *Of course,* Crasor thought derisively, *how could they have been prepared for something like us?*

Apparently the soldiers stationed in the buildings were beginning to panic, because shots were going wild at an increasing rate. *Shooting at things that defy physics might cause such fear,* Crasor supposed. No matter, whether they shot true or shot wild it wouldn't harm the five Breakers.

In a few more minutes the group was finally at the grand entrance of the Governor's mansion, its black columns supporting the round dome of the roof. The whole building was a large oval, three stories tall, black facade gleaming in the mid-day light. The front door was even an oval, large enough for several humans to pass through at once. Crasor hit it in the same way he had hit the gates, only not quite as hard. The doors performed the same trick as the gate, and Crasor strode into the mansion.

The first person he encountered inside was a young male Initiate, his fatigues fresh and newly issued. *And they set an inexperienced soldier at this critical point because?* Before the Initiate could act, Crasor reached out with what he thought of as his soul and touched the man. He caressed the man's essence, as if he were a lover touching his dearly beloved. When the man's soul gave a response of revulsion, Crasor had his answer. He leapt forward, bringing a flying forearm into the Initiate's face. He heard bones break and knew instinctively that the blow had been enough to kill the man. Without even looking back, Crasor continued his hunt for the Founder's little puppet. His acolytes wanted to feed on the Initiate—he could feel it in them—but he wouldn't allow it. There were more important things to do, and feeding could come later.

He ascended a grand set of stairs and walked down several extravagant halls without seeing anyone. *Strange...* He opened a door to a large antechamber and found the ambush. There were upwards of fifteen soldiers in the room, all poised for action. They fired, simultaneously, and the roar of projectiles breaking the speed of sound deafened Crasor. Thankfully he had not reversed the effects of the space-time warp, because if he had, there would be nothing left but bloody mist. Even so, he felt the warp strain as the projectiles encountered it, shuddering under the massive force.

The fact he had wandered into the ambush infuriated Crasor, but he knew there was no one but himself to blame. Instead of self-incrimination, Crasor focused his rage externally. He reached out again with his soul, lovingly caressing each foe's life-force in turn. His acolytes performed the same feat, but at a much slower rate. They, being four, had delved only half in the amount of time it had taken Crasor to do the remaining half.

Three of their current opponents responded in the same way as the young Initiate in the entry way. The rest loved his touch and lusted for more of it. Even now he could see they wanted it, *needed* it. *It is such a beautiful thing,* he thought, laughter rising within him.

Equipped with the knowledge of who needed the Seed and who needed the Blackness, Crasor and his acolytes sprang into action. He directed them to kill those marked for Blackness first and then subdue the others. The odds of succeeding without any Breaker causalities weren't good, but it was too late to turn back now.

Crasor released the warp and focused his mind on a different task. He reached out to those who needed the Seed, splitting his soul into what he thought of as a hand with many fingers. He caressed and stroked the group, subduing them with a blissful tranquility. As Crasor did this, his acolytes went to work, battling the remaining soldiers. After a brief struggle, three human corpses lay on the floor, blood pooling from their torn throats.

Crasor carefully approached each of the remaining solders in turn. He stabbed his elongated fingers into the left side of their chests. Seed flowed through the digits and into their hearts, beginning their conversion. Crasor loved watching them change. He saw the fire enter their eyes, saw joy and savagery manifest in their countenance. It was a sight that warmed his heart more than serving the Founder ever had.

With the task of Seeding complete, Crasor had access to each of the new acolyte's minds. From this he learned the man he sought was inside the apartment that adjoined the antechamber. He strode across the large room with the gait of a conquerer, his head high and triumph in his eyes. This world had only one small, flimsy door protecting it from his total conquest.

Crasor's blow caused the privacy door to splinter into fragments. It was wood. *Surprise on surprises. They make it so easy.* When he entered, he saw a man, a woman, and two small children. The delving was performed and Crasor wasn't surprised at the results. The man and the woman for the Seed, and the children for the Blackness. He had yet to delve any young children who were bound for the Seed.

Crasor intended to savor this moment. He would not caress them into docility. He wanted to enjoy the flavor of their emotions. It was time to use pure domination and will to humble this tool of the Founder and his wife. "Governor," Crasor said, nodding to the lean man with dark blue eyes and tawny hair. "And lady wife," he said, this time nodding towards the short woman with auburn hair and hazel eyes. "How nice it is to meet you both."

He intentionally ignored the children, as they were fit for nothing. Mentally, he directed his acolytes to seize them. The governor and his wife made an attempt at resistance, but gave up easily. *Either they are heartless or very good at hiding their emotions,* Crasor observed.

The four acolytes firmly grasped the younger child, a girl, and this broke through the mother's stoicism. The child began crying, and her mother reached out a trembling hand towards her. One of the acolytes took hold of the girl's head and slowly began to twist it. The mother started to gibber, spouting nonsense words. The girl screamed and cried as her head was forced past the point of comfort. There was a loud pop, and the child went limp and silent. Her mother wailed, a long keening noise that was music to Crasor's ears. Again his face was etched with the parody of a grin and laughter rose within him. The girl's father did nothing however, face still a mask of disaffection. The acolyte continued to twist, around and around, until the girl's head was finally torn from her body.

Crasor guessed the Governor's weakness and directed his acolytes to do the same to the boy. The shock of seeing the child's head held aloft by its brown hair was enough to provoke him. He strode up to Crasor and produced a rail pistol out an interior pocket of his coat. He raised it, but the move was slow and clumsy. *Apparently he isn't used to having to wield death himself.* Crasor caught the governor's wrist easily and with a quick twist the man dropped the pistol, wrist broken like a dry twig.

"A pity you are destined for the Seed," Crasor said offhandedly. "You are a weak individual, a failure. Unfortunately, we need everyone we can get." Crasor lifted his right hand, the one with the elongated, specially evolved fingers, and plunged them into the Governor's heart. After the Seed flowed into the man, he fell to the floor and convulsed for a moment, eyes lolling back in his head.

The fit only lasted for a short time, and when it was over, the Governor awkwardly rose to his feet. He shambled towards his wife, a moan escaping his lips. She backed away from him, fear blazing in her eyes. Before she could move far, Crasor was upon her, fingers questing for her heart, injecting the Seed. The woman repeated the same process as the man, spasming on the floor until she rose.

"Meh tha dahn be bruken," she said, the words guttural and barely recognizable. She saluted Crasor, her movements halting.

"May the Dawn be broken," the assembled acolyte Breakers roared, their voices loud even in the large room.

Crasor nodded his head, lop sided grin etched on his face. He had conquered a planet, true, but what was that in perspective of all the might of the Ashamine? And what of the Entho-la-ah-mines? They had an empire too. Perhaps before too long both of those mighty civilizations wouldn't be quite so great. He had taken one planet, why not more? Why not all of them?

30 – CAZZ-AK-TAK

Cazz-ak-tak felt the star go supernova. The Great Thought felt it through him and mourned the devastating loss. Its fragility had been well known. The larger star's greed for the matter of its smaller binary companion had been a subject of discussion amongst the scientists of the Entho-la-ah-mine for quite some time. To Cazz-ak, the impending loss of Haak-ah-tar felt like a condemnation to extinction. They had brought forth the new queen, but that only ensured the species' continued existence until she perished. They had fought so hard to birth the new Queen and now it was all for nothing. It was a measure that merely staved off the inevitable. Depression and anxiety flooded the Great Thought. Despair threatened to destroy them all.

With the loss of the crystals and the cave that contained them, there was no way to bring forth a new queen. Perhaps the cave might survive the shock wave, but the scientists weren't optimistic. It was small consolation that the humans would be wiped off the planet as well. Cazz-ak didn't like to see any creature suffer, even the humans who had harmed his species so much.

Even if the cave is destroyed, I will do my best to keep the Queen alive, Cazz-ak thought. *We must not give up hope. I will not let the sacrifice of the escort vessels be wasted.* Every single one of the support ships that had come with him to Haak-ah-tar had been destroyed by the humans. The other vessels had done everything they could to distract the humans so Cazz-ak's mission could succeed. Now, Cazz-ak's ship was alone and fleeing a dying star. *I wish their sacrifice hadn't been required,* he thought, mourning the loss of life.

Cazz-ak mentally sent a course adjustment to Raa-alk-mi, and the huge bi-pyramidal ship changed course slightly. Cazz-ak hoped it would bring them to distortion clearance distance a little faster than the prior course would have. Many ships, both large and small, fled with them, trying to get to the area that would allow them to escape the shock wave. Cazz-ak wasn't worried about most of the vessels, many being of a type that the humans used for utilities and transport. One of those streaming away in the evacuation was making him nervous however.

The battle cruiser close behind them was a type and size that could quite easily destroy their ship. *This is the one that killed my people,* Cazz-ak thought, seeing images of the human vessel through dying Entho-la-ah-mine eyes. So far the battle cruiser hadn't threatened them and was fleeing like everyone else. Cazz-ak hoped they would continue that way and that everyone would choose different paths once they reached the distortion area. If they were attacked, it would most likely end in the complete destruction of his ship and crew, either from the human weapons or from the delay allowing the shock wave to overtake them. It was not a pleasant prospect in either case.

The feeling on the command deck of the Entho-la-ah-mine ship was one of guarded optimism though. Since the humans had yet to attack, everyone hoped they would continue to think only of their need to escape and forget about the large alien ship that flew ahead of them.

Elth-eo-lan stood next to Cazz-ak, the new Queen beside her. She sent out gentle, calming messages to both Cazz-ak and the new Queen. He was glad to have her there, her comforts much needed in this stressful situation. The Queen was eager to explore everything around her, the newly formed connection to the Great Thought making her mind hunger for information and knowledge. She asked many questions of Elth-eo-lan and the guardian was doing her best to answer them all. Cazz-ak hoped the young queen's birth into the midst of war and turmoil wouldn't taint the naturally gentle and peaceful nature that was the archetype of the species.

When the Entho-la-ah-mine ship finally made it to the distortion area, Cazz-ak immediately set all his Hax-ax-ons to the task of generating the warp. The unified force began gently encouraging the space to condense and fold, to warp and stretch, to form a tunnel. As they worked, Cazz-ak tried to think of the best place to go. He didn't want to lead the pursing battle cruiser back to an Entho-la-ah-mine home world, and the lack of safe havens in the galaxy for his species left few options. The time was drawing near for him to give the location for the other end of the distortion, but he was still unable to think of anything acceptable.

Cazz-ak was beginning to despair of finding a good location when a stray thought lodged in his mind. Not a thought of his own, but a thought from outside of him, from outside the Entho-la-ah-mine Great Thought all together.

"We will be safe at Eishon-2," it said, the thought hopeful, positive. Cazz-ak saw lush forests and gently rolling hills in his mind. A small contingent of humans inhabited the place, but they were friendly, kind in heart and good in spirit. Under all the images ran a current of peace and safety. He couldn't tell exactly who was projecting these strong images, but he could feel the person somewhere near them, most likely a human fleeing from the supernova shock wave.

If he delayed any longer, the distortion wouldn't go anywhere and the whole Entho-la-ah-mine ship would fly into timeless non-existence. With no time left to consider, Cazz-ak passed on the images of the lush landscape and peaceful people to his Hax-ax-ons. They took the information and used it to carefully manipulate the distortion. With mere seconds to spare, they flew through the newly formed path between Haak-ah-tar and Eishon.

Before Cazz-ak could close the distortion behind them, the human battle cruiser entered it. Smoothing the distortion now would send the humans into timelessness. Cazz-ak knew leaving the human ship near them posed a monumental risk, but he could not order his crew to doom the humans that way, even if they had killed so many Entho-la-ah-mines. They had not attacked the Entho-la-ah-mine vessel yet, and perhaps they wanted peace. "Smooth the distortion as soon as the human ship is through," he directed.

The battle cruiser cleared the distortion and his crew began closing it as he had ordered. Just as the process was set in motion however, another human craft entered the pathway. Nothing could be done for them though. The distortion was smoothing and there was no way to stop it now. Cazz-ak, through the eyes of his crew, looked back at the doomed vessel. It was small and decrepit, its hull pitted, and obviously in need of repair. Cazz-ak knew little of human ships, but this was the worst one he had ever seen. It surprised him it was still capable of flight.

They aren't moving fast enough to make it in time, Cazz-ak thought, sad it was at least partially his fault for the future the humans were about to embrace. To his surprise, the small ship managed to stay ahead of the quickly dissolving distortion. As he watched in amazement, the decrepit vessel shot out of the pathway just as the end unfolded and became the smooth fabric of space.

Cazz-ak and his entire crew gave a collective sigh of relief, happy they would not be responsible for loss of life. The relief was short lived however. The battle cruiser was turning on a heading Cazz-ak knew meant impeding attack. Beside him, Elth-eo-lan began to grow nervous, her stream of comforting thoughts interrupted. The new Queen, rather than being frighted, grew more interested and exhilarated by this development.

Cazz-ak, along with Elth-eo-lan and the entire crew, knew their lives were nothing compared to that of the new Queen. With the elimination of the crystal temple on Haak-ah-tar, it was even more imperative she survive. If the species were to have any hope whatsoever, her life and health must be preserved.

Knowing he had no other choice, Cazz-ak, through his Hax-ax-ons, began to lay the foundation for the newly developed Entho-la-ah-mine weapon. He was reluctant to do so, but the humans were forcing him to fight. He gathered strands of the Great Thought, using the Hax-ax-ons to magnify his strength. Cazz-ak could feel the entire Entho-la-ah-mine species watching the situation unfold. Every individual in the galaxy stopped what they were doing and added their concentration to the effort.

The battle cruiser continued to draw closer and closer to the Entho-la-ah-mine bi-pyramid ship. Cazz-ak knew his vessel would soon be within range of the humans' metal throwing weaponry. This was not his first time in this situation, but he had the nagging feeling it might be his last. This ship was larger than anything the Entho-la-ah-mine species had defeated so far and it had easily destroyed the other bi-pyramids. The psionic weapon had never been used on a ship of this size and Cazz-ak didn't know if they had enough power to damage it. The opposing ship grew larger and larger as it approached, and Cazz-ak's optimism for successfully bringing the Queen through the engagement shrank proportionally.

He redoubled his efforts at gathering the strands of power in the Great Thought, his Hax-ax-ons doing all they could to help. He wove the strands together as he went, the thread growing to a string, then to a rope, then to a cable. Cazz-ak knew at any moment the human ship would be within range to use its weapons, but he was gathering the strands as fast as he could. If he tried to use the weapon too soon, it would be ineffective and he would have to start all over.

As Cazz-ak continued to work, the battle cruiser fired every weapon it had. The bright trails of color that signaled death streaked across the distance between the two vessels, the sight as beautiful as it was deadly.

Quickly melding the many strands of Great Thought together, Cazz-ak formed a rod. He carefully folded the rod back onto itself several times, forming a gigantic shard of mental energy. Once the shape had been properly formed, Cazz-ak took a steadying breath. With his mind completely focused and fully aware of the lives he was about to end, he thrust the shard directly at the oncoming battle cruiser.

The effect was instantaneous and devastating. It was as if a massive sword had cut the human ship in half. The severed segments began to fly along differing courses, explosions and venting atmosphere propelling them in ever changing, erratic trajectories. Cazz-ak immediately ordered his ship to take evasive maneuvers, hoping to avoid both the rapidly approaching barrage of weapon rounds and ship debris.

Unfortunately, the bi-pyramid couldn't move fast enough. The metal slugs fired from the human ship hit first, punching massive holes through the lightly armored hull. The impacts of the rounds and the subsequent venting of atmosphere caused the ship to jerk and shudder, knocking many of the six legged, stable footed Entho-la-ah-mines to the floor. Cazz-ak, already weak from his massive use of the Great Thought, was knocked into one of the walls of the command deck.

As he was rising to his feet, Cazz-ak saw Elth-eo-lan and the new Queen a short distance from him. Looking past them, he saw the oncoming debris of the destroyed human ship. While most of the larger pieces of the human vessel had spiraled off in different directions, one distressingly large piece remained on a collision course. The current state of the crew would prevent any maneuvering of the ship, leaving them dead in space. The damage and death caused by the human weapons were too severe to overcome in such a short time. The impact of the fragmented human ship would finish the destruction of the Entho-la-ah-mine vessel, and Cazz-ak knew it.

Small jets of venting gas drew Cazz-ak's eyes to the foremost chunk of human ship. At first he couldn't tell what was happening—*Perhaps some of their supplies are exploding?*—but then he realized it was some sort of escape system. He had never seen such a thing used before, but he immediately grasped that having such a system would save many of his people from death. Unfortunately, Entho-la-ah-mines had never needed such a device before, and because of that, had never developed the technology.

When he looked back down at Elth-eo-lan and the new Queen, he could immediately sense their terror, and more deeply, an unfaltering trust in him. *I cannot help them,* he mourned, feeling like a failure. Had the Queen not been aboard it would have been a terrible loss, but with her death, he would be responsible for the extinction of the species. In that moment, he felt a loss and pain so intense his connection to the Great Thought began to sever.

The Queen's voice in his head brought him back, both to reality and the Great Thought. "Cazz-ak-tak, you were chosen for this duty because you would not fail." Her voice was light and soft, encouraging, yet firm. Cazz-ak almost responded that he was already failing and they were already dead, both those on this ship and eventually the rest of the species. It was feeling the Queen's trust and Elth-eo-lan's hope that made him push aside his despair and self-condemnation. He was still alive, so he would fight until all strength left him.

He had no idea how to save the Queen, but a second look back at the human escape system gave him a flash of inspiration. He set about making it so, time being essential. It would be a matter of a few short minutes before the fragments hurtled into the Entho-la-ah-mine vessel. Cazz-ak had much work to do.

31 – WAKE

It was taking quite some time for the Ashamine's Bane to jump from system to system, stopping each time to decoy its worm impression. Wake often found himself deep in thought as he waited, trying to come to terms with the new life he had chosen. The small ship held little in the way of entertainment, so he needed to find other ways to occupy himself. His thoughts felt like a black hole, threatening to suck him in.

The crew didn't need his help, so that option was a dead end. All the ship's systems were up to date in good repair, so Wake couldn't pass the time in enjoyable technical pursuits. Talking was a good diversion, and he struck up conversations whenever possible.

"What is our final destination Captain," Wake asked on the second day.

"Eishon-2," Malesis replied. Wake hadn't heard of it before. "It is kind of a wild place," Captain Malesis continued. "There are many political and religious factions located there, and they run the spectrum from ambivalent to hostile in their feelings towards the Ashamine. The Brotherhood maintains a fairly large complex on the planet. Our leader, Parick Olvold, should be there. He moves from world to world, staying ahead of the Ashamine, but Eishon is a relatively secure location and he spends his down time there."

As time passed, the crew grew more accepting of Wake and started including him in their conversations and banter. They swapped stories and told him everything he wanted to know about the Brotherhood.

"Alnos Azak-so started the group," Ralen said, his voice taking on the tone of an experienced story teller. "He was a small merchant who lived thousands of years ago. When all the merchants in his area formed a guild to help their interests, Alnos gladly helped in its organization and funding. After a few years however, some larger merchants in the guild decided to begin a system of price fixing on all the members. Common goods became extremely expensive, causing shortages and protests amongst the poor population.

"Alnos Azak-so spoke against the price fixing, arguing it was unfair to the buyers and unnecessary for the merchants. The leaders of the guild threatened him, also promising to kill his family if he did not get back in line. For a time he was silent, not scared into passiveness, but focused on devising a plan. When everything was in place, Azak-so struck and the guild leaders were dead, their entrails spilled by Alnos Azak-so's small blade. The price gouging stopped and Alnos Azak-so was the people's hero."

Wake wondered if Azak-so had been a real man or just a legend, but in the end he supposed it didn't matter. The principle of the story remained true in any event. After having more time to think, Wake now felt he had been hasty in joining the Brotherhood, but he was still happy with his decision. He had been greatly impressed by Captain Malesis, Ralen, Carson, Qul, and Terron, both for their selfless effort to rescue him and in their great skill in doing so. If they were any representation of the Brotherhood as a whole, he would be content to be part of the organization. Besides, he could always leave if he decided he didn't like it.

After a few more days in empty space, the conversation amongst the group died off, leaving Wake with free time he had no idea how to fill. He didn't want to fall back into the trap of over thinking, so he once again looked for something to occupy him. Since the ship needed nothing and he yearned for a technical pursuit, Wake began examining the Clothing of the Iconoclast.

Upon closer inspection he determined it was indeed ancient, but he had no way to figure out exactly how old it was. Its crimson exterior was decorated with ornate silver scrollwork, perhaps indicating it was made for someone in a position of power. Wake's attention was drawn to the fact this ancient environmental nominizing suit contained many electrical components, but none were functional. He also discovered it was armored, something rare in an ENS. "Fascinating," he said to himself.

While digging around inside the suit's systems in an effort to make it functional, Wake saw a module that caught his attention. It was out of place, newer than all the surrounding parts. Its connection to the suit was brutish, hardly in keeping with the rest of the intricate circuitry. Curious of the module's function, he carefully disconnected it. Initially, there was no difference, but after a while he heard a light rushing noise coming from inside the suit. Tracking down the noise revealed the ENS was now processing air, something that had apparently been disabled in order to turn it into an execution chamber. With this new development, Wake was one step closer to being able to use the ornate suit as a fully functional ENS.

Another thing he noticed was an inscription on the back of the helmet. It was worn and looked old, just like the rest of the armor. It was hard to make out exactly what it said because the letters were in an odd script the years had not been kind to. *Callhis Hnghlwing* was his best guess at the first line. The second, after some scrutiny and reasoning, read: *By this, you will know honor.* After puzzling over the first line for some time, he was willing to wager it was probably a name and it was on the helmet because it was once owned by that man.

Having never heard of anyone named Callhis Hnghlwing and thinking it was a strange name—*Did I get some letters wrong maybe?*—he wrote it on a portable terminal and set out to find Captain Malesis. Not finding him on the command deck, Wake knocked on the door of his quarters. "Come in," Malesis said and Wake did so. After some small talk about how Wake was finding his accommodations on board the Ashamine's Bane, they settled down to the matter at hand.

After looking at what Wake had written on the terminal, Captain Malesis' expression grew puzzled. "You say this was on the helmet of the suit we picked you up in?" Wake nodded his confirmation and Malesis thought for a moment. "Would you get it so I can take a look at it?"

Wake retrieved the helmet and returned to Captain Malesis, his mind beginning to grasp that perhaps the ENS was interesting for more than just its technical aspects. Captain Malesis studied the helmet, turning it over and over and pausing to take a look at the inscription now and then. "I think you wrote the name down wrong, even though what you wrote matches perfectly with the helmet. Some letters are worn through and it seems there is some scratching as well." His voice had a bit of a quaver in it, although Wake could see no reason for that. "The name is Calthis Brightwing." He paused, looking at Wake expectantly. When Wake said nothing, Malesis spoke again, breaking the silence of a moment before. "You've never heard of her?"

"No," Wake replied, "I didn't even know it was a woman's name, let alone who she was."

"Calthis Brightwing was the wife of Orick Brightwing, a legendary leader of the government that preceded the Ashamine. She was his battle commander, a genius of warfare and tactics. The legend says she wore a battle suit of cobalt blue, not crimson. I suppose this could be some coincidence, but that seems highly unlikely. What you possess is very valuable." Wake was speechless, thinking through everything Malesis had said. "Some would seek to take this artifact from you," Captain Malesis continued, "but I promise you none of the Brotherhood will do such a thing. I will have to report finding it to my superiors, but they will allow you to keep it, especially due to the circumstances by which you came to possess it."

"Thank you," was all Wake could say.

"If you would, please continue to study it and report anything you find to me. And if you desire to sell it, please give the Brotherhood the first chance. This is a valuable artifact, assuming of course it is authentic, and it is especially valuable to our order. More so than you can probably understand at this point."

Wake regained his composure somewhat after his earlier astonishment. "For now, I would like to keep it and see what it can do. It's truly unlike any ENS I have ever seen."

"Of course, of course, take as long as you like. The Brotherhood would love to hear anything you can tell us about it."

So Wake began to work in earnest, trying to determine what the individual components of each system did. It was slow going due to the fact that most of the technology was unlike anything he ever seen before. The suit lacked any sort of power supply Wake could find, so he rigged up a small battery to get it up and running. Only the most basic systems would power up, and the more advanced features continued to allude him. When he tried to access them through the face plate interface, the whole system simply shut down. There were some features of the suit he believed were related to combat, but he couldn't determine how they operated. Their presence confirmed some of what Malesis had said though, and for that Wake was grateful. Before he could really get in depth with the suit, they neared their destination and Wake was asked to operate one of the ship's stations.

When they entered the worm area near the Eishon system, Ralen let out a startled shout, jumping slightly in his seat. Even the usually silent Terron cursed loudly at the sight unfolding in front of them. A huge Tarton class Ashamine vessel was pursuing one of the strange Entho bi-pyramidal ships, both vessels still inside the worm area. A worm hole was closing behind the enormous human ship, but before it could close for good, a battered and dirty little vessel sped out. "They sure did cut that one fine," Captain Malesis commented dryly. Wake agreed, knowing if they had lingered for a moment longer, everyone on the ship would have been lost forever in the folds of space-time.

"Ideas anyone?" Captain Malesis asked, his voice sounding angry at finding his once peaceful system invaded by intruders. "I don't think we can ju—" but whatever he had been about to say was cut off as the human ship sent a volley of tungsten slugs towards the Entho ship. The ionic tracers in the rounds glowed blue and green as they streaked through the blackness. "Damn Ashamine should burn in the hottest fires of the dark star," Captain Malesis fumed, whatever he had been saying earlier now forgotten.

Wake was at a loss for ideas of what to do next. Their ship was far too small to engage in the battle that was sure to come. One single round from the huge ship would be enough to turn them into particles. Lacking anything else to do, everyone aboard the Ashamine's Bane watched the conflict unfold, hoping against hope the persecuted Enthos might somehow escape. Wake held no special love of the Enthos, but he supposed the foe of his foe was his friend. Considering the prowess of the Enthos, that wasn't much of an alliance however.

The Ashamine ship and its tungsten rain were swiftly bearing down on the Entho vessel. Wake thought the Enthos lost, knowing they had no weaponry aboard their ships. It would be a short battle. But then something unfathomable happened.

The viewing angle wasn't optimal, but to Wake it looked like a massive, invisible blade was cutting the Ashamine ship in two. One moment it was bearing down on the Entho bi-pyramid, and the next it was separating, explosions and venting atmosphere sending the pieces off on erratic trajectories. It was impossible to see what caused the damage, but the evidence of its existence was easy enough to see.

The Tarton class ship was mortally wounded. Those on board must be coming to the same conclusion, because shortly after the blade had done its work, escape vehicles jettisoned away from the vessel. Some vehicles were obviously damaged and Wake wondered how long they would be able to survive. He shuddered at the thought of being in the void again, no air, lungs spasming in a vain to draw breath.

"Move it, move it, move it," Ralen chanted at the Entho ship. After a few moments it was as if the Enthos had heard him and finally realized their danger, slowly moving out of the threatened area. They didn't move fast enough though. The tungsten slugs were unforgiving, punching huge holes into, and in some instances through, the bi-pyramidal ship. It began to lurch and jitter as atmosphere vented into the void. Thankfully, their meager effort had helped them avoid most of the debris from the Ashamine ship. It looked as if they might be able to survive the encounter.

Many of the escape vessels that had left the Ashamine ship were on a course that would end with them smashing to pieces on the large bi-pyramid. He could see small winks of light as some escape vehicles tried to maneuver around the larger ship, their efforts in vain.

Wake, realizing he had a perfectly good terminal in front of him, directed it to scan the path of the Entho ship and its on coming debris for anything large enough to threaten it. After a moment the terminal returned its results and Wake saw a huge piece of the Tarton class' hull heading straight for the Entho vessel. "Fires of the dark star," he muttered. The fragment looked like a battering ram and its effect on the vessel would be nearly the same. There wasn't enough time for the Enthos to get out of the way.

"Good gods..." Captain Malesis muttered, eyes wide in amazement as the bi-pyramid collided with the decimated hull fragment. The piece drove through the Entho ship, piercing it. There were no dramatic explosions aboard the Entho vessel, but there was death. Wake knew thousands were already dead on both sides, were dying at that very moment, and all they could do was watch. Wake mourned at such useless loss of life. The fact there was one less Ashamine ship prowling the galaxy didn't seem to comfort anyone. It certainly wasn't a trade any of them would have chosen.

32 – FELAR

Getting into the APC felt like coming home after a long journey, even though it had only been a standard day since Felar had left it. She breathed a deep sigh of relief as the engine powered up and they began the journey back to AF Command.

"Make sure you latch your seat restraint," she told Lothis, feeling the strange protectiveness that had sprung up inside her the first time she had seen the boy. He looked at the straps as if he had never used them before, but quickly figured out how they functioned.

Felar had never wanted children, so why this mothering instinct now? She found it deeply puzzling. At this moment, the information she had retrieved from the installation was more important. *It's dangerous to keep the data square.* Lothis seemed happy to remain silent, so Felar spent the long drive back thinking about what had been revealed to her down in that horrific research station.

***

"The boy is to be sent up to the Founder's Hammer," Felar's commanding officer said. "He will be debriefed and taken care of there." Felar, who'd normally have been fine with that decision, was skeptical about what it meant exactly.

The loyal, patriotic Felar had vanished when she had viewed that terminal screen inside the research facility. She hadn't dared to access the information she had stolen onto the data square. Felar worried there was some kind of flag tied to the files, that AF Security would know she had extremely confidential information she wasn't cleared for.

"Request permission to escort the boy back to the Hammer," Felar replied to her CO, hoping it would buy her some time to figure out how to rescue Lothis from the Ashamine.

"Negative, Enlightened, the boy has an escort inbound to Haak-ah-tar."

"Request permission to see the boy. I feel talking to him would be useful for a tactics debriefing." She thought no such thing, but she needed a reason they would accept. She felt her heart would break if she didn't see him soon. *Careful, Felar,* she told herself, *you'll lose your edge if you journey further down this path.*

"Permission denied. The boy is to be kept in isolation until his escort arrives."

Felar had to disconnect her emotions from the boy. He would be off world soon and she'd be issued new orders. She couldn't quit thinking about him though, no matter how hard she tried. She kept seeing his face in her mind and then the information from the facility would flash through her consciousness. The agony was like watching an asteroid flying towards your home planet: slow, inexorable, and in the end, deadly. The boy had been rescued from what amounted to living in the fires of the dark star, had been saved from the ravages of those monstrous creatures Director Kasol had created, had been taken back to a civilized and ordered culture, and now he was to be sent back to his creators, to be enslaved once again to the will of the Ashamine.

When they had arrived back at the AF base, Felar had been quarantined and searched. She had barely been able to keep the data square hidden. *They probably would have brought out the Clothing of the Iconoclast for stealing that information.* The search was not a normal post-mission procedure, but it made sense given what she knew about the facility's purpose. *Good thing the square was small enough to swallow.*

The files Felar had uploaded onto the square contained the kind of information that turned loyal citizens into rebels, and she was at that point. Simply put—and that was extremely hard to do considering the amount of content she had briefly skimmed—Lothis was a clone of the original Founder. Felar had a hard time wrapping her head around that little tidbit, but it did make a great deal of sense when she noticed the boy had the fabled orange eyes, the same color of that notable leader. The citizens of the Ashamine had been provided with much news about the present Founder's son and it appeared all of those stories were just that—stories. She had found the truth in the research facility.

This also didn't appear to be the first time a clone had been made. She had downloaded information about all the Founders and their origins and from what she could remember, every last one of them had been clones of the first. What was different about Lothis were the new protocols that had been implemented in his upbringing. Further reading informed her he was being kept at the installation for what was euphemistically referred to as "raising". What it amounted to was programming. She had also found files that hinted at some type of experimental therapy that was being performed on the child, but she hadn't had time to read them. *I wish I could open this data square on a terminal,* Felar thought, knowing there was much she had downloaded that she had yet to read. There was information about what Director Kasol had been up to in his labs. Felar had no desire to relive her experience in that dark place, so she doubted she would ever read them. Having seen those creatures and Kasol himself was enough to convince her the man was evil and maniacal.

One of the files she had skimmed while down in the facility was unrelated to both Lothis and the monstrosities. It contained information about some form of military technology Kasol was developing. The information had been vague, but it seemed he was creating some form of super soldier nano-tech and it was nearing its final stages. The file indicated the experiment had been moved out of the facility and was now being continued on the Bloodsport asteroid. Felar hoped once she could open the data square she might discover more. If it worked, it would change how the entire AF operated.

Felar lay awake that night, unable to sleep. She couldn't allow the boy to fall back under the control of the Ashamine handlers. Her superior officers wouldn't allow her to escort him, eliminating any possibility of her spiriting the boy off and hiding him en route. Felar tried desperately to figure out a way to help Lothis escape, but she didn't even know where he was being held. She fell into a fitful sleep, her dreams an endless loop of running from misshapen forms in the dark.

The next day, Felar was summoned to appear before her commanding officer. She was filled with sorrow as she entered his office, knowing she would never see the boy again. *I wonder if I'll be dispatched to train a new group of Inits,* she thought, thinking about what her next assignment would be.

"I'm sending you and a new squad of Inits out to recon what the Enthos are doing," her CO said after she sat down. "Satellite data shows they landed a ship out in a remote patch of desert. We have no idea what they are up to out there. It appears they went down into some type of cave."

"Yes, that seems very important," she said, trying, and failing, to muster some of her old enthusiasm. A chime sounded from the CO's terminal and he was silent for a moment as he read a notification.

"Well, you can rescind that assignment," the CO said, sounding puzzled. "I just got orders from AF Command that you are to escort the boy up to the Hammer. I'm a bit puzzled at this change, being it's so last minute." He entered a few commands into the terminal and turned to look at her. "You're transferred to the escort detail effective immediately.

You are assigned to be the boy's personal protection. Be ready to ship out in a standard hour. Someone will come to get you when the shuttle is ready to leave for the Hammer."

Felar was even more puzzled at the last minute shift in orders. The Ashamine Forces didn't normally operate that way, but she supposed sometimes anomalous things happened in an entity as large as the AF. Even under the strange circumstances, she was glad her assignment had been changed. It would be nearly impossible to find a way to steal the boy from the rest of the escort, but she would try as best she could. She cared too much to do otherwise.

Felar returned to her quarters, packed her few belongings, and was ready well before the aide came to escort her to the Hammer's shuttle. After entering the small craft, she saw Lothis was already on board. His blank expression momentarily brightened in what was probably supposed to be a smile, a look more akin to a grimace. Felar smiled back her biggest grin. Seeing Lothis again strengthened her resolve to free him.

The contingent of soldiers on board the shuttle had it packed to capacity, and as the shuttle left the surface of the planet it was escorted by several fighters and a heavy gun ship. Both the soldiers and the heavy air support disclosed just how valuable Lothis was to the Ashamine. *Perhaps this will be harder than I thought,* Felar lamented. One thing her instructors forcibly instilled in her while going through the rigorous training for the FCs was that you had to have an extreme amount of luck to pull through the tough situations. And the definition of luck? Preparedness meeting opportunity. She set about preparing numerous plans in her head, knowing it was vital to be ready when the opportunity came.

Even though the cabin of the shuttle was packed, she outranked all the other soldiers. Her seniority made it easy for her to get the seat next to Lothis, displacing a hulking soldier that vaguely reminded her of Initiate Alexhion from back on Ashamine-4. She wondered momentarily what had happened to Alexhion and a feeling of revulsion came over her. Then the shuttle took off and her negative feelings were quickly forgotten.

The ride was short and easy. Lothis was silent, looking intimidated by all the people surrounding him. Felar could understand. Going from no human contact for most of your life to a ship packed full of sweaty, smelly soldiers had to be intimidating. Actually, now that she thought of it, he was doing quite well.

Every so often she would hear him speak some isolated word or phrase, but when she turned to look at him, he would be silently staring off into space above the soldiers' heads. None of the tightly packed soldiers around them noticed, so Felar figured it was her nerves and began ignoring the fragments. Soon they seemed to stop, but Felar was too busy thinking to pay attention to small distractions.

When they were finally outside Haak-ah-tar's atmosphere, she caught her first glimpse of the ASN Founder's Hammer. At first it seemed like the ship was in low orbit. As time passed and it continued to grow larger and larger, Felar realized the extreme size of the ship made it appear closer than it actually was. It had to be the largest ship she had ever seen. That realization drove home, viscerally, just how badly the Ashamine, and probably more directly, the Founder, wanted this boy. A momentary wave of despair washed over her, but she rallied after seeing the look of love in Lothis' eyes. She was amazed at how quickly the boy was picking up on his surroundings. *He must be every bit as intelligent as the files said,* she marveled.

Once the shuttle had docked in the massive vessel, Felar and Lothis were shown to their quarters. The other escorting soldiers were stationed in a ring around them. This would pose a bit of a problem for some of her plans, but Felar hoped it would only be a minor setback. *Preparedness meets opportunity,* she kept chanting.

Soon after settling in, Felar and Lothis were summoned to a meeting with the commander of the ship, Captain Talnavis. Talnavis was an older man, understandable for the commander of such an exalted vessel. His eyes had a burning fire in them, but whether it was a burning of devotion or of madness, Felar couldn't tell. After a salute to Felar and a smile to the non-responsive Lothis, the captain addressed them. "Welcome to the Founder's Hammer," he said, his voice hoarse, probably from a lifetime of yelling orders. "We're honored to have you on board."

Felar gathered from his welcome and ingratiating manner that he knew Lothis was the Founder's child, but she doubted he had any inkling to the manner in which the boy had been conceived. "Thank you for your service to the Founder and Ashamine," Felar said, trying to summon a front of the old patriotism that used to be her heart and soul. "You have quite a ship, you must be very proud to command her."

"Indeed, indeed," the captain rasped out. "The Hammer is an amazing vessel. There is no other ship that can best her in combat, perhaps no two ships paired together could equal her prowess. She may not be indestructible, but she is damn near close."

"Well if her size is any indication," Felar said, faking an enthusiasm she didn't feel, "she very well might be." This sentiment encouraged the old commander and he began to tell Felar and Lothis all the technical details of the ship and its systems. Felar tuned the man out, still nodding and expressing the same fake enthusiasm in all the right places. Lothis, true to form, said nothing throughout the whole conversation.

"So you see," Talnavis was saying, "the ship is perfectly suited to exterminate Enthos." The mention of the Enthos brought Felar back to the conversation and she began to listen closer. "We've caught several of their ships around Haak-ah-tar and we drilled them with tungsten slugs." The look in his eyes had definitely swung over to the side of madness. But no, that wasn't quite right. Felar decided it was probably more like devoted madness. *Big difference,* she thought as the man recounted the destruction of the Entho ships. He obviously enjoyed the slaughter of a largely innocent species. Felar herself felt the war with the peaceful alien species had been a poor move on the part of the Ashamine. When she saw men like this, it made her wonder how the government could keep from destroying itself. The populace of the Ashamine had been whipped into a frenzy against the Enthos by government propaganda, but the troops knew better, at least most did. Apparently, Talnavis wasn't one of them. Felar wished she could feel her old patriotism, but the way the government was handling the lack of resources by stealing the Entho home-worlds, made it hard. *And what they did to Lothis is more than I can forgive.*

It took quite some time for Talnavis to finish his monologue, but once he was done, Felar and Lothis returned to their quarters. The fact Lothis had said almost nothing since they left Haak-ah-tar frightened her somewhat. The boy had to have a fragile psyche and all this turmoil couldn't be helping. The ship offered much in the way of recreation, but Lothis was content to stay in quarters, so they sat in the two rooms that had been given them. Felar didn't mind though. Lately, the more she saw of the Ashamine, the angrier she got.

Just as she was settling back on her bunk to relax—good soldiers knew to rest whenever the opportunity presented itself—Lothis' voice startled her back from the threshold of sleep. "I can feel him...Them...All..." The boy's voice sounded eerie and strange in Felar's ears. She looked at him and his normally vacant expression had a quality of rapture in it.

"Lothis," she said tentatively, and she realized these were the first words she had said to him all day. The boy turned to look at her, but she realized he wasn't really *seeing* her. His expression gave her chills, not because it was frightening, but because he looked so elated. He also looked *gone* somehow.

"They have her on their ship and she is lovely. She will save them, but he will save her first, must save her." Upon hearing this, Felar began to feel fear deep down in her stomach. *What is he talking about?* she wondered. Before either of them could say anything else though, a loud alarm began to blare.

After a few moments of ear splitting volume, the alarm dropped a few decibels and the voice of Talnavis came over the address system. "Attention all crew. We've detected an Entho bi-pyramid and are in pursuit. Assume ready stations. We will destroy the enemy craft and resume the primary mission." The rough voice ended and, thankfully, the alarm stayed at its lower volume.

If Felar had to put currency on it, she would wager this was not an approved diversion. The captain was simply fulfilling his desire to kill and he would say something like, "That's what this ship was made for, how can I deny its use?" In war, killing the enemy was certainly desirable, but doing it while you had the heir to the Ashamine supreme leader on board was folly.

Upon consideration, Felar decided this new development might provide additional opportunity for escape. *Surprise is always the best thing to have when attacking, but chaos is also a useful ally.* Deciding she would know nothing if they stayed in their quarters, Felar decided to venture out. She took Lothis, who was now back to himself, and they left for the command deck. The rest of the guard escort followed them closely, maintaining a tight perimeter.

All was operating efficiently on deck when they arrived. The captain was issuing orders and his under-officers were carrying them out. The huge Tarton class ship was being brought around on a course to follow the Entho craft. This would give them a better attacking position. Then Lothis began to scream.

The boy's agonized wails were guttural and sounded strangely deep for someone so small. He fell to the floor and Felar followed him down, attempting to comfort him while holding him in her arms. For a brief moment everyone on the command deck was mesmerized by the child's outburst. The escort guards rushed in, looking concerned, but unable to do anything. A few seconds later, the comms officer turned from gazing at the boy to stare at his terminal. He was focused, obviously listening to the communications set he wore. After a moment or two, his face grew pale and a look of frightened amazement replaced the concentration that had been there a moment before.

"Captain Talnavis," he yelled over Lothis' screaming, "Captain Talnavis I have a priority communication from Haak-ah-tar." It took a moment for the captain to notice his communications officer, his attention was enthralled by the screaming child in the middle of his command deck. *Probably not used to having suffering children this near,* Felar thought as she comforted Lothis. *He's always had them on the other side of his guns.*

Once Talnavis finally realized his comms officer was yelling for him, he strode over to the man and bent close to hear what he had to say. The news blanched his face the same way it had his under-officer. He strode back to his terminal, only now his walk was shaky and tremulous. "Attention all hands," he broadcast ship wide, his voice sounding like it had aged twenty years since the last transmission. "We've just been informed the Haak-ah-tar Primary star has gone supernova." Everyone on the bridge was staring at Captain Talnavis, their expressions incredulous. "We must get to the worm area as fast as possible. We have vital cargo on board that must be safeguarded at all costs." As the captain was speaking, the navigation officer was frantically making calculations. When he concluded, he gave a thumb up to Talnavis. The captain, seeing the signal, continued his announcement. "I've been informed by navigation that we should have enough time to get clear of the system before the shock wave catches us. Unfortunately, there will be many lost on Haak-ah-tar itself, as well as many ships that are not fast enough to escape." A look of anger began replacing the pallid shock that had been on his face a moment before.

Talnavis stepped away from his terminal, and Felar saw the calculation and cunning in his old man's eyes. By this time, Lothis had subsided to soft whimpers that were more awful than the screams.

"You'll be alright honey. Everything is going to be OK," Felar said, trying to comfort the boy, but feeling inadequate for the task.

"I don't know how they did it, but these *Enthos*," Talnavis said the word with as much scorn and malice as humanly possible, "had something to do with this supernova. They caused it, they are using the star as a weapon to wipe us out! That's what they were doing under Haak-ah-tar."

Felar could see the madness returning to the captain's demeanor and it made her even more on edge than Lothis' screams had. The captain strode back and forth across the deck, gesticulating franticly as he did so. "We will hunt down the vile, filthy creatures who did this and convert them back to the polluted atoms they came from." All those on the deck responded with loud curses directed at the Enthos. The escort guards lost interest in Lothis and joined the mob, their profanity even worse than the deck crew.

Felar knew it was ludicrous for anyone to believe the Enthos could have caused the supernova. Ashamine scientists had warned the binary stars of Haak-ah-tar were bound to do just such a thing at some unknown time. Talnavis had seized upon the situation to justify pursing his own goals and his troops were just as blood thirsty as he was. *Insanity.*

Lothis was becoming more responsive to Felar's attempts to calm him, and now the boy's eyes were actually seeing. Felar had no idea what had caused Lothis to start screaming, but the timing of the supernova seemed too close to be a coincidence. "I felt it," she heard Lothis say, but the boy's lips didn't move. "I felt the supernova and it hurt me." This time she was looking directly at his face when she heard it, and yes, the boy's lips did not move even a fraction of a millimeter. Lothis must have seen the look of frightened amazement dawning on her face because he spoke again, only this time with his voice. "We need to go some place safe. Something bad is about to happen. We *have* to go some place safe," the boy repeated, and Felar could see he meant it.

She lifted the boy in her arms and headed for the door that exited the command deck. Thankfully all the escort guards were still caught up in the frenzy of hatred against the Enthos and didn't notice her leaving. Felar had to push past several crew members who obstructed her way, but they were far too focused on the pursuit of the Entho ship to notice her. "They're opening up a worm hole," she heard as she was exiting the deck.

"Follow them through! If we don't, we'll lose them," Talnavis said, full of angry eagerness and excitement. Then the doors slid shut and the sounds of the command deck were cut off.

"Is there a way to get off the ship?" the boy asked, a look of concern on his small face.

"Well, if we were able to get a shuttle—which is doubtful—we wouldn't be able to get far, plus the shock wave would wipe us out anyway. I think we are stuck on this ship, at least for the time being. I know you don't like these people, and neither do I, but—"

"You don't understand," he said, cutting her off. "This ship is going to be destroyed, and we don't have much time."

"I'm almost certain we are going to escape the shock wave, and it's impossible for that Entho ship to take us out." She was trying to reason with the boy, trying to show him that even though their present company was unpleasant, at least they were safe. That was more than could be said for their time under the surface of Haak-ah-tar. She knew she had to get him out of the grasp of the Ashamine, but now wasn't the right time. "This ship was built using the latest and best Ashamine technology. The Enthos don't even have any real weapons on their ships."

"Don't they?" the boy asked, and his voice had gone cold. She'd never heard him speak like that and it chilled her deeply. "If we don't get off this ship soon, we are going to die." He said the words with a finality that jolted Felar. She didn't understand how it would happen, but the sheer conviction in Lothis' eyes told her this high tech battle ship would be turned into space junk.

She let out several nervous laughs before she could pull herself together. It was unlike her to lose her composure so drastically. When the boy heard the laughs, the cold focus left his eyes. In an instant he looked like the frightened little boy she had taken from the facility under Haak-ah-tar. The stony faced avatar of power she had been looking at moments before was gone.

Escape pods. That had been one of the plans that had occurred to Felar. If this ship was going to be destroyed, it was the perfect place to go. She had no idea where the Hammer was heading, but she held hope there would be someone to retrieve them from the pod before it ran out of air.

Continuing to carry Lothis, she hurried towards the nearest pod array. There was one quite close because of the command deck, so the trip didn't take long. She didn't encounter many crew members, but those she did gave her odd looks, most likely due to the fact they had never seen a Founder's Commando running through the corridors with a small child. Felar didn't stop or even slow for these encounters. She knew now there wasn't much time. Every second counted.

When they reached the pods, they encountered their first real obstacle. A guard was stationed in front of the large doors that opened on to the chamber where the pod hatches were located. He was a brawny man, tall and fierce looking. The time for deception and trickery was long past. Felar set Lothis down onto his feet and strode directly up to the beefy guard. "How may I hel—" he was saying as she slammed her fist into his solar plexus. He was totally unprepared for her strike and Felar's shot was devastating. The man crumpled up on the floor, a sickly wheezing gasp escaping his lips as he tried to recover the wind that had been knocked out of him.

"Lothis, get this door open," she meant to say, but only got as far as the boy's name as she turned from the guard. She saw the boy was doing just that, diligently working at the small terminal located to the side of the door. A few moments passed and the guard began adding moans to his wheezing gasps. Soon, the large doors slid open and the boy cried out in triumph. "Good job!" she praised as they ran through the doorway. He said nothing, but looked up at her and smiled in reply. She noted he took much joy from her approval and the thought made her glad.

When they got to the first bank of pods, they stopped. The pod hatch they stood in front of slid up smoothly, and Felar looked inside the craft she hoped would save them from the disaster that was quickly approaching. The vessel was designed to hold six, so they would have plenty of space, but she disliked the thought of floating in the void, powerless to do anything about their fate. *There isn't enough time to devise a better plan.*

Once inside the pod, Felar initiated the protocols to launch the vessel. Normally, all pods were locked down until the captain gave the abandon ship signal, but Lothis quickly bypassed this requirement. The boy's skill with electronics seemed limitless. Felar strapped him into his seat, securing his harness. That task finished, she performed the same procedure for herself.

Just before she tapped the "Initiate" command on her terminal screen, Lothis shook his small head at her. "Don't do it yet," he said, a focused look of concentration wrinkling his brow. She waited for a full minute, growing increasingly nervous as time passed. The guard could be calling reinforcements. Even now they might be tracking Lothis' hashes and disabling them, rendering the pod inoperative.

"I really think we should—"

"Wait." The word was final, and the look of coldness reasserted itself on his face. *In for a finger, in for the arm,* she remembered her mother saying. She had gone this far, why not a little farther? Another full minute crawled by. And then another. And then a fourth. Now Felar was beginning to panic, her cool resolve and focus being eroded by the acid of uncertainty. Just as she was about to speak again, Lothis said, "Go." She stabbed her finger down on terminal screen so hard it bent back and jolted with pain. She wondered fleetingly if she had sprained it.

The pod accelerated quickly, the inertial forces shoving them back hard into their seats. Then they were free of the Hammer, streaming off into the void of space.

33 – LOTHIS

As they drifted, Lothis reflected on the events of the past few days. Since he'd been exiled from his prison, he'd discovered many things about the world. One of the most important was that those who had control of him relied on terminals and the information they provided. Changing that information to suit his desires proved to be amazingly easy. Even their "secure" systems were effortless to manipulate.

He remembered back to when he had found out they would be taking Felar from him. At first he thought she was abandoning him and he became despondent. Seeking more information, he hashed the terminal in his temporary housing. Gaining access to the high security systems of the Ashamine Forces took a couple minutes, but eventually he was reading documents that showed Felar was being sent on a mission to track down Entho-la-ah-mines. *I can't lose her,* Lothis thought, accessing the systems that would allow him to change the orders. Immediately, the terminal went into an extreme level of encryption. *I made it lockdown,* Lothis panicked. Then, he blinked. Immediately, the terminal's display changed. That wasn't quite right though, because the display stayed the same, but now he could read it. Something had focused in his mind—that was all he could determine—but how or why it did was beyond his understanding. He had made a few quick changes, assigning Felar to his escort and making sure all the procedures were properly authenticated. No one would know it had been him who had issued the orders.

Being able to read the encryption was just one of the many things that had been happening to Lothis that were outside his understanding. His *connection* to the supernova baffled him. The pain had been incredibly intense, far greater than anything he had ever imagined possible. Lothis had somehow tapped the energy of the dying star, had allowed it to flow into him. He had fought back against the energy, had tried to escape from it, but couldn't. When he had been able to open his eyes, Felar had been there, comforting and caring for him. Without her he didn't how he would have survived. Her tender kindness had helped him shut the door—*gateway*—to the energy from the dying star. Had she not done this, perhaps the energy would have filled him until there was nothing left. That was certainly a frightening thought.

He was glad he had sensed the impending destruction of the Founder's Hammer. When Lothis had reached out to the Entho-la-ah-mines and their queen, he could sense they were preparing to destroy the Hammer. Felar hadn't wanted to listen to his warning. He had told her they needed to leave, but she either didn't understand or didn't believe him. That had made him angry, extremely angry. He could see just how angry he was by the way she reacted to him. Finally, she had listened and they made it to the escape pods.

Time passed as they continued to drift away from the Hammer, the pod's separation motor having cut out just before they exited the ship. Each second that passed found them further and further from the ship of his captors. "Look at that," Felar said, her voice low in the manner Lothis had determined to mean she was talking to herself. In spite of that fact, Lothis looked anyway.

His viewing angle was optimum, Felar having rotated the pod so its large front window faced towards the Ashamine vessel and its Entho-la-ah-mine counterpart. She had also decreased their forward thrusters, wanting to get away from the Hammer while still conserving as much fuel as possible.

Lothis determined Felar's exclamation most likely had to do with the large amounts of glowing ions that were streaking from the Hammer towards the bi-pyramid. He looked at them for a moment and then realized what they were. He had seen a diagram for a rail weapon before and this situation fit its use quite well.

As the slugs approached the huge Entho-la-ah-mine craft, Lothis began to feel another stirring in his mind. This one felt different from the supernova, but somehow it was akin. It was *outside* somehow. And while the feeling wasn't painful, it made him uneasy. Almost losing himself on the command deck of the Hammer gave him a right to be cautions, at least until he understood this thing. *The Entho-la-ah-mines are about to strike, but I don't understand how.*

The stirring in his mind grew as the slugs streaked towards their target. Soon the stirring grew to a humming vibration and the vibration rose towards a crescendo. Lothis knew somehow that if he still had the gateway open when it reached its highest pitch, it would kill him. The signal began to rise exponentially, and Lothis grew frightened. His fear must have shown because Felar looked at him and asked, "What's wrong Lothis? You look upset." He didn't answer her, couldn't answer her. He was using all his mental strength to shut the gateway between himself and the Entho-la-ah-mines. He strained against the force, using all of his ability to try to cut off the link. It wouldn't budge and Lothis sensed the pitch was almost at its highest. *Must. Push. Harder!* he thought, redoubling his efforts. And then it closed, snapping shut with a violence that dazed Lothis. He felt exhausted, drained, empty.

"I-I don't really know," the boy stammered, his arms hugging his slender legs to his chest. "Buh-buh-but it's gone now." She stroked his hair and gave him a kind look.

"Maybe soon we can get you to a doctor and he can figure out what is causing these—" she stopped to try to think of the right word to use, "these episodes. Maybe it can be cured." He looked up at her and smiled, but inwardly he had grown scared.

What if the signals were taken away from him? That thought scared him to the core. Yes, the signals frightened him too, but they were so sweet to listen to, turning the mundane blandness of the world around him into something beautiful. No, he wanted the signals, but somehow he would have to learn how to control their effects on him. And perhaps he could learn to better control which signals he tuned into. *Why did I never have these experiences while down in my room?* he wondered. *Did they have me shielded somehow?*

All thoughts of the signals left his mind as Lothis saw something begin to happen to the Founder's Hammer. It was as if the giant ship was being torn in two. Felar, seeing the look of wonder on his face, turned to look out the window. The Hammer was splitting into several large sections, some of those pieces fragmenting even further. "Founder bless them," Felar said, awe and astonishment in her lovely voice. Lothis didn't comprehend how it happened, but the Hammer had been destroyed. It had to be connected somehow to the signal he'd been tuned into earlier. *How did the Entho-la-ah-mines do it?* What he saw in the chaos unfolding before them put his mind on a different track.

Many pods were ejecting from the human craft, but they were not faring as well as Lothis and Felar had. Some flew straight into the wreckage of the ship, battered to junk before they could even attempt to maneuver through the debris. Some were damaged before they escaped the Hammer, atmosphere and propellant leaking from their compromised hulls. It looked like few, if any, would survive their birth into the destruction engulfing the Hammer.

Their attentions were soon drawn to the Entho-la-ah-mine ship as it tried to perform evasive maneuvers to escape both the slugs and the oncoming debris of the Hammer. It seemed as if the alien craft was starting to move out of danger, but it maneuvered too slowly. Slugs perforated its hull and the ship began to shudder as atmosphere vented through the rents. Lothis watched, stunned by the continuing destruction on display right before his eyes. He saw no escape pods, nor did he see any of the fire or explosions that were now engulfing portions of the Hammer. The slugs had done their work and it was evident the Entho ship was crippled. Several of the hull pieces bearing down on the bi-pyramid were obviously going to change the state of the ship from disabled to destroyed.

"We don't need to see this," Felar told him, her voice quavery. Lothis turned away from the destruction and noticed a tear in the corner of her eye. He decided to say nothing about it, knowing he couldn't console her. "What we need to do is to find a way to get the bugger out of here. We're running on limited air and fuel." Somehow he knew what she wasn't saying, "*Now that both ships are destroyed, we have no one to rescue us.*" The thought scared him, but he had learned how to deal with fear down in the terrible facility under Haak-ah-tar. Felar was still with him and she would protect him. Of that he had no doubt.

They began working the terminals next to their seats, scanning the surrounding area for other ships. They found none. They looked for the beacons of other escape pods and had the same result. It was not an encouraging picture.

"In all the rush of pursing that Entho vessel, I doubt anyone on the Hammer signaled our location back to Ashamine High Command." Felar paused, looking as if she was wondering if she should go on. "When HC doesn't hear anything from the Hammer, it will be assumed the ship was destroyed by the supernova. In other words, no one will be coming to look for us." Felar's voice sounded bleak, but Lothis was still sure she would find a way to save them. She had done it before and he was confident she would do it again, no matter the odds.

Once they had done everything possible on the terminals, they turned to look at the battle field again. It was a desolate sight, huge pieces of both hulls floating amongst smaller debris. It looked like death. It felt like death.

Lothis continued to stare at the swath of space, feeling like he was missing something. Finally, he caught hold of it. There was life out amongst the destruction. The signal was faint, but now he had found it, he knew for sure. It felt familiar to him, like the signal he had felt before the Ashamine ship broke up, but different somehow, calmer. It was Entho-la-ah-mine. He didn't understand how to do anything more with that signal, so he let go of it for the moment.

Time passed as they waited for rescue, and Lothis grew bored. There wasn't much to do in the pod, so he continued to explore the surrounding signals. He reached out to them, caressing their energy and trying to find the source. Soon, Lothis discovered a characteristic that allowed him to distinguish two types of signals. Most originated from unintelligent sources, such as stars, planets, terminals, and mechanical objects. These he ignored for the moment. Far more interesting were those coming from intelligent, aware creatures.

Quickly, he determined this was how he had felt such a strong connection to Felar before they had met. He could sense the goodness of her energy even now. He wanted to probe deeper, but was worried about what would happen. Instead, he focused his thoughts on the space outside the pod. The Entho-la-ah-mine energy was still near them, as vibrant and alive as before. He pushed his mind further out, past the wreckage, past the planet, as far out as his newfound ability would let him. And then Lothis felt something *different.*

It was a fleeting glimpse, a tug at the edge of this new sense. Someone or something was watching him. Not understanding how, Lothis pursued the signal. It almost vanished before he could latch onto it, but once he did, there was a connection to a source unlike any he had sensed before.

Lothis saw a group gathered around a table, bright beings of shining light. The signal hurt his head, but he held on to it tightly. Curiosity forced him onward.

"This is the boy from the prophecy, yes?" Lothis couldn't tell who was speaking, couldn't distinguish any characteristics of the forms.

"Indeed, and he grows much quicker than we ever could have imagined," a new voice said, lighter, more airy than the previous speaker. The scene before Lothis flickered, the lights surging and dimming at a rapid pace. Everything in this place had a strange, foreign feel to it.

"If he has traced us back here, he has gone exponential," a third, deep voice said.

"Did we give the rest of them enough guidance?" the first voice asked. Everything surged and flickered again, like electricity coursing through a wire.

"The soldier saved the boy, the girl rescued the convict, and the engineer will soon find the protector. They all seem to be converging quite well." The last was spoken by a new voice, one rich and full off authority. "But we shouldn't be talking about these matters with *him* watching." Lothis felt the group's attention shift towards him, and the energy surrounding him surged. The flicker oscillated more rapidly, reaching a driving crescendo that overwhelmed him.

Full consciousness rushed back into Lothis' body, and he tried not to gasp from the sensation. The pod was as still and boring as before. Felar sat aimlessly looking out the large view window. He had so many questions about what he had just overheard. Thankfully, it seemed he would have plenty of time to think while they waited for an unknown rescuer.

34 – MAXAR

What a day, Maxar thought, wondering what would happen next. Their worm generator was permanently broken. Jaydon had told Maxar that the "blighthearted buggering piece of equipment is terminally buggered." The drive had nearly cost them their lives, but everything was working out OK so far.

The arrival of the Entho bi-pyramid had surprised everyone on board the Revenge, but seeing the huge Ashamine ship behind it was terrifying. They had believed, as stupid as it sounded now, that the Ashamine had sent the battle ship to recapture Maxar. Once they thought about the situation however, they realized the Ashamine craft was tailing the Entho ship, not their own. Everyone shared a sigh of relief, but they were still left with the problem of their inability to escape the supernova shock wave.

It had been Tremmilly's idea to slip through the Entho worm hole after the Ashamine ship. The maneuver was extremely risky, but it held better odds than the alternative. They had barely made it through, and that was a generous way of saying it. Maxar was surprised the decrepit old craft had survived. Still, making it to Eishon-2 before all of their atmosphere slipped out of rents in the hull would be a close thing.

Their fun little escape had been further complicated when they saw the battle between the Ashamine ship and the Entho bi-pyramid. Maxar felt no remorse for those who had perished on the Ashamine side. He knew they deserved no pity. He did feel bad for the Enthos, but sometimes that was how things went.

Ironically enough, the Revenge had ended up in the very system they had wanted to go to in the first place, Eishon. Maxar watched Tremmilly go pale when they realized where in the galaxy they were. He hadn't understood why, and all she would say in answer was to mumble, "Leading or intuition?". *She is one strange girl,* Maxar decided. Not that he didn't thank both her and the drunk Jaydon for getting him off Bloodsport, but he firmly believed they both had issues. Somehow, the two were growing on him though, and Maxar didn't know how to feel about that. At least he could leave them once he got off this shabby ship.

Tremmilly's home planet was small, out of the way, and lightly populated. He'd never heard of it, so chances were no one would know who he was or that he'd been sentenced to Bloodsport. Since an Ashamine vessel had been destroyed in the system, investigators would soon be nosing around, but they had no reason to come down to the planet. It would be a great place to lie low for a while.

They were on their way towards her home on Eishon-2 when Jaydon let out an exclamation of surprise. "I fund shomthing," he said, but it was unclear what his feelings were on the matter, at least from his tone. Both Tremmilly and Maxar were engaged in a game of Castle, but rose and went to see what the constant drunk had found.

When they arrived, they saw nothing interesting, at least initially. After they had a closer look at the terminal screen, they realized why Jaydon had called them. The terminal showed a stationary blinking dot in near proximity to them. It was located along the path the Ashamine and Entho ships had followed after leaving the worm. Maxar thought he knew what it meant, but Tremmilly didn't understand. "What is it?" she questioned.

"It's han scape boat," Jaydon returned, his words partially slurred from alcohol.

"You mean someone actually survived that... that..." Maxar said, uncharacteristically at a loss for the word to sum up the battle.

"Well, ushually those sings honly blip lihike that when there is shomething shtill kicking insidesit." The owner and captain of the A'Tal's Revenge was fairly close to being drunk and his words came out in a rush. Maxar had spent little time with the man, but already he was realizing the captain had a heck of a thirst for booze, any kind of booze, at any time of the day or night. "Do ya whanna gho pickit up?"

The question hung in the air momentarily, neither Maxar nor Tremmilly answering. Maxar was ready to tell the drunk to keep them flying towards Eishon-2, but before he had the chance, Tremmilly answered. "Yes, if we can help someone, we should do it."

"The margin of safely making it to the planet before we suffocate is precariously thin. Adding more people will slice the margin further. Is it worth the risk to rescue unknown, possibly hostile Ashamine personnel?"

"Maxar, we can't just leave someone to die out here," Tremmilly responded, a disapproving look on her face.

Jaydon, not seeming to care either way, began piloting the ship towards the pod. Maxar turned to the girl and spoke, making sure he was loud enough so Jaydon was included in the conversation. "If we take Ashamine soldiers back to your planet, they will bring a lot of hurt down on us. Anyone who watches much Bloodsport will recognize me, and if one of those solders is a fan, another Ashamine battle cruiser will be breathing down our necks in no time. Even if none of them recognize me, at the very least we will all be questioned about the destruction of the Ashamine ship. We will be required to testify. I for one don't look forward to doing anything like that, especially since I so recently escaped incarceration."

Maxar thought he had never seen someone look at him with so much incredulity in their eyes. "You, of all people should be able to empathize with someone in need of rescue. I still don't understand why I came to get you, but I can see a clear reason for going to get whoever is in that escape craft." Maxar was never one to allow himself to be corrected, but Tremmilly's words cut him deep. He didn't let it show, a trait he had learned from being pitted against some of the most vicious criminals in the Akked Galaxy.

Jaydon dutifully brought the ship towards the Ashamine escape pod, only weaving the vessel slightly in doing so. The time to cover the intervening distance passed largely in silence. Maxar didn't feel like finishing the game of Castles, and Tremmilly didn't seem interested either. Jaydon continued drinking, something he apparently did as a hobby.

The hull of the pod was intact and they could see no visible damage or atmosphere leakage. Maxar still thought taking any survivors with them was a bad idea, but he held his tongue, not wanting to provoke Tremmilly's wrath any more than he had already. *Why does this girl have that power over me?* Jaydon tried hailing the small craft, but received no reply in return.

"I whonder if heir rhadio got damaged or shomething," Jaydon remarked, the seriousness of his tone almost lost in his drunken slurring. It was getting impossible to understand him.

Before he really thought of what he was doing, Maxar bent over a terminal and initiated the radio between the two crafts. "Listen," he said, his voice cold and commanding, "if you don't talk with us, we aren't going to pick you up. If we don't pick you up, you are going to float out here for a very, very long time."

When he had finished speaking, a voice that sounded like a young boy came over the speakers of the Revenge, "We are running from the Ashamine, will you help us?" The directness in the boy's words took Maxar aback. While, he was still contemplating his answer, an older voice came on, one of a woman. "I'm sorry, my son is somewhat distraught and doesn't realize what he is saying. We were running from the supernova, not the Ashamine. May I ask who it is we are speaking to?"

Maxar honestly had no idea how to answer that one, so he shut his mouth. This time, Tremmilly answered, "We are friends and we'll get you and your son out of there and to safety." Her voice sounded odd, and while she spoke, she reached her hand up to her head as if she were experiencing a headache. Maxar shook his head in amazement. He had never been around someone this strange. In the short time since he had met her, there had been many episodes of weirdness. That was OK he supposed, at least that trait had caused her to come to Bloodsport to save him.

"Thank you very much," the woman in the escape vessel said. He could hear something familiar in that voice, but couldn't quite place what it was. Had he known this woman before? That sounded impossible, but he guessed it wasn't totally out of the question. Then, after a moment of consideration, he understood. The reason the voice sounded so familiar was the way she had spoken in a clipped tone, not quite emotionless, but close. It was the tone of someone used to getting respect. Perhaps she had been a Bloodsporter? But then why would she have been on the Ashamine ship? Most likely she was some type of officer. Regardless, her tone spoke of someone used to authority of some type, and Maxar would do well to stay on guard.

Amazingly enough, Jaydon didn't smash either the Revenge or the small escape vehicle in the tricky docking procedure. Maxar didn't care what happened, so he was largely relaxed, but Tremmilly was high strung, uttering nervous noises every time Jaydon narrowly avoided smashing the two crafts together.

The docking complete, Jaydon rose to go usher in his new guests. He promptly fell back into his seat, his balance lost due to the alcohol coursing through his body. "Will yhou both khindly welcome the new ar-ar-arrivals?" he asked. Maxar could barely understand the sot, but he made out the words. He didn't want to do it, but he supposed he couldn't expect Tremmilly to go alone or with only Beowulf for support. It was possible those on the escape vehicle would make an attempt to capture the ship, but Maxar thought it unlikely.

Tremmilly led the way to the docking port, Beowulf and Maxar trailing behind her. She pressurized the short section of corridor connecting the two vessels and then opened the ship's end. The escape vehicle's end was still closed, the fresh paint of the door making the disrepair of the Revenge more apparent.

Maxar, standing behind Tremmilly, saw her raise her hand to her head in much the same way as she had done on the command deck. "You got a headache or something?" he asked, trying not to sound exasperated because of the delay of the escape vehicle's hatch.

"No, not really," she said absentmindedly. Maxar waited for her to continue, but when it didn't seem likely she would do so, he spoke once again.

"Well it's just that you keep putting your hand up on your head, like it hurts or something. Are you feeling OK?"

Still taking little note of what Maxar was doing or saying, Tremmilly did manage to answer. "Yeah, I'm fine. Just a little distracted. It's a strange feeling. I can sense something on the other side of this door." Beowulf emitted a high pitched whine as Tremmilly finished speaking, causing Maxar to start. What had she meant by feeling something on the other side of the door? He decided, yet again, that the girl was definitely not right mentally. Sure she looked great, but by the Founder she sure did have a strange personality. *Can't let myself get too attached to her,* he thought, and then was surprised when he realized he needed to warn himself at all.

The sound of the escape vehicle's hatch opening broke into Maxar's thoughts. The woman who stepped through immediately impressed him as a hard headed, stiff necked, by the books kind of person. Hence the dislike that rose in him. He couldn't tell exactly why, but he still felt his instinct to leave the escape vehicle had been the correct choice. Then he noticed her military fatigues and all his first impressions were confirmed. *Military. Just great,* he thought sardonically. Things hadn't gone perfectly in escaping the Bloodsport, but they had gone well enough. Now he feared all of that had been for naught.

Maxar carefully schooled his face to look neutral and betray nothing of his inner turmoil. This was not difficult, being something he practiced plenty back on the Bloodsport. When the kid stepped through the hatch though, it became exponentially harder to maintain his passive expression.

The kid was small and scrawny, his black hair messy and unkempt. His clothes were clean for the most part, but they hung on him, making him look even smaller. These qualities weren't what disconcerted Maxar so much however. It was his eyes. They were orange, just like the Founders. Maxar had never seen such eyes anywhere but in the vids and pix of the Founder. And this kid took the Founder's direct and penetrating gaze to a whole new level. The kid's eyes were boring into him, digging down to his soul. He gazed into those eyes and couldn't pull himself out. Deeper... Deeper...

Then the woman spoke and broke him out of his trance. "I'm 3rd Class Enlightened Felar Haltro. This," she said, pointing to the twig Founder, "is my son Jon." Everyone stood motionless in the silence that followed. Tremmilly, waking from her previous strange behavior, broke it.

"My name is Tremmilly, and this is Maxar," she noted, pointing to him. "This large dog here is my friend Beowulf. Don't worry, he's big, but his kindness is as massive as he is." *Sure it is,* Maxar thought, *good story. Ignore the fact you saw him tearing out throats back on the orbital dock.* The woman Felar and the twig boy Jon noticed the big wolf-dog then for the first time, and they reacted as if they had heard Maxar's thought. Twig boy let out a high pitched yelp and clutched at the woman, who, reacting with a fighter's reflexes, reached for a weapon that was not holstered at her belt. Maxar noted the movement, filing the slice of knowledge away for further analysis later.

"Don't worry, he won't hurt you. I promise. See?" Tremmilly was now stroking Beowulf, his long, lustrous coat flowing through the girl's fingers. The wolf-dog normally looked quite intimidating, but with the gorgeous girl petting him, the animal lost some of that ferocious look. He even had the good sense to roll onto his back to further the illusion of harmlessness.

Twig boy poked his head out from his mother, and after watching for a few moments, cautiously walked to the dog and began petting him alongside Tremmilly. Beowulf's right rear leg began to kick the air in pleasure, but the boy, not understanding the movement, jumped away in fright. "No, no, he just does that when he likes what you are doing," Tremmilly said in a reassuring voice. The boy then resumed petting the dog which was quite brave considering all the previous scares.

"This isn't my ship," Tremmilly said, standing up from her position near Beowulf and walking towards Felar, "but make yourself at home. If you would like to meet the captain, he is on the command deck."

Felar was looking at her surroundings, seeming to have decided none of them were imminent threats. The look on her face made it evident she thought about as much of the ship as Maxar did. "Alright," Felar said curtly. She seemed to note the near hostility in her voice, because when she spoke again it had vanished. "We are both so grateful you picked us up." Felar gave Maxar an appraising look and then asked, "Are you military?"

The directness of her question caught Maxar off guard and he didn't immediately know what to say. "No. Why do you ask?" She looked at him suspiciously, but what she saw apparently didn't match her thoughts, because the look left as quickly as it had arrived.

"You have the look of a soldier about you," she said dismissively. Maxar stole a look at Tremmilly out of the corner of his eye and gave silent thanks the girl wasn't giving anything away in her expression. Given she was so transparent most of the time, it was a minor miracle in his opinion. "What caused the holes in the hull of this ship?" Felar continued, catching Maxar off guard yet again.

"In our haste to escape Haak-ah-tar, we accidentally flew through some garbage an Ashamine ship had jettisoned. Must have torn us up pretty good because we're venting atmosphere. Should have enough to make it to Eishon-2 though." He tried to say the last bit as nonchalantly as possible, hoping she would drop the subject.

"Really," was all Felar said in reply, sounding less than convinced.

"Well, let's go see if the great Captain Jaydon is still conscious," Tremmilly said cheerily, smoothly transitioning them from the awkward silence that had followed Felar's last statement. Maxar let out a single bark of laughter at the girl's pronouncement.

They all followed Tremmilly as she led the way through the litter strewn ship to the command deck. Maxar brought up the rear, not wanting the soldier woman or the twig boy behind him. Beowulf amicably trotted at his side, happy with Maxar's companionship.

When they reached the deck, they found Jaydon unconscious, the bottle he had been drinking from lying on the floor, some of its contents having spilled on the deck. Beowulf trotted over and began licking at the clear liquid. When Tremmilly realized what he was doing, she scolded him and he came trotting back. Maxar even thought the wolf-dog looked somewhat abashed, although how that was possible he couldn't tell.

"Is your captain always this way or is this how he welcomes his guests?" Felar's tone was hard to interpret. He couldn't tell if she was joking or if she was being sarcastically cutting. She continued in her hard tone, and it quickly resolved his indecision. "I thought the maneuvering of the ship was erratic. It was highly irresponsible for you to allow this man to pilot a ship while intoxicated, let alone attempt a rescue. Jon and I could have been killed by his reckless flying." *Ingrate,* Maxar thought to himself.

"He is usually like this," Tremmilly said timidly, answering Felar's original question, "although I haven't known him for long." Whatever Felar made of this answer, she gave no outward sign. Instead, she started a new topic.

"What is your destination? Can you fly the ship or must we wait for the captain to sober up?" Maxar could see the woman was trying to think her plans out several steps in advance, always a desirable trait in a soldier. He had never thought her inept, but a small amount of respect arose in him for her wisdom.

"Well, we are headed for Eishon-2. There aren't a lot of flights off that world, so I don't know how long you'll be stuck there, but it's better there than being in space right?" There was a note of hopeful conciliation in Tremmilly's voice, apparently wishing the older woman would forgive her for Jaydon's drunkenness.

"That's fine," Felar responded, too quickly. She tried to stay emotionless, but Maxar picked up the momentary flash of desire that had crossed her face. This too was filed back in his mind for later review. Then something clicked.

Why is someone who is on active military duty traveling with her son? It was obvious the woman was on duty due to the fact she was in uniform. The Ashamine Forces only wore their uniforms when on duty. Something about Felar and the twig boy didn't add up. Maxar didn't want to figure it out though, he just wanted to get away from them. Anyone connected to the Ashamine would have a duty to subdue him and barring that, at least report him.

"Either myself or Maxar can fly this craft though, so don't worry about having to wait for Jaydon to come back to the land of the living." Tremmilly was still trying to lighten up the situation and her latest effort was having a positive effect.

"That's great, real great," Felar said, a smile finally gracing her face. Maxar noted how beautiful it made her look, but it did little to change his desire to put as much distance between himself and the woman as possible.

Maxar turned to look at the boy, only to see him staring directly at him. That gaze was disconcerting in the extreme and Maxar wished the kid would quit using it on him. The fact the boy had said nothing the whole time he had been on the ship was even stranger still. Plus, other than his initial fright of Beowulf, he was unnaturally calm. A normal kid would be flapping from all the drama of having to escape a ship that was smashed to pieces and then float around helplessly in the void for a while. *Not natural, not natural at all.*

After carrying Jaydon to the cargo hold, Maxar took a crate back to the command deck. He sat in the corner, watching Tremmilly switch the system over to auto-nav. Beowulf lay down next to him, and Maxar began petting the shaggy wolf-dog. Soon, Tremmilly and Felar got over their initial awkwardness and were talking, discussing their pasts and the current situation. The twig boy Jon kept staring at Maxar, his orange eyes piecing. *This is going to be a long thirty minutes,* Maxar thought, trying to ignore him.

35 – TREMMILLY

An alarm began to blare and Tremmilly turned her attention to the console. A surge of fear coursed through her. "We just hit the critical level for air." She reached forward and selected an option to silence the alarm.

Maxar stood from the crate he'd been inhabiting in the corner and checked the display. He looked thoughtful for a moment and then announced, "It's gonna be close, but I think we'll make it."

Silence descended over the command deck. Tremmilly was still nervous. The thought of being trapped in a space with no air kept running through her mind. *I have to focus on something else,* she thought. *There is nothing I can do about it now.*

"Where were you stationed before the Founder's Hammer?" Tremmilly finally asked Felar, resuming the conversation they'd been having before the alarm sounded.

"Ashamine-4. It's the AF training world. I was an instructor there for a while," Felar replied, looking up from Jon, a concerned look on her face.

Tremmilly too was worried about Jon. He had been focused inwardly the entire time he'd been on the ship. "Is she the girl? And which one is the convict?" he said to himself, alternating looks between Tremmilly, the doorway to the cargo hold, and Maxar. *How does he know there is a convict on board?* His orange eyes reminded her of something she couldn't quite grasp hold of.

"Ashamine-4 sounds like an interesting place," Tremmilly replied distractedly. "I've never been anywhere but Eishon-2 and Noor-5. That's why I'm excited to go back. It will be great to see Psidonnis after so long." Maxar returned to his seat in the corner, seeming content to be silent. He hadn't said much since Felar and Jon had come aboard. *I bet he's still worried Felar will turn him in.* Tremmilly had no such worries. The woman had dropped her stern exterior, and she felt a kinship with the Ashamine soldier.

The ship's terminal beeped loudly, signaling their proximity to Eishon-

2. Tremmilly looked out the window, tearing up with happiness. "Those oceans are pristine," she said, pointing out the view window, "clean blue water stretching out as far as you can see. I've never sailed on it, not many do, but I have been to the beach. If you follow the line of those snowy mountains south, you'll see a vast plain bordered by forests on three sides. We are headed to the western edge of the plains. That's where my home is."

"I'm excited to see it," Felar said. Maxar nodded and smiled in response.

"There are a few things I should probably tell you about my village." Tremmilly said, growing nervous as they approached the grass landing area outside the village. "It is made up of mostly Dygars. Their customs are strange. And I'm not sure what they will say to you. I just wanted to warn you not to be offended."

"Do they sacrifice humans?" Maxar asked, mock horror on his face.

"No," Tremmilly said, laughing, "nothing like that. The priests can just be an odd bunch, that's all."

"I'm sure we can handle it," Felar said. "And maybe Jaydon can get counseling from Psidonnis or another priest. He obviously needs it."

After a few more minutes of conversation, the ship set down gently and went to standby. Tremmilly walked back into the cargo hold, hoping Jaydon would be awake. He hadn't moved and was still passed out, clutching his bottle.

"Well, guess you'll have to catch up with us once you wake up," she told him. Tremmilly hoped Jaydon would decide to stay on Eishon-2 for a while. The peacefulness of the place would help him heal, even if he decided against talking to a priest. "You still owe me the story about who I remind you of. I'm holding you to that," she said with a sad smile, hitting the button to open the hatch.

Felar, Jon, and Maxar followed her outside and Tremmilly was surprised to see a priest standing a short way off from the ship. Her heart soared as she walked towards her old friend Psidonnis. The man was old and bald like him, but as she drew closer, she realized it wasn't Psidonnis. In fact, it wasn't anyone she even knew. "Terra bless you children," he said in a beatific tone. "I am Brother Torvold. Father Psidonnis sent me to fetch you. He foresaw your coming." Tremmilly noticed Felar and Maxar exchanging looks, but was thankful neither one said anything. The boy took it all in stride, his penetrating orange eyes absorbing everything going on around him.

"Terra bless you too, Brother Torvold," Tremmilly said, bowing her head slightly in respect. "Thank you for coming to escort us." The priest bowed in return and began walking towards the settlement, gesturing for them to follow.

"While you were off planet, Brother Psidonnis was raised to a Father," Brother Torvold said as they walked. "His prophecy accorded him great honor and prestige. Terra manifested through him, showing us all her favor." Brother Torvold then fell silent, looking as if he had something he needed to say. Tremmilly kept quiet, a sinking feeling building in her stomach. "Shortly after the ceremony, Father Psidonnis suffered a stroke. The Healing Father looked at him, but said there was nothing to be done. He has been resting in his cottage ever since."

Tremmilly, upon hearing these words, broke into a run towards the settlement, tears streaming from her eyes. Beowulf ran easily at her heels, empathetic of her grief. Her desire to see Psidonnis narrowed her vision, and she failed to notice any of the familiar sights that greeted her homecoming. When she entered the cottage, Tremmilly gasped in horror.

Psidonnis, while never a robust individual, now looked withered and atrophied. He was obviously being well cared for, but looked terrible. Tremmilly rushed to him, all the fears that had been conjured by Brother Torvold's words now made manifest before her. When she sank beside his cot, a choked sob escaped her lips. Psidonnis' eyes came open and he smiled. A jagged sliver of pain was driven into Tremmilly as she saw that one eye didn't open as far as the other, that half of the formerly radiant smile didn't exist. The stroke had done considerable damage, one side of his face no longer cooperating with the wishes of his brain.

"Hello Trem," he said, his voice slurring the mellifluous tones she had heard her entire life. This, more than anything else, drove home the realization that he was damaged. She wanted him to get up, to quit giving her that inadvertent sneer of a smile, but it wasn't going to happen. She felt helplessness and despair engulf her.

"Hail Psidonnis," she said, returning the greeting they had performed so many times before. "I wish I had never gone. This wouldn't have happened if I had stayed here," she said, tears coming to her eyes. *How could he have changed so much in just six weeks?*

"You had no control over this," Psidonnis said reassuringly. "There was nothing you could have done." He raised his left arm and used it to gesture her closer, embracing her as best he could. "I sent you away. Great Terra has shown me much of your journey though. I know you brought someone back, a few someones in fact." Tremmilly didn't know how to respond to this, so she sat in silence.

"You did a great job Trem," Psidonnis continued. "I knew you would. It is scary going off world, but you did it. I'm afraid, however, there is more work to be done."

At these words Tremmilly stiffened, ready to fight his judgment. "I'm not leaving you again, especially not when you are like this. I won't let you die." Her words tasted bitter in her mouth.

"Tremmilly, I am going to die," he said bluntly, the slur of his voice reducing the severity of his tone. Tremmilly was surprised at his words, momentarily stunned.

"I'll take you off world so real doctors can take care of you. They'll fix you, reverse the damage." This idea revitalized her, gave her hope. Even before she had finished speaking he was shaking his head though.

"That's a great idea Tremmilly and we could go right now if it weren't for the fact that time is precious and growing short. There is no time for you to waste on me."

"Waste?! Waste?!" she shouted back, her voice becoming shrill. "What is more important than saving the life of my most beloved friend? Tell me!"

"If you had the choice between saving me and saving everyone in the universe and all the generations to come, what would you do?" he asked, some of the slur replaced with a commanding tone. Tremmilly calmed considerably, responding to his authority.

"That question makes no sense and has no answer," she replied, refusing to give in. "I'm not the Founder, able to influence the galaxy. I can merely love and help those closest to me."

"Even the smallest pebble may change the course of a mighty river if it is close enough to the river's source. I know you want to take care of me, but you must not. You don't have the time. I'm telling you that great and terrible events are ahead of us, and you are but a small pebble. You must try to get as close to the river's source as possible, must divert it so we are not all swept away." Some of the vitality was beginning to drain from his eyes and he was growing more exhausted as she watched.

"You need to rest. You look tired," she implored him, feeling drained herself.

"Yes, yes," he replied distractedly, his eyes, both the open and the veiled, taking on a far off look that didn't ease her fears at all. "Just remember that I will always love you." She rose from beside his cot and walked to the door.

"We can talk more when I get back," she said, fighting hard not to begin sobbing. "I'm going to go get some blankets or a cot so I can sleep near you, that way if you need anything, I can get it." He didn't seem to notice her leaving.

When she returned to the cottage, Psidonnis was dead.

***

The memorial for her greatest human friend was held two days after, during a sunny afternoon. The wind was blowing gently, rushing through the full green leaves of the trees. Tremmilly thought it a fitting day to remember a gentle and kind man. When they laid him to rest in mother Terra, his flesh bare and ready to receive her embrace, Tremmilly quit trying to resist her emotions. She cried and cried, great sobs wracking her small frame. Her parents had passed before she understood what death meant. That loss had been dulled with time, but this—this was fresh, deep, and raw.

As she was leaving the memorial, a hand snaked around her own, squeezing it tightly. When she was able to blink away enough tears to see, she saw Felar standing next to her, her son Jon following close behind. She squeezed Felar's hand back, grateful she had a new friend to be with as she said goodbye to an old one. Maxar and Jaydon soon joined the group, bringing more light to Tremmilly's darkness. Jaydon's movements were graceful and he didn't have his bottle with him.

They all walked in silence for a while, taking in the bright sunshine and fresh air. "We're sorry for your loss," Maxar said, as Tremmilly stopped near the bank of a stream. The water coursed through well worn rocks, the sound soothing her raw emotions.

"Thank you," was all Tremmilly could think of as a response.

"I hate to have to talk about it right now," Maxar said awkwardly, "but we all need to discuss what happens next." He paused for several moments, and when no one responded, pushed on. "Felar, what do you think the Ashamine response will be?"

Felar thought for a moment, then replied, "I doubt anyone on the Hammer had time to transmit their location to Ashamine Forces Command, so they'll have to send out ships to look for it. That will take time, but Eishon-2 is a known worm location, so they will be here before too long. Once they find the debris, they'll send out an investigative team." She paused for a moment, looking unsure.

"What is it?" Tremmilly asked, the discussion drawing her out of her grief.

"Well," Felar said, hesitatingly, "the Hammer was carrying some pretty important cargo. I'm guessing the Ashamine will send out more than just a team. They'll probably dispatch a whole battle group to recover it."

"Great," Maxar replied, shaking his head.

"What kind of cargo?" Jaydon asked, his coherent question surprising Tremmilly.

"It was classified above my level," Felar answered.

Maxar had a resigned, disappointed look in his eyes. "Whatever it is, they'll be crawling all over Eishon-2 asking questions, looking for it. I had hoped to be able to stay here for at least a little while, but now it's really important for Tremmilly, Jaydon, and I to head somewhere outside the Eishon system."

"You all did nothing wrong," Felar said, looking puzzled, "why not wait a while? Tremmilly is in the midst of her grief and the ship is in dire need of repairs."

Tremmilly looked at Jaydon and Maxar, hoping one of them would explain. Neither did. OK, *if they aren't going to fabricate a good lie, I'll tell the truth.*

"Before I left Eishon-2, Psidonnis made a prophecy. It's the whole reason I left in the first place. I only understand parts of it, and I'm not even sure I have those right. Even though I loved Psidonnis, I have mixed feelings about the prophecy. Initially, I only followed it because I wanted some excitement in my life. In the end, I got more than I wanted, but I also met all of you. I don't believe in gods, but it seems like *something* is leading me. Maybe it's just my intuition and chance." She felt like she wasn't making sense, but Felar was giving her an encouraging look, so she continued.

"Anyway, following the leading or whatever took me to the A'Tal's Revenge and Jaydon." Tremmilly paused and she could see Maxar tensing, knowing what she was about to say. "Jaydon helped me get to Bloodsport, where we rescued Maxar."

Felar looked over at Maxar, unsurprised. "I figured as much. Your story about being a merchant on Haak-ah-tar was pretty flimsy. You're a warrior and it shows. If it makes you feel any better, you don't have to worry about me reporting you. I don't owe the Ashamine anything."

"You're an Enlightened. That's not exactly a new conscript," Maxar said. Tremmilly could tell he was angry with her for telling his secret, but Felar had responded how Tremmilly thought she would. It would be much easier now she didn't have to keep a secret. Tremmilly hoped she hadn't damaged her growing friendship with Maxar.

"You're right," Felar answered, her voice level, "but lately some things have made me question my allegiance. Those events have also put me into a position where I need to stay away from the Ashamine investigation as well. The truth is, I kidnapped Jon from his father. He was an abusive man, but highly ranked in the Ashamine. If they find Jon, they'll take him back to his father and I'll be put to death."

This revelation surprised Tremmilly, but made sense when she thought about it. The woman's tough exterior, the boy's quietness: everything fell into place. "I'm so sorry," Tremmilly said, putting her arm around Jon. The boy reluctantly accepted her affection, eyes focused elsewhere.

"So," Felar said, a wan smile on her face, "it looks like Maxar and I at least have need to stay away from the blighthearted Ashamine. Tremmilly, you could probably remain here though. All record of you and Jaydon's presence at the Bloodsport was likely destroyed in the supernova."

"I have no reason to stay here," Tremmilly replied, trying not to start crying again. "Besides, there is the prophecy. Captain Jaydon, is your ship still for hire?"

"Ain't nobody paid me yet, and it's busted," he said, "but yes, I'll continue to let you all fly my ship around the buggered Akked. Drunk in a dock or drunk in space, doesn't matter one bit to me."

"The hull of the Revenge needs a day or two of repair work," Maxar said, "and we'll need to find someone to repair the worm drive, if that is possible."

Jaydon thought for a moment. "If I stay sober, we can get the hull done in a couple hours." Tremmilly doubted that would happen. *I'll do my best to help him stick to it.*

"And what about this prophecy?" Felar asked. "Am I in it?" Her words sounded like she was joking, but Tremmilly could see the underlying seriousness.

"I'm not sure." Tremmilly's embarrassment returned. *They're my friends, they'll understand.* "The best way for you to know is to listen and see for yourself."

Tremmilly began a recitation of the prophecy, completely from memory and exactly as Psidonnis had told her originally:

"When the Breakers rise, there shall be six on whose choices the worlds do lie. The choice of virtue or corruption will bring an ancient existence to many, death to more still. Persevere and strive, the Acclivity will bless those who survive.

"Six shall have great influence, many choices when the Breakers rise. Woe to six, that Breakers have experience when they have none. Six shall have need of all their will.

"The first be of a light most bright, spirit most pure. Her life touched by death before cognition, her desire only for peace. She shall start the fire that kindles the worlds to the Acclivity. Woe to the Breakers.

"The next shall have hands that shed blood, his blood in motion with machines. He does not know his heart, yet through course of life he shall learn what to see. He shall be the strong hands that guide the Acclivity, albeit he is not gentle. Woe to the Breakers.

"She of battle will fight beside the hands, her heart ferocious, yet kind. Her path has been strange, her child not of her blood. She shall be a strong pillar, the Acclivity magnified through her strength. Woe to the Breakers.

"Next is a man of character, the dead that is found, wearing that which is ancient, the icon of legends long past. His heart is good and powerful, a mighty man to lead the Acclivity. Woe to the Breakers.

"He that is green has strength of mind, his people are his weapon. He is dissimilar, but his heart is good; send him not away. He shall unite a people unspoiled, he shall be the salvation of those of his kind. He shall bring his kind to the Acclivity, and the worlds will tremble at their might. Woe to the Breakers.

"Last is he smallest of all, but a boy in the eyes of the world. He is descended from power, full of power, wielding power. His mind is a weapon, though his hands be frail. His heart is strong, though his body may fail. He has the power of life, the gift of death. The Acclivity rests on his shoulders. Woe to the Breakers.

"All six shall have friends and foes alike, some from within and some from out. Many more shall sway the Acclivity, many more essential. Some will live and many more will die. Come forth you adventurers, you seekers of battle. The Acclivity calls, though the Breakers may yet decide the fate of the worlds.

"But to you who would stay in comfort and safety, not yielding to the call: Blightheart shall establish itself on you and the worlds will be sundered by the Breakers."

36 – CAZZ-AK-TAK

Cazz-ak-tak knew that he, Elth-eo-lan, and the new Queen were the only ones left. He was surprised they had survived the destruction of their ship. His last minute effort had been the only thing standing between the Queen and complete annihilation. He could feel appreciation coming from both of his surviving ship mates.

In a way, Cazz-ak was sorry he had made the effort. He had spared them from a quick and possibly painless death in favor of one that would be slow and agonizing. The harder he fought death, the worse the potential outcome became. He kept all of this inner turmoil from Elth-eo-lan and the Queen, not wanting to demoralize either of them.

At first he had been able to draw on the Great Thought to move their small orb through space. Now, with the death of the rest of the crew on the main ship, he had lost the focused power of connection to the Great Thought. The three of them alone could barely move the small craft, its interior cramped, dark, and devoid of gravity.

"Come stand next to the hull," Cazz-ak had directed back on the bi-pyramid, before the debris had hit them. Elth-eo-lan and the Queen had done so, trusting him to save them. Focusing through the Great Thought, Cazz-ak molded a portion of the hull around them, creating a small escape vessel. *This will save us,* he thought hopefully. Now it seemed as if their salvation would become their doom. When they ran out of breathable atmosphere—which, considering the small space, would not take long—the end would come quickly, but not painlessly.

"My name is Na-ah-co," the new Queen said mind to mind, breaking into Cazz-ak's thoughts. At first he didn't know what to make of her declaration. It came out of no where and was outside custom. Usually the queen was named by a council of elders, her name symbolic of the times she lived in.

"It means, 'She who mocks adversity'," Elth-eo-lan sent, breaking into the momentary pause that had developed after the Queen's declaration. Her voice sounded happy and Cazz-ak had no idea why.

"It is for the elders to decide your name," Cazz-ak sent, a slight note of disapproval in his tone. "Please do not be hasty, my Queen."

"It is not for you to rebuke me," she sent, her voice stern and developed, surprising in one so young. "I am your Queen, I am Na-ah-co, she who mocks adversity. I see no elders here to name me."

"As you say, my Queen," Cazz-ak replied, bowing his head down slightly in deference. He supposed in reality it mattered little what her name was or who picked it. What mattered was that she was strong and growing stronger by the minute. It was good she was healthy, good she had the makings of a powerful queen.

"You fear you have brought us all here to die, that it will be painful. You believe it would have been better to have a quick death on the ship in a flash of light as opposed to dying in the dark of this orb." She had brought out his thoughts exactly, thoughts he had tried to keep from her. Was she that strong or had his mental shield slipped?

"As you say, Queen Na-ah-co. I only fear for your safety," Cazz-ak sent.

"Calm your fear. Even now, as you despair, there come those who will take us to safety. They try to contact us with electro-magnetic signals." Cazz-ak wondered how she knew this, but he remained silent. The hull of their small orb was thick and opaque, making it impossible to see out. She must have sensed them with her mind, but that was a feat Cazz-ak had never heard of. The detection of life other than Entho-la-ah-mine had never been demonstrated, the sensing of frequencies outside visible light thought impossible. This young queen had somehow done one, the other, or both. Of course she could be imagining it, perhaps out of desperation or hope.

"No, do not doubt me. They draw near," she replied to his unvoiced doubts. He was transparent to her it seemed.

Just as he was about to apologize for his doubt, Cazz-ak felt the orb drop slightly and crash against something. Everyone fell into a pile at the bottom of the orb. Cazz-ak realized, dazedly, that there was now gravity. He guessed they were inside another ship, its artificial gravity effecting them.

This thought of the ship made Cazz-ak wonder who it was that had picked them up. It was most certainly humans, and from Cazz-ak's experience, most humans were menacing, angry beings. He wondered briefly if death in space would be better than what these humans probably had in mind. "No," the Queen once again sent, "they are friends, at least for the moment." That statement puzzled Cazz-ak.

A light tapping on the hull announced someone was outside their pod. "Join your minds to mine," Queen Na-ah-co sent. She took up the threads of their thought and strengthened them, focusing it into a shape that resembled a thin knife. As both Cazz-ak and Elth-eo-lan watched, the Queen cut an opening large enough for them to walk through.

Once the section of hull fell outward to the floor, the Queen stepped boldly through, not waiting to see if her caretakers were going to follow. Cazz-ak beat Elth-eo-lan to the new hatch, immediately catching sight of their hosts.

They were tall, at least from Cazz-ak's perspective, but then all humans seemed that way, except for their immature form. There were two of them, one somewhat taller than the other. The taller one had dark brown hair that came down to his odd human ears. Cazz-ak thought his eyes were a strange, penetrating gray color. It made him think of the frozen worlds he had been to, of gray ice. The shorter man was slightly smaller than was average for a human. His hair reminded Cazz-ak of fire.

"I'm Wake Darmekus, Brotherhood of Azak-so," the taller one said audibly, bowing slightly towards the group of Entho-la-ah-mines. "This is Ralen Call, also of the Brotherhood of Azak-so. You are on board the Ashamine's Bane." Once the man had introduced himself and his comrade, the room fell silent. No one spoke, either audibly or mentally. Cazz-ak knew the right of contact was reserved for the Queen, but then he realized perhaps she wanted him to handle the negotiations.

"My name is Cazz-ak-tak," he finally replied via mental link. Both men were somewhat startled, their manner becoming more wary. They looked at each other, trying to confirm that what had just happened had not been some type of hallucination. "This is Elth-eo-lan and Na-ah-co," he sent to both men, motioning to each when he said their name. He deliberately omitted the title of queen from Na-ah-co, suspecting that would be the wisest course of action until the humans showed their intentions.

"I'm not meaning to be rude, but is this the manner in which you communicate? The reason I ask is that I have never been near any Enthos and am unclear on any customs or procedures that need to be followed." The man named Wake was cautious in his speech, talking calmly and with respect, other than the use of "Entho", which was a common derogatory term. This was not Cazz-ak's first time dealing with humans, but it was going better than any previous meeting he had ever been a part of.

"We have no ability to speak via sound waves," Cazz-ak explained. "Having our mental capabilities, the function never evolved."

"Ah I see," Wake said, a contemplative look crossing his face. Cazz-ak had studied humans as much as was possible for someone in his position. Knowing how they acted and reacted was important in dealing with this species. Learning their language had helped tremendously. Much of what they thought and felt was displayed clearly on their face, but language, with all its tones and inflections, added an even greater advantage during negotiation. "At any rate, we wish there were more of your kind for us to pick up, but our sensors tell us you are the only living things out there. There was another vessel that came in behind the big Ashamine ship. They picked up one of its escape vehicles and sped off to Eishon-2." Wake seemed to realize he was rambling and stopped, looking over to Ralen.

"Well, we'd be real happy if you'd follow us up to the command deck," Ralen added. The Captain would like to speak with you. He wants to know a little about you and what you'd have us do now that you're on board." Cazz-ak could see Ralen's small frame grow more relaxed as he spoke.

Cazz-ak gave his assent to the plan, Elth-eo-lan and Na-ah-co remaining silent. They followed Ralen and Wake through some narrow passages and onto the command deck of the Ashamine's Bane. It was a small space, and there wasn't enough room for all of them to go in at the same time. Cazz-ak, not receiving any instructions from the Queen, continued to lead the situation. He walked into the command area, stopping in front of a well muscled human with short white hair and blue eyes.

"Captain Malesis here," he said, a smile on his face. Cazz-ak thought the smile looked friendly as opposed to menacing, something rare in his experience with humans.

"Cazz-ak-tak, Elth-eo-lan, and Na-ah-co," Cazz-ak said by way of introduction. Malesis didn't seem surprised by their mental communication and Cazz-ak guessed this was probably not the man's first encounter with Entho-la-ah-mines.

"It's truly a pleasure to meet you all," Malesis said, still sounding genuine. "We brought you in because it looked like you could use the help."

"Indeed," Cazz-ak said. "We thank you for your kindness and for going out of your way to help those who are scorned by your kind." He said the last part so he could judge Malesis' reaction to it. The man took no offense at the statement, indeed, he agreed with it.

"There is much humanity has done to wrong your species, and for that I'm truly sorry. I, and the whole Brotherhood for that matter, do all we can to make up for the injustice and harm caused by humankind." Captain Malesis was genuine, but Cazz-ak had one more thing to say in order to satisfy himself this man could be trusted.

"Xenocide, you mean." Most humans would deny any such thing was happening, that the humans were merely defending their interests on planets "Enthos" occupied. What they always failed to mention was that the Entho-la-ah-mines were there first, the human colonists came without permission, caused problems with their "Entho" neighbors, and then sat back in satisfaction when the human ships came to wipe out the "Entho" population.

"Yes, that is truth," Malesis said matter-of-factly, looking directly into Cazz-ak's eyes. Cazz-ak decided Malesis, and possibly the Brotherhood, could be trusted, only a little to begin with, maybe more later if they earned it. Telling him about Na-ah-co being the last queen was still not wise, but Cazz-ak was confident these humans weren't going to just kill them all outright.

"Our question now is what to do," Malesis said, breaking the silence that had descended after his blunt agreement with Cazz-ak's observation of xenocide. "We have the feeling since you destroyed that huge Ashamine ship, they'll be out here soon to investigate. We have our own reasons for wanting to avoid the Ashamine," his eyes flicked a quick glance at Wake, almost too fast to notice, "so we'd prefer to stay as far away from them as possible."

"Agreed," Cazz-ak stated.

"We could drop you off on an Entho-la-ah-mine world, but those are becoming few and far between and we need to stop on Eishon-2 for some business. You could come along with us and we could decide what to do once the situation clarifies somewhat."

Considering he had no better options and his fate was firmly in their human hands, Cazz-ak decided this was as good a plan as any. He needed time to think and confer with both Na-ah-co and Elth-eo-lan about what their next move was. At least now they were safer than they had been drifting along in the escape orb. *Our life expectancy has gone up,* Cazz-ak thought hopefully.

"That sounds good. Thank you," Cazz-ak sent, trying to make the thought a happy one since he had no physical way to express that emotion to the humans.

"It's agreed then," the Captain said happily, a broad grin splitting his face. "We are going to the Brotherhood installation on Eishon-2. It's in the foothills near the southern pole of the planet. Eishon-2 is a warm place and very hospitable, but there aren't many inhabitants. The planet is mainly made up of the misfits of the galaxy, the Brotherhood included." This he said with a fond look in his eyes. "The Ashamine leaves this neighborhood of the galaxy alone for the most part, so it's a good place for people who don't care for them. In other words, perfect for some Entho-la-ah-mines who want to hide from the Ashamine until something better can be arranged." He smiled genuinely at Cazz-ak and his companions before he turned back to his terminal and started entering commands.

The human vessel resumed its course towards the planet, and as time went on, the features of Eishon-2 began to grow larger. As they entered the atmosphere, Cazz-ak sent a message to his fellow Entho-la-ah-mines through the Great Thought, telling them of their location and the status of the Queen. A flurry of good will and happiness came back through the connection, along with no small amount of hope and fear.

37 - THE FOUNDER

The Founder threw the heavy prismatic cube in rage. It ricocheted off the wall, narrowly missing the aide's head. "Get me someone who is competent before I kill you!" he roared, spittle flying from his mouth as he did so, vivid orange eyes ready to burst from his head. The female assistant fled, bursting into tears as she left the Founder's office.

He stared down at the report he had just been briefed on by the aide. The terminal screen listed "complete destruction of the planet" and "loss of at least 90% of personnel and space borne assets". The ships that had escaped the supernova were now scattered all over the galaxy. Pandemonium reigned. The Founder's Hammer, the newest and finest ship in the AF fleet, had not been heard from since it reported it was in pursuit of an Entho bi-pyramid ship in Haak-ah-tar space. The supernova and subsequent disappearance of the Hammer and its precious cargo had pushed everything else aside in the Founder's mind, including the communications black hole that had become the Noor system.

"Why can no one find this ship?" he yelled after her, not expecting an answer, but wishing to vent some of his frustration. The ship itself was expendable, especially since the new mines on formerly Entho worlds were up to full production. The cargo on the Hammer, however, was not easily replaceable. He had to have his heir. The Founder had thought he had lost the boy once before, and going over his options then had looked grim. He had thought the Hammer a safe place to keep Lothis, but now his namesake ship was failing him. Some reports said Captain Talnavis, the commander of the ASN Founder's Hammer, could be overly ambitious and sometimes lacked a necessary cautiousness. The Founder hoped the bastard hadn't done anything to endanger the boy.

If he could have sent Crasor, the Founder would have been confident the man would keep the boy safe and escort him back. Crasor would not take Lothis on an unnecessary chase after some blighthearted Enthos. The

Founder had given up on expecting Crasor to return however. *Crasor is dead,* the Founder decided. That disappointed him, but it certainly didn't grieve him. He still couldn't find anyone who was capable of fulfilling the role of Facilitator. *I cannot settle for a mediocre candidate.*

The fact the Bloodsport had been destroyed also irked the Founder. The Ashamine would lose a great source of income because of it. All the Ashamine Forces on the planet itself were a total loss as well. *At least now I won't have to dispose of Felar Haltro,* he thought. *That's one good thing to come out of this catastrophe.*

The longer the Founder thought about it, the greater the realization there were more things going wrong now than ever before in his long tenure as Founder. Was this coincidence or were there people conspiring against the Ashamine? The Founder dismissed this as paranoia. The thought of someone instigating a supernova was ludicrous.

The Divisionists were another matter entirely. Their ranks still continued to grow, and Crasor's mission seemed to be aborted due to the earthquakes that had shaken Noor-5. The Founder hadn't heard of any "acts of retribution" carried out against "enemies of the Ashamine" by "loyal zealots" on any other planets. That was the mission, a task Crasor had obviously failed to carry out. Not only that, but the whole Noor system had undergone a communications blackout shortly after the earthquakes. No transmissions or ships had left the once busy system. *It's located on a major shipping lane. What has happened there?*

The curious archaeological discovery on Traynos-6 was also on the Founder's mind. Thankfully all potential security risks had been eliminated. Apparently, the man they had set up to take the fall had miraculously escaped his execution, but that mattered little. Wake Darmekus didn't know anything about the discovery deep in the mine, and all the miners who did know anything about it were dead. This was one situation that was, at least for the moment, under control. Once things became more stable in the Ashamine, he would be able to allocate more resources to exploiting some of the mysterious technology deep under Traynos-6.

An aide, this time a male, came into the Founder's office, somewhat timidly. "Sir, we just received info on the Hammer," he said, voice quavery.

"Yes, yes, yes," the Founder said in atypical impatience. "Get on with it."

"Well, it appears to have been destroyed sir," the aide said, cringing as he did so.

"WHAT?!?" the Founder screamed. His reaction was livid, causing the aide to take a stumbling step back, almost falling in the process.

"One of the other ships from Haak-ah-tar saw it go through a worm hole after an Entho ship, just before the hole closed. We had our analysts compile a list of probable places and sent out recon drones to track the Hammer down." He was quivering, shaking, feeling the waves of wrath emanating from the Founder. *Good,* the Founder thought with savage glee, *at least someone respects me and does their job.*

"One of the scout ships went to the Eishon system. It wasn't high on the list," the aide explained, "but they found the remnants of a massive battle. Apparently—" he said, stopping for a moment to gulp and try to regain his composure before going on. "Apparently, both ships annihilated each other—completely."

"How is that even possible?" the Founder shot back, one decibel shy of screaming. "The Enthos have no weaponry, and as I remember, there is nothing in the Eishon system other than a bunch of religious wacks."

"Ye-ye-yes sir," the aide stammered. "Just so." He looked down at the report he carried on his portable terminal, apparently refreshing his memory. The Founder was growing even more impatient and angry, but continuing to shout at this young man would accomplish nothing, he decided. After the aide had found what he was looking for, he began to speak once again. "We don't know what happened, but the scout drone recovered the Hammer's secure records unit and is transmitting the information to us as we speak." As the Founder seemed to grow less angry, the aide became more confident and less nervous.

"Ninety percent transferred," he said after a moment. After a few more seconds, "Transfer complete. Decrypting." Another minute passed, the Founder trying to calm himself and regain control over his wildly flailing emotions. "Decryption complete. Would you like for me to read the report sir?"

"No, I have my own terminal in case you hadn't noticed," he snapped. Even as he was speaking, he brought up the report at his desk terminal. The secure records didn't really hold any more information than what the aide had already told him. Everything was normal up until a minute or two before the secure records unit lost its connection with the ship. At this point the device recorded an extremely large object striking the ship, but it listed the Entho bi-pyramid as being too far away to be the object. It also reported that many escape vehicles had launched. Hope surged into the Founder. *Perhaps the boy is safe!*

Digging deeper into the records, he found a discrepancy. Somehow, an escape vehicle was launched *before* the ship had been struck. The file showed Lothis and a soldier, 3rd Class Enlightened Felar Haltro, had boarded one of the escape vehicles near the command deck several minutes before the collision. *How did they know to get off the ship? And why was she with him? I ordered she be kept on Haak-ah-tar until I could deal with her.* It was clear they left at a precise moment, waiting in the vehicle so the timing was close to the destruction of the ship. Had they left sooner it would have alerted the captain and had they left much later their chances for survival would have decreased dramatically. *Where are they now?*

"This is the same Enlightened Felar Haltro that extracted the boy from the facility," his voice was a flat statement, not a question, but the aide felt it needed to be answered.

"Yes sir," he stated eagerly, looking up from his portable terminal. The Founder merely rolled his eyes, something the aide failed to notice.

"Why don't you do something useful and answer a real question," the Founder asked, voice brimming with mock and scorn. "Why did they leave *before* the damage occurred to the ship?" The aide was somewhat puzzled at this question and thought for a moment before answering.

"Perhaps they left early because they saw the danger of whatever struck the ship?" he said, voice halting.

"Possible, but then why would they have waited so long to launch the pod?" This time the Founder gave the young aide no time to answer. "Obviously, you idiot, the woman was kidnapping the boy and timed her escape with some sort of external collaborators. Or perhaps they were within the AF. Either way, they had it timed so she might escape in the chaos, taking the child with her. She must have found out who he is." He thought for another moment, and the aide was smart enough to keep his mouth shut. "Perhaps it was those religious lack wits? But how would they have the power to destroy a Tarton Class ship? I suppose it's worth investigating, given there are no other leads. And while we are at it, we can take care of that dirty little corner of the Ashamine. The woman couldn't have gotten far in the escape vehicle, so unless they had transport on a ship with a worm generator, they are on Eishon-2." That logic felt quite sound to the Founder and a little of his anger subsided.

The Founder began sending commands through his terminal, creating formations of ships and issuing orders. Troops were summoned, armored vehicles gathered, and atmospheric fighters ordered to assemble for transport. "Please, if you can find it within your less than adequate brain to perform a task successfully, request that my Ascended commanders come to me. Inform them it is urgent, security level five." The Founder turned back to his terminal, continuing to analyze his military forces and issue orders. "Oh," he added just as the aide was about to leave, his voice cheerful, "remember that if you even *think* of breathing a word of this to anyone, your life will be the *first* thing you'll wish I had taken from you. You've done an adequate job so far, but don't think that will even come close to saving you if you breech security." The aide blanched and left the room hastily. The Founder smiled tightly, a small bit of pleasure having been added to his day.

Soon enough, he thought excitedly, *those buggers and rebels on Eishon-2 will see what happens when they conspire to capture the heir of the Ashamine. They should have kept their heads down and maybe we would have left them alone for another fifteen years.*

38 – CRASOR

Crasor Tah Ahn was drunk on power, high on power, enthralled to power. The Breakers, though not yet fulfilling his wildest fantasies, had provided him with the tools to reach those dreams. The army he controlled was not as big as the Ashamine, but it was far more loyal, absolutely loyal in fact. True, he only controlled one planet, but he held its land, its sea, its air, and its people with absolute control. The only thing remaining were the ships in Noor space.

"Prepare yourselves. Remember, the highest priority is securing the command deck and its comms equipment," Crasor told his small, hand picked squad of Breakers. They were on a supply ship, preparing to dock with the Ashamine Forces vessel that had just arrived in Noor space. *Once we capture this ship, we will be able to secure the rest of the vessels in the system. And with the jamming abilities on board, we can secure all comms. The next stage of operations is imminent.*

Crasor stood in front of the airlock, ready to enthrall the soldiers on the other side as soon as the door opened. It would be a short, but intense struggle. The ship wasn't large, but the danger it posed and the opportunities it presented were worth the risk. *We need as many worm capable ships as possible, plus, this one is armed and armored.* Crasor was surprised this was the first AF vessel dispatched to the Noor system. The Founder must be really busy to ignore the comms black out for this long. *All the better for us.*

The airlock door hissed as it opened, the slight difference in pressure between ships equalizing. Crasor shoved shards of thought at each of the soldiers, causing their minds to overload with ecstasy. He quickly caressed them and sorted the Seed from the Blackness. His squad rushed in and dealt with those bound for Blackness as Crasor continued on towards the command deck. He would give the Seed later.

Before he got to the command deck, Crasor wrapped space-time around himself, causing light to pass by him instead of reflecting off him. He became effectively invisible to anyone who was not a Breaker.

"What's going on with the supply transfer?" the captain asked as Crasor entered the command deck. At first, Crasor was startled, thinking the man had seen him and asked the question.

"No word back yet. They are taking a lot of time to report," his XO responded. Crasor, moving silently because his shielding only worked on the visible spectrum, crept up behind the captain. As he did so, Crasor scanned the room, probing the inhabitants' psyches. *Oh captain,* he thought, drawing a long knife out of a sheath at his waist, *you are far too pure for my liking.* Crasor sunk the blade into the man's back, aiming for his heart.

The captain gurgled, his body letting out its last bit of life. Everyone on deck turned to see what was making the strange sound. Crasor knew the sight would be quite strange, a blade protruding out of their captain's chest, glimmering red in the bright light, its origins unknown. It would be as if it had simply appeared there.

The XO, although bound for the Seed, was still loyal to his captain. He didn't know what was happening, but he knew how to react. "Comms, send word to AFC that we are under attack." Crasor sent out his shards of thought, attempting to dazzle everyone on deck. As he did so, he looked for the comms officer, knowing if he got the message off, the entire Breaker species might be destroyed by the Ashamine.

Something was wrong with Crasor's mental persuasion however. He could feel someone resisting it, and he had the sickening suspicion it was the comms officer. *This could ruin everything,* Crasor panicked, frantically searching through the personnel seated in front of the ship's terminals.

He finally found the man, hurriedly trying to send the alert. Just as he was about to press "Transmit", Crasor sunk his knife into the man's brain stem. The officer fell lifeless on to the console and blood flowed across his terminal. Crasor quickly reached down and hit "Cancel". He let out a sigh of relief and summoned the squad to come dispose of all those bound for Blackness. *How did the comms officer resist my compulsion?* Crasor wondered. It was the first time anything like that had happened.

After he and his squad had finished taking over the Ashamine ship, they used it to capture the rest of the vessels in Noor space. It was easy to disguise themselves as AF and board each of the vessels in turn. A few of the civilian ships had small weapons on board, but none were a match for Crasor's mental control.

With the domination of Noor-5 and its surrounding system complete, it was time to begin the next phase of his plan. Crasor knew instinctively that he needed to search the newly converted population of Breakers to find those who were developed enough to learn to Seed. He spent days searching out his chosen underlings, carefully selecting those best suited for the exalted position. Once he'd found three, he began cultivating them. Their psyche had to be altered so their bodies would mutate the ability to produce the Seed. It was hard working with the selected lieutenants as they had yet to fully evolve out of the "dumb" phase. They were slow and had a hard time understanding tactics or higher thought. Teaching them was proving to be nearly impossible. Crasor stayed patient though, waiting for them to develop the mental capabilities they needed to progress. He trained them throughly, eager to be off to complete his own goals, but making sure they were equipped to do the work he needed of them. He would be able to communicate with his lieutenants, but they would need to make quick decisions on their own while they conquered new planets.

Finally, after a week, their training was complete and Crasor felt good about putting so much responsibility on the shoulders of his three Descended—his mocking term for the similar Ashamine rank. He watched as the Descended summoned forces to the orbital dock and loaded them on ships. The shuttles were packed during each trip, crammed full of partially developed Breakers. Their minds were still imperfect and slow, their bodies halting and clumsy. They would do well enough though, Crasor supposed. He had directed the Descended to go to weak, less populated planets early on. Using this tactic, they would build their forces from the populations of the conquered planets without suffering too many casualties. The first three on the list were Taggardt-6, Eishon-2, and Qi-3, all planets that lacked a military presence. Crasor knew the Breakers would have no problems on these worlds. He hadn't been to any of them except Eishon-2, but he trusted his secure reports from the Ashamine. *They still haven't restricted my access,* he thought, a sneer of disgust transforming his handsome face into ugliness.

"All forces loaded," came into his mind from the Descended leading the force going to Qi-3. "We are ready to depart." Thankfully the Descended could communicate using their minds, because their voices were still quite harsh and guttural, slow and hard to understand. Using one's mind was so much easier.

"Break the Dawn," Crasor replied by way of permission to depart.

"May the Dawn be broken," the Descended responded, the engines on his ship coming to life.

Very good, Crasor thought in celebration. His dream of power was finally bearing fruit, and not because of the Founder or the Ashamine—*What have they ever done for me?*—but because he had won it by the might of his own hand. He knew the condition of the Ashamine government and to his eye it looked like an eager whore ready for a buggering. All the meetings he had attended with the Founder, confidential information he knew, all of that would be crucial now. Bringing down the Ashamine—*and let's not forget the decrepit human species in general*—was his prime goal. A new order was descending upon the universe, *his* order.

The other two Descended finished loading up their ships and left as well. There was still a huge population of Breakers on Noor-5, reserves if anything went wrong on the expansionist missions Crasor had just sent out. He hoped everything would go as well on the other planets as it had on Noor, but you never knew until the work was done.

Crasor boarded his own ship, a small speedy vessel that had been owned by an Ashamine courier. While his mission was one of expansionism and conquest just like the others, his would have to be done alone. First he would go settle his business with the Founder, fulfilling a desire that had been nagging at him since he had become a Breaker. With that out of the way, he would try to corrupt and exploit the Entho group mind he had discovered. Both objectives were tantalizing goals to Crasor.

Removing the Founder would be complicated and dangerous, but its rewards would be great. Without the strong leadership it was totally dependent on, the Ashamine would crumble and the Breakers would sweep through the universe, devouring the resources, both living and inanimate, they needed in order to continue to grow.

Subjugating the Enthos would be a new task altogether. Crasor's Breaker mind had no recollection of how to deal with these creatures, but his covert viewing of their group mind made him crave their energy. *Soon I will be strong enough to break through their mental barriers and then we shall see,* he thought. He didn't know whether or not they could be converted, but they either had to be made one with the Breakers or completely destroyed. They were certainly much too powerful, intelligent, and evolved to be left alone. He needed to gather more information about them. *Perhaps some "hands on" experience will enlighten me.* He looked forward to that task.

As the small craft moved away from the orbital dock far above Noor-5, Crasor reveled in his new found power and worshiped the entities that had given it to him. *I never would have risen this far keeping allegiance with the Ashamine and the Founder.* The leader of all humanity had never truly seen the value of all of Crasor's many abilities, had never given him a position with the chance to grow and have real power. Now Crasor's time had come. Now he would Break and the worlds would quake to their very foundations.

Noor is a small fire that will grow and consume the universe, a small spark that will ignite the cosmos. All that do not burn will be refined, purified, exulted. He smirked, an ugly look that had begun to fit his face more and more each day. *The Dawn has come, and I have come to break it.*

###

WANT MORE?

Become a Patron and get exclusive short
stories, essays, poems, and art. Rewards
include digital & paperback novels,
commissioned works, Q&A videos, as well
interactions with me!

ⓟ patreon

Patreon.com/ZachariahWahrer

Find more of my writing and art
(including the Dawn Saga) at:

ZachariahWahrer.com

Dear Reader,

Thank you for investing your time in my fiction! If you enjoyed this book, I'd really appreciate it if you would share the experience with your friends and leave a review at your favorite retailer and/or Goodreads.

If you'd like to get in contact with me, you can email: **zachariah@wahreroftheworlds.com**.
My website, **www.zachariahwahrer.com** *is a great way to find more of my writing. If you are more of a social media person, I'm on:*
Facebook: www.facebook.com/ZachariahWahrer
Twitter: www.twitter.com/ZachariahWahrer
Medium: www.medium.com/@ZachariahWahrer
and **Instagram:** www.instagram.com/ZachariahWahrer

May the fires of the black star be quenched in your life,
Zachariah Wahrer

***

ABOUT THE AUTHOR

Zachariah Wahrer spent the first twelve years of his adult life doing various jobs around the United States, such as eBay salesman, punk rock musician, horse halter craftsman, and rock climbing gym route-setter.

Near the end of 2014, Zachariah moved into a Honda Odyssey with his wife Sarah and began traveling the United States and Canada, seeking inspiration and adventure while writing and rock climbing full-time. His first novel, Breakers of the Dawn: Book 1 of the Dawn Saga, was electronically published in December of 2014.

When not deeply immersed in imaginary worlds, Zachariah loves to experience the outdoors as well as read about science, futurology, and trans-humanism. He also enjoys home-brewing and creating digital art to accompany his writing.

While writing this novel, Zachariah lived in: Bellefontaine, OH; Dublin, TX; Colorado Springs, CO; the Honda Odyssey; and Benton, KS.